AMAZING DISGRACE

James Hamilton-Paterson

AMAZING DISGRACE

Europa
editions

Europa Editions
116 East 16th Street
New York, N.Y. 10003
www.europaeditions.com
info@europaeditions.com

Copyright © 2006 by James Hamilton-Paterson
First Publication 2006 by Europa Editions

Library of Congress Cataloging in Publication Data is available
ISBN 1-933372-19-2

Hamilton-Paterson, James
Amazing Disgrace

Book design by Emanuele Ragnisco
www.mekkanografici.com

Printed in Italy
Arti Grafiche La Moderna – Rome

F+AM

b173398824

CONTENTS

For Mark Sykes and David Pirie

And, after more than forty years,
high time too

Why should I let the toad *work*
   Squat on my life?
Can't I use my wit as a pitchfork
   And drive the brute off?

   —PHILIP LARKIN, "Toads"

AMAZING DISGRACE

1.

The trouble with sitting quietly under your pergola in splendid isolation is that before long restlessness sets in. True, the vindaloo blancmange at lunch might have something to do with that (and very good it was, too: an intriguing marriage of the incandescent and the gelid). But there's more to it. Up here among the crags the world is oppressively silent. Drops of brilliant late-spring sunlight trickle through the vine leaves overhead and splash onto the marble table, pooling around a coffee cup and blotching a thick pile of manuscript. For some time now this gross slab of paper has come to feel like my own tombstone that I have been engraving with such lapidary skill—my own, despite its being the story of someone else entirely, a person I loathed from the start.

The perennial problem, of course, is *work*. Philip Larkin famously saw it as a toad: a chill, ugly weight that squats on us all, blotting out most of our scant allowance of days. And nor is it the sort of work like fetching water and planting rice that is plausibly useful for survival. On the contrary, nearly all employment is the civilian equivalent of the sort of punishment once meted out to recalcitrant squaddies, such as digging one hole to fill another or whitewashing coal. I'm amazed we kick up so little fuss about the awesome futility of the work most of us do. Writing novels, for instance. Fictioneers, with their dim penchant for social relevance, like to dwell on such minority afflictions as love, erotic misconduct or being brought up white in Southall, while the daily work that lays waste the lives of the majority goes largely ignored. So I shall boldly break with tradition and deal with the lump of human coal I have recently and so laboriously been attempting to whitewash. Sadly, there's nothing fictional about *her*.

The personal toad beneath which I have suffocated for years requires me to write other people's books for them. A thankless task, you will agree. Yet I can modestly claim they are artfully agreeable books about largely disagreeable people, and the one on the table I have just finished is no different. In fact, it is the odious toad's very repetitiveness that now leads me to gaze dejectedly out over the view from my house, a view that would by rights send many a Tuscany groupie into ecstasy. The terrace ends in space. Many miles away on the far side of an immense gulf of air the Mediterranean is visibly frittering its time away, lying glazed and inert in its bed at two o'clock in the afternoon like a teenager who has been out clubbing all night. From time to time flashes of light prickle amid the general glare along the coast as the sun catches the windscreens of unseen vehicles crawling about in the ant heap far below. Human beings in their desultory pursuit of happiness, that archetypal wild-goose chase, in default of which they will have to make do with mere wealth . . . Samper, Samper, whence this spleen, this ennui? The bloody sea, probably, the very sight of which these days reminds me of things I would as soon forget, such as the company I have been obliged to keep these past fourteen months. It's hard to convey the sheer awfulness of these people I write about in order to keep my still-youthful body and raddled soul together. My latest subject has been freakish even by recent standards. Picture to yourself a nut-brown amputee in her late fifties with skin that makes Brigitte Bardot's look like a Clinique ad and habitually deploying the vocabulary of a lesbian trucker. What, I ask you, has Gerald Samper to do with such denizens of a netherworld? He of the refined musicality, the culinary inventiveness, the trim buns (if he does say so himself)? Didn't he long ago resolve that things could not go on as they are?

He did. Yet by a series of cruel misfortunes not a single one of my ingenious ploys designed to escape earning a living by such humiliating means has come to fruition. With what opportunistic delicacy did I arrange for the great Italian film director Piero Pacini to employ me as his biographer! My acquaintance with him, though brief, was intimate enough. I last saw him lying on a beach south of Viareggio at night, surrounded by the exploding set of his latest film, his green plastic eyeshade welded by heat to the back of his head as he was cradled by his toothsome son Filippo. ("Call me Pippo, Gerry," this wonder boy had urged me from the controls of his family's helicopter only that afternoon.) Frankly, my heart leaped up as I beheld distress rockets in the sky. This was the sort of episode any biographer longs for. Surely these pyrotechnics also presaged the start of a new era in my life when at last I would begin to move in glitzy cultural and artistic circles worthy of my talents. Only weeks later I was relieved to hear that Pacini was making an excellent recovery, albeit after a certain amount of skin grafting. And the next thing I knew, I was staring at a headline in *Il Tirreno*: "Morto il Cav. Pacini da un infarto." And immediately there came the image of John Cleese as Basil Fawlty shaking his fist at the ceiling, shouting through clenched teeth: "Oh *thank* you, God! Thank you so very much!" The first real chance of a break and my subject has a heart attack and dies, taking with him all the gossip and stories and malevolent asides that are so crucial to a lively biography. Typical.

At this point it becomes clear that the recent blancmange is, in the phrase of my late mother's late charlady, *very searching*. I hurry indoors and, once at ease, can't help yet again admiring the taste and artistry with which I have redecorated the downstairs bathroom. My original scheme was a deliberate mockery of provincial British chic: call it Laura Ashley meets Imelda Marcos. This time I have done it out as a jeu d'esprit. Walls, floor and ceiling all flat white except for the close-spaced wooden rafters overhead which are now biscuit, prolonged by stripes of the same colour and width running down the walls and across the floor in matching tiles. The effect is like being airily caged within light ochre bars or of being done up in a benign protective parcel. Gazzbear, my American teddy with built-in flatulence, sits on the lavatory cistern wearing his little blue waistcoat, holding his chubby arms aloft either to greet all comers or else in a marvelling gesture at the elegance of his place of confinement. I notice from the little label stitched to his groin that although his inspiration came from Pennsylvania, he was made in China. Not for the first time I find myself wondering what on earth the Chinese labouring peasantry—so recently escaped from the night-soil-haunted fields of the provinces to work in the satanic mills of industrial cities—must think of the people they make these things for. The farting teddy bears, the mechanical masturbators, the battery-powered Jesus Christs, the transparent acrylic lavatory seats with genuine banknotes embedded in them: what do the Chinese who devise cheap ways of manufacturing these fatuous objects imagine their customers must be like? Brain-damaged aliens, possibly. One day we might learn. Probably it will turn out that they long to have such things themselves. Still, somewhere behind these thoughts a theory of cultural shame may be trying to articulate itself. After all, if we would be loath to admit to friends and family that a machine designed to plunge or suck at the flick of a switch was hidden beneath crusted towels at the back of our wardrobe, why should we be any less embarrassed that foreigners might think such things represent our national character?

The vindaloo blancmange having made good its escape, I

am now definitely in the market for a pick-me-up. Time was when a neighbour of mine could be relied on to turn up at all hours bearing a bottle of Fernet Branca, her favourite tipple. The poor dear *was* pretty far gone. I have since switched to prosecco as being the only thing one can drink all day in an Italian summer and not become incapable of coherent living. Accordingly I go to the fridge, fetch a bottle of Bisol's admirable "Foie" (which, since we are in Italy, translates as "lusts"; life's about *pleasure*, stupid), and return to my dappled terrace. The view—distant torpid ocean, neighbouring crags silently cracking apart as the sun inserts its myriad stealthy chisels—is the same, but now the Samper spirits have some prospect of recovering in the company of a chilled bottle in its cooler and a moisture-beaded glass. I was going to explain about the tombstone manuscript on the table and why the sight of both it and the sea have the power to plunge me into gloom. I have lately been earning a living by ghosting the auto-biographies of temporarily famous idiots, mainly "sports per-sonalities," to use the generic term. Luckily no one reading this book is likely also to have read *Downhill all the Way!*, which concerned Luc Bailly, a burnt-out skier. Nor, I trust, will they have read *Hot Seat!*, my recent oeuvre detailing the charmless life of the Formula 1 driver Per Snoilsson, a murderous little turd with the brains of an earwig. I'm not proud to admit that this last effort has sold appallingly well, the punters seemingly hooked by its shameless kiss-and-tell accounts of what racing drivers would like people to think they get up to after dark. Sales have depressingly confirmed the mentality of my reader-ship.

"Nice for you," you're probably saying with bitter magna-nimity as you regard Samper in his vine-shrouded Tuscan eyrie, sipping prosecco at two-thirty in the afternoon. And so it might be if mine were a purely humdrum job, one that—like an airline pilot's—involved a minimum of human contact while now and then staying sober. But you're overlooking the horrors of the task. Think about it. In order to ghost celebrities' lives one needs to spend actual time in their company, often traipsing along with them from continent to continent in their lurchy little executive jets together with their quarrelsome but lickspittle retinue. One has to let them maunder into a tape recorder at snatched opportunities—as it might be at two o'clock in the morning in a hotel room in Kuala Lumpur, where they are grumpily smashed on Chivas Regal because they've had to leave their narcotics at home out of a craven fear of execution. One also has to visit obscure Swedish villages or places like Berwick-upon-Tweed to meet their families and be shown endless photo albums containing pictures of the subject as a child engaged in activities (such as sitting at the wheel of a pedal car) that will inevitably merit the weary caption "The shape of things to come."

In ways I could never have predicted and may never be able to convey to you, my latest subject has managed to be the worst of the lot. You will find it especially hard to believe this if you are already one of her millions of cretinous fans. Yes—Millie Cleat: the celebrated around-the-world one-armed yachts personality. And I can give you a sneak preview of the genealogical part of my book's first chapter by assuring you that it really is her name, "Cleat" being a felicitous instance of what *New Scientist* has dubbed "nominative determinism." In brief, since by now most of you will know the story all too well, she taught herself to sail Albacores on Ruislip Lido in her thirties. Finally leaving her husband—a poor, shell-shocked creature—to look after their two teenaged children, this steely harridan flew to Australia "to get in touch with her spiritual side with an Aboriginal tribe," as she mendaciously told the *Daily Express* once she had become famous. Like ectoplasm at a Victorian séance, Millie Cleat's spiritual side only ever materializes at interviews, and with equal credibility.

One afternoon she went swimming off Perth and lost her right arm to a petulant shark. The first lifeguard to reach her, wearing two pairs of his wife's tights to protect him from jellyfish, had no sooner grabbed Millie than she was stung on the neck by a box jelly. It was just not her day. She survived, however, although she later ungratefully ascribed this to "a miracle" rather than to excellent Australian medical care. The incident turned her into a local celebrity; she then became nationally known by announcing her intention to build a yacht and sail it solo back to England.

By now this woman, who I suppose was not unhandsome if you like that sort of thing, was attracting admirers. One of these was a Sydney businessman with a stump fetish and a great fortune. Lew Buschfeuer offered to sponsor Millie, who gratefully accepted and spent most of the next eighteen months down at the boatyard ensuring the trimaran taking shape there was the best someone else's money could buy. Her mentor had behind him the global resources of *Vvizz* Corporation, which will give you some idea of why she specified a titanium hull. By the time she was launched, *Beldame* had cost him nearly thirty-five million Australian dollars, much of which had gone on the hi-tech goodies with which it was stuffed. These included electrical gadgets halfway between a bosun's chair and a Stannah stairlift to winch her painlessly up the masts for emergency repairs.

You might well ask why a tycoon, even one erotically motivated, would pay so much to build an oceangoing racing yacht for a grandmother—for such Milly had recently become. The answer was that, to him, thirty-five million dollars was nowhere near serious money. Besides, he had detected in this weird Englishwoman a ruthlessness, as well as an armlessness, of which he stood in awe. So there came a day when Milly anointed her nose with a white splodge of factor 50 in the tribal markings of Australian sportspeople and, wearing a gimme cap and a dauntless grin, pressed the button that set the main-sail. Alone on her boat she left Sydney harbour on a "trial spin" non-stop around Australia. To general incredulity she not only succeeded but did so in record time. Long before the voyage was over her progress was being followed by TV audiences well beyond Australia.

Of course you know the story, even if you pretend otherwise. Once she had broken that record there was no holding her. She re-provisioned and, like Nelson before her, set sail for England, home and beauty. She managed this trip in record time also. By now Millie Cleat was bankable. It was natural that the husband to whom she had returned after an absence of almost three years would urge her to set off immediately on a non-stop circumnavigation of the globe. So, too, it was for *Vvizz* Corporation. TV audiences worldwide had become fixated on the familiar image of this one-armed granny, as brown and furrowed as a monkey left out in the rain. They were hooked on the endless *intime* Webcam pictures of her plotting her course or snatching a meal. Helicopter shots of *Beldame* heeling into creamy waves had become a ritual part of newscasts. The great green-and-gold sail across whose paunch the giant *Vvizz* logo blazed was iconic. The corporate slogan written across the foredeck, "No Worries," was a token of faith. In the face of all this there was, as Margaret Thatcher had once famously remarked, no alternative. The ratings demanded it. Millie entered the next round-the-world race.

And without seeming to try, she won it and broke the record, too, making the fastest-ever solo circumnavigation. After she had been setting a brisk clip for several weeks the media turned it into an epic race against time, against the elements, against human frailty, against history itself. Once "The Battling Granny" and "Heroine of the Deep," she now became simplified as just plain "Millie." Ask "How's Millie doing?" in any pub in Britain and only the truly disenchanted would have had the nerve to respond irritably, "Millie who?" Well, disenchanted, c'est moi. Mind you, that was before I was appointed as her ghost and disenchantment turned to well-earned loathing as she stood me up for appointments, changed her story, lied, disparaged my dress sense and made other personal remarks unnecessary to repeat here. One thing I really resented was the sheer technology involved in her record. It wasn't just that practically everything in the way of navigation, steering and sail-setting was done for her by *Beldame*'s computers and servo motors. No, the really sad thing was that the satellites tracking her every inch of the way made it impossible that sooner or later we would discover she had faked it, like Donald Crowhurst sailing his mad circles in mid-Atlantic in the late sixties. Had she done that my admiration for her would have changed everything.

Instead of which the whole thing became a cliché, as was inevitable given the press coverage. Almost from the first the newspapers had had to suppress the phrase "single-handed," although it still slipped out now and then from journalists' keyboards with the self-conscious qualifier "no pun intended." The pillory ought to be reinstated for people who append "no pun intended" to their facetious gaucheries so we could all visit them in our lunch hour and pelt them with mule droppings. If they didn't intend the pun why did they write it, print it, proofread it and have it published? But I don't wish to wear us all out with rancour. The afternoon is hot; the prosecco is working its mellow magic; and I fear that more about this insufferable woman must inevitably emerge as we go along. For the moment you will just have to take my word that a *chasm* extends between the persona the press and public connived to invent for Millie and the foul-mouthed Cleat whose story I have had to dig out. As she neared the Solent and the finishing line of her famous voyage, a lone journalist with enough courage and independence to suggest that her peers found her an arrogant sea cow alluded to Millie as "the *Beldame* sans merci." I can add that from the point of view of the elementary social graces she is also a *Beldame* sans s'il vous plaît.

Enough. It's time to think about more important matters, such as what I shall eat tonight, bearing in mind that lunch turned out to be the gastronomic equivalent of a strip search. Something light, then. Among the treasures waiting for me in the freezer is a little creation that only last week I finally brought to perfection: Lambs' Lungs with Surgeon's Fingers. I don't know about you, but I have always thought of offal cookery as being almost the chef's supreme challenge. It is all too easy to wind up with a plate of tubing or nodules reeking of the farmyard. I mean, look at andouillettes: suicide to eat without first checking for an all-night chemist, unless of course you're French with the necessary antibodies. The mind becomes panicky with images of microbes and sphincters. Rillettes is hardly much better, coming into a similar category of jowls-'n'-bowels. They used to serve it on toast with gherkins to blue-chinned workers in French cafés: a terrible brawn containing shaving-brush tufts, the white gleam of cartilage, the odd broken tooth. The graphic American name "headcheese" says it all. No: my dainty lambs' lungs have nothing in common with such seven-franc dishes. On the contrary, they have about them a refined innocence that is positively arcadian. Nothing to do with the gamy old goat-footed god with the shaggy thighs, of course. I'm thinking more of little brown boys piping artlessly to their flocks. My dish of lungs exhales an aura of myrtle-dotted pasture and Attic sunshine redolent of herbs and dalliance. For the moment I am unfortunately going to have to keep mum about the exact technique whereby I convert the raw lungs' pink sponginess to a texture that yields to the side of a fork. I have asked Frankie, my agent, to look into the tricky legal area where copyright law overlaps with patent law. If one can patent an industrial technique, why not a new dish or a new technique for cooking it? Could I collect royalties from cooks who prepare my inventions? Here we are in the province of intellectual property, you understand.

In any case, all I shall say for the moment is that Samper's way with lambs' lungs owes something to the "plastination" technique of Dr. Gunther von Hagens, whose flayed chess players have done so much to raise the morale of school outings all over Europe. As for my "surgeon's fingers," these are digit-thin rolls of savoury delight based on minced quinces, garlic, pine nuts and bay, all stuffed into lengths of ox artery, tied off and boiled. There is no doubt they will perfectly complement the lungs, whose preparation includes olive paste. To go with this brilliant dish a white wine is surely called for—something lively and with enough acidity to cut through the little organs' big taste. A Frascati, I fancy, which is what the Romans have always chosen to accompany their own offal dishes.

2

The reason you caught me at a low moment yesterday afternoon, sitting outside with a typescript, is that I had finished the text of *Millie!* only that morning and had just despatched it via cyberspace to my editor at Champions Press. Normally it's quite nice to sit and gloat for a bit once a book is finished, but the sight of this one only made me gloomier. Today, though, I realize it's off my hands at last and I have definitely begun to banish the megrims. So much so that as I take my daily measurements I find myself singing the exultant yet tragic aria the dying Giancarlo sings to Nutella, the peasant girl from the hazel forest, as he gives her the magic pill that will make her live for ever—the very pill whose daring theft from the Alchemist's cave will guarantee his own demise. "Conservare in luogo fresco, ben asciutto e pulito," he implores her. "Do this for me, Nutellina mia, for me, for me, do this, this, this. Tenere fuori della portata dei bambini." His voice breaks on the word "bambini" as he and the audience acknowledge the pathos of his demand that she keep his priceless gift out of the reach of children. Nutella, a hopeless innocent, is the only person in the opera house who doesn't realize the purloined pill that will give her eternal life will also make her sterile. She is not the sort of person who reads about side effects on the label. Don't you find that at these moments of high drama you naturally become quite carried away, singing alone in the kitchen? I, too, choke on "*bambini*" even as my stupendous top A leaves a vase on the dresser ringing in sympathy.

A couple of years ago I acquired a neighbour who secretly admired my voice, although she could never quite bring herself to admit it. Marta was from Voynovia—a composer, as it turned out, and living much too close for comfort in the only other house up here for miles. Perhaps out of jealousy, and with a streak of cruelty I hadn't known was in her, Marta caricatured my singing and used her travesty in the score she wrote for Piero Pacini's film. I was very put out at the time and fell self-consciously silent for months afterwards, as anyone would. But after she disappeared—victim, I am now convinced, of that disgraceful American security programme worthy of Stalinist Russia and known as "extraordinary rendition"—my confidence and eventually my voice gradually returned. Since when I have occasionally sung from a kind of tarnished elation, like this morning. But these days my arias tend mostly to be sad. There was nothing I could do to discover where Marta had been taken, or by whom. She simply vanished back in January while I was away one weekend, leaving her house unlocked and her coffeemaker boiled dry on the hob. The gas was still alight when I found it, having burnt a hole in the caffettiera's aluminium bottom. There were also unmistakable drops of dried blood on her kitchen table. I knew dear Marta's housekeeping habits made those of a hobbit look dainty, but this was eccentric even for her. Her mouse-coloured car was still in its shed, too, implying that she hadn't left under her own steam. Although I believed completely in her innocence there was no denying she was from a very rough-diamond Voynovian clan with connections to organized crime and no doubt with Middle Eastern links as well. I called the carabinieri, who came promptly enough and briefly inspected her house with the occasional incredulous snigger but refused to be alarmed. "Undoubtedly the lady will come back," an officer told me. "I believe she has done this before?" Which of course was true; but on that occasion I'd known roughly where she was and why she'd gone and in any case she was back within a fortnight. It seemed to me that the police, who had got their fingers burned when they once improbably tried to arrest her as a call girl, were keen to keep Marta and her Voynovian connections at a distance. Not only did she surprisingly turn out to be vouched for by grandees, but I could imagine these local policemen had concluded she might be trouble in ways they would prefer not to know about. What they wanted was a simple life followed by early retirement. "You must let us know if she doesn't return, Signor Samper," they said, putting on their gloves again. "When you think she's really missing."

"But she's really missing *now*," I insisted, even though I already sensed it was useless to go on. At what point in a policeman's imagination does an absent person turn into a missing one? Each week I phoned them up to remind them; each week I was fobbed off with bland reassurance. As a rule I am deeply resistant to conspiracy theories, but I did begin to get the feeling that someone higher up had told them the case was closed. And then one day in Camaiore I ran into Signor Benedetti, the weaselly estate agent who had speciously sold both Marta and me our respective houses. After our normal exchange of florid disrespect I mentioned to him that she had disappeared. He had suffered a dented reputation for having spread malicious fables about her and surely had no reason to feel well disposed towards her, yet he told me a story I can't believe he invented. He had chanced to be at Pisa airport one Sunday afternoon, waiting in the viewing lounge for his wife's flight to arrive from Rome. As he incuriously watched passengers embarking on a British Airways plane down below on the stand he noticed a woman with a shock of frizzy hair who certainly looked very like *la* signora Marta being escorted by three young men to a white Gulfstream jet parked some way off on its own. But then, of course, he couldn't be certain. The way Benedetti recounted this made me think it was only beginning to take on significance for him now I'd remarked that she had disappeared.

"'Gulfstream?'" I pounced disbelievingly. Benedetti merely smiled.

"A Gulfstream V. Probably a C-37A," he said in a tolerant, know-all sort of voice. "Aircraft are a hobby of mine. There was a very small 'N' registration number on the tail. Definitely not Italian. In fact, almost certainly, you know, *them*. Military or government."

"But good heavens, we must tell the carabinieri at once. It could be very important."

He looked me in the eye. "I very much regret, signore, that I am absolutely unable to confirm my identification of the lady, so it will be impossible for me to support your story if you go to the police."

"Signor Benedetti," I said, making an effort to preserve the niceties. "Please tell me I am foolishly mistaken in presuming that a man of your evident truthfulness and moral courage could consider denying the eyewitness account you have just given me with your customary transparent sincerity."

"Esteemed Signor Samper, you may presume what you like. I shall deny everything even though I have told you the truth. Now if you will excuse me?"

And rodent-like, he scuttered away. Cowardly bastard. Still, I was pleased to notice his hair-weave could do with tightening. That's the worst of these high-maintenance cosmetic vanities. Since they're essentially a form of lying there's no going back: you just have to keep reweaving the tangled web. But his bombshell left me with nothing to do and no one to tell. The mild paranoia that the architects of the fatuous "War on Terror" have done their best to instil in us makes the law-abiding citizen markedly reluctant to become involved. Rather quaint when you think about it, that a vital piece of street wisdom for living in today's democratic, free societies should be

"Keep your head down." I tried to comfort myself by reflecting that Marta always was a darkish sort of horse, what with that sinister Eastern-bloc clan of hers on the loose in unmarked helicopters. I really think she did her best to keep them at arm's length, being an artist, but who knew? The fact remains that these days I can hardly bear to think of her because the images that spontaneously crowd into my mind's eye are not those of when life up here at Le Rocce was normal. All I can see in my imagination is poor frizzy Marta hung up by her thumbs in some bare, cement-walled shed while outsourced Middle Eastern interrogators do unspeakable things with their electrodes at the behest of a freedom-loving government six thousand miles away. I banish these thoughts by singing, since they are of no help to her and only distress me utterly. She has been gone almost five months now. All I can do is go over to her shuttered house from time to time to make sure the roof isn't leaking and that no one has broken in. I bought her a new caffettiera and amaze myself—given what a pain in the neck she actually was as a neighbour—by hoping against dread that one day the old girl will come back to use it. And oh, the inventive "Welcome Home" cake I shall bake for us to eat amid giggles in the laundry-heaped squalor of her kitchen! But until that moment I try to put her out of my mind.

There's something that's nagging you, though, and it has nothing to do with Marta. It's sharp of you to have noticed that casual little phrase I foolishly let drop about "taking my daily measurements." So now that cat's out of the bag and won't be stuffed back in I shall have to explain something embarrassing, not to say delicate. How can I best go about this? Start at the beginning. Well, it began by my being assaulted with spam. Each time I opened my e-mailer it was swamped with resistible offers ("Hair Pies stuffed with Hot Meat!!") or else with importunate messages implying (such are the dismal times we live in) that my penis could do with enlarging. Since it is fatal for any man *ever* to comment on, still more protest, any allegation with the word "penis" in it, I shall simply say the extravagant claims of enlargement being made aroused my forensic curiosity. Were they even legal? How could such a thing work? "Which of you by taking thought can add one cubit unto his stature?" my evangelical stepmother Laura used to quote, dumpy little number that she was. Still is, actually, and even more so now age and piety have begun to shrink her. I soon found out that taking thought is not one of the options being touted on the Internet. Taking pills, yes. Taking exercise, certainly. Taking up springs, weights, pumps and even surgery, most definitely. But not thought. The competing therapies' copywriters must be making the regular pharmaceutical industry green with envy, able as they are to imply promises that directly address their patients' anxieties. "Thicken Ur DICCKY!" they urge. "Pack More Veal!"

It's pathetic how insecure most men are on this point. Over the years many an intake of breath and murmur of quiet surprise—even of outright admiration—has led me to assume Samper is in that lucky minority who need never fear the deadly epithet "average." (As in: "I am average; you are understandably worried; he is the subject of an entertaining case study in *The Lancet*.") So it really was in a purely detached spirit of scientific enquiry that I sent off for a sixty-day course of the least harmful-sounding pills. Not that the ingredients of ProWang's Pow-r-Tabs™ sounded very reassuring when they duly arrived, containing things like "Horny Goat Weed (*Epimedium sagittatum*)," stinging-nettle leaves and "orchic substance," which I can only assume is ground-up testicles. Whose, I wonder? Moreover, the pills themselves smell very rank, like a chapel in which a Black Mass has just been held. Nevertheless I have reserves of fortitude that people often find startling and I am now thirty-four days into the course. To my great surprise I find they do seem to be having some very slight effect after all, chiefly in the circumferential sector. A purely localized reaction, I expect: a minor local distension that is enough to get Mr. and Mrs. ProWang off the hook for making false claims. I have no doubt the swelling will go down the day after the pills run out. Meanwhile, I do slightly wonder what the ingredients may be doing to the rest of me, but having got so far I'm not going to stop now. I see myself in the tradition of those great nineteenth-century men of science who drank glasses of sea-snake venom to see what would happen and then wrote dispassionate monographs about it. This is definitely the Samper attitude, even if there is something a bit wonky about the enterprise. Onward and upward regardless of the outcome, like Longfellow's obsessive mountaineer carrying his Excelsior! banner into the alpine snows, unashamed of its grammatical solecism. Surely the pious monks of San Bernard must have had *some* Latin and could have told him the word he'd chosen to mean "Higher!" was unfortunately an adjective and not an adverb? But they were probably so shocked they decided to let him carry on up the mountain to a well-deserved fate. Anyway, if at present I had a banner it would read "Maior!" or even "Maximus!," and I do believe many a pious monk would welcome me with open arms.

Another thoughtful lunch on the terrace. The sky is blue, the world lies at my feet, I am preoccupied. As always when preoccupied I distract myself with goodies. In this case I start with a glass of chilled prosecco into which exactly *one* drop of Angostura bitters has been allowed to fall. On no account must the mixture be stirred, otherwise more fizz will come out of solution. The thing to do is to watch appreciatively as the smoky brown bead unravels into ruby skeins and paler wisps, is carried away by the tiny convection currents and dispersed into a uniform shade so the prosecco is scarcely pinker than before. Nor is the taste much different: certainly no bitterness and merely the faintest hint of something aromatic, as if the grapes had been laid briefly on a cushion of herbs before being pressed. Today this drink goes admirably with a cold collation rounded off with a chunk of sensational cheese. This is a pecorino with a history, not just a sheep's cheese that has been racked on wooden shelves for a fortnight to harden up. Nowadays when everything is done at a rush, a mere month's ageing can earn a pecorino the epithet "stagionato" or "mature," which is absurd. The pecorino I am now eating spent its early days on shelves, but then it was taken to a cave in the mountains of Sardinia and carried down to a particular grotto blessed with low humidity and absolute darkness. There it was racked on trestles with a ten-centimetre air space between it and its companions and left to contemplate its soul's progress for seven long months in an unchanging ambient temperature of nine degrees Celsius. After that formative experience in the caseous equivalent of Purgatory it was gently reawakened by being carried back into the warmth and light of the upper world, where it acquired the label "Grottino" and in due course found its way onto Samper's luncheon table. The rind is thick and dark and mottled with mould but the cheese inside is the innocent colour of raw linen, not dry, but fracturing easily into geological chunks with the consistency of a stiff but friable wax. The flavour is divine: strong and deep and with none of the mouth-burning qualities of certain elderly Cheddars. In the ever-blander world of today's mass-produced comestibles one embraces a pedigree Grottino with the enthusiasm of, say, a lost alpinist greeting a Saint Bernard.

While eating I indulge an innocent pastime. Fifty minutes' work with pencil and paper yields four anagrams of "penis enlargement." I'm pleased with "Men's pie entangler" and "Gentlemen, a sniper." There's concealed historical drama to be read into the headline "Temp enrages Lenin!" and I'm definitely reassured by the implied promise of "permanent sin glee." But, yes, underneath it all I'm preoccupied. I can't any longer conceal from myself that I fear Millie Cleat is not going to like the book I've written her, and the prospect of having to rewrite until she is satisfied is dismal verging on intolerable. At the extreme she might even prevent publication, when the remaining third of my fee happens to be payable. I am, of course, an old pro and understood from the first that this wasn't a warts-and-all life but a ghosted autobiography. When we originally met, talked the project over and eventually signed the contract I did tell her that even the most devoted fans like their heroes and heroines to come with a smattering of warts because such private revelations make them seem more human, more like the readers themselves. Otherwise, if the account is too sanitized, it simply degenerates into hagiography and there's little mass interest these days in saintly lives. "Sure, sure," she kept saying. "I don't care what you write." Boy, had I heard *that* before. Those are precisely the people who bring an action three days before publication when thirty thousand copies of the book have to be hastily purged from bookshops and warehouses and pulped. And once an author has done that to a publisher he may as well hang up his word processor.

Frankly, I should have thought the average reader's overall reaction to the Millie Cleat who springs feistily from my pages would be one of "*Eeughh!*" It's impossible to disguise the central facts of her character, which are that she's grotesquely ambitious, manipulative, without scruple and completely besotted by her own image. She makes Narcissus look self-effacing. However, perhaps I'm wrong to assume that everyone will automatically find her character distasteful. I've made this mistake before. In both my Luc Bailly book and *Hot Seat!* there were incidents that shed some pretty dubious light on the heroes, yet both Bailly and Snoilsson seemed happy to let them stand. Mind you, I never was convinced that Snoilsson could read, so he might have missed them. But the point is, I gather readers actually admire these tales of their heroes' ruthlessness. They think them "sharp" and "enterprising."

Is it me, or is it my readership that's changing? For years I thought most people wanted their sporting heroes and heroines to triumph not just over their own mental and physical limitations ("no pain, no gain!") but also over the moral squalor of today's professional sport. Call me a romantic, but I still warm to Britain's admiration for gallant failure as opposed to the transatlantic worship of unscrupulous success. Wake up over there! It's *because* history is written by the winners that it's bunk. Trust him; old Henry Ford knew. I also thought I understood that the heroes of my books were supposed to be ordinary people with extraordinary talents who got to the top without having to resort to screwing their coaches when they were twelve, like gymnasts, or brutally fouling each other in full view, like footballers, or standing in the slips quietly telling the batsman that his wife's a terrific lay, like Australian cricketers. These days I don't think the readers care. People expect their sporting heroes to lie and cheat and foul and stuff themselves with performance-enhancing drugs because if they don't it means they've stopped short of a total commitment to winning. "It's the money these days," they say, as if that not only explained but excused everything. Actually, they're all shits, the lot of them—sports personalities, fans and my readers alike, and it's time Samper got *out* of this sordid business.

3

You think I'm exaggerating. You think when it comes to beloved Millie, the world's nautical darling, I'm over-stating my case. So I will indulge your verdict by not protesting. I am even willing to agree that simple job dissatis-faction leading to total burnout has distorted my view. But there is an unarticulated popular belief that a lone woman doesn't brave the world's oceans without mysteriously being rinsed free of the baser human motives. It is as though pro-longed and intimate contact with nature automatically made people grander and purer instead of stupider and redder in tooth and claw. Being a one-armed grandmother only hallows Millie still further in her public's eye: a gallant old sea dog rather than a poisonous old sea bitch. "It may be that the ghosts of Sir Francis Chichester and perhaps even of Drake himself were standing by her and gave her strength in her hours of lonely agony off Tierra del Fuego," intoned the *Daily Mail* (or was it the *Express*?), cunningly conflating Cape Horn with the Garden of Gethsemane. I don't remember anybody writing in to point out that Jesus Christ had not been miked up, watched by Webcams and pinpointed by satellite, nor is there any record of his having taken frequent nips of Glenfiddich from a plastic bottle on a lanyard around his neck. It's this aura of sanctity attributed to the woman that finally I can't bear. Like any professional ghost who writes about popular heroes I've naturally done my best to suppress the truth; but in order not to do further damage to my blood pressure it has now

become a matter of principle to present to her credulous public an alternative Millie Cleat.

Principle? I hear you cry, and I'm duly grateful that you
scoff. Under normal circumstances Gerald Samper is indeed
the very last person to invoke principle. In fact, if I had a personal motto it would probably be "Expediency Always
Trumps Principle." I now think this might look rather well on
the stonework above the sitting-room fireplace: *Semper utilitas
virtum superat.* Only the sentiment might make the pious
monks of San Bernard shudder (if they still exist); the grammar
is impeccable. If I had such a thing as a core this would probably qualify as a core belief, but mercifully I haven't so it will
remain a private rule of thumb. In any case I hope shortly to
convince you that present circumstances are not normal and
that I have a duty to blow Millie's gaff.

To that end, let me recount an incident that is for me
unadulterated Cleat, and one which I have loyally and shrewd-
ly omitted from my book. It is a story I succeeded in documenting in unusual detail, backed up by tape-recorded interviews with twenty-three oceanographers, many of them sober.
So vivid were their accounts, but so far removed from most
people's lives their activities, I'm afraid I shall need to do a little background scene-setting once I have fetched a fresh bottle
of prosecco from the fridge. Like millions before me, I find
alcohol is inseparable from anything to do with the sea.
Certainly there's no possible way I could have written *Millie!*
sober. As Churchill noted in relation to the navy, there abideth
rum, buggery, the lash, these three; but the greatest of these is
rum. Admittedly there have been a good few moments in my
life, especially in Morocco, when I would have challenged his
priorities, but just at present some prosecco will do nicely. The
glass brims, the tiny bubbles ascend in wavering chains, so let
me begin.

A few years ago there was one of those awesomely tedious

panic stories that nowadays hit the headlines with increasing frequency and tell of the different versions of imminent doom that are probably in store for us, as if we cared. Sometimes it's rogue asteroids, often it's dread epidemics, and eternally it's global warming (or, in my preferred version, a growling lamb or even a grim ball gown). This particular story concerned a volcano called Cumbre Vieja or "Old Peak" on the island of La Palma in the Canaries. The diverting scenario on offer was that Cumbre Vieja might be seized by a sudden fit of vulcanism such that its already fractured slopes would fall off into the sea, causing a tsunami of epic proportions. It would be goodbye to time-share cottages in Lanzarote as the wall of water sped off to lay waste the west coast of Africa before fanning out across the Atlantic to do the same to the eastern seaboard of the United States. Until the story hit the news, such vulcanological work as had been done on Cumbre Vieja was not imbued with much sense of alarm. Suddenly, however, having learned of the damage the wave might also cause low-lying coastal areas in Europe, the EU decided to fund an urgent geological survey of the seabed around La Palma to see if it could yield advance warning of disaster, and to deploy some instruments that would enable permanent monitoring.

This project, the European Atlantic Islands Geomorphological Instability Survey (or "EAGIS" for pronounceability), duly rose through the usual bureaucratic strata in Brussels from the depths of feasibility into the sunlit realm of implementation. That it did so with unusual despatch was surely a measure of how worried Brussels functionaries were about their time-share cottages, not merely in Lanzarote but in Funchal over in Madeira to the north. The declared aim of the survey was "to produce a three-dimensional model of the volcano's submarine roots by using acoustic signals to penetrate several kilometres into the earth's crust and reveal the faults leading down to the magma chambers of molten rock." Can you *seriously* imagine this as a plausible ambition? Others could, it seems, for EAGIS recruited oceanographers from several countries and disciplines and finally put to sea late in the year in no fewer than four seismic-survey vessels. These were specialized craft of massive and hideous design known as ramform, being wedge-shaped with an extremely broad stern over which as many as twelve streamers of sensing instruments could be towed simultaneously. What with fuel tankers and other supply vessels, it was a fleet of a dozen ships, hired under very tight time restrictions and with overrun penalty clauses, that finally set sail out of Rotterdam. If they were lucky the scientists would have a bare sixteen days on site. A series of Atlantic squalls would be enough to abort the whole programme and write off some eight million pounds. True, this was merely cash from the bottomless sack of that perennial Santa Claus, the European taxpayer, so it was literally of no account. Yet if the enterprise failed somebody somewhere might be forced to account for it, so everyone duly assumed a serious expression while it was planned.

So also did the EAGIS scientists as they put to sea, daunted but eager. They were daunted because the area around La Palma to be surveyed was large, but as scientists they were licking their lips expectantly because it was an unheard-of luxury to have four survey vessels at their disposal. In the normally cash-strapped world of oceanography they were used to making do with a single converted Hull trawler towing a limited amount of often elderly equipment. This was a golden, never-to-be-repeated opportunity that the Good Fairies of Brussels had sent them, and they had gleefully designed experiments to take maximum advantage of it.

Some people's ideas of excitement seem designed expressly to astound the rest of us. My informants assured me that their most ambitious and enterprising scheme was to have all four ships abreast, working in pairs. One of each pair would tow a dozen streamers on the sea's surface: thin polythene tubes up to four kilometres long with sensors embedded in them at regular intervals. The other ship would be towing a variety of air guns. These were heavy metal cylinders that produced detonations of compressed air at different depths and at various frequencies. The echoes of these sound waves from deep below the seabed would build up a 3-D picture of the volcano's roots. I was told that to appreciate how difficult it was I had to imagine four ships moving slowly abreast with a rigorously maintained distance between each, all towing four kilometres of streamers exactly parallel with one another so as to build up a seismological map with equal accuracy in all three dimensions. Apparently this is hard enough when going in a straight line but still harder when the ships reach the edge of the survey area and need to turn in order to come back and do a swathe in the reverse direction. They said it took these boats nearly thirty kilometres to turn safely and re-group at the end of each leg, which was why everyone in EAGIS was worried about time. Anything that added further delay to the difficulties of maintaining this balletic synchronization day and night might scupper the entire enterprise.

For a fortnight luck was with them. According to those I interviewed no equipment malfunctioned, nobody goofed, the weather remained calm and blue. The Canaries are on much the same parallel as Kuwait and New Delhi, and even in the Atlantic in November it was hot on deck as the oddly shaped vessels steamed back and forth while the scientists watched the winches with their precious spools of streamers. Below decks they slept in shifts and stared at the banks of monitors in the labs as the streams of data came bouncing back from deep below the earth's crust. Day after day the familiar bulk of Cumbre Vieja and the island of La Palma shifted from port to starboard as the ships turned and turned again, sailing their grid pattern with the precision of a military manoeuvre. And day after day the volcano's even bigger undersea bulk slowly took shape on the laboratory plotters like a giant composite X-ray of a rotten tooth. Anyone other than a scientist would have been bored out of his skull.

On the morning of the fifteenth day an alert Marine Mammal Observer aboard *Scomar Seismic* spotted a whale dead ahead. Regulations required that each ramform carry two of these MMOs who had the power to bring the survey to a halt in mid-leg if need be, and to order the immediate silencing of the air guns to avoid damaging the cetaceans' hearing. Aboard survey vessels MMOs are generally about as popular with the scientists as the lollipop ladies who patrol street crossings outside schools are with commuters. Despite the beasts' fearful halitosis most marine scientists feel a vague benevolence toward whales, just as many drivers do toward children. But the aura that surrounds MMOs and lollipop ladies, compounded of virtuousness and the smug certainty that any jury will find in their favour, can induce in those pushed for time a nearly irresistible urge to accelerate. This particular whale off La Palma brought the survey to a temporary halt. If the wretched animal could have received the blast of the combined ill will of several hundred EAGIS scientists it would have shrivelled in an instant to the size of a herring. As it was, aborting the leg left incomplete a crucial portion of a huge unsuspected fault that was being revealed deep below the volcano. After hasty consultations over the ships' radios it was unanimously agreed it was vital to re-survey this last leg. The whale, whether from malice or indolence, seemed disinclined to leave and was soon joined by another. Eventually they both swam away and disappeared off the sonar screens, but what with re-grouping and getting the equipment synchronized again it wasn't until ten o'clock at night that the four vessels could begin surveying once more.

This was where my informants' story began to degenerate

into one of those Alistair MacLean-style narratives that manage to infuse mild drama with the spirit of pure wood. Unfortunately, in order to protect Samper Enterprises legally I dare not deviate far from the taped accounts they gave me. I am perfectly aware their conversation lacks sparkle. On the other hand the event these scientists witnessed is of importance and piquancy, as you will soon appreciate.

At two o'clock in the morning the ships' radars picked up the faint blip of a small craft approaching. On the bridge of the *Scomar Explorer* a British oceanographer, Valerie Geddes, was standing with a cup of tea beside the short-range scanner, keeping an eye on the four vessels' relative positions. The detail of the cup of tea struck a note of homely realism, I suppose, which was why people remembered it. You can be sure that had she been picking her nose or reading Kierkegaard they would have edited it out as irrelevant. This is why adventure stories are often so boring to read. From her instruments Dr. Geddes noticed that a brisk wind had got up, an offshore breeze that no doubt brought with it the parched smell of the Sahara Desert, although nobody mentioned it. This breeze obliged the ships' navigation computers to compensate in order to keep them on course. The need to keep checking explained why nobody paid any attention to the insignificant blip on the radar until it was only a nautical mile off *Explorer's* port quarter. Valerie immediately got on the radio to her counterpart in the neighbouring vessel to starboard.

"What do you think it is, Patrice?" she asked. (From his name I at once imagined a tall, clean-cut, aristocratic Frenchman with blond hair, practically an aftershave model. When eventually I met him he was a tubby Belgian with eczema in his beard.)

"It's making about twenty knots, very low profile. I guess it's got to be a speedboat of sorts. Maybe a Zodiac?"

"Well, we're not getting any acoustic signature. We've got a zillion hydrophones out there so one of us ought to be picking up propeller noise, or at least some of the frequencies of engine noise. How about you?"

"Nothing here, either. We're going to lose it on radar any moment now. Your hull's about to screen it from us."

By now others in the ships' radio rooms were trying to raise the mysterious craft on a variety of channels but without success.

"Ought we to send the chopper up?" Each ramform carried a helicopter which could be launched fairly quickly in emergencies. But this was the middle of the night and at a moment when every waking person's attention was focused on the survey. Did a tiny blip on the radar overhauling them at a rate of twenty knots constitute an emergency and justify putting a helicopter with two men into the air? It all had to be balanced against the requirements of COLREGS. Survey ships are as rigidly bound by the International Maritime Organization's collision regulations as any other vessel, but ramform skippers have better reasons than most for being reluctant to abide by them. Apparently if a ramform stops suddenly its streamers begin sinking and may easily be lost.

While they were dithering, others were outside on the port wing of the *Explorer's* bridge with night-vision binoculars trying to see the interloper's navigation lights, but without success. It was a moonless night, and the various lights on nearby La Palma and some inshore fishing vessels in the lee of the island further confused the issue. Suddenly from the bridge came Valerie's cry, "For Christ's sake, now *we've* lost him—he must be right on top of us. Use the searchlight." The light came on, swerved about the sea off the port bow, flashed over something billowy and lurched back to illuminate the immense green-and-gold sails of a trimaran yacht below them and shockingly close, a mere eighty metres away and heading straight across the ship's bows. Collision seemed inevitable (this phrase is now out of copyright). On the bridge there was a burst of incredulous profanity as someone overrode the autopilot, spun the tiny helm hard to starboard and sent the engines to Full Astern. The Collision Imminent alarm whooped deafeningly until someone turned it off. The starboard searchlight came to life and caught the yacht barely scraping past the ship's forefoot with centimetres to spare. The profanity became a chorus as other alarms went off and warning lights flashed, telling everybody what they already knew: that the ramform's course had been irretrievably corrupted and the leg once again ruined. Valerie was still on the radio to the *Scomar Navigator*.

"Can you *believe* this idiot?" she was raving. "No lights, no radio, and he's totally screwed us. Have you got him on visual? If he's going to try and race you too he isn't going to make it, Patrice. He'll go slap across your streamers. You'll sink him with your buoys."

It had been explained to me that each streamer had at least one navigation buoy halfway along its length as well as a tail buoy at the end. These were towed along on the surface and it seemed impossible even for a yacht with a draught as shallow as that of a trimaran to cross twelve lines of streamers without colliding with one or more of the sundry solid objects hissing along behind the survey vessel. Whoever had the *Navigator's* helm also had a matter of seconds to decide what to do. He decided to go hard a-port, hoping to turn the ramform inside the yacht's oblivious course and shield it from the equipment it was towing.

Unfortunately, when a ship towing many tons of cable and equipment goes abruptly to Full Astern the equipment carries on under its own inertia for a while. And if the towing vessel just as violently changes course at the same time, the carefully maintained spaces between each towed streamer become chaotic. As it happened, the yacht did implacably maintain its course and the *Navigator's* turn probably did save it from ploughing through the lines of streamers and being sunk. But the cost to the EAGIS survey was fatal. At least one searchlight followed the green-and-gold sails as the trimaran rapidly disappeared.

"*Beldame*," read somebody with a pair of binoculars. "Isn't it that goddamn lone yachtsgranny, whatsername, Millie Thing?"

"Cleat! Sodding Cleat!"

But they had more urgent things to worry about than Millie Cleat. For even as *Explorer* and *Navigator* skilfully avoided colliding, their combined twenty-four streamers and towing cables fouled one another in a gigantic spaghetti-like tangle four kilometres long. God alone knew how many hours it would take to sort out and carefully retrieve the monstrously expensive equipment. So God alone knew how much penalty time it was all going to add to the ships' hiring. But it was already clear that a final and vital part of the volcano's geological structure would remain unknown. This survey would be incomplete, with Cumbre Vieja just beginning to appear even more menacing than had been feared. Dawn found the EAGIS fleet's crews sullen with disappointment and rage.

By the time the scientists had salvaged their equipment and reached the Bay of Biscay on their delayed homeward course to Rotterdam, Millie Cleat had arrived off the Solent to an ecstatic national welcome. The shark-pruned brown figure dwarfed by her bellying viridian sails had easily broken the world record for a solo non-stop circumnavigation. From now on and for an indefinite period she could do no wrong. "When I picked up that wind off Africa I just knew I was going to do it," she told the cameras. "It was as if some wise power had taken over the *Beldame's* wheel."

"*Wise power?*" the EAGIS scientists yelled as they watched her on satellite TV aboard their four ramforms. "No lights, no radio, no warning, clear breach of COLREGS Rule 18 by cutting straight across the bows of a vessel 'restricted in her ability to manoeuvre' and clearly marked by its lights as towing gear, plus causing Christ knows how many thousand pounds' worth of damage, and that's a *wise power at the wheel?*" Furious as they were, it was already quite obvious to them that no amount of official remonstration on their part would make the slightest difference or, indeed, would even be listened to. For the foreseeable future the woman who had ruined their survey was untouchable. As much good expecting water to flow uphill as to denounce Millie Cleat for abysmal seamanship.

4

If ever you were mean enough to suggest that Samper makes a fuss about nothing, I submit the previous chapter as evidence of the bizarre worlds I'm required to come to grips with in order to write these ludicrous books. Any masochists among you who read *Hot Seat!* will realize that I needed to become marginally au fait with many indigestible mechanical details of Formula 1 engines. And now, too, for *Millie!* I was obliged to scrape acquaintance with a lot of maritime technology I never knew existed. Part of the deal, I'm afraid, so I'm not ashamed of having to pass it on. Never let it be said that my books lack an educational aspect, even if it does concern knowledge one could live exquisitely without. On the other hand I do owe some reasonably abject apologies for the occasional pulp-fictional tone of the narrative just related. As already explained, I thought it safer to stick as closely as possible to my transcripts of the twenty-three scientists' own accounts when I tracked them down some months later. Vastly entertaining as many of these characters turned out to be—and in one case quite amazingly attractive in oilskins—they are mostly not the sort of people who express themselves in polished dialogue.

I have already intimated that any sea story without alcohol is like a kiss without a moustache, as the Saudis say, and I don't believe a single one of the oceanographers I met was a closet teetotaller. Naturally, therefore, my own bottle of prosecco has long since been swallowed in the retelling of this shameful maritime incident and I am now in urgent need of something else to take the taste away. I'm afraid we're not yet quite done with this little contretemps in the Canaries. In a spirit of fairness and balance normally quite alien to me but temporarily forced upon me by Britain's Palaeolithic libel laws, I will present la Cleat's own version of the story. But not yet. It can wait until tomorrow. Right now, an early gin and tonic on the terrace is imperative and then, I think, will be the *moment juste* for the unveiling of a marine speciality of my own humble devising whose ingredients are unwittingly awaiting their apotheosis in the fridge. Since posterity demands that I bequeath it the recipes of my more inventive dishes, I shall jot this one down right now on the terrace, in between tinkling sips of g-&-t when ice cubes jostle the upper lip to produce a sensory satisfaction almost unknown since one left off being breast-fed.

Before that, though, a brief word about mood and food. I have never yet read a cookery book that attempts to match dishes with one's emotional state. Insofar as the TV cheffies' latest productions exhale an affect of their own, it is invariably one of breezy intimacy, as though the hair-gelled oiks who wrote them had stepped through the screen and were right there in your kitchen, filling it with blokeish bustle and yo-dude matiness. Any suggestion that one might like to devise a dish to harmonize with one's emotional state would go unheard in flurries of exclamation marks. "What gets me all excited is real down-to-earth nosh!" they bawl, banging down pots and pans with the licensed abandon of someone whose old friend Giovanna has been making homemade pasta in her little Umbrian village ever since she was tall enough to roll it out on the kitchen table. "Nothing poncy, nothing fancy, but hey!" Whatever it means, this swamping patter claims that the best cooking is dead simple, the implication being that if something is good enough for canny old peasants like Giovanna it's surely good enough for Essex boys like us. Well, I am a Shropshire Samper and think only an idiot would pretend that all the best dishes are simple, just as only an oaf believes cooking must always be quick and *fun*, as opposed to interesting and complex and hard work to get right. Sometimes one's mood requires a reflective silence in the kitchen, broken only by the snicking of a knife through vegetables as one works one's way towards a dish that carefully expresses the moment.

My point about food is simply that one occasionally wants something that has its own aura of high seriousness (offal), or faint melancholy (rhubarb), or earnestness (lobster). (Synaesthetes, who never agree about any of their associations, should block their noses when I tell them that, for me, dishes involving these particular three foods come to the table in the keys of D flat, B minor and F sharp, respectively). One's emotional state surely has everything to do with what one wishes to eat. If I'm in frivolous mood I don't want to eat haggis, and if downcast I don't want spring rolls or, for that matter, anything with a single bean sprout in it.

It seems there must once have existed a British tradition of the colour coordination of food and mood. The manuscript of William Blake's "Jerusalem" refers quite legibly to England's "dark Satanic meals," but owing to a typographer's error he has been misquoted ever since. In any case this ancient and sensitive style of cuisine died out in England although it thrived fitfully on the Continent, particularly during the Age of Decadence. A well known example is the black dinner that Des Esseintes throws in *À Rebours* as a funeral banquet in memory of his own virility, "lately but only temporarily deceased." The guests at this extravagant caprice are waited on by naked Negresses "wearing only slippers and stockings in cloth of silver embroidered with tears." This is not only silly but much too extravagant for a mood that is merely downcast. Besides, there is nothing wrong with the Samper virility that naked Negresses could possibly cure. No, tonight this whole Millie business has left me feeling *spiritually* dark-hued, so my dinner will match it:

Death Roe

Ingredients

450 gm cod or similar roe (but not sturgeon)
16 ml squid ink
1/2 aubergine
Bottarga
Black rice
Black currants
1 whole nutmeg
1 lime
1 tbsp olive oil

Squid ink is easily bought in 4 gm sachets as *nero di seppia*. Bottarga is the second-greatest thing ever to have come out of Sardinia, only narrowly edged out by sardonicism, the convulsive laughter ending in death that the Greeks said was induced by eating a particular Sardinian plant. Tying for third place come Grottina pecorino sardo and sardines, especially fresh ones eaten straight off an insanitary griddle in a Mediterranean port (it's important to keep our antibodies frisky). Bottarga is the dried roe of either tuna or the flat-headed grey mullet, *Mugil cephalus*. The original Arabic word for salted roes, *batarikh*, became adopted and mispronounced all over the Mediterranean; but the Sardinian version of the thing itself is a refinement of the crude original. To make bottarga you hand-massage the roes to expel all the tiny pockets of air that might harbour bacteria and make them go bad. This takes hours. Then you salt them thoroughly and press them between wooden planks heaped with marble weights. This takes a week.

Finally you dry them in the sun, which takes up to two months. You are left with a sublime hard substance that can be grated over dishes, especially pasta, to make them redolent of sun and sea. A good bottarga is the marine equivalent of truffle and has the power to scent things even in small quantities. Tuna bottarga is sharper, saltier and more pungent than mullet bottarga, which is subtler and sometimes has an almost almondy aftertaste.

Black rice is a variety originally grown in China and comes accompanied by that slight frisson of taboo that often goes with gourmet Chinese food. We understand this is because it would once have cost us our head to eat it unless we were royal. Black rice was, predictably, so incredibly rare and hard to grow it was reserved for the Emperor and inevitably became known as "forbidden" rice, along with forbidden monkey-picked Tie Guan Yin green tea and forbidden hundred-year-old pickled panda labia. Undaunted, the Italians have simply taken up growing black rice in Piedmont, where Principato di Lucedio sells it as *Venere riso nero*. Quite what it has to do with Venus escapes me; but then the same thing goes for that reliable human activity known as *Venere solitaria* which keeps us sane and thankfully has nothing to do with anything as transient as love. Black rice takes a lot of cooking, sometimes up to 30 minutes, and comes out of the pan a deep purplish black and smelling of freshly baked loaves.

So if we summarily switch off the winsome TV cheffies in mid-grin it will leave the limelight and work space to Gerald Samper as he prepares his gloomy masterpiece, Death Roe. We start by taking the fresh roes (do not on any account remove their outer membranes) and immersing them for 19 minutes in a simmering mixture of the squid ink with the juice and zest of a medium lime plus just enough water. Once the roes are seething put the black rice on and start slowly grilling half a well-oiled, large, unsalted aubergine. When it is done, scrape the pulp out and set aside. Its delicious seared and wrinkled skin must also be reserved. When the roes are ready, remove their outer membrane. You will find that despite it the squid ink will have penetrated and turned them black to their hearts. Using a fork, blend the aubergine pulp with the roes and a tablespoon of olive oil. As you work it, gradually incorporate a small quarter of a nutmeg that you have previously pressure-cooked. There, *that* would have wiped the indulgent smiles off the cheffies' faces. It would simply never have occurred to them to pressure-cook a nutmeg. This is because they have less imagination and curiosity than a stick of celery. After 45 minutes of slow pressure-cooking a nutmeg changes intriguingly from being as chewable as teak into something that crumbles dryly while still retaining wonderful aromatic properties. You will find that the water it cooked in is barely discoloured and scarcely even smells of nutmeg. Whatever the chemical changes that take place, they do so inside the nut; and while it remains identifiably nutmeggy in flavour it is now mellower, less aggressive, more brooding. A small quarter of this cooked nut should now be crumbled and blended with the roes, aubergine pulp, oil and a sparing benison of grated bottarga. This process must be done by hand. If you use a mechanical blender you run the risk of winding up with a peculiar stiff *taramasalata* looking like a dollop of bitumen. Ideally, the individual fish eggs should remain intact.

Death Roe is clearly one of those dishes whose presentation is everything. The Samper way is to get out his precious matte-finish black Wedgwood trencher and heap the crumbled roes in the grilled aubergine skin at the centre of a bed of black rice. A few black currants scattered artistically not only look well but constitute tiny land mines of unexpected flavour. It is a sable meal for a discoloured mood, and may be further set off by being eaten with a sharp and dazzling white yoghurt. As you eat it on a terrace in the company of a bottle of chilled, slightly acidic Valpolicella, you may pleasurably imagine the cheffies' expressions as they creep off home to put something safe in the microwave, probably deep-frozen pizza. They are also going to need quantities of reassuring pudding, achingly sweet and intensely lemon-flavoured. But then, they never were fit company for adults with adult moods.

*

This morning I am definitely chirpier. There's something calming about these matutinal rituals: coffee on the terrace, doing my measurements, planning revenge. A pair of buzzards revolves around an early rising thermal, no doubt looking for a tastily rotting carcass, the raptorial equivalent of coffee and croissants. Even in May up here in the mountains the early sunlight smells of ozone: an invigorating smell that makes me want to stretch and brings to mind long-ago summer holidays I spent in shorts trying to catch lizards. I was very fond of the smell of my bare knees and forearms in the sun. How sad are these childhood memories! The internal record is still vivid and intact but it has become buried beneath the years' accumulating ordure.

Which reminds me. Today, as threatened, I have to give you a sneak preview of the passage in *Millie!* where bos'un Cleat has her own yarn about that dark and stormless night in the Canaries. Her dazzlingly guileless version goes as follows:

I now knew I was on the home stretch. Even faithful old *Beldame* seemed to be tugging at her leash like a weary dog at the end of a long "walkies" who suddenly recognizes her own street. Exhausted as I was, my mood definitely gained a fillip from knowing that, barring adverse winds or some unthinkable disaster, I ought to make the Solent with maybe as much as five days in hand. God willing, I thought, this is the big one! If I break the record I shall definitely dedicate it to Clifford and the kids.

As soon as the weather modeller made it obvious that the wind was simply going to run out on my original course up the Atlantic, Barry came up with the major course change that brought me five hundred miles further east than we'd anticipated. According to him MetSat was giving good winds up the west coast of Africa for the next fortnight and we decided to go for broke. Sure, we'd lose time crossing over, but if I stayed on our planned track I ran the very real risk of being stuck way out there in mid-Atlantic. No one could admire and respect Rufus Rasmussen as a sailor more than I do, but since he was my closest rival I'm afraid I was overjoyed to see him miscalculate and slow to a crawl far to the west of the Cape Verde Islands. With any luck he'd shortly be completely becalmed. I know it sounds harsh, but that's the nature of friendly competition! As you know, Millie's motto is "It's an ill wind that blows somebody else more luck than me!"

So we updated my AutoNav and bingo! the closer I got to Africa the better the wind became. By now *Beldame* was really getting the bit between her teeth. I decided that between us we'd go for a record that no one else would be able to beat for years and years—if ever. It now felt as though every yard counted. As I came up on the tip of El Hierro in the Canary Islands I decided not to go up the west coast of La Palma but to cut inside and graze its eastern shore. This was a calculated risk on my part. To judge from the map I guessed there might be more inshore fishing craft on this eastern side of the island, but the charts were predicting the boost of a three-knot northwesterly current coming up between La Gomera and Tenerife and it could make all the difference. Recognizing my plan as a masterstroke, Barry okayed it at once.

It was night as I sped up off La Palma. *Beldame* was really soaring, touching 28 knots. To my dismay I could see an awful lot of lights in the water up ahead, including what looked like four gigantic Christmas trees the size of aircraft carriers in line abreast. To be honest, I had to sneak a look at the chart of the various light combinations to decode the signal they were all showing. I managed to translate it and understood they were towing gear of some sort. God knew what that meant, except that it put me in a fix. Even though the ships only seemed to be making a few knots, for me to cut across to starboard and go right around this strange strung-out fleet could lose me as much as an hour, and quite probably longer if it also lost me the current. But if I were to sneak up to port and slip through on the inside between the island and the inshore ship I could maintain my course. So, being a feisty gal and used to taking calculated risks (as only a born sailor can who is supremely confident of her seawomanship!), that was what I did. As I snuck up and overtook them I was awed by the size of the vessels. Compared to poor little *Beldame* they looked as big as oil rigs, chugging along slowly with all their deck lights ablaze. I'd never seen ships like these before. Their sterns were enormously wide and I noticed huge spools with cables disappearing overboard. Something mysterious connected with the world of communications, no doubt. As I overhauled the nearest behemoth I couldn't help a feeling of pride at how efficient the millennia-old technology of simple ropes and sails and flimsy hulls still is. Modern technology has its efficiencies too, I dare say, but the heavy thudding of engines and the stinking pall of diesel smoke that marked these ships' laborious passage seemed, well, strangely old-fashioned! Little *Beldame* soon showed them a clean pair of heels and the great monsters fell astern without, I suspect, even being aware of my presence. Soon their heaps of blazing lights dwindled to a faint haze on the horizon and I was past La Palma. I fervently thanked whoever was at my helm that I hadn't lost a second by sticking to my course.

"Whoever was at my helm," my foot. Servo motors, actually, carrying out tiny course corrections from the *Beldame*'s computers at the rate of three every second. "Simple ropes and sails and flimsy hulls," my arse, as if they had been borrowed from the *Kon-Tiki* or the *Cutty Sark* instead of being respectively polypropylene, nylon and titanium. And . . . but no. Why protest further? I know perfectly well what awful tosh it is. The style! The shriek marks! The clichés! Not to mention the downright disingenuousness of the whole thing—little Miss Innocent slipping by unnoticed. I know, I know: it's grotesque. But in my defence I was being faithful to the account of her voyage that the winsome Millie Cleat (whose name can be re-arranged as "I melt all ice") gave me not long after I had signed the contract to write her book. In those days I was still making an effort to feel benignly towards her. In those days she hadn't passed certain opprobrious personal remarks about my hair and one or two other things. And in those days I hadn't yet heard the oceanographers' accounts of her passage through the Canaries. As soon as I had, I realized how utterly pointless it would be to tackle Millie about it. It would have been akin to taxing Mother Teresa with skimping on personal hygiene. By then Millie had been beatified, remember, and sometimes when I took issue with her version in one of our sessions I thought my ears caught a restless rustle like that of a flock of vultures adjusting their plumage: the sound of lawyers' robes billowing in the distance.

5

The days pass. My nicotine-stained agent Frankie rings from London to say how much he has enjoyed reading *Millie!* But he would say that. When has an agent ever told an author his latest book isn't up to scratch? He isn't paid to make discouraging judgements. He waits for the publisher's reaction and then assumes a series of rubberized diplomatic postures calculated to mollify both parties. We've still heard nothing from either Champions Press or Millie herself. Ominous, I call it.

And so whole weeks go by and June begins to steepen with the sun, which often seems vertically overhead as though Le Rocce were Nairobi. It's hot even up here in the mountains, where for long hours nothing seems to move. One after another the days are transfixed by a blazing needle like ranks of identical blue butterflies in a cabinet. Time that manages to be static yet will not come again, etc. Terrific. Down there beyond the crags and the diminishing S-bends of the road, down among the twinkling greenhouses and windscreens on the coast, people are laughing and gossiping and smearing each other's inaccessible parts with sun oil. Ironic self-knowledge comes with the job, so I can't pretend I haven't got exactly what I schemed so hard to get a couple of years ago: splendid isolation, distance from the world. And the same irony obliges me to say that sometimes I really wish old Marta were still over in her house, thumping the stuffing out of that Cold War piano of hers. Gross and preposterous though it was in so many ways, her behaviour, and not least her Voynovian cuisine, kept one on one's toes as well as on one's lavatory. It piques me even now to think of her traitorous theft of my private singing voice, to say nothing of her clumping seductiveness. But the other week when I went over to check her rural slum my threadbare conscience drove me upstairs to make sure that rats weren't nesting in her mattress. Suddenly, I was taken unawares by the pathos of her silent bedroom: by the hairbrush still clotted with her dark frizzy wires and the way it brought the horrid euphemism "forced grooming" to mind. I was even touched by the handful of dreadful cosmetics she must have bought off a barrow in Viareggio, all with Italian names like Hot Passion and Silken Princess. I admit that when I thought of what might even then be happening to the poor creature in some cement-block oubliette my eyes did fill, rather. Gerald *Samper's*? I know; but only for a minute, until I supposed philosophically that that was what came of being born into an eastern European (I nearly said western Asiatic) mafia clan. No matter that you're a talented composer with no interest in a life of black helicopters and Kalashnikovs, your family will always drag you down in the end. It's nothing to do with blood being thicker than water, just that the child you were fatally haunts the adult you never quite will be. Guilty by association.

Something has to change. I can't go on like this. In a short while I shall have to face my fortieth birthday—inconceivable!—and there's no way I can enter my fifth decade while still writing about sporting heroes. My books are nothing but cunningly crafted lies, yet avoid being honest fiction. But neither are they attempts at objective history since fantasy figures *have* no objective history. No, as befits this squirmy, relativist age they fall uneasily somewhere between. Not nonfiction so much as un-fact: the genre that encourages celebrity paste to pass itself off as diamond. One reason I think Millie Cleat is pure paste is that before beginning her book I read a little around the subject of lone yachtspersons in order to put her into some sort of historical perspective. Way beyond the call of duty for my kind of writing, of course, but one needs to alleviate the tedium of the eternal record-breaking *now* in which sporting heroes live. It was salutary to learn that an American, Joshua Slocum, had not only sailed single-handed around the world over a century before Millie Cleat but that he had the taste and good sense not to do it without stopping occasionally. I admit I find something simpatico in this idea of lone endeavour. But it has to be done self-effacingly, otherwise it's like donating to charity and making sure your name gets published. You choose to set off into the planet's great salt wastes, and your life *is* that odyssey. Nobody knows where you are and nor do you know how it goes with family and friends, which is how you want it. Your competence, like your life, is self-contained. It is your skill at dealing with navigation, sails, hardship and your own company that enables you to survive—or else prove unequal to the elements and disappear for ever, as Captain Slocum eventually did.

I don't know whether this is courageous. Maybe certain people are simply born not to be landlubbers, so the alternative of a comparatively safe life ashore never arises. Maybe they don't need daily human bustle in order to acquire themselves. In Slocum's days no one confronting the sea alone could ever be other than humble, and setting off by yourself in a sailboat was voluntarily to slip from human sight and almost from human mind as well. It is precisely the relentlessly high public visibility of Cleat and her ilk that violates this ideal—that and every item of hi-tech hardware that sails their boats for them. Far from disappearing, they are in all-too-constant touch, watched on Webcam by millions around the world night and day, their position known to within centimetres courtesy of GPS, their course plotted by computer, their sails set or taken in by little motors. Undoubtedly it's still a dangerous activity compared with pony-trekking or billiards; but then surely one ought to run *some* sort of risk to earn all that unstinted adulation? Being privy to an overview of la Cleat's recent loud whizzings about the ocean has made me admire all the more the strong, silent nutters of yesteryear, bearded and lined, who did these things the hard way in rancid oilskins. My admiration (but definitely not envy) is reserved for the Shackletons of the world who achieved epic journeys with lousy or nonexistent equipment, for men like Whymper or Mallory who went walking on the Matterhorn or Everest largely unwatched by the world and wearing not much more than an old tweed jacket, plus fours and stout boots. Millie's yacht cost thirty-five million Australian dollars; Slocum's thirty-six-foot sloop, *Spray*, probably a few hundred American dollars. I rest my heavily biased case.

Yes, the days pass. I know they do because my sixty-day supply of Pow-r-Tabs™ is visibly dwindling. I wonder if this isn't taking over from calendars as a way of keeping track of time in a pill-popping age? No more tearing off the days; one's steady tramp towards the grave is made visible in the increasing rows of empty pockets in bubble packs. The rattling residue in my brown plastic bottle is not the only thing to make me thoughtful about what either time or Horny Goat Weed may be doing to my body. Something is having an effect, and quite startlingly so. The only thing to have shrunk is my scepticism. In my role as heroic nineteenth-century scientist I examine myself daily with a dispassionate regard for scrupulous bodily measurement, like Francis Galton and his anthropometry. Well, not quite dispassionate, maybe. Just the first feathery wisps of concern. Nothing to really worry about, of course; but all the same I go on the Internet to look up this *Epimedium sagittatum* and learn there are quite a few *Epimedium* species, including *E. pubescens* (which sounds enticingly rejuvenating) and *E. brevicornum* (very much less promising). Horny Goat Weed

inevitably turns out to be a Chinese herbal medicine, pronounced in Cantonese "yam yong fok," which perhaps means
"forbidden." It "nurtures the kidneys, fortifies the yang, expels
wind-damp-cold and improves one's ability to resist a lack of
oxygen," so maybe Mallory and Whymper took bundles of the
plant with them in their knapsacks to chew at altitude. It also
improves blood flow to the penis and causes erection, which
might be unwelcome while climbing Everest although it's true
I know nothing about Mallory's later relations with Irvine. *E.
sagittatum* also does wonders for menstrual irregularity.

But the clincher is this guileless assertion: "Small amount
promotes urination; large amount inhibits urination." As far as
I'm concerned this sums up the essential vagueness at the heart
of all herbal medicine. It's not just that the effects of a single
plant can be utterly contradictory, but that phrases like "large
amount" are never explained. It's pitiful. Just try imagining this
principle applied to cookery: "Blend large quantity of flour
with a lesser amount of butter and a number of eggs." Here
we're talking about potent weeds that might induce parts of
the body to run amok, or just unstoppably to *run*. Looking at
the other formulations of Horny Goat Weed on the market I
can't find any uniformity of dosage. Mr. and Mrs. ProWang,
who make my pills and whom I now see as a hardworking
Cantonese couple forever chopping dried herbs in their tiny
kitchenette in Guangzhou, don't mention any quantities at all
on their label. It's true I haven't yet noticed any urinary irregularity, but I shall be seriously displeased if I begin to have
periods at my time of life. I realize that taking any pharmaceutical is a lottery, but at least the stuff that doctors prescribe
comes in standardized strength and dosage. Until they take the
trouble to isolate a plant's active ingredient and weigh it properly, I can't see how herbalists can ever be certain their patients
won't see-saw arbitrarily between floods of urine and acute
retention, not to mention appalling gusts of wind-damp-cold

that in restaurants would give rise to long, incredulous stares over the tops of menus.

On balance I'm inclined to dismiss Horny Goat Weed as a threat. I'm much more anxious about the "orchic substance" the ProWangs are adding to their pills. A classically educated pedant like Stephen Fry would point out that *orchis* is Greek for testicle, but that it is also the name of a family of orchids because of the shape of their root tubers. Frankly, I would sooner know the "orchic substance" I'm ingesting daily is of strictly vegetal origin. Still, maybe there's a recipe in all this: a hitherto-untested combination of *animelles* with orchid roots. There's something intriguing about the union of testicles and suburban greenhouses. Hortiball Stew? I shall have to find out if orchid roots are toxic.

Then comes the morning when Frankie rings up with his customary salvo of coughs. People sometimes ask him if he isn't afraid of cancer. "Good God no," says Frankie. "Far too obvious. No, I shall die of mortality"—a beady glance—"just like you." Today his tone is not very breezy. Ominous, didn't I say? As usual, Samper was right.

"I've just had some feedback from Weetabix." This is our whimsical private name for my editor, Michelle Tost, a.k.a. the Breakfast of Champions.

"She hates the book," I say gloomily.

"She does no such thing, Gerry. She says it's witty and dis-creet and Champions Press are honoured as always to have another title from you. No, what she says is that Millie herself wants a few changes."

"Oh God. *How* few?"

"Oh, not a lot." Breezily evasive. "You know these people, Gerry. They make no end of a song and dance about an entire chapter and it's often curable by removing a single sentence. Remember Per Snoilsson."

I remembered. The Flying Swede had thought my vivid

account of how racing drivers disported themselves between races, especially when playing the notorious "Pit Stop Game," would bring him into disrepute. Disrepute! The man who charges around the world's circuits leaving behind him a welter of skidding cars and flying wheels; the man everybody knows was responsible for the death of that sweet little French champion François Bidet at Monaco. In that instance artful old Gerry, casting a jaundiced eye over his own prose, adroitly removed the single appearance of the word "knickers" from the chapter and Snoilsson passed it.

"I wish not to have anything more to do with Millie Cleat," I say firmly.

"Mm."

A long pause, in which we both silently acknowledge that it really doesn't matter a row of beans what I want, provided I want to get paid for this book. That I do; and so does Frankie. Best get it over with as quickly as possible so the book will be ready in plenty of time for the Christmas market and I can embark on something worthy of my talents. Grit the teeth, Samper. "But I'm not having that woman in this house."

"And why should you?" said Frankie emolliently. "You just need to agree between yourselves on where you're going to meet. It may only take an hour to listen to her objections and—"

"Objections? You said changes."

"Of course, that's what I meant, Gerry. Absolutely not complaints as such. Just probably silly quibbles about matters of emphasis."

Vintage Frankie: just probably silly quibbles. Has anyone ever been reassured by reassurance?

"I'll talk to Weetabix. So where's Millie at the moment? Brisbane?"

"No, here in London," says Frankie. "Apparently Lew's over on *Vvizz* Corp. biz."

I have a pretty good idea what that involves—not that I am

about to strike moralistic attitudes. Indeed, when the hugely wealthy CEO of a multinational corporation squires a married global celebrity around town these days the whole starry scene transcends morality entirely. It even lends morality a faint aura of pathos as being about as relevant in the twenty-first century as a mediaeval chivalric code governing the correct wearing and throwing down of gauntlets. In fact, I thought how pleased Millie's husband Clifford would be. Far from being a poor cuckold stuck in Pinner while his wife underwent transfiguration by limelight and headline, he would be mightily relieved. Clifford was the only member of the Cleat clan I liked. In the early days of researching the book he and I would slip off to a half-timbered twenties pub that sixty-five years ago was probably spoken of as "that roadhouse on the way to Hendon aerodrome." A great barn of a place now drowning in suburbia, with waves of balti houses, Chinese takeaways, shish-kebab joints and betting shops breaking against its mock-Tudor brick walls, I expected it to be full of rorty wide boys driving stolen BMWs. Instead, the saloon bar was rather quiet, bizarrely lined with glass-fronted cabinets of stuffed weasels, some of which held miniature cricket bats and wore MCC ties, and a lot of signed black-and-white stills from "The Wizard of Oz." Oh whoops, I thought. Could it be we have fallen among the friends of Dorothy? The place was quite well patronized by people I assumed were regulars since they greeted Clifford as one of them. Presumably the hubbub surrounding his wife's recent around-the-world record had abated by then, for I noticed nobody made any reference to her. Quite evidently Clifford was not thought of just as Mr. Millie but as someone with an entirely separate identity.

In all, I spent several evenings in his company and far preferred it to that of his wife. I flatter myself that this was true for him, too. Not that there was much self-flattery involved, since if the marriage Clifford described to me had been made in heaven it bespoke a heaven with quite a malign sense of humour. Millie had been three or four years older than Clifford when at twenty-three he abandoned a career in the Navy to marry her in 1979. "Stupidest thing I ever did," he said disarmingly. "Not that I'm not fond of the kids, don't get me wrong. They're great. But Millie and me, well, I suppose we weren't cut out to be shipmates. I was having certain, um, problems in the Navy at the time, plus I wanted to come home. I was born pretty much here, you see, just over in Kenton. I'm a Middlesex man, Gerry. In every sense."

Ah yes. Enter Dorothy, discreetly, wearing mufti. But I liked the way an ancient county, once the eponymous home of the Middle Saxons and brutally zoned out of existence in the mid-sixties, still lingered to define something that persisted just beneath the surface, even close to the heart.

"When I married her I liked her spirit. We were good chums, really. Not a lot of the other, if you get my drift." Clifford stared intently into his beer. "We were neither of us much on that sort of thing. Well, it was four years before Pauline was born, then Jack a couple of years later. Millie was thirty plus by then. And then—ironic, really, when you think about it: it was me introduced her to sailing. Basically, I was happy to get her out of the house. All that stuff in the papers about her being a seawoman born and bred is a load of bollocks. I'm not saying she didn't take to it like a duck to water and it wasn't long before she outgrew poor old Ruislip Lido. But bred to it she wasn't. I doubt if she'd ever put bum to thwart in so much as a rowing boat until she met me. From then on, though, she was bloody unstoppable. Always off sailing, she was. I did most of the kids' upbringing myself. Not that I resent any of it, it was just the way things turned out. I suppose it's the same for all of us in one way or another. We always wake up too late to who we really are, and by then we're stuck with living a life belonging to someone else entirely."

I could sense Dorothy sidling closer. "And from then on Millie just drifted further away each year?" I suggested, not much caring but being professional all the same: an author temporarily stuck with someone else's life entirely.

"Drifted, my arse. She'd set her course and headed off over the horizon. She knew where she was going, all right. Not even that Aussie shark could stop her."

"Lew Buschfeuer?"

"Now, now. I'm referring to the brave animal that lunched off her arm. Better man than I am, Gunga Din, and all that. I wouldn't have had the nerve. You probably haven't heard Millie swear? I mean, really have a go? We used to sound off a bit in the Navy, but we were just kids compared to Millie. I bet that shark's ears are still ringing. Like I said, you've got to admire the woman's spirit. She's way beyond all this, now." Clifford's gesture took in himself, the cricketing weasels, the entire pub and its encroaching tide of eateries, as well as a large tract of northwest Greater London. "You know she's got a new house near Chichester? She did ask if I wanted to move down there, which was nice of her, but to be frank I'd sooner die. Poncy lot. Weekend sailors and the pink-gin set in designer yachting caps. Either that or wearing more wool than the average sheep. They look like extras from a film about Dunkirk."

"So what do you think she'll do now? She can't go on with this long-distance yachting caper, surely? Not at her age. And anyway, she's already broken the only record that matters."

"Christ, Gerry, don't let her hear you say that. There are dozens of other records, and to people like her they all matter. But you're right—even she can't go on for ever. I've asked her, naturally, and so have the kids, because obviously we worry about her. When you think about it, it's ridiculous, really, a one-armed grandmother sailing around the world. But she's always vague about the future. I don't think she knows herself. Two things I'm certain about, though. One, she's never going to come home to Pinner, and between you and me I can live with that because she's not the only one to have a life of her own." He shot me a complicitous glance. "You must meet Terry sometime."

Nothing discreet about old Dottie now, waving her underwear triumphantly over her head. Samper's gob remains utterly unsmacked. "And the other thing you're sure about?"

"Oh, just that although she might well retire from yachting she won't retire from the limelight if she can help it. Not Millie. You know how jealous she is of her rivals, especially that Rasmussen fellow she left behind in the Atlantic. She really hates him. No, she'll have to find something to throw in their faces. I dread to think what it will be."

All this zips through my mind in compressed form as I sit on my Tuscan terrace talking to Frankie on a mobile phone. I am resigned to going over to the UK and spending as little time as possible with Millie at whatever mooring she chooses. Happily, it is more likely to be Brown's Hotel than Pinner. I just hope it won't be Chichester. I wonder if I will ever see Clifford again and find myself undismayed to think I mightn't. Just another dysfunctional sporting family, the Cleats. I seem to collect them.

"I'll call her up," I tell Frankie resignedly. "And come over. Obviously I shall have to pay the fare myself," I can't help adding in my role as poor, put-upon Samper. Completely bogus, of course. We both know perfectly well that I am paid well for these writing jobs on the understanding that I persevere until all parties are satisfied with the text. All parties but the author, that is.

"There's a good boy," says Frankie.

But after he rings off I have to deal with something that has been nagging me ever since my after-breakfast session with the tape measure. I repeat the measurements and there's no doubt. Only two pills to go and Samper is definitely packing more veal. Obviously this process will stop when the course finishes, but all the same I'm glad the experiment is nearly over. However, it does do something for the masculine spirits. I'm beginning to wonder how I shall look in that new pair of Stiff Lips jeans I bought the other week in Florence. The last word in fashionable, of course, and they cost a fortune; but now I hear that Homo Erectus jeans are sold in Essex outlet villages it's time to switch my allegiance. While nerving myself to call Millie Cleat in London I essay the electrifying curse that Adriano flings at Elena's head in one of the most impassioned outbursts in nineteenth-century Italian opera. "A thousand tortures fall upon you! / May you carry your children to the cemetery one by one, / The Host turn to marble in your faithless mouth!" Rattling good stuff, but unfortunately today my voice isn't up to Ficarotta's taxing score and I'm obliged to give up, panting. I content myself with repeating the opening phrase, *Mille atroci tormenti*, which little by little turns into *Millie atroce Cleati*. Childish, no doubt; but it puts me right in the mood for phoning her.

6

It is not Brown's Hotel but the London Hilton, a suite affording a glimpse across Constitution Hill into the sacred precinct of Buckingham Palace garden. I gather that when the hotel was built in the early sixties there was one of those huge public outcries that exist mainly in the imaginations of a few noisy journalists, to the effect that our dear Queen (as she was then known) would have her privacy invaded by vulgar Americans in their skyscraper hotel spying on her from its upper floors. Since when, nothing has exceeded the vulgarity of our own homegrown press where the royal family is concerned—except that of the royal family itself, of course, whose indiscretions have seldom been conducted anywhere as tastefully secluded as a private garden. In this whole business of spying and being spied on the Brits really have been outstandingly stupid, even for them, and have lost all sense of where the demarcation might be between public and private. We have renounced our privacy with an almost audible sigh of relief, as though shedding an intolerable burden laid on us by the centuries. (Such are the insights afforded a jaded exile by a view from the forty-third floor, or whichever this is.)

Millie is herself also standing at the window with the short, thick telescope she carries everywhere, a prop too naff for further comment. It is three o'clock in the afternoon and she is wearing a garment that only plebeian queens like Noël Coward ever affected, a sort of cross between a housecoat and a dressing gown all in crimson Chinese silk with dragons rampaging over her knobby little chest. The empty sleeve is pinned up to the shoulder with a dramatically large safety-pin. Thespian, that's what she is, I realize with surprise. I haven't actually seen her these past six months, owing to my having been busy writing her pestilential story, and in that time she has changed. Gone is the plucky grandmother from Pinner. The creature standing at the window languidly surveying her domain is, good Lord, *queenly*.

"Gerry darling," she cries, turning and coming forward to gather my two hands in her one. Where did she learn that? How can she possibly avoid a guest-star appearance at Chichester Rep's next Christmas panto? She leans down to pat the thick folder of manuscript sitting prominently on a coffee table. "Your book! So wonderful. So naughty, too. The things you so nearly say. Delicious. Now sit down and tell me all about yourself. It's been an age." The telescope hangs from a lanyard around her chicken-skin neck and bounces heavily off the dragons as she sits down. I notice scurf on the shiny brown shins that gleam beneath the hem.

Numbly I grope for a chair. Am I going to have to play Miss Mapp to Millie's Lucia? Or worse, Georgie Pillson? I decide resolutely to remain the last of the Sampers.

"*Millie!* You look like Lord Nelson got up as Somerset Maugham. All you need is an admiral's hat and a cigarette holder."

At this she frowns slightly, reminding me that she dislikes levity unless it's her own. "Same old Gerry," she says with a glint. Too late it occurs to me that she may never have heard of Somerset Maugham and probably dares not ask in case the truth is even worse than she suspects. Some West Country delicacy, perhaps, like a Cornish pasty or Devon cream, only more disreputable?

"Well," I reply cautiously, "the same old Gerry has gathered that, kind as you are about his book—our book, *your* book—

you feel there's the odd bit of rejigging still to be done. I'm sure
you're right. When one bakes a beautiful cake it's essential to
get the final artistic details of the icing absolutely spot-on,
don't you think? Decorations are vital. The least sign of slop-
piness can have a subtly discouraging effect on the mind of the
person eating the cake and can actually change its taste. Finally,
everything comes down to where you put your little silver balls.
Like life, really."

(Here I am going to employ a technique that is wholly novel
in modern British writing and leave it up to the reader to supply Millie's foul language. From this point on and throughout
the rest of the book you should simply pepper her sentences
with the sort of expressions that make you feel jaded and
slightly ill to see in print.)

"It's not your little silver balls I'm thinking of," says the raddled yachtsdiva tartly. "Although in my opinion quite a few
have found their way into your cake. Now, all the stuff I told
you in those long conversations we had with your tape
recorder—you know, about my family, my accident, how
Beldame came to be built and so on—all that stuff's okay, obviously. No—I'm talking about your fantastic stories, how I only
learned sailing in my thirties on Ruislip Lido, that sort of thing.
Those are definitely not okay. I can't imagine who the hell
you've been gossiping with. It wasn't bloody Clifford, was it? I
warned you not to believe half of what that man tells you. He
likes his yarns—it's something he picked up in the Navy. Not
the *only* thing he picked up in the Navy, as a matter of fact,
but unfortunately I didn't know about that until well after we
were married. Anyway, the facts speak for themselves: I'm a
seawoman born and bred, everyone knows that. So those bits
will have to go. But more than that, Gerry, what really bothers
me is the way you manage to make me sound like somebody
who's just another around-the-world sailing legend. And I'm a
lot more, as we both know, and as the British public knows."

Strewth. If I flatter myself—and it *has* happened now and then—it is because, almost alone in this hack trade of mine, I have a reputation for making two-dimensional sporting heroes seem briefly three-dimensional despite everything they can do. Take that downhill skier, Luc Bailly. When I first met him he was nothing but a crippled priapist in his late twenties with a factory making hideous sportswear and a private round-the-clock team of deft-fingered nurses. But by the time I'd finished with him he was Monsieur Renaissance Man. Even the group sex orgies, the clysters in Klosters, had been airbrushed into something hazy and artistically stylized, like one of those huge brown old canvases of the Rape of the Sabine Women.

"I'm mortified to hear about the book's shortcomings, Millie," I tell her dangerously. "Perhaps if you will be a bit more specific we can pump up the portrait accordingly. Is there any particular aspect of your fascinating personality you would like elaborated? Your maternal qualities? Cookery skills? Kindness to animals? Sense of humour?"

Surely this time I have gone too far and I fully expect her to give me one of her nautical tongue-lashings for impertinence, facetiousness, etc., but she just looks thoughtful.

"I'm thinking more that you haven't taken me seriously as a *spiritual* person." She waves her hand at the incriminating folder on the coffee table. "As your version stands, our hero-ine gets bitten by the long-distance sailing bug and goes for gold, driven by her extraordinary determination, competitive-ness and raw courage. Do you really think that's me, Gerry? After all the time you've spent with me?"

"You're saying you're *not* determined, competitive and courageous?" I grope, flummoxed by her having spent the best part of a month last winter telling me she was exactly all those things.

"Of course not," she snarls, reverting reassuringly to type. "How could I possibly have become world-record holder and the most successful yachtswoman in all history otherwise? But I'm other things *as well*, you must have noticed that? Really, Gerry, wake up! You're missing the whole point, if I may say so. Perhaps it's because you're a man. Sort of. Sort of because you're a man," she adds quickly.

Yeah, and packing more veal, is what I'd like to retort. My ex-analyst, who retired badly bruised after only three sessions many years ago, would have been interested to learn that what pops into Samper's mind at this instant is a vision of himself wearing his new jeans, the crotch distressed beyond the designer's intentions. And over in Guangzhou an elderly couple look up from their tireless chopping and bundling and beam with pride. But I don't want things to degenerate still further. I want to get briefed, go away and amend the book and then get the hell out of Millie Cleat's life for ever and ever. Samper knows when to swallow his pride. I notice the sun has broken through the London overcast outside. Millie notices, too, with her weather eye. She gets up and goes to the window with her engorged telescope and resumes her Horatia Nelson act, scanning far horizons.

"I had a dream, Gerry," she says loftily. Goodness gracious; forget Nelson, it's Martin Luther Queen. "I'm quite certain I must have told you. Even in Pinner the sea was calling me. It was never to do with winning races, you know. It was something almost, well, *mystical*. About being alone, just me and the elements. About being blown on my way to an unknown destination. Unknown to me, I mean. But perhaps not unknown to the wind . . . I wonder if you can understand? Feeling one's life is on course for the grandest voyage of all?"

This claptrap is punctuated by the reassuring sounds of London normality filtering through the double glazing from outside: the growl of buses and the sudden familiar bray of a police siren. I am not an urbanite but I find myself nostalgically pleased to hear them. Sometimes the silence up at Le Rocce can become oppressive.

"I assure you this is the first time you've ever mentioned this, Millie," I tell her. "And what's more I have all your tapes to prove it. Obviously, had you made it clear that this side of you is so important I should have written about it. Of course. But you never did."

Horatia Queen half turns from the window and gives a pitying little smile. "*Men*," she murmurs.

I do some more pride-swallowing. "Then what you and I need to do is arrange to have a session in the next day or two when you can give me all this new stuff properly and I shall ingeniously incorporate it into our text. Not in lumps, I mean, but properly spread throughout. I'm sorry, Millie, but I never asked you about your religious views because you never gave the slightest hint that you had any." Quite true. And anyway, it's not the sort of thing one asks people these days for fear they'll tell you.

"Very well, Gerry. Since I can see you're taking notes you might scribble a reminder to yourself to ask me about the Canaries. Just write Can—"

With a deafening crash the door bursts open, slamming back into the wall, and four immense policemen wearing black flak jackets irrupt into the room with drawn pistols. One kicks open the bedroom door and yells "Clear!," then does the same to the bathroom beyond. The others fan out and cover us, shouting "Freeze-freeze-freeze!" Into the room behind them trots a breathless pink man in a suit. For a moment everything does freeze. Tableau.

"You with the scope!" shouts one of the men to the pop-eyed Millie, paralysed by the window. "Where's the weapon? The gun, the *gun*!"

Everything in the room becomes treacly, as though slowed by a rising tide of testosterone and adrenaline that has already reached our waists. I find I can't move my legs. In this instant of total fear I feel something like a small sac burst somewhere inside me and hot liquid run down. To her credit Millie snaps out of her paralysis first.

"What gun? There is no gun, you moron! Just what the hell do you freaks think you're up to?"

Briskly the nearest freak pins her to the wall by the window with a forearm across her chest while he runs a huge shameless hand over her scrawny frame. He whips the telescope off her, examines it, peers through it and tosses it onto the sofa.

"Your name?" he demands, stepping back. He could hardly have asked a more welcome question. Millie draws herself up, her hand clutching at the place where her telescope had hung as though feeling for a microphone.

"I am Millie Cleat!" she bawls. "*Millie frigging Cleat*! Does that ring any bells in your tiny brain? Ocean racing? Around-the-world yachting? That sort of thing?"

It was the pink man's turn. "Er, quite true," he says, coming forward. "I can identify the lady. This is indeed Millie Cleat. And, madam, I really must apol—"

"Who the hell are you?"

"I am the duty house security officer. My ID."

The gigantic policeman studies the plastic folder incredulously. "Your name is ffitzgammon-Pithers?"

"It is. Ignatius ffitzgammon-Pithers."

At this welcome touch of farce the scene begins to sort itself out. The testosterone and adrenaline leak rapidly away. The policemen relax and holster their pistols, leaning against the wall, sweating and trembling with reaction. It turns out that "a highly reliable report was made" of a telescopic rifle sight seen behind the window of this room. "Naturally these windows overlooking the Palace are under constant surveillance." I thought he was going to add the automatic "for your own safety and convenience" that today functions as a sort of amen at the end of most nannyish public announcements. After a while the police gather themselves to leave with a breezy "Better a false alarm than the real thing," which in the absence of anything more penitent has to serve as an official apology. They also take our names for their incident report even though it was an incident of their own making. I suppose we should be grateful we don't have to supply DNA samples. With admirably misplaced nerve one of the men asks Millie if she'd mind autographing the back of an envelope for his little boy. Like Medusa, she paralyses him with a glance and he has to be tugged from the room by his colleagues, mountainous in their uncouth gear, their waists thickened with innumerable pouches of ammunition and stun grenades. When I was a boy they were still public servants; these days they are swaggering lictors. It is a perfect parable of Britain's progressive social decay—or so I think as my heart rate subsides towards normal and ebbing panic induces an elderly querulousness (What on earth have we come to?).

Pink Mr. ffitzgammon-Pithers is also distressed as he examines the hole in the plasterboard wall made by the door handle slamming back. "Really!" he says, half to himself. "It's all too much. That's the second time this week. It's like living in Baghdad."

"Been there, have you?" asks Millie rudely. She, too, has been badly rattled.

"Oh yes," says the security man mildly. "I'm only temping here until I can rejoin my regiment. Just until the medics give me the okay. Touch of shrapnel from an IED—improvised explosive device—that's all."

To my pleasure this upstages Millie even more, and only an emetic display of abject servility on the part of the day manager, who bustles in wringing his hands, brings her back to normal. Even without her telescope she becomes very haughty indeed, Lord Nelson playing Lady Bracknell. I leave halfway through the manager's ritual self-abasement, at the point where he starts handing out free passes to the bars and restaurants and saunas within his gift and explaining that "the dear lady" need not fear she will be presented with anything as unseemly as a bill when she leaves at the end of her delightful stay.

"*Delightful?*" queries Lady Bracknell.

"It has been a great delight for us," the wretched man assures her mendaciously.

As I totter off down Park Lane I realize that in its curious way the afternoon has been a bit of a delight for me, too. It's never much fun for an author to learn that he still has work to do on a book he thought was finished, but there's a good deal of compensation in watching his subject being mistaken for a regicide at the very moment she is laying claim to a deep spirituality. I just have to tell someone, so I flag down a taxi and manage to catch Frankie before he leaves the office. We spend a hysterical hour over glasses of the agency's Glenmorangie dreaming up tabloid newspaper responses. "Millie in Sniper Drama," "Panic Ahoy!," "Millie Sails into Hilton Storm." "A special security squad assigned to the Palace had egg on its face after a raid yesterday afternoon when it mistook for an assassin the nation's heroine, Millie Cleat, widely tipped for a peerage in the next Birthday Honours List. The feisty granny's response was unprintable . . ."

"Oh dear," says Frankie, wiping his eyes after laughter has brought on a near-terminal coughing fit.

"And this, mark you, the woman who wants me to rewrite her book so she comes across as the Mother Teresa of the high seas." I am not quite so crippled by laughter as Frankie. I keep remembering how absolutely terrified I was up in her room, not to mention that it is I who am going to have to do the writing.

"Don't worry, Gerry. Of course you're not going to rewrite

the book, only doctor it a bit here and there. We'll resist on the grounds that she never made any mention in her tapes of this allegedly vital aspect of her character. That was her responsibility and if she left it out it's either down to her own negligence or she's just invented it. I'll call her in the morning and tell her you're happy to be briefed about whatever emendations she wants but that the biographical facts in the book depend on her original taped accounts, so she can't now make radical changes without our renegotiating your fee very substantially. Also, of course, I can imply that a serious amount of work on your part would take a lot of time, in which case she might have to resign herself to missing the publication slot for Christmas. That should do the trick. If I've got her aright she can't wait to see herself in print."

Good old Frankie. That's exactly the stuff an author likes to hear from his agent.

*

Next morning I am slightly disappointed to discover that the Hilton episode has in fact earned no mention anywhere in the papers. I tell myself it has been hushed up for security reasons, which could well be true. Anything that makes the police look silly might compromise security, which makes it de facto a security matter and so it's securely sat on. When I come to think of it I realize it is probably in Millie's interest to keep quiet as well, just as it is in the hotel's. When all the self-righteous protest and expostulation have died down, nobody is going to emerge looking particularly dignified. Millie will be given a new tennis-court-sized suite and told to live in it buckshee for as long as she wants just so long as nothing is said about having been roughed up on the premises in the name of security. She and Lew will be able to gorge themselves on freebie meals and become sodden in saunas for as long as they can stand it. Strange how these things only ever happen to people with so much money it's completely immaterial to them.

At any rate, something this morning feels different. Something has changed. Maybe that little internal sac I distinctly felt burst when Millie's room was raided was the reservoir for a gland that anatomists have hitherto overlooked in their studies of the endocrine system? Tucked away somewhere along the rugged coastline of the thyroid isthmus, within sight of the brooding islets of Langerhans, must be the *vas malevolentiae* or the sump of malice which ruptured yesterday afternoon and has flooded me with electrifying ill will. I have had Millie Cleat up to here, and beyond. The woman is nothing but black trouble. In his relentless efforts to look on the bright side Frankie thinks it will just be a matter of adding a nifty sentence here and there throughout my text to satisfy Millie's claims to be taken seriously as a deep and mystical human being. But I know Millie, and yesterday I read the signs. Something or someone has got to her in these last six months; and the pared-to-the-bone, ruthlessly competitive sailor has begun to give way to something more grandiose and complex. You can't fool an old hack like Samper. Somebody has been putting ideas into the woman's head: alien imports that, unless quickly rooted out, will run riot and destroy the defenceless native ecology of her tiny brain. That question I asked her husband Clifford last year has become more pertinent than ever: What do you think she'll do now that she's getting too old for competitive sailing? Obviously, I don't give a stuff what the answer is except insofar as it affects getting this book off my hands.

7

Certain people—since axed from my Christmas-card list—have hinted that my frequently voiced exaspera-tion over the subjects of my books arouses a similar degree of exasperation in them. "So what is it you *would* like to write about?" they ask a little fretfully. "And why don't you go and do it?" All very well to be fretful, I reply, offering them a disarming plate of scrumptious deep-fried mole crickets from the Philippines, but it's not that easy. True, it's no doddle wringing a book-length story from a monosyllabic tennis play-er whose brain's two hemispheres consist of clay and grass. But millions of people know the player and tens of thousands want to buy the book as a Christmas present for a sedentary relative, and several hundred may actually want to read it. This makes for quite a decent living for G. Samper. The people I should vastly prefer to write about tend to be more than halfway intel-ligent and connected with the arts. However, books about art command rather small sales: generally speaking, the higher the art the lower the sales. Sometimes they don't sell at all, although it helps if the high artist had a low life. Coffee-table books can be the exception, and *Genital Decorations of the World—Part II: Equatorial Africa* in Thames & Hudson's authoritative photo-essay series is tipped to do well this Christmas. This is not what I have in mind, though, being notoriously a person of intellectual refinement.

Marta, the wild-haired Voynovian composer who was my neighbour at Le Rocce until indefinitely detained by the

Powers of Darkness, claimed to have been at Moscow Conservatory with the fabulous Russian pianist Pavel Taneyev. I once thought I might have a lot in common with him as a potential biographee—he is unmarried, for a start. But although Marta would have been the ideal person to introduce us, the indolent old bag never got around to it. Shortly afterwards events in our respective domestic lives became so hectic that I never pursued the idea. I have often regretted this failure bitterly, and never more so than when signing the contract with Millie Cleat. As far as I'm concerned Taneyev is a god of the keyboard, not by any means one of those post-Soviet vulgarians who help poor, naïve Scarlatti along with extra notes, fatuous rubatos and general editorializing. A bit in the Richter mould, perhaps, he produces wonderfully cool and limpid Shostakovitch preludes and fugues but does occasionally let rip in the grand manner with an old warhorse like Balakirev's *Islamey*. His account of Prokoviev's Eighth Sonata is a dream.

Extending the phrase "connected with the arts" to its absolute maximum of looseness, I did begin to be professionally involved with the boy-band singer Nanty Riah, a.k.a. Brill, late of Freewayz and now lead singer of Alien Pie. The circumstances in which we met were so bizarre I shall not trespass on your credulity by recounting them here. The fact is, young Nanty as good as commissioned me to write an account of his life that would transcend his temporary idolization by millions of teenagers and eventually lift him into the ranks of those seamy old pop musicians who survive long enough to be knighted for services to themselves. It was Nanty's ambition to become one such and to be numbered among those raddled rockers who fondly believe they are respected for their views on balls-aching things that serious people don't want to waste their time thinking about such as Africa, the drug problem and rain forests. Accordingly, we hatched a plot to write an account of his life to date that would give him some credibility on the long and winding road towards knighthood. Indeed, I had already begun to sketch an outline of the book when, as you will recall from last year's media frenzy, Nanty was shot during an art theft in which three Van Goghs were stolen from his private Lear jet on the tarmac in Rome. Not fatally shot, I'm glad to say, because I've grown quite fond of him; but the idol of millions was nonetheless soundly perforated in one or two fundamental places and had to lie in a pool of his own gore on the Wilton rug in his plane's cabin while the thieves took their time unscrewing the pictures from their frames on the bulkhead. Since when the poor fellow has apparently made a good recovery from the gunshots, but the incident has done nothing to improve his mental stability and the book we were supposed to be working on is on indefinite hold. Worse, it has proved impossible to induce him to sign a contract, and my agent has sternly forbidden me to write another word of his story until he does. "The richer they are," Frankie said from his bottomless supply of folk wisdom, "the more the buggers want something for nothing. Not another word, Gerry."

So *that* project has stalled, too. And now I'm ready to answer the question of who, ideally, I should choose to write about. Currently, I think that would be Max Christ, who for my money is the greatest orchestral conductor since Toscanini. Still only in his forties, his meteoric career has included his extraordinary move from the Berlin Philharmonic to Colchester, where as everyone knows he famously built up a symphony orchestra to be the perfect vehicle for his sound. Today the CSO is one of the finest orchestras in the world, and their accounts under Christ of Schumann's symphonies, in particular, are quite simply the best ever and completely give the lie to those who thought Schumann's orchestral writing was inept. Cretins, in short.

Ah, Christ, you say, because even you (with your secret preference for "world music" and its banal fusion of Hopi hip-hop,

Moroccan rockin' and Papuan rappin') even you have heard of Max Christ, pronounced to rhyme with "wrist" and almost as glitzy as his legendary namesake. And I agree; because when you say "Ah" in that tone it implies that, dazzling though Samper's prose so obviously is, he may not have either clout or qualifications enough to write the Max Christ Story. No one is more aware than I that a world-famous conductor in search of a biographer is unlikely to enlist the services of a sports writer whose track record consists of books about track records. He naturally fears his life story might wind up being called *Hot Podium!* or just plain *Christ!* He also fears that the English-speaking world of letters doesn't know that the German name for the pale Galilean is "Christus" and will ignorantly tarnish him with impiety. My uphill task will be to convince this great man that Samper is eminently qualified for the job—that his sporting biographies are merely an aberration, the enforced and temporary prostitution of a talent really saving itself for marriage to a subject worthy of it. I am not entirely without hope, for I have been concealing the fact that I do have a way into Max Christ, as they say: tenuous, but definitely a link. You many remember my mentioning that I interviewed all those EAGIS oceanographers whose seismic studies in the Canaries Millie Cleat comprehensively ruined. There was something in the appearance of one of them when he was in his Southampton office trying on a bright yellow suit of oilskins while I interviewed him that drew us into a closer rapport. Indeed, young Adrian Jestico is now one of the rare, regular guests whom I'm happy to receive up at Le Rocce. In a casual conversation he asked me about a watch I had recently bought in Germany, and I said I had found it at a branch of Christ's in Frankfurt—Christ being a well-known chain of jewellers and watchmakers with shops all over Germany and Switzerland. "Oh," said Adrian casually, "my sister Jennifer's married to one of them. You may have heard of him, the conductor Max Christ?"

Just like that. I couldn't believe my ears. When I could, I gathered the couple had met when Max was starting to knock the Colchester Symphony Orchestra into shape. Jennifer Jestico was a young violinist good enough not to have to pose in a wet T-shirt on the front of her first CD or peer from behind a curtain of blonde hair with slightly parted glossed lips as though auditioning for a garage calendar. Apropos, it surely can't be long before we are given the first nude performance of Mendelssohn's violin concerto at the Proms. I mean, what is the point of prolonging this pretence that the whole of Western culture isn't drifting inexorably towards a generalized state of pornography, its true bottom line finally revealed? The first all-nude account of the St. Matthew Passion should likewise be not too far away, with the entire orchestra, choir, soloists and conductor in the buff ("Convincingly seemly"—*The Gramophone*. "The reminder that we all stand naked before God was deeply moving and added yet another layer of meaning to Bach's protean masterpiece"—*Music & Musicians*. "St. Matt's Nude Passion"—*Sun*). According to Adrian, Prokoviev's third violin concerto brought his sister Jennifer and Max Christ together, and together they have remained. Adrian has assured me it wouldn't be hard to arrange an introduction to this fabulous conductor, who has risen to the top by virtue of sheer overwhelming talent. Without having had to remove a stitch of clothing, or conduct in trademark pink tails, or wear so much as a diamond nose stud, Max Christ has become acknowledged as arguably the greatest conductor under the age of eighty. In my typically shy and retiring way I have so far done no more than drop a discreet hint to Adrian that I would be forever in his debt were he to make it known on the family grapevine that Max Christ's ideal biographer is only a phone call away. We can all dream. Anyway, in the prosaic meantime I have to rid me of this troublesome Cleat. And overnight the inspiration for a little mischief has occurred to me.

I now call up Dr. Adrian Jestico at BOIS, the British Oceanography Institute in Southampton, and ask him if he would send me a copy of a strange picture I had noticed pinned to a board in his office when I originally interviewed him. It was a grainy, black-and-white outline of a face, caught three-quarters on and staring out with a bulging eyeball beneath a partially eroded thatch of hair. It was cavernous, mournful and demonic. Its blurred features, all of which could be read in so many ways, conveyed a peculiar charismatic power. Adrian said that he and his colleagues knew it as "The Face," and that it was an artefact of a side-scan sonar map of the bed of the Pacific Ocean somewhere near Hawaii. He explained that the seabed had been more than three thousand metres below the survey vessel and that the apparent face was simply an illusion created by the sonar impulses striking the geological features on the bottom, forming light areas and shadows according to the angle at which the echoes were reflected. Everything depended on this viewing angle, as was proved by an adjacent track of the survey that partially overlapped the same outcrop and revealed nothing but random rocks. It was exactly like one of those faces one can see in outline on a mountain range that disappear if viewed from a different standpoint. In fact, there was an analogous example in the famous case some years ago of the "Face on Mars" which, as soon as a subsequent probe flew closer and photographed it from another angle, was revealed as an ordinary flat-topped mesa. Naturally, this didn't stop devotees going on believing it was a giant sculpture or a sacred icon placed there by a lost Martian civilization or some such nonsense. It's really pathetic what people will believe in their scramble to ditch reason and embrace blah.

Adrian is delighted to oblige, bless him. In due course this frame of the original scan appears as an e-mail attachment and The Face glares back at me from my computer screen as though daring me to call the bluff of its nonexistence. It is quite a startling image until you know how it was made, and all the better for not being the amended version I had seen in Adrian's room which had a facetious speech bubble drawn in felt-tip coming out of its mouth saying "I can see your bow thruster!!" Scientists' humour. I pop round to Frankie's, blow the picture up, borrow the office printer and make a good hard copy the size of a small poster. I also contact Millie to make a date to see her so she can brief me on the spiritual angle of her character from which she now wishes to be viewed. I suddenly realize that mine is to become the art of the side-scan biographer, expected to conjure up a different portrait by viewing her from a different slant and tinkering with light and shadow. She agrees to see me later in the week when she has "prepared her thoughts." Mine are already prepared, but I prepare them still further with a few hours' research in the London Library.

*

Inevitably, my session with Millie Cleat turns out to be an anticlimax. She really hasn't anything much to add after all. She is absolutely typical of virtually all my clients, few of whom know what they want, most of whom give me the authorized version of their story, and all of whom think I have got the facts completely wrong when they read the final draft. It is true that in Millie's case I did rely on her husband Clifford for some background stuff, especially as regards her introduction to sailing. Not having been born yesterday I even took the trouble to find an old boy who had given her lessons back in her Ruislip Lido days. Now Millie wants me to write that her parents used to take her on holiday to Salcombe, where she began to mess about in boats from the age of three. I've no doubt it's all baloney, and tell her frankly that we don't have the time to track down some octogenarian Devonian skipper who might remember her and give a plausible Cap'n Birdseye performance. I shall incorporate this wholly uncorroborated claim as part of the gospel according to Cleat. No skin off my nose, after all. I've long since given up hoping I shall never knowingly have to lie in print.

As for her alleged new spiritual side, Millie's not much help in documenting this, either. What it looks like to me is that some time over the last year she has been taken up by a clique of worshippers who see in her everything she sees in herself, and then some. I get an impression of grizzled ladies with cabin cruisers and small, irritable dogs who spend a lot of time in chandlers' shops looking at galley stoves and stout clothing. With them are younger ladies, busily shedding ill-advised marriages and struggling for self-expression. Swathed in pashminas, they bring a New Age soulfulness to the gin-and-gaspers ethos of their older companions. All of them adore Millie Cleat. They think she is a total heroine because she has scorned the elements, triumphed over anno Domini, shaken a fist at losing an arm, risen above family life and forged an intimate private relationship with the ocean such that something of the divinity of nature has rubbed off on her. I now suspect Millie has become quite dependent on these admirers to bolster her view of herself. It's one of the great pitfalls of celebrity: terrific for the ego but dealing a deathblow to both intelligence and a sense of humour. I gather there is an authoress whom similar fawners have convinced she is practically a reincarnation of Shakespeare. Poor Millie may be becoming equally delusional.

Admittedly this theory is my own invention, based simply on trying to read between the lines she spouts with a faraway look in those sun-bleached eyes of hers. We are sitting in her new Hilton suite—this time with a view over nothing more sensitive than the rooftops of Mayfair. I notice her telescope has vanished and with it her Horatia Nelson persona. Today she is rather plain and earnest, rambling on without coming up with any new information. She merely repeats that on her record-breaking voyages she has often felt as though she were in the hands of a benign, powerful force. This is not much in the way of grist to the mill of a malign, powerless biographer, but we work with what we're given.

"The Canaries," I say when at last there's a lull. "The other day you asked me to remind you to mention the Canaries. What was that about?"

"Oh yes. You know I told you that on the last leg I sometimes felt it was like somebody else's hand on the helm?"

"Um," I say cautiously. "As I understand it, Millie, for most of the time you didn't exactly have your own hand on the tiller anyway. Wasn't it under computerized control?" The next thing we know, she'll start hoping to see her Autopilot face to face / When she has crost the bar.

"There you go again, Gerry. I don't *literally* mean I felt something had taken over the steering. More that it felt as if my fate was out of my hands."

"Or hand, to be precise," I stopped myself from saying. "And this happened around the Canaries, is that it?"

"To the south. About a day before I reached La Palma. I suddenly felt we could do no wrong, me and *Beldame*. We'd picked up the wind just where I'd predicted and we were really beginning to fly. It was as if the wind and the sea had joined forces just to get us to the Solent quicker than I could ever have managed on my own. Really. But there, I've always been super-sensitive to the ocean's living principle. You see, Gerry, I've absolutely no doubt that the sea is alive in some mysterious way. A sentient entity with a mind of its own. And I think that we, the human race, are committing the utmost folly in the way we are rubbishing the oceans, polluting them with chemicals and noise and trashing the animal life for our own selfish and shortsighted ends. I've always believed this, Gerry, and it's missing from your book. It's a vital part of what makes me the world's best. When I sail, I sail with humility and respect. And it pays off. The ocean knows I'm on its side."

Golly, what hubristic poppycock! How right I was! The old girl's been got at. A year ago it was all "She'll be right!" and blistering curses she must have picked up from Antipodean friends and boatyards. Now it's "the ocean's living principle" and "a sentient entity": the pashmina phrases of people who have dabbled their fingers in the Age of Aquariums. "We, the human race." Blimey.

"Okay," I say in the brisk and businesslike tone of the cosmetic wordsmith called in to advise on a difficult case, "we can fix that. But can you give me any idea of when you first felt this coming on? I remind you that you never mentioned it last year. It's all new to me."

"If I never mentioned it in so many words, Gerry, it must be because it's so much a part of me. There never was a moment when I 'felt this coming on,' as you put it. I just am by nature a spiritual person and always have been. I can't help it."

"Fine. Well—I'm thinking aloud here—how would it be if, instead of my trying to shoehorn little reminders of your native spirituality into the book as it stands, we were to write an entirely new short chapter about it and stick it in the middle? Something with gravitas and weight to give stability to the rest of the text? Like lowering a centreboard," I add with the offhand ease of a master of metaphor. Maybe after all it is G. Samper who is the reincarnation of W. Shakespeare.

"Brilliant, Gerry!" exclaims Millie, and would have clapped her hands. "That's a marvellous solution. A chapter all about my soul and its relationship with the sea, and let that speak for the rest of the book. Good. How soon can you do it?"

You may be thinking that, despite wanting to get shot of Millie and her wretched book in the shortest possible time, I am letting myself in for far more work. Surely writing an entire new chapter will be much more laborious than inserting snippets here and there? No, actually. It could take for ever to add soulful asides without doing grave damage to the overall tone, which is one of ghastly can-do breeziness masking a steely determination. It will actually be far easier and more plausible to change gear radically somewhere in the middle to invoke a different Millie, a hitherto unsuspected Millie, a Millie full of spiritual rapport with the oceans she sails over. It matters not that I can feel my breakfast borne upwards on a surge of gastric reflux at the thought of the piffle I shall have to write. This is the professional's way forward. And it is also part of Samper's master plan.

"You know, Millie," I say in a tone somewhere between earnest and deeply moved, "maybe you and I have more than a little in common after all. Tell me, do you believe in Neptune?"

"Wasn't he the ancient god of the sea?"

"Quite right. Neptune was the name the Romans gave the much older Greek god Poseidon. When the universe was divided up between his brothers and sisters, Poseidon was given the sea to rule. He was also the god of the winds and earthquakes and was notoriously temperamental. When in a good mood he made the sea calm and commanded new land to emerge from it. In bad moods he would strike the land with the gigantic trident he carried, causing earthquakes, storms at sea, shipwrecks and drownings. He lived in a palace on the seabed off the biggest of the Greek islands, Evvoia, where he kept his chariot and a stud farm for breeding horses."

"Sea horses?"

"Not at all. The real things. Poseidon seems to have been the god of horses as well, and he certainly identified with them. When he wanted to have sex with his sister Demeter she turned herself into a mare in the hopes of thwarting his advances. She should have known her brother better because he simply changed into a stallion and advanced all the same.

Some time later she gave birth to a foal. They led complicated lives in those days."

Millie is giving me a puzzled look. "Why are you telling me this, Gerry?"

"Because if you're interested in the sea being, um, sentient and divine, mightn't you want to reflect on your own feelings having ancient roots common throughout pre-Christian history? Maybe those are what you're tapping into now. A sort of Jungian thing. Of course, I'm only throwing this out as an idea for bulking out this new chapter I have to write. A different Millie and so on, in touch with primordial deities."

Now she becomes a bit more animated as the implications begin to dawn on her. "But that's marvellous, Gerry darling. It means I didn't imagine it and that people have always felt like me. I can relate to that, all right. I don't mean the palaces on the seabed stuff, obviously, though I know lots of people who believe in Atlantis."

I bet she does. "Most of them probably think Atlantis is an archaeological site they hope will be found one day. A sort of drowned city where a fabulous civilization once lived. No doubt the very looniest are expecting there to be people in togas strolling its streets beneath two thousand fathoms of water. Forget Atlantis, Millie. It's a complete red herring."

"Right. Of course I don't believe myself in people walking about on the seabed. But the idea of Poseidon being some sort of . . ."

" . . . Gaia figure . . . ?"

" . . . Gaia figure, exactly, Gerry. A spirit of the deep, a sacred principle of the sea. And those with the right sensitivity can harmonize with it. And that's what happened to me off the Canaries. That's why I broke the record. It was the strangest sensation."

"Well, anyway," I say, thoroughly disgusted with myself but thinking that several pages of wacky discourse along these lines will enable me to polish off this new chapter in fairly short order, "I'll just leave you with these thoughts. Oh, and with this as well," and from my briefcase I produce my rolled-up printout of "The Face." Without unrolling it I say: "This is a picture taken from a sonar scan of the seabed off the Canaries. It was made during an oceanographical survey that was taking place as you passed through. Remember—in the book you thought the ships you saw might have been cable-laying vessels? They were actually doing a big seismic and bottom-profiling survey. On one of the passes they made they saw this on the seabed over a thousand metres down." This is, of course, a lie: the scan came from somewhere off Hawaii. But what the hell, what I need is the effect. With quiet drama I unroll the poster and hold it up. And I must admit that even I feel a curious chill as the creature's eyeball and haunted gaze stare out across Millie's Hilton suite with its baleful charisma. "Strange, isn't it? It's just an artefact of the technology—a trick of the way the sonar pulses were scattered around the rocks on the bottom. I can't remember the scale offhand but that image will be several hundred metres across, maybe even half a kilometre. Anyway, I'll leave it with you and see you again in a few days' time when you've had a think about things."

On this disreputable mixture of cod mythology and half-truths, exit G. Samper.

8

You catch me in a sunny mood today. Not only do I not have to see Millie Cleat, but Adrian has called to say I shall soon be able to meet the great Max Christ. His sister Jennifer has promised to arrange a dinner either in Suffolk or up here in London at their pied-à-terre. The mere prospect of meeting Christ makes my knees suddenly weak. I fear I may not be worthy of him. It's preposterous. Can you imagine Gerald Samper in a crisis of confidence? The man whose Norman ancestors, on encountering British cuisine for the first time at Hastings, earned the name "Sans Peur"? Nevertheless, I'm fearful of my own anxiety. I'm anxious to make a good impression and for my professional life to take a steep upward turn, and there's nothing more potentially disastrous than wanting something too badly. I do hope Jennifer lets me know in good time where our dinner will be because I shall have to go shopping first. The one thing one learns from living in Italy is the paramount importance of clothes. It's not that they say anything important about you, but that people believe they do.

While in London I'm staying with Derek, a complete slut and old friend who works in Josiah Corcoran's, the Jermyn Street hair salon so fashionable that people wait for months for an appointment, by which time heavy-duty scissorwork is necessary. For all that Corcoran's trades behind discreet gold lettering as befits the generally austere, bespoke dignity of Jermyn Street, it is informally known to its employees and certain of its customers as "Blowjob." Derek's life is seriously haywire and most of the time I have his flat to myself, where with my customary kindness I carry out the basic maintenance and DIY work he's utterly incapable of. Last night he stayed out, no doubt to bump uglies, so this morning I can take my measurements in the bathroom without fear of interruption. By some magical synchronicity today also happens to see me rupture the very last hymen of silver foil on the very last bubble pack of ProWang's Pow-r-Tabs™. I should never live it down if Derek were to burst into the bathroom at this critical juncture: it would simply confirm his fantasy that I'm vain. Mind you, anybody wanting to maintain a minimal presentability would appear vain to Derek. We're much the same age, give or take, but to be brutally honest you would hardly know it to look at him. It surely can't just be genetic. It must have something to do with our respective lifestyles: his in the fleshpots of the metropolis and mine in the pure outdoor spaces of a Tuscan mountainside. I once lent him a pair of my treasured Homo Erectus jeans when he wanted to cut a dash, poor lamb, and instead of their denim contours filling nicely with the accustomed trim Samper posterior they just hung on him so that his buttocks looked like a couple of grapes in a paper bag, creases and crinkles everywhere. Being one of nature's diplomats I assured him he looked marvellous, and off he pranced to Wimbledon Common or Hampstead Heath or somewhere too dark for it to matter. Somehow Derek seems to have reversed the old adage and has managed to use it and lose it. But he's good company in small doses and I now think he should seriously consider a course of silicone shots in his bottom.

These lighthearted thoughts grow a little heavier as I ply the tape measure and suddenly become relieved that my own course has ended. Since I have conducted this scientific experiment on my own behalf and not on yours I decline to give exact figures. I will say, however, that overall growth has been consistent and still shows alarmingly few signs of slowing down. I should emphasize that things were perfectly satisfactory in the first place and it was only sheer curiosity that induced me to try out the Chinese couple's miracle pills. Like all people of sensibility I'm a great believer in the aesthetic appeal of perfect proportions. One has one's new Stiff Lips jeans to think of, and enough veal is enough. I'm content to settle for the happy medium, or *Epimedium* in this case. It's the orchic substance that's worrying. I think it may have set off a storm along that endocrine coastline of mine. I can all too vividly picture the waves of hormones breaking along the grim cliffs of the thyroid isthmus, the islets of Langerhans now hidden behind scudding curtains of spray. For the first time I'm wondering if there's an antidote.

But the thought that I shall soon see Christ banishes these few trivial clouds, and as I go about preparing something with which to greet Derek when he deigns to come home (for house guests have certain obligations), I find myself singing. Did you ever see *L'uomo magro* when they did it at the ENO as *The Thin Man*? It was one of Ficarotta's early short operas and it's sometimes paired with *Cavalleria Rusticana* or *I Pagliacci*. Good plot, with all sorts of Sicilian banditry and lost inheritances to spice things up, but the central story is that of Lieutenant Gasparo, who wants to marry Cinzia. Gasparo has recently returned to his town after a year away fighting the Turks, but hardly anyone recognizes him because he has become prodigiously fat. Last year's willowy young officer now resembles Monty Python's Mr. Creosote. His military campaign was highly successful and his troops won all sorts of victories and booty, which included a number of eager, hairy women and a Turkish-delight factory. But Gasparo has a weakness that soon betrayed him and, leaving the women to his equally hairy and eager men, he took to spending entire days in the deserted factory, pining for Cinzia and comfort-eating his way through hundredweights of sugar-dusted, gelatinous cushions of *lokoum*. The result is that when Cinzia first glimpses him rolling like a dirigible across the town square she is so horrified by his appearance she swears a solemn oath she will never marry him until he is once more as slender as when they had first met by moonlight. To that end his family, keen on her dowry, walls him up in an old fort, leaving a single entrance to his cell so narrow that only a thin man could squeeze through. Until he loses enough weight to come forth as *l'uomo magro*, Cinzia will remain unwed.

Normally the role of Gasparo is played by a tenor wearing a fat costume, and after his spell in the fort they pull his bungs out behind the scenery and he whistlingly deflates in time for the triumphant last wedding scene. There is a great studio recording of *L'uomo magro* by Pavarotti and Muti with the La Scala orchestra, but for obvious reasons Pavarotti has never been able to play Gasparo on the stage. The aria I like best, and the one I choose to sing this morning as I bustle about trying to spruce up Derek's grubby little kitchenette, is Cinzia's "Seguire," which she sings to Gasparo outside his cell one night. It is an aria of plaintive longing and encouragement, while not lacking in a degree of admonition. She is a very determined young lady who doesn't relish the prospect of waiting so long for him to slim down that she loses her looks before he can regain his. "*Seguire*," she urges him, "*seguire un'alimentazione quotidiana sana ed equilibrata è importante per mantenersi in forma.*" Towards the end her words are punctuated by her starving lover's pitiful howls from inside the cell in a masterly tragicomic duet.

As I sing and scrub away my mind is busily flicking through a mental card index of recipes to find something suitable for greeting Derek on his return from work. He has pretensions to being a gourmet, despite the condition of his stove which he has certainly not cleaned since my last visit many months ago. Remembering that he particularly likes fish, and recognizing that it will require some deft shopping in the excellent fish shop around the corner, I decide on a Samper classic:

Eels Flottantes

Ingredients
1 kg eels
Whites of 5 eggs
400 gm samphire
Thumbnail-sized lump of fresh ginger
2 large sticks of rhubarb
Small piece of nutmeg
400 gm okra
1 tbsp gelatine
Lime juice (optional)

The eels I find this morning are alive but disheartened and, back in Derek's kitchen, squirm sullenly in their mucus. It is possible that by some misunderstanding you have formed the impression that Samper's approach to the natural world is callous and uncaring, especially where it intersects with gastronomy. This is a calumny, as will be evidenced by my concern to take these poor eels' lives in a way that causes me no pain even as it kills them instantly. I reject at once both the two commonly used methods. The first is to put them in a deep bowl and sprinkle them liberally with salt. This is claimed to do for them inside two hours and to remove much of their slime as well. I submit that any method of execution that takes up to two hours to work is dismally inefficient. Also, it is improper to punish still further any wild creature that has already had the misfortune to wind up in a zinc tank off Marylebone High Street. What is more, eels that have been "brined" in this way have often been found still alive eighteen hours later. They are verte-brates with an advanced sensory system and it is safe to assume they suffer. A more popular way of despatching eels is simply to chop their heads off, probably using for the first time that chopper bought on impulse in a supermarket in Chinatown because it looked so professional and was so cheap. It will come as a shock, however, to learn that severed eel heads may still be showing signs of life up to eight hours later. That's what comes of anthropomorphism. We assume that what seems to kill us quite reliably will do the same for any other creature. You will note I say "seems" to kill us, because in 1905 an unsqueamish French doctor named Beaurieux conducted experiments with the freshly guillotined heads of condemned murderers. One involved a convict named Languille with whom Beaurieux had previously agreed a code whereby the victim promised to try to respond to questions by opening and closing his eyes. The blade fell and the doctor addressed Languille's head, twice calling out his name. Languille's eyes duly opened twice. On the second occasion, "the eyelids lifted and undeniably living eyes fixed themselves on mine with perhaps even more pene-tration than the first time." (This is a true story, although I grant it's an odd coincidence that Languille is French for "the eel.") Presumably if a very sharp blade transects the spinal cord precisely between two cervical vertebrae, thereby causing minimal physical shock, consciousness would not necessarily be lost instantaneously. All of which goes to show that cooks should think twice before reaching for their Chinese choppers and lopping off bits of live animal under the impression that they are being humane. They should try to imagine what goes through an eel's mind when it suddenly finds itself missing from the neck down and then swept away into the aromatic darkness of a kitchen pedal bin, being intermittently doused with showers of onion peelings and coffee grounds for eight hours until things mercifully begin to fade.

To kill eels instantly, strike them smartly on the back two-thirds of the way down with a rolling pin. *Then* cut their heads off. Wash the headless corpses thoroughly in cold water for up to half an hour, carefully scraping the slime off. Gut them normally, not forgetting to prolong the cut to an inch beyond their arseholes because a sort of kidney-like organ is lying doggo down there. Wash them again and cut into slices about as thick as the length of the top joint of your middle finger. Now lightly boil the okra, samphire and rhubarb separately in barely enough unsalted water to cover them, in the samphire's case until the leaves slide off the stalk (probably 10 mins. but depends on the season). When all three are done, put them without draining into a liquidizer together with the small lump of root ginger, blend them, add salt and pepper with a sparing hand (samphire is already quite salty) as well as a squeeze of lime juice if you have any, and put the mixture aside to cool in a large bowl you would not be ashamed to see on a dining table. The colour will be predominantly greenish; the shade can be intensified by stirring in a few drops of food colouring.

Now fry the eel slices gently in the merest smear of olive oil (their own fat will mobilize as they heat up) until they begin to brown and the skin is easy to separate. Still without removing the skin, set them aside as well to cool. When they are cold enough put them in the fridge and go out and buy yourself the tie you noticed on the way to the fish shop and have been thinking about ever since. It costs nearly eighty pounds, and it has taken the fit of introspection caused by slaughtering innocent eels to talk yourself into deciding that it is a killer item essential to the Samper wardrobe. A summery little number, it resembles Shredded Wheat in both colour and texture and is allegedly made from the undyed silk secreted by caterpillars fed on biologically farmed mulberry leaves, if you can believe the blarney on the little card attached. For eighty pounds they should have fed them on honeydew and the milk of Paradise;

but it's a spiffy tie and represents the upside of my dismal literary activities.

Back in the kitchen once more, take two cups of the green broth and heat one and a half of them. Soften the tablespoon of gelatine in the remaining half-cup of cool liquid and then dissolve it completely in the hot. Stir it well into the rest and put the bowl in the freezer to set. I know full well that this gelatine method is cheating. In the authentic original version I pioneered some years ago (on the same day as my exquisite Mackerel & Blackberry Loaf), I used freshly made chicken stock for cooking the vegetables. When rendered from a whole chicken gently simmered for three hours, this stock sets naturally when refrigerated and is unquestionably preferable. This present version is a slightly disgraceful makeshift for those pressed for time: a recourse that I realize is perilously close to TV cheffie cookery. Banish this thought if you can by taking five eggs from inside the door of Derek's fridge and praying they were laid later than 2004. Separate the whites and beat them until they stand up (the Robert Mugabe approach to cookery). Bring a little milk to the boil and grate barely enough nutmeg on the surface to leave a fine film. Then with a wet spoon toss blobs of the egg foam onto its surface for a few seconds. They cook almost at once and turn into quenelles of meringue imbued with the merest ghost of nutmeg.

By now you are home and dry, which is more than can be said for Derek who has just rung to say he's been caught in a shower near Berkeley Square and is presently huddled in a doorway because, not having his brolly with him, he daren't risk getting his hair wet. Rugged outdoorsman that I am, I do my best to keep any contempt for such feebleness out of my voice. Still, I suppose when you haven't much hair to start with and what remains has been frisked and dolloped into a texture considerably like meringue, you do better to lurk in doorways rather than risk collapse. This gives me ample time to remove the now-set bowl of liquid from the freezer and admire its trembling, rubbery surface as well as its beautiful deep-green colour. On it I now dispose with the utmost artistry the roundels of cold eel, topping each with a cap of meringue. And there we are: Eels flottantes! Now the point of leaving the skin on the slices becomes apparent. It is entirely a matter of aesthetics. The meringues seem to float like icebergs on their little black rafts of eel meat, themselves buoyed up on a fathomless green ocean. And maybe the scrupulous addition of one or two of those famous silver balls to the meringues' peaks will give this great dish its final touch of fantasy.

It is true to say that when Derek finally does arrive and has restored himself with a hair dryer and gin he is not in the ideal mood for gastronomic adventure. I now realize that in his way he is really rather unenterprising. He certainly eats what I have spent so much of the day preparing in his honour, but in a pettishly tentative and dispirited manner ("like snacking out of a pond"). But he perks up on hearing that I shall soon see Christ. "We *are* moving in exalted circles these days, Gerry," he says with elaborate unconcern, and then can't stop himself adding: "Did I tell you I styled Pavel Taneyev the other day? He's over here for ages because he's doing a complete Bach at Wigmore Hall over the next six weeks. Difficult, difficult hair. I think ideally he wants to look Byronic—you know, shoulder-length, wide open collar. But it's far too fine and he's really just too old for that look, poor boy. His is that wretched kind of hair that lacks all body, and he really shouldn't wear it long at all because otherwise it has to be whizzed up to make it look bigger and he risks turning into Dame Edna Everage. Whatever else she did, she never played the *Goldberg Variations* in Wigmore Hall. He's so sweet, though, ever so generous with complimentary tickets to his concerts. We all call him Pauline. Leslie, who washes him, says he adores being shampooed. By the time I get to cut and style him he's all flushed and rosy. I always think Russians are so sensitive."

Stories about sensitive Russians always make me think of Stalin and the account given by his dentist. Being Stalin's dentist must have rated as the world's least desirable job, with the gulag or the executioner's bullet lurking behind one's every move with the little silver probe. And as for *drilling* . . . Years after Stalin's death his dentist admitted it had been nerve-wracking, and made worse by the dictator's own terror of having his teeth seen to which led him to babble endless Georgian jokes to postpone having to open his mouth. A dental appointment with Stalin ran to several hours. Knowing Blowjob, I expect hair appointments with Pavel Taneyev take quite as long. It's typical of Derek that he feels compelled to try to upstage me, even as he must know that Max Christ easily outranks Taneyev in terms of visibility and general recognition. But there we are, and it costs me nothing to allow for poor Derek's being a hairdresser with collapsed nether cheeks. Still, I can't quite bring myself to admit that I should very much like an introduction to Taneyev myself, and it's a bit of a shock to hear that a person I would adore to write about has so easily swum into Derek's ken. I suppose I was still hoping to reach him via Marta. Taneyev remains a hero of mine; and while it's all very fine pinning my immediate hopes on Max Christ, it may well be that some earnest German is already halfway through writing the conductor's official biography. So I certainly ought to have an alternative subject up my sleeve. As if I needed reminding of the awful fate that awaits me if I fail, Frankie mentioned the other day that Champions Press has had an enquiry from an international rugby player who wants his story told and they thought of me. *Can* it get more humiliating than this? The essential Socratic dignity of suicide is something that is beginning to take hold of me with quiet conviction.

"I must say, Derek, if you can lay your hands on any of those complimentary tickets I shouldn't at all mind going along to hear Taneyev at least once. When does he start?"

"Next week sometime. The first evening's the Partitas, I think. He's booked me for that afternoon. He says nobody in the whole world understands his hair as I do."

"A well-earned compliment on your intellectual achievement." I'm not about to give gratuitous hostages to Derek's malice so I shall say nothing about my wanting to meet his illustrious client—not unless he first tries to wangle an introduction to mine. I shall simply buy a ticket to one of Taneyev's less popular evenings, such as when completeness obliges him to play those dreary early toccatas, and then slip off backstage afterwards. I expect I shall go in a corduroy suit of a restrained shade—probably that bitter chocolate one I noticed when I bought the tie this afternoon. It's vital to understate when choosing ultra-soft fabrics, otherwise one risks looking like Big Lord Fauntleroy or plain flamboyant. Discretion is the better part of velour.

The next day, a Wednesday, Adrian's sister Jennifer rings to say there's a sudden loophole in her husband's calendar and could I manage dinner with Max this Friday? Can I ever?, I think as I gracefully accept with a tiny lurch of the stomach. My apprehension becomes more marked when Jennifer explains that unfortunately Adrian won't be coming as well because he has just rung to say he's flying straight off to join some survey vessel that's having instrument problems. Naturally, I've been relying on the promise of his moral support for this critical evening. Well, that does it: I shall go out and buy that corduroy suit right now. What is seven hundred pounds when one's future is at stake? No sooner have I put the phone down than Frankie calls to say Millie Cleat's keen to reach me but doesn't have Derek's number. Certainly she doesn't, I say, and nor must she. I suggest he tells her I shall be out of touch for the rest of the week. "She's not used to being kept waiting," says Frankie delightedly. "Exactly," I say.

Cities inhibit me. I look out over the cobbled mews at the back of the flat and feel trapped. Just before he left for work this morning Derek found a letter pushed beneath his front door from his imperfectly literate landlord, a smarmy, tone-deaf immigrant who lives upstairs. He was complaining about "a very bad yoweling" yesterday morning that disturbed his patients. "Were you singing, Gerry?" Derek asked me crossly. "After I asked you not to?"

"I forgot," I admitted. "Only a little aria from *L'uomo magro*. Why shouldn't I? What patients, anyway? What is he—an analyst? An abortionist?"

"An irrigator. He insists on absolute calm when doing it. He offered me a freebie once after I'd just moved in, but he's too creepy. He eats those Japanese breath-freshener pastilles all the time. Also, his flat's obsessively neat and full of deodorizers and incense burners. I simply fled. He's not pushing rubber tubes up me, not even to reduce the rent. How can one be an anal retentive *and* an irrigator, that's what I want to know. But I don't need trouble, Gerry, so no more singing, *please.*"

Thus admonished I now creep silently about, gathering my wits before sallying forth to buy clothes suitable for dining with Christ. I'm already sick of London and miss Le Rocce, where I can wear what I like and sing what I like and cook what I like. With a small pang I find myself wondering if old Marta's back yet. But then, she wasn't too keen on my singing, either, and took a terrible revenge for which, if I live long enough, I may yet forgive her.

9.

"I hope you don't mind taking the train to Woodbridge," my hostess had said, "but Max has to be in Colchester on Friday afternoon and it seemed more logical." For them, yes. I buy the best bottle of prosecco I can find and wrap it myself because shops here won't wrap anything properly, not even gifts. It is only when one has lived abroad for any length of time that one appreciates what a peculiar place England actually is. I catch a late-afternoon train, allowing masses of time because I hate being rushed and flustered. I'm hoping to arrive early enough to spend an hour or two in a friendly hostelry at the other end, putting my thoughts in order over some Dutch courage. Before catching the train I remind myself to sit bolt upright for fear of creasing my new corduroy suit, which I have to say is drop-dead luscious and flatters the Samper physique to the point of sycophancy. And my new dull-Shredded-Wheat tie is simply made to go with it. However, these precautions have turned out to be wholly irrelevant. Not only is the train so dawdling and delayed that I become seriously alarmed, it is also so crammed with commuters that the question of how or even where to sit is purely academic. With a certain hauteur I resign myself to standing the whole way and try to minimize physical contact with my fellow straphangers to keep my beautiful suit unsullied. In any case I shouldn't have dared sit because almost as soon as they got on most of the passengers began tearing open plastic packages of noisome snacks and have dripped and spurted mayonnaise or ketchup over each other ever since.

My instructions are to get a station taxi to Crendlesham Hall, "a little out of town towards the Crendle and Swythings," whatever they are. Am I right to detect something excluding, even mildly hostile, about these opaque directions? When we finally arrive in Woodbridge the sauce-spattered horde pours out onto the platform with me in their midst trying to hold myself poised and aloof, like Liszt's *St. François de Paule marchant sur les flots*. The result of his stately passage is that by the time he reaches the taxi rank Saint François finds himself fresh out of transport. When at last he gets a cab it is five past eight and he is already late for this crucial dinner. The driver is not some ancient Suffolk dunce but a young Pakistani or something, very swift and civil. I implore him to hurry still more. "It can't be far," I tell him to reassure myself.

"About twenty minutes with luck, sir," he says.

"Twenty *minutes*? 'A little out of town,' they said," as if by quoting this I could magically shrink the distance. "And what's a Crendle? Or Swythings, come to that?"

"The Crendle's a hill where they used to execute horse thieves, sir. Rough lot they were in those days. You don't want to hear how they did it." He is watching me in the driving mirror.

"Yes, I do."

"Ah. Well, what they did was stuff the fellow as full as they could with freshly grated horseradish root, at both ends, sir, if you follow me, *and* in his eyes. That would be dreadful agony, as you can imagine if ever you've taken a tiny bit too much with your roast beef. All ablaze and choking, he'd be. And then they'd peg him down to the ground and have a Suffolk Punch sit on him. That's one big mother of a shire horse, you know, sir. Weighs over a ton. They say the horseradish would shoot out of him, oh, twenty feet or so, even his eyes, too, sometimes, pop-pop. There wasn't much horse-thieving around these parts. That's the Crendle over there now, sir." He nods towards a low crepuscular hill. Again I catch his gaze on me. "Would you care to stop, sir?"

"*Stop*? Absolutely not, I'm late as it is. You can't go too fast. Pardon my saying so, but you're amazingly well informed."

"For a Pakistani or for a taxi driver, sir?"

"Just very well informed," I say warmly but warily. "For a Briton." I am not about to have my multiracial correctness quizzed. "And Swythings?"

"They're what we call a particular area down by the Deben. That's the river here. Swythings is an old dialect word meaning 'quick to mow.' Probably peasant humour, sir, since the land there was so often flooded."

He's much too knowledgeable to be a mere unlettered local; he's obviously an autodidact. I muse on this and forget about the time and suddenly we're turning into a lane—no, a drive—and pulling up outside a large half-timbered, barn-like building. A naked bulb hangs over the porch and its light, together with that of the rapidly deepening dusk, illuminates an immense heap of sand, a cement mixer and various wooden pallets of materials shrouded in polythene. *Can* this be right? Does the world's greatest young conductor throw dinners at a building site? It's a hopeful sign of eccentricity for a potential biographer, if a little discouraging to a potential diner. I pay the driver, who gives me a card and hopes that I enjoy my evening. Right now the chances feel slim. Because Adrian flew off to join his ship before I had a chance to ask him, I'm still unsure exactly what he has told his illustrious brother-in-law about me. As the front door knocker comes away in my hand I reflect on the awkwardness of being invited to dinner by total strangers unless there's some pretext that everyone acknowledges. So it is reassuring that the woman who answers the door is recognizably Adrian's sister. "You must be Gerald," she says, taking the immense horseshoe from my hand. "Don't worry, it's always coming off—it's just something temporary we rigged up. As you can see, we've got the builders."

"Inside as well as out." The house looks immensely old, such of it as is visible between dust covers and sheets of plasterboard leaning up against the wall.

"Yes, I must apologize. We ought really to have met in London after all. I'm afraid I've got so used to it that I forget what a pigsty this place is. Oh, and the lavatory in the cloakroom here is kaput. Josh has put one of his dinosaurs down it so I'm afraid you'll have to go upstairs like the rest of us. To your left at the top of the stairs." Jennifer waves a hand towards a broad wooden staircase while leading the way to the kitchen, which is a welcoming womb of warmth and light and delicious cooking smells. And there, sitting reading a newspaper beside the immense Aga range, is Christ himself with a cat on his lap.

"I'm so sorry I'm late," I say. "The train took hours and hours."

"We're quite used to it," says the celebrated man, getting to his feet and apologizing to the cat, which lands on the pale brick floor looking blank and cross like a suddenly woken child. The great Max Christ turns out to be surprisingly small, with greying curly hair that could use some of Derek's attention. "They're doing something to East Anglia's signalling system or something. Everyone's late all the time." His English is impeccable.

We shake hands and I'm about to hand over the prosecco to Jennifer when I discover to my horror that I must have left it in the taxi. My hosts make light of this and press a deeply welcome gin and tonic into my apologetic hands. "The driver gave me his card so maybe I should ring him up and ask him to leave the bottle at the station," I say lamely. I find I don't care much because now they both know I brought something it has already served its purpose. Still, £15.99, a grotesque price. "A pretty odd sort of driver," I add. "He told me all about the Crendle being a hill where they used to execute horse thieves. Asked me if I wanted to stop there, if you please, at twenty-five past eight at night. A Pakistani, he said he was."

Jennifer and her husband exchange glances. "So Khurshid's out again, is he?" says Max. "I wonder if it's remission or probation this time? He's just a harmless sex offender. Perfectly polite and nonviolent. Sometimes he stops when he has a lone gentleman in the cab. You were quite safe. Rather a gifted man. Certainly very inventive. He makes up stories about the places he drives past."

"Horse thieves, indeed," says Jennifer, lifting a shoulder of mutton out of the oven. "The Crendle's actually a stone monument near a crossroads about two miles from here. Nobody knows quite what it commemorates. It's so weathered it's a complete blank on all its faces. You can just recognize it in one of Constable's paintings."

"Ach, Quatsch, Hannele!" says Max. "Don't listen to her," he urges me towards the plain scrubbed kitchen table laid with an assortment of ancient cutlery with yellowed handles that looks as though it was assembled from local junk shops. "Jennifer's as bad as Khurshid when it comes to making things up."

"Well, what are Swythings, then?" I ask her, a little bemused. "Khurshid said it meant 'easy to mow' or something."

"What nonsense! It was a mediaeval land-tax system. People could graze their cattle on 'swithen' land for nothing, although they did have to donate a cow each Christmas to the Bishop of Bury St. Edmunds."

"You're *such* a liar, my dear," Max tells his wife fondly.

I can't get the measure of any of this, like the victim of an obscure practical joke. I'm tired and hungry, too, what with the nervous strain and late arrival, although the g-&-t is working its customary magic. I suppose I was expecting something more along the lines of a formal dinner with maybe one or two household-name glitterati trying to be witty by candlelight. The sort of company where at last I could be myself and feel at home, maybe even shine a little in my modest way. Instead here we three are, sitting at the kitchen table, tucking into a large and succulent mutton roast. I should think that after a good searing this piece of friendly old sheep we're eating must have gone into one of the cooler bottom ovens at around two o'clock this afternoon. In that enormous iron casserole with water in its sunken lid to keep the contents moist it would have been just about ready by seven. Max (as he insists I call him) has produced some bottles of Donnafugata's '02 Tancredi, a sumptuously glowering Sicilian red that looks almost black in the glass and makes me want to weep it's so good, although that may be partly due to the gin that preceded it. I can feel myself beginning to relax a little, especially when Jennifer compliments me on my suit. My exquisite corduroy sheathing, expressly designed to go with silver and heavy linen and august company, has actually been contributing to my unease in a subliminal sort of way. One does not take onto a building site seven hundred pounds' worth of Blaise Prévert's dark-chocolate corduroy (or cordureine, as Derek ungrammatically and gratuitously called it this morning, jealous faggotino, he of the absentee bottom who couldn't wear a suit like this in a million years). On every surface in this house one risks the contagion of plaster dust and worse. But now after a glass or two of the Tancredi I find to my surprise that I have begun to view the suit as having something in common with my late lamented bottle of prosecco in that it is proof of my taste and good intentions, and whatever its physical fate it has already made its point.

A further surprise is Max's apparent disinclination to talk about music. This seems not to be the bluff, Elgarian defensiveness that insists on discussing horse racing while the avoided topic broods like a thundercloud above the table. Max's attitude is more that of the man who doesn't wish to consider work outside office hours. This is awkward, since I am naturally eager to establish my own musical credentials, such as they are; although I dare say there are not too many people who can sing most of *L'uomo magro* from memory, to say nothing of *I froci di Firenze.* So I tell Max how wonderful I think his Schumann symphonies are, trying to sound thoughtful rather than fulsome. I say I am particularly impressed by his going back to the autograph of the Fourth in its 1841 first version, which is so much more spontaneous and transparent in texture than Schumann's overworked later version with its thick wind doublings.

"Oh," Max says modestly through a mouthful of mutton (though I can tell he is pleased), "I was only following the trail blazed by Nikolaus."

Harnoncourt, I presume, and am about to carry on with what Brahms said about these two versions of the D-minor symphony when Max abruptly changes the subject.

"You know the person I really admire?"

"Celibadache?" I hazard.

"Sergiu, yes, of course; but I was thinking of Adrian. My brother-in-law. I always wanted to be a palaeobiologist, did you know that? I realize Adrian's an oceanographer, which is rather different, but he manages to do a lot of field work. I'm envious."

"When you say you always wanted . . ." I prompt, with a glance at his wife to see how she is taking this. Is this to be another joke at the expense of their earnest, overdressed guest? But she is unconcernedly helping herself to mint sauce from a child's porringer at the bottom of which some merry bears can be glimpsed cavorting dimly beneath the vinegar. It reminds me how easily my stomach can sometimes be upset by acidic food, and my new trousers do suddenly feel remarkably tight.

"I mean it was what I always wanted to be as a child," says

Max. "Only alas! my talents were all musical. When I was seventeen and already at the Conservatory I met this marvellous American scientist, Valeriy Bogdanov, who had been on a joint expedition to what was then Soviet Siberia to investigate the prehistoric animals buried intact beneath the permafrost. He was a scientist, all right, but he told me that at the time he'd really gone more as a clandestine missionary for one of those weird American sects—Jehovah's Adventists or Seventh-Day Witnesses or whatever they are. But he became so fascinated by the perfectly preserved remains they found that he gave up hoping to spread his gospel and instead concentrated on the beautiful science."

"Ye cannot serve God and mammoth," I venture. "It's well known. It says so in the Bible."

"We're still in touch, you know. Professor Bogdanov's very eminent these days, but he still gets out to do field work. He's offering to take me to a place he himself discovered in Siberia quite recently which is a real mammoths' graveyard. And do you know how he found it? By his nose," says Max, tapping his own as though I might have forgotten what it was called in English. "He was going along offshore in a rubber boat looking at these low cliffs and suddenly he smelt this terrible stink of decay. So he went in and found an inlet with permafrost banks about ten metres high. Only the permafrost was melting, and all the ancient frozen animals were thawing out and decaying. Global warming, you see. Extraordinary, don't you think, to smell an animal decaying that has already been dead fifteen thousand years or so? I'd love to see them for myself. Red hair and long tusks. Valeriy says he has actually eaten woolly-mammoth steaks from a frozen specimen."

"A classic case for Aga cookery," I say. "Stewed very slow with big juicy onions, I should think."

"Adrian tells me you're a brilliant cook," Jennifer puts in.

"Not brilliant, perhaps," I concede, "but *interested*. I like inventing things, although not all of them are necessarily edible. Sometimes one gets tired of the old tried-and-trusted, don't you think? The obligatory British meat and two veg?" Oh, well done, Samper! Like leg of mutton with mint sauce is a new culinary departure? "At other times, of course, a classic like this fabulous roast is exactly what one needs," I add firmly.

"I'm afraid we find ourselves regressing a bit these days," admits Jennifer. "It's what comes of living on a building site with a five-year-old. Kids are conservative anyway, and just at present with hardly a properly habitable room here Max and I seem to need reassuring food. When he's away on foreign tours he usually has a grim diet—you know how awful protracted hotel and restaurant eating becomes. You long for a simple bacon sarnie. Anyway, I did think of having veal tonight but Max said you probably have all the veal you want. Living in Italy, I mean."

"No lack of veal there," I agree feebly, hoping I'm not blushing.

"Adrian tells us you're also a brilliant writer." Max is refilling my glass from deep down the second bottle of Tancredi. "I apologize that I've not yet read any of your books."

"Keep it that way!" I cry in alarm. "No, really, I mean it." In case this sounds like false modesty disguised as jocularity, I add: "Not unless you're interested in sporting heroes. What can I say? It's a living. For now."

"Quite a good one, I should think. We hear you're writing about that yachtswoman at the moment—what's her name, Hannele?—Millie, that's right. Millie Cleat. So what's she like? As a person?"

"One-armed."

"Oh, you don't have to be tactful," says Jennifer eggingly. "Adrian's already told us about what she did in the Canaries. They're all still hopping mad at BOIS. Though I suppose competitive sport is a ruthless business these days. Presumably it doesn't much matter what you do so long as you win."

"The people who believe that are the ones who keep parroting that history is written by the winners. Unfortunately, it's history's least interesting and significant version." I can feel myself on the edge of becoming sententious, which will never do since I really don't give much of a toss who writes history so long as it's readable. I'm afraid alcohol has that effect on me and I must be careful lest too much Tancredi writes Samper's future as a loser. For even now I'm aware of something else making itself felt that may be due partly to the wine but mainly to a combination of nerves and mint sauce: one of those internal crises the malicious fates send to afflict anxious dinner guests in strange houses. Something I have eaten or drunk is proving to be searching to the point of unabashed interrogation. The waistband of my Blaise Prévert trousers, recently so snug, now feels definitely constricting. I am, I fear, going to have to leave the table briefly.

Normally, of course, I feel not the least diffidence about such things, which anyway are much less embarrassing in Italy where physical functions are treated matter-of-factly and in a way that cheerfully acknowledges that we all share a human common denominator notorious for making forceful demands at inconsiderate moments. In the Britain of my childhood public lavatories were often euphemistically signposted as "public conveniences" as though they were just rather handy things to have around instead of Meccas of desperation. But circumstances tonight are not by any means normal. I still haven't the least clue as to whether things are looking hopeful for me or not. I can't make out if these civilized, amiable people are merely indulging me as someone wished on them by an absent member of the family or toying with me as part of a testing procedure. I don't even know if maestro Christ wants his biography written by anybody, let alone by me. For that reason I'm reluctant to leave the table at all because I can't bear to think what they'll be saying once I'm out of the room. On the other hand I recognize that if I don't go *now* I shall precipitate rather more than a mere career setback. So I excuse myself and get to my feet in a clenched sort of way.

"Up the stairs and to the left, I think you said?" I drop my napkin beside my empty plate with frantic languor.

"Shall I come and show you?" asks Jennifer, the perfect host. "It's all a bit chaotic and some of the lights are dodgy. They promise it'll all be over by November, but I have my doubts."

"No, no, it's quite all right. I'm used to building sites. Don't forget I live up a mountain. For a long time I would offer guests a spade and show them the great outdoors." By now I am halfway out and heading at a fair clip for the stairs, which at least are well lit. At the top is a sort of gallery off which leads a beamy corridor. Almost immediately to my left there is a half open door through which I glimpse the unmistakable welcoming gleam of porcelain. And not a moment too soon. The light doesn't work and the door won't close completely but by now I am beyond caring about such trivia. It is a lavatory, and that's all that matters. Within seconds Blaise Prévert lies around my ankles and after a Homeric detonation I realize Samper is saved. As I sit there catching my breath and blissfully suffused with relief I keep a wary eye on the slightly open door's strip of light. I think I glimpse a small figure flit silently past on little pink feet but for the moment I'm still too much under the influence of Tancredi and easement to care. Enough light filters in for me to realize that their bathroom, too, is a building site. There is a step ladder propped next to the lavatory and several buckets with distemper brushes in them are ranged nearby. From next door comes the sound of flushing and the little pink feet whisk past the door again. That's odd, I think, as I cast around for the toilet roll, my hand patting the bare wall to either side. Why would anyone have *two* lavatories so close togeth–? And then it sinks in. I rock experimentally on my throne and my worst fears are confirmed. This lavatory bowl is not plumbed in. This lavatory bowl is either waiting to be plumbed in or has just been removed from the bathroom next door, it hardly matters which. Well, well, Samper: by far your greatest social move to date. The perfect dinner guest who dumps at random in holes and corners about the house and then wonders if his illustrious host would like him as a biographer.

For a long moment it is uncertain whether I am going to sit there in frozen misery and maybe begin to cry, or else start laughing. Actually, it's not really much of a choice for the last of the Sampers, and I'm soon rocking with desperately stifled hysteria on—and over—my illicit stool. It's when things can't get any worse that real hilarity begins. When at last I wipe my eyes I can make out that by the merciful dispensation of fate there is across the room an industrial-sized roll of paper towelling such as builders might use to clean their brushes. I duck-waddle across bent double, trying to hold Blaise Prévert off the dusty floor, and avail myself of it in liberal handfuls. I finish off by stuffing wads down the bowl on top of the evidence, which I'm hoping is trapped in the deep S-bend behind. Another wad at the unplumbed end ought to tamp it in. My eyes having adjusted to the semi-dark, I can now see that not only is the lavatory further out from the wall than normal but at a slight angle to it. However, these helpful giveaway details were rather too little and much too late. As I adjust my dress before leaving (as public notices used to urge gentlemen) I'm aware that I now have a delicate decision to take. Do I go down and confess all? That would obviously be the decent, manly thing to do. But I have always found decency and manliness dragging their feet when all instinct is screaming at me to keep quiet and get the hell out. Just go as soon as is humanly possible; give up the whole doomed enterprise as one bad job brought on by another. After

all, sporting heroes aren't really so awful. Their own behaviour
is mostly reassuringly atrocious, plus they pay top whack and
anyway, who honestly cares a row of beans whether Schumann
doubled the woodwind in his revised version of the Fourth
symphony? Well, actually, *I* do; but perhaps not enough to conduct a shamefaced confession downstairs in front of the Aga
like a child who has had an accident. I can feel the thought rising hotly that it wasn't my fault, dammit. It wasn't my fault I
had to flounder around an unlit building site to find a usable
lavatory. What kind of a way is this to treat a guest? Why
couldn't we have had a perfectly civilized, businesslike evening
together in London instead of enduring this hideous farce in
darkest Suffolk, a county clearly full of idiotic dialect and perverted taxi drivers? Was it for this I spent seven hundred
pounds of my hard-earned money on a suit, not to mention
£15.99 on a wasted bottle of prosecco and practically a week's
wages for a rail ticket granting me the generous privilege of
standing in a train for three hours? Why did I ever leave the
quiet sanity of Le Rocce?

But even as the protests surge through my brain I know it's
just rhetoric. Jennifer is Adrian's sister and I most definitely
wish to remain friends with Adrian, and sooner or later the
thing will get out and oh! what a tangled web, etc. The adage
"least said, soonest mended" clearly doesn't apply to a dinner
guest who has copiously mispooped in the spare room.

So, quietly leaving the scene of the crime I go downstairs
like a child prepared to own up. My opening phrase, "I'm
afraid I've just done an awful thing" is ready and waiting as I
enter the kitchen and see the table is now laid with a large bowl
of syllabub, a deliciously crumbly-looking Stilton wrapped in a
cloth and yet another bottle of Tancredi. Before I can utter a
word, Jennifer says:

"You found your way all right? Incidentally, Gerry, I forgot
to say we're taking it for granted you'll stay the night."

"Oh, no. No, really." I am prepared to confess, but then to scuttle away into the decent absolving darkness. A taxi ride, a late train and many, many miles placed between myself and the time bomb upstairs. "You're very kind but I can't possibly."

"But neither can you possibly go," she says reasonably. "It's far too late. I don't even know if there are any trains from Ipswich after midnight at present, thanks to the work they're doing on the line. No, you must certainly stay here, Gerry. Besides, Adrian would never forgive me. I know you're used to roughing it and all that, but I've made you up a bed anyway."

And because my confession has been thwarted—*confessio interrupta* as the pious monks of San Bernard probably knew it—it has now become utterly impossible to make it. The right moment, once past, is irrecoverable. By half past midnight I find myself, freshly sponged but still unshriven, in bed in my underwear in Max's study at the end of the upstairs corridor. There are ceiling-high shelves of scores and all sorts of musical memorabilia, but I'm too emotionally exhausted to inspect them. As I lie in the dark I am thankful only that I'm not having to sleep in that room next to the bathroom, which I now think of as Ground Zero. That would have been rough justice indeed. As I start to drift off there comes into my mind a lugubrious hymn my stepmother Laura used to sing around the house, only tonight with words supplied by my own bruised and self-pitying ego:

> Amazing Disgrace! My best hopes brought
> To nothingness and grievings.
> An entry to Christ's house I sought
> But fouled it with my leavings!

I confess I am not greatly looking forward to the unmasking the morrow must inevitably bring.

10

Not enough hours later, something that takes its time re-congealing into Gerald Samper awakes to the creak of the bedroom door and the sound of breathing. Then there is a diminishing patter of footsteps and a piercing child's voice in the distance announcing: "Mummy, there's a man in Vati's study." A sleep-sodden mutter of adult voices, then: "I said I won't go in, didn't I?" More approaching pattering, more breathing, more retreating feet. "He's still there. He looks funny."

My watch tells me it is five past six. My heart tells me King Herod was one of history's underrated heroes. My brain tells me very little, except to convey a vague presentiment of disaster. Then last night's events come back with a rush and I remember exactly why I don't wish to be in Crendlesham Hall in deepest Suffolk this Saturday morning. Through the half-open door comes the sound of heavier, parental footsteps, a gasp and the muffled expletive "Heagood!" of a Bavarian who has trodden in bare feet on a plastic stegosaur. Evidently Christ has risen, and with any luck he'll put some coffee on. Okay, Samper: the order of the day is to get the hell out as soon as you can. These are thoroughly nice people, much too nice for the likes of you. It's too late to make a confession now. We have entered that arrested, umbrageous world of adult mores where things are simply presumed not to have happened.

Seven-thirty finds me downstairs in the kitchen with a cup of coffee, talking with Max Christ the world-renowned conductor who is standing by the Aga in a puce dressing gown scraping cat food out of a tin with a clotted fork while the cat stands on its hind legs, mewing. "An Guadn!" says Max kindly, plonking the saucer down on the floor, and the cat tucks in. "You know I'm not keen on anyone writing my biography?" he turns to me apologetically. "I don't like any of this personality-cult business. I'm really interested only in doing my work as well as I can. Nothing beyond that. Of course it's nice when things go well and turn out successfully. I'm happy when people are pleased, and I'm delighted about Colchester because now the orchestra's got a life of its own and will go on quite happily if I drop dead tomorrow. But even when I'm on tour I'm counting the days when I can come home. I'm a family man, Gerry. I know this place looks chaotic at the moment and hardly like anyone's home. But I think it will be very nice when it's done. There's a barn out at the back that we're converting to a studio big enough for small chamber concerts and with good enough acoustics for instrumental recordings. I'm planning on travelling much less in three or four years' time. I'd like to do more work with the CSO and encourage people to give master classes and recitals here, a bit like Britten did at Snape. Truthfully, Gerry, I've no interest in seeing stuff published about myself. I frankly dislike all that commercial mythmaking. You know, like the way RCA built up Horowitz as the world's greatest pianist when he was nothing of the kind. Amazing technique, no question about that, but so often incoherent and vulgar in his interpretations. Just think of those awful blind octaves he added at the end of Chopin's B-minor Scherzo to make it sound flashier."

"Although the late Scarlatti recordings were surprisingly modest and good."

Max nods. "But perhaps by then he occasionally tired of his own shallowness, not to mention that of his awesome wife. She was Toscanini's daughter, as you know. I had to call on them once," he says reminiscently. "I was just a kid in New York doing some semesters at the Juilliard and I was summoned to the Horowitz apartment. They kept me waiting until after two A.M. I say 'they' because Wanda—what's the expression?—wore the trousers in that household. Given the chance, Vladimir would definitely have worn a dress." Max sips coffee and smiles at the memory.

"Well," I say after a pause for some silent cursing, "I do understand. Anybody sane and serious is reluctant to go along with the celebrity rigmarole. I just regret, as a professional writer, that your stories may go unrecorded." Now, careful here, Samper. Don't connive too easily at your own rejection. "But you know how things are, Max. Sooner or later interest in certain public figures reaches the point where biographies get written willy-nilly, with or without the subject's consent. And even, well, *family* men as you describe yourself don't always come off lightly. You know: trouble with lovers, mothers, others," I wave a hand suggestive of juicy scandals. "Would it not be preferable to have the process more under your own control? It's true that unofficial biographies tend to imply sensational revelations while official biographies suggest ponderousness, even hagiography. But in my experience" (this is a complete lie) "there's a happy medium to be struck where the subject has control over much of the factual stuff and the writer preserves the editorial independence to give the whole thing an individual flavour." Awful nonsense, this, but probably not bad for eight o'clock on a Saturday morning.

"I shall give thought to this, Gerry," Max says. "I promise. You may well be—"

But at this moment a small figure wearing dinosaur pyjamas bursts in followed by Jennifer, ravishing in a black silk-and-cashmere dressing gown by Zoran, surely the ultimate in Jackie Onassis chic on a building site.

"Hä, Joschi, mogsd wos dringga?" Max asks his son, who nods violently while gazing at me.

"Max! Will you please stop talking Bairisch to him? At least let him learn Hochdeutsch."

"Okay. But what about you, Hannele? Deaf i Dia a Bussl gem?"

"No, not until you've shaved. Good morning, Gerry. I hope you got some sleep? I'm sorry our resident tyrant woke you at that unearthly hour. Actually, we were all lucky this morning. He usually starts at about five."

Family life, you see? Absolute death to an orderly existence. It's at moments like these that we bachelors smugly count our blessings.

"If you can wait a bit I'll give you a lift into Woodbridge," Jennifer offers. "Josh and I have to go in to do some shopping, don't we, Josh?"

They come and go, gradually putting clothes on in a piece-meal sort of way, eating bowls of cornflakes and slices of toast while leaning against the comforting warmth of the Aga. This is, after all, an English summer.

"Where's Luna?" Josh demands.

"She's had breakfast and gone out," his father says.

"I bet she went to do a poo."

"In that case it was kind of her to go outside for a change."

Suddenly I'm aware of this child's bright blue eyes fixed on me with accusatory confidence.

"Why did you do a poo in the dark room?" the little bastard asks.

"Josh!" his mother warns. "Now don't be silly, please."

"But why did he?"

"That's quite enough. Come on, now, eat up and put your shoes on."

"But he *did*, Mummy. I heard him. And it smells of poo in there. *Eeuwgh!*"

"Of course you didn't hear him. Poor Gerry! I expect you had a dream, Josh. And if it smells in there it's probably Luna.

She doesn't like to go out if it's raining," this explanation being added for my benefit as Jennifer glances at me apologetically. Not for the first time in this madhouse I hope I'm not blushing. The child is still staring at me with a tilted spoon in his fist from which milk is running up his sleeve. Serve him right.

"Dino's gone down the Klo," he announces. "But he's still there." Is there no getting this diminutive sod off the topic of lavatories?

"I'm sure Gerry doesn't want to know that," his mother tells him, but Josh is not about to relinquish his favourite subject so easily.

"He wanted to do a poo and I was helping him and he fell in. Mummy, will they get him out today?"

"I doubt it, darling. It's Saturday and the builders don't come on Saturday, do they? We'll ask Mr. Baldock on Monday."

"The fat one? Will he get Dino out?"

"I'm sure he will. Now come on, Josh, quick! Gerry here wants to catch a train and you and I have to go to the bookshop to see if Orlando's come in yet, remember? The big marmalade cat?"

God's teeth and knuckles, the little pest is obsessed! He's a positive fecal freak. My last chance has obviously gone of making an intimate confession and apology to Jennifer on the way into Woodbridge. There is absolutely no way I am introducing any topic remotely touching on defecation in front of this child. So be it. I take my leave of Max, who shakes me warmly by the hand while promising me again that he'll "think very carefully about the whole matter." Josh is firmly strapped into a kiddy-seat in the back of the car, although for some reason his mother omits to gag him, and off we set for Woodbridge. And all I can think of is an unplumbed toilet bowl and its festering contents that each turn of the wheels is leaving farther behind us. On the station forecourt Jennifer gives me a brief hug and I thank her for a delightful evening while I notice Josh's clear gaze fixed on me, silently telling me that I can carry on with such grown-ups' mummery all I like but it doesn't fool him. He *knows*. Shortly afterwards, the train's wheels are beating their retreat-from-Moscow refrain:

> Amazing Disgrace! How sour the cry
> That haunts the wretched Gerry!
> His prospects low that once were high;
> Downcast, who once was merry.

*

It takes me the entire weekend to recover, if only partially, from this ordeal. I found myself in a state of extreme frailty in which I could easily have been stunned by a falling moonbeam. The prevailing social climate nowadays is heartless and bruising. There was a time when it was considered perfectly proper for traumatized members of the intellectual classes to retire to darkened rooms with sal volatile, laudanum and an anodyne book. Fainting, swooning, pining and paroxysms of uncontrollable grief were all considered perfectly normal in the sensitive from time to time. They were merely evidence of a fine but overburdened soul. These days, of course, nobody has a soul, fine or otherwise, and any such behaviour is stigmatized either as "acting out" or else as a "symptom." A Samper naturally scorns a pharmaceutical crutch, unless it contains derivatives of the poppy, but he doesn't say no to darkened rooms, soft music and sympathy. He does not expect an old friend like Derek to corpse over the account of his dark night of the soul in Suffolk and to refer to it as my Waterloo, a particularly heartless phrase in the circumstances. I'm sorry to say there's a cruel streak in Derek; and while we all know that virtue is its

own reward he would do well to remember that the utterly callous do not go unrepaid, either.

But thanks to my splendid mental constitution Monday
morning finds me just about strong enough to cope with Millie
Cleat, who when last heard from was clamouring to speak to me.

"Oh, Gerry darling, thank goodness it's you," she bawls
down the line as if she were reviewing the Fleet at Spithead in
the days before they invented semaphore. "Gerry, I can't tell
you what a difference you've made. You've changed my life, do
you realize? You can't deny it now: you're definitely chan-
nelling. The spirit is working through you."

"I'm sorry, Millie, I'm a little slow this morning. I really have
no idea what you're talking about."

"The picture, silly. The Face, as you called it. I Sellotaped it
to the wall as soon as you left and it's been gaining power ever
since. Not only does that wonderful all-seeing eye follow me
around the room wherever I am, but the whole picture is surrounded by a glow. I'm looking at it at this very moment and
that's the only way I can describe it: a sort of shimmer. I'm not
imagining it, you know. Debra's been here and she recognized
it immediately. She says there's absolutely no question that it's
a sacred image. Don't you see? It explains everything. That
strange feeling I had when I must have sailed right over him
without knowing he was there."

"Millie, I explained this to you," I break in impatiently, hoping to stem the gibberish and recognizing the name Debra as
that of one of her chief groupies. "The Face doesn't exist. It's
an illusion. It's like an optical illusion, except it was caused by
sound waves instead of light waves. It's a chimera, a figment,
a—"

"Listen, darling," she breaks in earnestly, "you really must
drop this hard-boiled pose of yours of . . . of . . ."

"Brutal rationalism?" I hazard. "Rationalist brutality?"

"Of dismissing everything as though it can all be explained

by science. On its own, science won't get you anywhere worth getting to."

"It got you around the world and back to the Solent."

"Not *just* science didn't. There was also a small matter of superlative seawomanship." This is more like the Millie I'm used to. "But there was something else, something even more fundamental and important, working *through* me. Call it the spirit of the sea, call it Neptune if you will."

"I won't."

"Now you're being silly, Gerry. Because unless you open your mind to it you will never understand how to finish my book."

Ah. I see. Yes, that is a problem. Undoubtedly I must get shot of Millie and her book with all possible despatch. But I'm damned if it's going to require me to become an acolyte in a primitive religion recently dusted off by a lot of nautical dykes under the influence of gin and heroine-worship. Mind you, at another level I can't deny a feeling of malevolent glee. The plot is proceeding exactly as Adrian and I were hoping it would. Millie has swallowed the bait whole. Our plan, of course, is to let this intolerable and pretentious woman make a complete public ass of herself over The Face and then have some scientist—preferably not Adrian himself—stand up and announce that, sadly, Millie Cleat has allowed herself to become misled by a perfectly commonplace oceanographical phenomenon on a par with seeing faces in clouds which, presumably, no sane person these days would worship as manifestations of a Sky God, etcetera etcetera. To be followed by TV close-ups of Millie's blushes and stammering climb-down. After which even her greatest fans will surely have to admit she's a considerable numbskull, while Samper and the entire EAGIS team will be popping prosecco corks and throwing their hard hats in the air. That will also be the moment for giving the media the story of what *really* happened that night in the Canaries when an obsessive yachtsperson, the balance of her mind perhaps disturbed by solitude, dreams of victory and seabed gods, selfishly ruined a scientific mission that might have provided crucial information regarding Cumbre Vieja's potential hazard and the vulnerability of half the northern hemisphere to a tsunami of Armageddon-like proportions . . . To say nothing of the money . . . And all backed up with photographs taken from the *Scomar Explorer's* bridge clearly showing *Beldame* scooting across the survey vessel's floodlit bows with inches to spare.

"We really need to finish this book," I now tell her reasonably. "Otherwise it will miss the Christmas market. And that does matter because—and I hate to remind you of this—the more time that goes by, the more the image of Millie Cleat fades on the public retina. Next year it may be Rufus Rasmussen, don't forget." This unkind cut gets the desired effect.

"Over my dead body," Millie growls.

"Right. So we absolutely need that Christmas slot. I propose we have a final session together tomorrow, and I'll go home and do a week's work on the text, and then I shall e-mail the whole lot to Champions Press and that will be that." An inspiration strikes me. "It's your *next* book that will be about The Face and Neptune and the elevation of Millie Cleat to Grand High Priestess of the newest cult to sweep the globe. Don't forget that in this business you've always got to have another book in the pipeline. This present volume confirms you as the world's greatest yachtswoman. Your next will establish you as a spiritual giant, treading the world's oceans with humility and reverence as Neptune's avatar or whatever. That will make not only commercial, but artistic sense. But for the moment we mustn't clutter up *Millie!* with too much spiritual stuff, otherwise it will jar with all the technical detail and steel-jawed determination. Much better keep the themes a bit separate, don't you think?"

And before long, of course, the plausible Samper has prevailed and Horatia Cleat is well on the way to her apotheosis as Neptunia Cleat. I can practically hear her filling the tub in her Hilton suite in order to practise walking on water. When I ring off, a little exhausted with oratory and intrigue, I'm feeling more cheerful. I shall soon be home in Le Rocce, putting the final bogus details into the text of the book, and thereafter I shall be free. I consciously squash back down the nagging creature who bobs up to say, "Yeah—free to do what, exactly? We're not going to be writing about world-famous conductors any time soon, are we?" In my experience there's no time like the distant future for listening to these bank-managerial inner voices. It's the present that matters: the present that includes the sunny prospect of sitting in Tuscany and doing a bit of singing and cooking.

All the same, I'm aware of some cobweb-like apprehensions hanging around at the back of my mind. It's all very well making jocular proposals about Millie declaring herself Neptune's avatar, but there's always the possibility she'll take them seriously and I shall actually have to write that next book. I suppose in the last resort we will be able to expose her in time to prevent this fate, but I've known things not go according to plan. Still, let's not worry about what may never happen. The thing to do now is to get home as soon as possible.

11

And, of course, as I drive upwards through Casoli to my eyrie my spirits lift with every metre of altitude gained. It's always the way. There's something about these visits to my native land from which the person of sensibility needs to recover. I don't know what it is exactly. The boorishness? The whingeing fatalism about our bottomless decline? The ethical dereliction of the politics? My ruffled countrymen may well ask what's so special about contemporary Italy, with its view of literacy that scarcely exceeds the ability to decipher a telephone directory and a politics with the moral vision of a nineteenth-century South American caudillo. And my reply is simple. What's special about it is that it's *not mine*. The great advantage of being an immigrant is that one never worries as much about a host country's politics and social problems as about those of one's native land, which even now seem paler and less significant. Perpetually foreign but persistently European, one simply cherry-picks one's way through life, drifting hither and yon across frontiers at whim, feasting off the nice things on offer and ignoring the rest, just as people have always done. What else? For all its bathos, and in default of any serious alternative to this act of principled despair, lotus-eating is definitely the way forward.

I peel off the road and down the short track leading to my house. The familiar roof comes into view and across the chasm to the right the bulking grey crag from behind which the distant sea furtively emerges like a satellite photo of an indiscreet act.

But what is this? There is a flashy new Range Rover parked where the track forks to skirt my property en route to Marta's shack. Walkers? They do sometimes leave their cars up here while they ramble around. On the other hand it's not unknown for people to bring a car up here for less virtuous purposes and I scan the ground around it for dead Peroni cans, cigarette stubs and lust's latex fallout. Nothing. As I let myself through my barrier I wonder how young lovers up here before the invention of the motorcar managed to escape their cavernous sooty farmhouses full of inquisitive children and eagle-eyed grandparents. Was the same recourse on offer in the horse-and-buggy era? How carnal could they have become in the lee of a looming equine backside, the black purse of its anus periodically disgorging hot wet mulch and its velvet ears swivelling back against the starlit sky like furry radar dishes? Surely they would have felt too much surveilled by that great brute witness? The close presence of a living, breathing creature periodically gusting ammonia and methane would hardly have been less inhibiting than the peeping Thomism of the parish priest himself.

I drive in and stop beside my shuttered house. Off through the trees to my right runs the reassuring beechwood fence that demarcates my property and Marta's. It is a fence with a history. I built it for protection against my eccentric neighbour and very nearly with my own blood when, owing to an accident with a nail gun caused by Marta distracting me, I found myself fixed to it like one of Martin Luther's ninety-five theses, and no less eloquent of protest. Following that, my beautiful structure was torn down without permission when Piero Pacini was shooting a scene for his unfinished last film, and later replaced. Now I catch the murmur of voices from the other side. *Marta!?* Can it be? My expectations soar. Has the old slag returned at long last? I prepare myself to commiserate with her thumbscrew bruises and electrode burns and to welcome her home. With renewed cheerfulness I find my key to the door in the fence between us and hurriedly open it. And there, standing just outside Marta's back door, is someone I instantly recognize and wish I didn't: the weaselly house agent and amateur plane-spotter, Signor Benedetti. In deference to the hot weather he is jacketless in lightweight slacks and a designer version of one of those white short-sleeved work shirts affected by airline pilots and coach drivers, all epaulettes and breast pockets but tarted up with smoke-grey mother-of-pearl buttons and one of those obtrusively discreet monograms in white silk thread on the left-hand pocket. The entire shirt is a serious lapse of taste. On the other hand, not one of his woven hairs is out of place today. With him is a baggy pink man and a dumpy pink woman. Of Marta there is no sign and my expectations abruptly stall and nose-dive. Benedetti is clearly both startled and disappointed to see me, making it mutual.

"Good day, *ingegnere*," I say. "This is a surprise. I hardly dared expect the pleasure of your renewed presence up here. Really, I had no idea house agents remained so emotionally attached to properties that have so long been off their books. I suppose you must be the fond parent who can never quite let go of his children even when they're old enough to have passed into others' hands for ready cash."

"Signor Samper! Your exquisite fluency reminds me most pleasurably of the conversations we have enjoyed together these last few years. I'm sure you are feeling as well as you're looking? Such youthful elegance! You wear your years as you do your clothes, with admirable lightness."

"Be that as it may, Benedetti," I say, cutting to the chase in my ill-bred English fashion, "I find myself apprehensive lest your presence here with what I take to be clients indicates that you have some firm knowledge of my neighbour's fate."

"These are indeed potential clients," he says, ignoring my implied question. "What is more, they are countrymen of yours. May I present Mr. and Mrs. Baritoni?"

Baggy and Dumpy have meanwhile been standing there sweatily with the baffled smiles of Britons waiting for all this foreign babble to blow over. They have plainly not recognized Samper as any kind of kin, which is cheering.

"Apparently you're English," I say to them in that language. Expressions of relief cross their glistening faces.

"Oh, you too? That's right," says Baggy. "But we're not quite who he says we are. Not Baritoni but Barrington. I'm Chris, and this is Deirdre, my wife. I import motor mowers and she's a dental assistant. Now you know all there is to know about us."

I can well believe it but don't say so. We Sampers don't war gratuitously on flabby folk with estuarine vowels, but neither are we prepared to soften up merely on the grounds of having a passport in common. More to the point, though, I'm not under any circumstances having them as neighbours and I'm really disappointed not to find old Marta. I introduce myself curtly.

"Gerald Samper. I live in the house on the other side of this fence. Might I ask what you're doing here?"

It is Dumpy who answers and I have the impression that, like Wanda Horowitz, she calls the shots in this ménage. "We're looking to buy a house in this area and Mr. Benedetti has been kindly showing us a few to give us some initial ideas. You know—a grasp of the market."

"An odd way to go about it, given that that this particular house is not for sale."

"Oh, isn't it?"

"Certainly not. Did he tell you it was? It's lived in by a lady who happens to be away at the moment. Unless Benedetti knows to the contrary, that is." I turn to their tour escort and switch language. "Have you heard from Marta, then? Do you know what's happened to her? Is this house on the market?"

Some eighteen months ago this man and I had a run-in over

my peculiar neighbour, and I like to think he received a severe warning from his cronies in the carabinieri for spreading vile rumours about her. At the time he unquestionably retired wounded and I really imagined we had seen the last of him up here, his rodent confidence assuredly having been dented. Evidently I was wrong.

"No, signore, I have heard nothing directly. True, it is possible this house is not for immediate sale. But as we were in the neighbourhood I thought I would give Mr. and Mrs. Baritoni an idea of the kind of house they might find in this area in places off the beaten track. I was sure my esteemed former client wouldn't mind."

An unsettling thought strikes me and I revert to English. "Have you been inside?"

"We did have a little look round, yes," admits Baggy. "It needs a good deal of work but it's got real possibilities."

"No it hasn't," I correct him. "It has absolutely no possibilities whatsoever since, as I say, it isn't for sale. And anyway, I think it's charming as it is." Even as I speak I'm conscious of the irony of hearing myself defending Marta's rural slum after a history of slagging it off as a place suitable only for the commercial-scale cultivation of toadstools. It is, after all, the house whose bedroom the great Pacini used as a set when he wanted the interior of a dirt-poor fisherman's cottage for his film. "It's outrageous that Benedetti brought you here at all. I can't imagine what he was thinking."

"That wasn't our fault," Dumpy says reasonably. "We're new to the area. He's just driving us around."

"Certainly it's not your fault." I turn back to Benedetti who is now looking uneasy, as well he might. "I understand you have been inside this house, *ingegnere*, which means you must still have the key. Which also suggests that if as a matter of course you retain the keys of all the houses you sell, you still have the key to mine, too. Is this true?"

With a little start the house agent draws himself up, his honour impugned. For a moment he looks less weaselly and more like a goosed rooster. "Signor Samper, I must protest! I most certainly do not possess a key to your house. If I may say so, it is a suggestion quite unworthy of you."

"On the contrary. I have a nasty suspicious mind and such a question is entirely worthy of me. So if you don't have a key to this house, might I ask how you got in?"

He looks me levelly in the eye. The rooster has vanished and the weasel returned. "The back door was unlocked."

This is tricky. I'm sure it wasn't, because I would definitely have relocked it after my last look around. But I'm not so absolutely certain that I can make a direct accusation.

"*Ingegnere*, please allow me to be entirely clear," I say. "In my neighbour's absence and at her request I am acting as her caretaker here. She has naturally given me permission to enter the house and check it from time to time. So far as I'm aware she has given no permission to anyone to conduct guided tours with busloads of foreigners. And besides, even if you did find the door open, am I to suppose you have acquired the habit of just walking into houses that are obviously lived in and full of other people's belongings?" I turn back to my countrymen, as Benedetti was pleased to call them. "I don't suppose you saw how he got in, did you? I mean, was the back door unlocked?"

Dumpy and Baggy look at each other, trying to remember. "No," they shake their heads. "We followed Mr. Benedetti around the house from the drive but probably a bit more slowly because we were looking at the place. By the time we got here the door was already open. Is there a problem?"

"Not really. Or none that involves you. As I've just told him, I act as caretaker of this house and I'm just a bit unnerved to find people wandering around it when I wasn't here."

Soon after this they leave, but not before Baggy confides in an aside: "This isn't the first house we've seen with furniture and stuff, you know. Benedetti's got a lot of keys."

I'll bet he has. A regular little housebreaker, our weaselly one. The whole episode has cast something of a pall over my own homecoming. I was going to invent some irresistible delicacy to go with the prosecco on my terrace, but my heart's no longer in it. Poor Marta. Of course, I realize the Voynovian bat is nothing to do with me, and she has certainly never asked me to take the least responsibility for her house, still less to act as caretaker. But I worry all the same. I simply don't want anything awful to have happened to her and can't rid myself of the suspicion that despite his protestations of ignorance Benedetti might actually know something. I mean, what else would give the little turd the confidence to come and show prospective buyers over her house? Later that afternoon I call the local carabinieri, with one of whom I have developed quite cordial relations since the previous imbroglio, and mention to Virgilio that as I'm not always here it would be much appreciated if he could arrange to have the odd patrol car drop by from time to time in order to check on Marta's house, at least until she returns. I soon learn that, alas, the carabinieri seldom find themselves free to visit such isolated houses as ours in the course of duty and I would do better to engage a private security firm such as Metronotte to carry out regular patrols. However, Virgilio would gladly pass on the word and he is sure that occasionally a patrol car can come up to check on my neighbour's house when things are quiet and they have a bit of time to spare. I thank him and ring off. My real reason for the call is that it will automatically have been recorded; and in case there ever is a break-in at either of our houses it will be an additional piece of evidence to flourish in the face of our insurance companies.

*

I go to bed glummish and vaguely apprehensive but wake seven hours later to a different world of morning sunshine and mountain silence that has been wheeled into place overnight by the celestial scene-shifters. I'm not clear how this happens. Solitude and fresh coffee anyway make me cheerful of a morning, and not being in a London flat is a further bonus. People like Derek are naturally metropolitan, of course. Like rats they live in cities at great ease. They scamper through their daily mazes with no obvious sign of boredom, amply rewarded by decent food and a good deep litter in which to pup. Not that that particular detail is much of a selling point with Derek; but there's no doubt his monumental empress-sized bed covered in fabrics from Heal's represents about as much comfort as anyone could reasonably expect when vertically separated by a mere nine feet from somebody else's colonic irrigation. It's the being so much on top of everyone—or beneath them in Derek's frequent case—I find so hard to bear in cities. That and the constant din that wears me down so that merely going out to interview a leathery yachtswoman in her Hilton suite for an hour makes me feel, by the time I'm home again, as though I've run a marathon (Oh, rat-man!). No, give me the fluent silence of these hills where I can hear myself think, not to mention cook and sing.

So for ten days or so I rise early and steadily compose a graceful and also disgraceful new short chapter to insert in *Millie!*, in between waxing operatic and breaking for exquisite little snacks. I even indulge in a limited amount of DIY: domestic tasks I generally perform for reasons of thrift that are somewhat more fun to have done than they are to do. That being said, I would be falsely modest if I pretended not to have a knack for them. People expect writers to be effete creatures whose skills in the world of practical activity go little beyond falling off bar stools in the Groucho Club. In extreme cases these skills may extend to changing a light bulb, but this nearly always means the writer is a lesbian. (Super-lesbians like Ernest Hemingway don't really count as writers.) It is true that when it comes to the higher reaches of joinery and craftsmanship my own skills are merely those of the experienced amateur. But I'm neither afraid nor too proud to have a go, that's the point.

All of which means you won't be surprised to learn that I have decided to change not only my own front-door lock but that on Marta's back door as well. The more odious the idea becomes of strangers wandering around her house at will in my absence, the more I feel protective of both our properties. Meeting Baggy and Dumpy has reminded me that I could have many worse neighbours than a frumpish composer from beyond the River Vltava. Which reminds me, I wonder if hers is also Smetana's neck of the Bohemian woods? I still have no real idea where Voynovia is. I think it must be to the east of Ruritania: Hentzau and John Buchan country, but not quite as far as the thirty-nine steppes. I'm told the European Union's latest expansionist pounce has recently brought even Voynovia within its shining bounds, although of course that still doesn't mean it's in Europe in any meaningful sense. After all, some of the more addled denizens of Brussels seriously consider Turkey as part of Europe on the grounds that hordes of dervishes and janissaries once bombarded the walls of Vienna, disturbing Haydn's retirement and frightening his servants, and to that extent could be said to have had an influence on European history. This, mind you, a country of eighty million Muslims that only recently abjured torture and honour killing in order to qualify for EU membership, not because it thought them wrong. Think Osmin in *Il Seraglio*. As Derek once remarked, the only good Ottoman is one you can lie on. I suppose by comparison Voynovia could easily come to feel as unassailably Old European as France. Anyway, so far as I'm concerned Marta's real home is her slatternly castle here at Le Rocce rather than that of her family in the distant shadow of a mountain called Sluszic, and like any castle it deserves a good lock on its back door. So I go down to Viareggio where I buy something that looks more appropriate for a bank vault, with tungsten bars that simultaneously shoot upwards and downwards into sockets at the turn of a most peculiar key with raised pimples on it like a plucked turkey thigh.

While I'm down there I find I'm in the mood for culinary adventure and drop by the butcher for some calves' brains. Last night before falling asleep I dipped into one of my favourite bedside books, Emmeline Tyrwhitt-Glamis's *Emergency Cuisine*, written in the dark days of 1942 when heavily rationed Londoners had accustomed themselves to an unusual diet, and stray cats and dogs had all but vanished from the city's streets. These dumb chums were pressed into service as extras in the general drama of the war effort, passing through a thousand trusty Radiation gas ovens while acting out their selfless, unauditioned parts, which might accurately be described as casserole-playing. Dame Emmeline (as she later became in recognition of her bravery while working in the resistance to Woolton Pie) believed that austerity could be taken too far. From her house in Berkeley Square a stream of recipes poured forth, the less eccentric often being espoused by the Women's Institute and published in popular magazines. She regularly netted the gardens in the middle of the square to produce, according to season, owl tartlets, pigeon strudel, a fudge of robins, blackbird pâté and, on one notable occasion, nightingale fritters. She discovered that the antiaircraft battery gunners in Hyde Park were attracting rats with their National Loaf sandwiches and latrine pits, and it wasn't long before she was trapping the rodents in sufficient quantities to bake the celebrated Pied Piper pies she then sold to Fortnum & Mason, donating the revenue to the Red Cross. The animals' pelts Dame Emmeline cured with alum in her airing cupboard and turned into a cloak and mittens for her chauffeur, who was too old to be called up and was living in some discomfort in her vast Hispano-Suiza, up on blocks in a mews garage in Peckham for lack of petrol.

This sterling and freethinking spinster was unafraid to try anything, having inherited the scientific curiosity of her distant relative Frank Buckland, the nineteenth-century naturalist and experimental gourmet who had sampled nearly all the British vertebrates and lepidoptera. She agreed with him that while earwigs were foully bitter and bluebottles unspeakable, woodlice were a plausible alternative to potted shrimp. Emmeline Tyrwhitt-Glamis was undoubtedly the first Englishwoman to prepare and use cockroach purée in any quantity, naming it "Victory Paste." In her journal she herself described Victory Paste as having the flavour of "peanuts and vanilla, with a faint suggestion of sealing wax; altogether agreeable." It was a popular addition to servicemen's wartime diet, especially in the Royal Navy, where it became a staple as a sandwich filling for officers during action. *Emergency Cuisine*, first published by His Majesty's Stationery Office in 1942, is a collector's item these days, its rarity enhanced when most of the first edition was destroyed by an incendiary-bomb strike on the Hackney warehouse in which it was awaiting distribution. I treasure my own copy as much for the breezy Tyrwhitt-Glamis style as for her inventive recipes and her popular cry of "Buns Against Huns!"

When next you look she begins her instructions for making squirrel dumplings at a majestic beech tree or a spreading horse chestnut, spare a thought for all the mighty energy locked up in beech mast and conkers. Now think of the sprightly squirrel, his fur gleaming with health as he performs his lithe acrobatics high in the topmost branches. Whence comes this unstinting ebullience? Why, from the nourishment he draws from eating the seeds containing the embryonic forests of tomorrow! His little body is a veritable powerhouse; and it behoves Britain's fighting housewives to avail themselves of this energy. Have one of your estate workers procure you a brace or two of these nutritious rodents . . .

And so it is that while I'm down in Viareggio I buy calves' brains and one or two other impulsive odds and ends. Then, deciding I may as well eat down here, I have a delicious light seafood lunch on the front and watch the world pass by. The restaurant overlooks the beach and in the noonday glare the women come and go, probably not talking of Michelangelo but of Botox and liposuction. Nor, to judge from their expressions, do their escorts appear to be earnestly discussing the Mammon of Unrighteousness or even the problematic orchestration in the second act of *L'uomo magro*. Their whole demeanour is that of males who wish quite soon to enact the ancient ritual of passing on their DNA and are wondering how much they need spend on their girl's lunch to ensure it happening. No one seems to have done much swimming. The beachwear of all three sexes is outrageous, revealing acres of broiled flesh and graceless bulbosities creakingly restrained by wisps of designer nylon. It all reminds me uneasily that my own highly personal problem of packing more veal is going to have to be faced sooner or later. But still, time's a-wasting; so with my calves' brains in my cool-bag and some costly ironmongery to render both our homes Benedetti-proof in the boot of the car, I drive back up to Le Rocce with a sense of virtue and purposefulness.

12

Anybody who knows me at all will acknowledge that single-mindedness is a salient character trait of mine. I am not one of those people—and Derek, I fear, *is*—who channel-hop their way through life with attention spans that make bacteria look thoughtful. Today, for example, my priority is definitely door locks; so I put the calves' brains in the fridge for later and take a condensation-beaded bottle of prosecco and a glass out onto the terrace. The afternoon is hot and the wine I drank at lunch has induced a slight drowsiness that needs chilled refreshment to chase away. Take a tip from Samper: when planning locksmithery and the like the trick is never to rush but to get into the right frame of mind for the task ahead. So I sit and calmly peruse the instructions for fitting these two identical but complex locks that I've bought. In response to the usual cutaway drawings with arrows I fetch a Phillips screwdriver and remove flanged knob "A" on the inside of the lock, exposing the slotted arms for attaching the two long bolts that will secure the door top and bottom. Dead straightforward. Child's play. Time passes in which I reflect on the many successes of my DIY past. The prosecco is beginning to hone my concentration to a fine point so that I am able to read and reread each sentence of the instructions, which are written in the bizarre dialect reserved for such things. "Important: Knurled screw 'F' is mounting in association for downstriker plate 'L' only." What could be clearer than that? I read it many times with my enhanced attention and understand it in its fullest and deepest sense. Time for action! Leaving the empty bottle and glass on the table I dig out my tool kit, buckle on my tool belt with the power-drill holster, find the key to Marta's back door and sally forth to her hovel.

I keep saying "hovel," but in all fairness there is nothing flimsy about Marta's cottage. Like mine it is built of stone and to judge from its worn thresholds it has seen centuries of peasants come and go, a tradition her occupancy in no way interrupts. In common with many Italian houses the ground-floor windows are protected by iron grilles, making it look impregnable. Still, what is the point of iron bars if in your muddle-headed Voynovian way you leave the back door unlocked? I let myself in and pause in the gloom, inhaling that familiar scent I shall for ever associate with Marta: mildew and *shonka*, a lethal Voynovian sausage, as well as a deodorant she uses called "Witch," a pungent example of a cure that is worse than the disease. I check the front door, which already has a decent lock as well as one of those patent little deadbolt security things that require a separate key. I've no idea where that is. I think she never used her front door so it's really only the back door that needs attention. I spread my tools out on the floor in an orderly fashion and crack my knuckles like a flying doctor preparing for a bush amputation. Technically, I suppose, it might be taking a liberty to install a lock on one's neighbour's door without her permission, but really: this is someone capable of walking out of her house for days, weeks, *months* at a stretch, leaving all the doors unlocked and a gas ring alight. I'm betting the old bat is going to be pretty pleased by this token of neighbourliness.

The door itself is absurdly stout: massive chestnut planks that I can see are going to need intensive drilling to take the barrel of the lock. Hoping to throw much-needed light on the job I click the switch. Nothing. No lights anywhere. I find her fuse panel and all the switches are up as they should be. It then becomes obvious: with her stunning domestic incompetence

Marta has omitted to arrange to have her bills paid by banker's order every two months and ENEL have cut her off. I check her telephone, which I eventually find beneath a pile of unironed laundry. Dead. Same problem, no doubt. Telecom Italia have lost patience. I don't blame them. Wearily I trudge back to my house to fetch an extension cable and see if it will reach. Needless to say it doesn't, not by twenty metres or so. I find some other lengths of cable that will if someone can be bothered to join them all up. Sitting on the grass outside I busy myself with cutters and strippers and insulating tape. Absolutely typical, the whole thing. You get all keyed up to do a job but then find yourself having to spend hours laying on basics like electricity. To the end of the cable I wire in a block of three sockets so at least I can have light and use the drill at the same time. When finally it's all assembled I discover it just—and only just—reaches. Good enough. At last I'm set to make a start, although by now it's considerably later than I should have preferred.

However, I won't be hurried. The Samper watchword is "methodical." By the time I have it all marked up and the hole has been drilled in the iron-hard door I notice that late afternoon has elided into early evening. I return to my own house to collect another bottle of prosecco, which I definitely feel I have earned. Obviously I'm not one of those slightly pathetic types who need to disguise the seriousness of an alcohol dependency by whimsically referring to the sun as being over the yardarm. Not having a drink problem myself, I certainly don't watch the clock. Many days go by when I drink nothing but water. But sometimes a glass of prosecco gives a little fillip to the flagging DIY man who wants to finish a job and go off to cook his supper. Anyway, half the people who use the expression have no idea what a yardarm is. As the author of *Millie!* I can enlighten you. It is the pole attached at right angles to a mast from which a sail hangs. In northern latitudes the sun would have been high enough to clear the topmost yardarms of a square-rigged ship at around midday. The glass of prosecco that I'm now appreciatively sipping, sitting back on my heels in a scatter of wood chips and a small glow of achievement, is more of a sundowner. I contemplate the job I have done so far and, like the old Hebrew deity, see that it is good. The central lock is impeccably installed, if I say so myself, the keyhole outside with its brass surround neat and straight. All I need do now is cut the two bolts to the right length so they will slot neatly into the stonework top and bottom, and that will be that. Chalk up another item in the Samper tally of doing good by stealth.

Mind you, when I say "all I need do now," I'm making light of the difficulty of sawing tungsten-steel tubing. When I slip back to my house to fetch the angle grinder I notice how dark it's getting. Somehow this project has swallowed up the entire afternoon. With patience and showers of sparks I eventually manage to cut the tubes to the right length, attach them to the stubby arms that flanged knob "A" will eventually hide, and mark where to drill the sockets into which two metal cups ("S," provided) can be fixed with instant cement. I drill the holes in the stonework and painstakingly clean them up with a little chisel. The cups easily fit into them, so I close the door to see how well the bolts are going to slot in. There is nothing as satisfying as that oiled *snock!* of a piece of mechanism shooting home, in this case the central latch. It is a snug, precise sound that, as it echoes around Marta's grim hallway behind me, is a tribute to one's craftsmanship. In order to examine the top bolt better I tug the inspection lamp to get a last inch of play in the cable running in under the back door through the hollow of its worn threshold. The wretched thing promptly goes out and I am plunged in darkness. Goddamn. I must have pulled the plug out of the block outside. I'll have to go out and plug it in: I only need another few minutes' work here before

I can clean up and clear out. I scrabble at the lock to let myself out but can't find flanged knob "A." In fact there's no knob at all, just a hole. The knob is, of course, on the table on my terrace eighty metres away where it has been ever since I removed it. And I have nothing else with which to turn the tumblers of this very technical lock that so satisfyingly latched itself not thirty seconds ago.

There then occurs one of those peculiar moments when the brain splits into two. One half goes whirring around like a trapped moth, mentally visiting the locked back door, the locked front door and the barred windows in swift succession as realization slowly dawns that there may be no easy way out of this, while the other half remains strangely unsurprised as though it had known all along it was hopeless. By the time the two halves of my brain have united once more I am in no doubt that things have not gone according to the Samper plan. I still can't treat this as anything other than a mild inconvenience, though. It's simply a matter of letting myself out of one of the upstairs windows. A bit undignified, perhaps, but there's no reason why anyone should ever find out. However, once I have groped my way upstairs and opened a window I become seriously discouraged. It is a moonless night and the ground below is a dim blur. True, this top floor is not very high, and if I hang from the window sill before letting go the drop shouldn't be much more than two or three metres. I try to remember what's underneath, but can't. My impression is that there's a certain amount of Marta's junk scattered about. I'm not at all keen to risk jumping down without being able to see what I'm jumping on to. I have a vision of breaking an ankle on a brick or a lump of rock and having to crawl eighty metres through a pitch-black garden to my own house. It's a risk one would take only in a dire emergency such as fire. The obviously sensible thing to do is to wait for rosy-fingered dawn. So well done indeed, Samper. You now have to spend the night in Marta's unlit and unaired den, with no supper and probably nothing to drink. Nor can you call anyone for help because the phone's dead. There may not even be any water, since I'm pretty sure she has one of those systems that work on demand and require electricity for the pump. True, she might have left a bottle of something somewhere and maybe there will be a fossilized piece of *shonka* or other Voynovian delicacy that I can gnaw at, but the prospect is vastly different from the one with which I was planning to reward myself and to which I had been looking forward.

Luckily she still has a functioning gas stove because it's fed by cylinders. With a box of matches I light all the rings on the hob which throw out enough light for me to find a packet of peculiar fluted candles in a distant cupboard. At least I assume they're candles; one can never tell in this house. The writing on the box is unhelpfully in Cyrillic script but they look like candles and smell like candles. Still, I know from experience that this doesn't mean they mightn't be a Voynovian delicacy to be served after dinner with coffee. They might equally well turn out to be particularly punitive suppositories. However, they burn, and in a minute or two Marta's chaotic kitchen is lit with a kindly orange glow that reveals swags of cobwebs. Hoping she might have left something drinkable in the fridge I open it and immediately reel back, hastily slamming the door again. It must be months since her power was cut off, ample time for whatever she left in it to have unfrozen and brewed up. I retain the impression of a miniature landscape within: rolling hills of mould with one enormous nodding fungus gathering itself to spring. Enough of the stench has made good its escape to make one think of those crime scenes on television where a floater has been retrieved after many weeks in a river and detectives stand around upwind with handkerchiefs pressed to their noses while a team of medics tries to revive a police frogman with sal volatile. Whatever else, Marta is going to need a new fridge if and when she returns. Then in another cupboard I find my booby prize: two unopened bottles of Fernet Branca, Marta's favourite tipple. The kitchen having become uninhabitable, I retreat upstairs with a bottle and a glass together with the box of matches and a couple of spare candles and prepare myself for a long and cheerless vigil.

Sitting on the edge of her bed I stare glumly at the black pane of the window, seeing nothing but my own reflection and that of the candle flame. It is quite bad enough to be condemned to pass the night on Marta's bed, as effectively walled up as *l'uomo magro* was in the opera, without knowing that my own house, by contrast, is open to the four winds, standing there with doors and windows gaping like a hilltop *Mary Celeste*. I pour myself a stiff tot of Fernet. It must be over a year since I last tasted the stuff and I'm clearly out of training since it comes as a shock. Never mind: be thankful there's anything at all. A snatch of tune is running through my head and I recognize it as an irritating hymn my stepmother Laura used to sing around the house as she swept and dusted. Even some of the words come back: "Who sweeps a room, as for Thy laws, / Makes that and th'action fine." Huh. I haven't swept a room but I *have* put a new lock on Marta's back door and what's more it was done as for His laws because one of them, if you remember, involves loving thy neighbour as thyself. Th'action might have been made fine, but I have to admit th'outcome is something of a bugger's muddle. Yet the more I think about it while pouring myself another glass of masochistic balm, the less I'm willing to accept it as my fault. Really, the whole thing is squarely down to Marta. From the moment she arrived up here she has been nothing but trouble. Benedetti misled me from the outset, of course, when he lyingly described her to me as a mouse-quiet foreigner who was hardly ever here. In my experience, limited though it is, mice do not often play the piano outside a Tom and Jerry cartoon. Neither do they viciously lampoon one's private singing and turn it into a musical score for a film. Mice infrequently fly helicopters in and out at all times of day and night, destroying people's carefully nurtured pergolas as they pass overhead. Come to that, they seldom demolish entire fences without permission; and when they go away for arbitrary periods mice do not leave incandescent coffee pots on gas stoves and back doors swinging in the breeze. In such circumstances what is the good neighbour supposed to do as for Thy laws? Reach for the warfarin?

As I pour myself another liberal glassful I can feel the gratifying rush of righteous anger. After all, the entire point of my coming to live up here in majestic isolation was that I would be spared the world of suburban disruption and could get on with some work. Instead of which, although miles from anywhere, I have found myself living in a crazed soap opera, trapped in a version of *Neighbours* that has clearly been scripted by one of those writers with a ponytail, trembling fingers and pupils like wormholes. It's the *time* this blasted woman has caused me to waste. Most irritating of all is to have wasted it doing DIY jobs on her behalf when she might never return to benefit from them. For all I know her bleached bones may even now be emerging from a shallow desert grave as the thin wind strips the sand away, and serve her right. If there's a passionate conviction that never fails to overtake one in the middle of a DIY job it is surely that one was made for better things. *Was it for this?* the internal cry goes up. Was it for this that I bothered to learn about the Thirty Years War (1618–1648) at school? Does a working knowledge of the ablative absolute help one fit a lock to a door? Do Wordsworth's daffodils, fluttering and dancing in the breeze in their ineffably cretinous fashion? Does it even help to know that the very form of these questions constitutes a rhetorical trope whose name I have forgotten? No: none of it is of the slightest use. All the knowledge I laboriously acquired at those expensive schools my father sent me to (thereby excusing himself all parental duty for two-thirds of the year) has proved irrelevant and superfluous. In order to get by these days one needs a stretch in an establishment with its fingers firmly on the pulse—or better, the carotid artery—of the world. Somewhere like the Joseph Stalin School of Deportment and Manners in Lausanne, for instance. I have heard this establishment is very hard to get into, with a longer waiting list than either Eton or Harrow, and by no means every pupil who enters graduates. Some are never seen again. But those who emerge with the coveted *ruban noir* are assured of being more than equal to any task or situation that life has to offer. It is absolutely certain that no alumnus of the École Joseph Stalin de Maintien et des Manières would ever lock himself by mistake into his Voynovian neighbour's rural slum and have to spend the night there without supper, drinking Fernet Branca by the light of a guttering candle. Come to that, nor would he find himself condemned to a career on a sub-literary treadmill that entails writing about nautical haemorrhoids like Millie Cleat.

There are times when the genteelly educated who didn't go to school in Lausanne fall prey to black thoughts in the night hours. We are overtaken by darkness of the brain as images of pointlessness and defeat crowd in and all too accurately represent the teeming emptiness of being alive. We think of our dead. We think of our own inexorably approaching death. We think of the paltry and arbitrary work we are obliged in the interim to perform in order briefly to feed ourselves: work that makes an ox plodding in a circle to draw water seem rewardingly purposeful. And then we think of the Fernet Branca bottle beside the bed and discover to our surprise that it is now barely a quarter full. We pour ourselves another glass and try to pretend that we didn't blot our copybook with Max Christ; we convince ourselves that even now he is deciding—regretfully, maybe, but deciding (*Muß es sein? Es muß sein!*) that since a biography is inevitable sooner or later it may as well be written by Gerald Samper. At least that way it will be literate and unconventional. Maybe in the rush of professional and domestic life at Crendlesham Hall no adult has yet noticed the still-moist solecism lurking in the junk room next to the bathroom. Maybe if they have they will have taken it as prima faeces evidence of a bolshy builder making his feelings known at not being paid double overtime. Maybe pretty Adrian will be able to get his equally pretty sister to lean on Max and . . .? But I don't really believe any of it. People either want their biographies written or they don't. When they're as famous and distinguished as Max Christ they neither need nor wish for extra publicity. And now the thought of Adrian contrives to lower my spirits even further. Why isn't the rat here lending me succour and support instead of messing about on the high seas? I don't wish to remind myself that this is the sort of contract expected of lovers and partners rather than of just good friends. Ah well. Memo: find out tomorrow when he's due home.

I must have fallen asleep because something overcomes the Fernet in my bloodstream and wakes me. The candle has expired. I badly need to pee and remember that as the water's off it would be better not to use Marta's lavatory. I therefore resort to the time-honoured practice of rural areas and pee out of the window. No sooner have I started than there's an anguished bellow from underneath, "*Dio boia!*," a crashing noise and then a brilliant light is flashed into my eyes. This is the end. Maybe I'm still asleep? It's pure nightmare, whatever it is.

"You come down out of there!" orders a crisp voice in Italian.

"Who are you?" I ask, not much less brusquely.

"Carabinieri. We are armed and this house is surrounded! How many are there of you?"

"For heaven's sake! Just me."

"Do you have a gun?"

"Of course not. It's you that's armed, not me."

"He's lying," I hear an unseen companion say. "Watch out, Albé, he's wearing a holster."

A dull orange flash below is accompanied by a shocking bang. "See?" the voice shouts up as a bullet screams off into the night. "Next time it'll be you unless you throw your weapon down. *Do it now!*"

My fuddled brain is doing its best but it's like stirring porridge. I'm scared, all right, but I think the slight insulation from reality provided by residual sleep and Fernet prevents that little internal sac of terror hormone from bursting as it did during the raid on Millie's Hilton suite. It's all just a little too unreal. "It's not a proper holster," I call down reasonably. "It's for a power drill. I fell asleep wearing it. I'm Gerald Samper from the other house. I've been fixing a lock on this lady's back door."

A pause. "Well, come out at once with your hands up and we'll see. No tricks, mind. This is a lonely place and you don't want to cause an accident."

There is no mistaking the menace in this trigger-happy goon's voice. He keeps aiming the light at me and I keep aiming for a tone of sweet reason.

"I'm sorry, I can't come out. I know it sounds silly, well, it *is* silly, but I'm afraid I'm locked in."

"If you got into the house you can get out again, can't you? Who locked you in?"

"Um, it was sort of . . . I, uh, locked myself in, actually. I've just fitted a new lock to the back door, you see, and it locked itself and there's no knob on the inside to let myself out, and . . ." I hear my voice tailing off dismally. It's bad enough to have been caught peeing out of a window by the person you've peed on; if you've also locked yourself into someone else's house you inevitably look a complete prat into the bargain. Will these humiliations brought on me by my absent neighbour never end? How does this Voynovian witch manage to exercise her malevolent power at such a distance? Even, possibly, from beyond the grave?

"I think it's time we radioed for reinforcements," I overhear one of the men below saying, and I catch the word "*brigatista*." This is dire. If they really suspect I'm a member of the *Brigate Rosse*, the Red Brigades, they are probably scared too, which means there's a serious possibility I will be shot somewhere painful and incapacitating, possibly through the buttocks, while "resisting arrest" or "evading capture" before being dragged down in handcuffs for interrogation by the local agents of DIGOS.

"Look," I say with my hands still up, framed by the window embrasure in the blinding torchlight, "I'm an English writer. *Un artista*, not *un brigatista*. I live in the house over there on the other side of that fence. The thing to do is to let me out of this house and we can go over there and I will show you all my *documenti* and we'll call up Lucchese Virgilio. He will identify me."

There is another silence. "You know the *tenente*?"

"I do. Not well, but Virgilio has been up here before and he knows that this neighbour of mine is away. It was I who asked him to have the carabinieri drop by occasionally." Even as I say it the irony is not lost on me. It *would* be tonight of all nights they chose to patrol.

Muttering rises from the darkness beneath. The torch beam is still trained on me but it's obvious these men have been thrown off balance by my mention of their senior colleague.

"The thing to do," I go on, feeling that at last Samper is beginning to take charge, "is for one of you to trot across to my house, which you'll find open, and fetch the ladder hanging in the garage. I'll have to climb out of this window. Once I'm down we can sort all this out in five minutes."

And this is pretty much what happens. Once I'm on the ground and they're finally convinced I'm just some harmless foreign nutter without a revolutionary thought in his head the whole situation eases. They're obviously as relieved as I am. It turns out there are only two of them after all, just a couple of young patrolmen who were checking on Marta's house as an excuse for goofing off for forty minutes instead of tangling with the denizens of the night down in Camaiore. We go back to my house and I offer the fellow I peed on the use of my distinctive white-and-biscuit ground-floor bathroom while his colleague checks my passport and *permesso di soggiorno*.

"I'm awfully sorry about that," I say with a rueful nod in the direction of the closed door, from behind which come vigorous splashing sounds.

"Oh, don't worry about Alberto," says his partner with a disarmingly merry smile. "Does him good to get pissed on occasionally. The joke is that *he'd* gone round the back of the house to do the same thing. He was standing there enjoying *una ricca pisciata* of his own when you opened up overhead. We won't let him forget this in a hurry. But he can sit in the back of the car until he changes his uniform."

Later, after the sound of their Alfa Romeo has died away and I am belatedly lying in my own bed and wondering if I shall ever be able to get to sleep again, I work out that it must have been the noise the luckless patrolman made clumping around beneath the open window that had woken me. The episode ended amiably enough, and the two carabinieri could hardly have been more civil in the circumstances, given that one had had a drenching and both a bad scare. But it has all been at the cost to Gerald Samper of a great burden of indignity and nervous strain which, I can assure the bulging bint of Voynovia, has been faithfully entered on the debit side of her ledger. I'm still incredulous that my voluntary display of neighbourly goodwill should have led to such humiliating farce. I suppose I should be grateful that I'm not even now under police guard in the new hospital in Lido di Camaiore, face down as a surgeon repairs a bullet hole in my bottom, trying not to laugh behind his green mask. My stepmother Laura's charming habit in my boyhood was to stand over me after some painful accident involving a bicycle or a new sheath knife and, even before blood or tears were staunched, to say, "And what lesson do we learn from this, h'm?" Rotten baggage. I don't know that there's a lesson to be drawn from tonight's debacle, other than that urinating on policemen is one of those things best done sparingly. You might pass this bit of hard-won Samper wisdom on to your own son if you have one.

13.

It takes me several days to recover my equanimity after this distressing episode. The worst of it all is that, in my own mind at least, Le Rocce is fast losing its aura of unspoilt wildness that first attracted me to it. More and more it is becoming tainted by association with the most brutal kind of worldliness, principally helicopters and policemen. The following day I rang my friend Virgilio in the carabinieri to apologize for the night's events. He laughed it off, kindly but quite briskly; and if any good has come of the whole affair it is the distinct impression I have that as far as the police are concerned Le Rocce is going to be allowed to drop off their map. It must seem to them that each time they come they run the risk of tangling with completely loopy foreigners, visits that always end in their having to retreat in disarray or humiliation. Nothing short of the assassination up here of the Mayor of Lucca or the apparition of the late Pope Wojtyla robed in glory will readily bring the local cops to Le Rocce again. Fortunately, I can't see either of these horrid events happening in or around the Samper residence which, as we all know, is a haven of non-violence as well as of profound scepticism.

The other person I phoned that day was Dr. Adrian Jestico, now back in his Southampton office after his quick flip offshore. If you remember, his sister Jennifer had explained that he wasn't able to join us for dinner that night at Crendlesham Hall because he'd been called away to deal with instrument problems aboard a research vessel. Having interviewed him and his colleagues after the EAGIS trip, I now have a respectful grasp of the fortune it costs each day to run these ships and understand why there's a panic when things go wrong at sea. By a strange coincidence this particular vessel to which Adrian flew was also working in the Canaries, although it had no connection with EAGIS or volcanoes. The scientists aboard the R/V *Tony Rice* had been plotting deep-sea currents to the west of La Gomera using acoustic thermometry. Something to do with global warming, apparently. Suddenly, their work was disrupted by ten-minute bursts of loud incoherent signals coming at irregular intervals from the seabed some way to the north of their position. Puzzled, and preferring to do some detective work before abandoning their measurements, the scientists eventually tracked down a singular train of events.

Three months earlier a freak wave had washed a consignment of thirty new transponders off the deck of a container ship bringing them from the United States to Rotterdam, en route for some European research department. The transponders were packed in a ten-foot container and the wave swept it into the Atlantic where it drifted for weeks before its seals began to degrade, water leaked in and it gradually sank. This is apparently a common enough occurrence for floating containers to constitute a real danger to oceangoing yachts. For a long while they remain buoyant enough to float barely submerged and as invisible as blocks of ice. What made this container a hazard to oceanographers was its consignment of transponders that had already been profiled to form a network for detecting seismic events. Each transponder had been set up to chirp at a different frequency so that the events could be pinpointed using triangulation. Once deployed, they would remain silent until they detected a seabed tremor, whereupon they would switch themselves on and interrogate each other for ten minutes. While their container was sinking in stately fashion to the sea floor off La Palma, the water pressure activated the transponders. When the container touched down on the bottom, the bump was enough to set them off in a ten-minute burst of activity.

Since then, each minor seismic event beneath the seabed has triggered them again, and since in that area such events happen several times a day they have made themselves heard a good deal. There they are in their container, sending out wild bursts of data and each responding to the others' acoustic bleeps in a recursive stream of feedback. Their chatter is unstoppable and fills the water column with the weirdest tweetings and cheepings. The scientists aboard *Tony Rice* have tried sending commands to them to turn themselves off or otherwise commit suicide, but without success. They continue to sit like a group of housewives at a coffee klatch, compulsively gossiping down there in their little room in the dark. And there they will continue to gossip until their batteries run down or some method is devised of shutting them up. In the meantime they are making any further acoustical experiments in the area impossible.

Since Adrian is in charge of the thermometry project he had to jet out to Las Palmas and be helicoptered aboard the ship to see what could be salvaged. The weather on site was unsettled and Adrian found the *Tony Rice* tossing fretfully, a state of affairs that he said applied equally to the vessel's complement. The lost container is on the bottom in a place described as virtually inaccessible. The sea is very deep at that point and the seabed a chaotic jumble of volcanic detritus. The scientists have concluded there is little chance of retrieving the container and any salvage attempt would cost vastly more than the transponders are worth.

All of a sudden I saw the possibilities this story of oceanographical woe offered. Perhaps my sense of grievance—normally the most quiescent and least visible side of my nature—had been gingered up by the awful contretemps at Marta's house. But at once I spotted how a costly but minor maritime upset could be turned to Samper's advantage. So I rang up Adrian and told him my plan, extracting his promise to come and visit me shortly. However, I rang off without telling him about my recent night of shame. I'm still a little nervous of his laughter, to be frank, and before recounting tales at one's own expense one needs to be comfortably à deux and with a fair slug of prosecco under one's belt. I thought it judicious to wait before making him privy to my amazing disgrace.

That was three days ago. Since then I have looked at my new chapter for *Millie!* with renewed satisfaction, confident that I have produced a recognizable portrait of one of the outstandingly bogus characters of our day and age, a portrait I'm certain she will read entirely differently. As I explained to her in London, it would be impossible now to alter the text throughout to make it look as if she had been motivated from the outset by her numinous relationship with the ocean deities. That is not what drives world champions, and everybody knows it. My new short chapter, though, invents some soulful moments and blows a little dust from the road to Damascus into the middle of the book. There's no actual moment of blinding revelation, no voice from the sky talking about pricks and persecution. Instead, there's a growing awareness on Millie's part of something that only the very successful and overpraised need be told: that there may possibly be more to this world than their own egos. Something in the starlit nights and the hiss of phosphorescent water past *Beldame*'s three hulls succeeds in making her feel marginally uncertain about where she is going and why. A step further involves her entertaining the novel idea that treating the ocean as the mere racing circuit on which the engrossing saga of her personal achievements has unfolded is not merely bad taste but plain sad. My aim in this new chapter is to do little more than introduce the concept of a lone yachtsperson with Doubts, and maybe scatter a few seeds of callow spirituality that, by the time a sequel comes to be written, will no doubt have grown tall and can be harvested as a rich crop of orient and immortal bollocks.

I give my new chapter a final going-over and must admit it deftly strikes just the right note. As I say, Millie will read it as straight. Anyone else with more brains than a greenfly will marvel at the unseemliness of a one-armed mid-fifties grandmother only now beginning to wonder whether her domineering competitiveness may not have shrivelled the rest of her like a parched pea. I'm so pleased with it I e-mail it off at once to Frankie so that he can print it out and have it biked round to the Hilton for Millie's approval, which I'm confident she'll give. She'd better if she wants to catch the Christmas market.

That done, I can turn my attention to other things. One of these is not easy to think about because it brings back the other night's events with too much clarity for comfort. It has to do with the spectacle I must have presented when first transfixed by the policeman's blinding light and his blasphemous bellow. I have to ask myself whether my unconscious, having made sure I was woken by the policeman's footsteps in the first place, mightn't maliciously have driven me to expose myself at the window. For when on approaching his fortieth birthday a man suddenly finds himself packing more veal, it is possible that his unconscious might revel in it in a jock's locker-room sort of way even as his ordinary self would cringe at so juvenile an urge. And of late I have found myself cringing whenever I remember my recent experiment with Mr. and Mrs. ProWang's potent little pills. This is not so much from shame, since it's hardly a cause for shame to wish to push back the boundaries of scientific knowledge, but from worry. *Where will it end?* That's what I want to know. Like Topsy in *Uncle Tom's Cabin*, it growed, and as yet shows no sign of stopping.

The question is, at what point do I go to a doctor and confess what I've done? As an insecure nineteen-year-old one might get away with it; but at thirty-nine the confession that I'd belatedly decided I was under-vealed would be embarrassing, to say the least. I also doubt whether anybody would believe me ("Yeah, yeah, a scientific experiment. I mean, come on, Mr. Samper. Pull the other one"). But to admit that the re-vealing process had grown out of hand might be to invite the medical profession's most scathing weapon, derision ill-masked as professional sympathy. I suppose I might write to Mr. and Mrs. ProWang in Guangzhou—or, better, c/o their Internet site— and . . . and what? I can't possibly complain that their pills have done exactly what they claimed they would, and more. Maybe they could start work on an antidote to arrest the process? Yet for that I would need the evidence of a medical examination, which brings me back to that consulting room and the medic struggling to maintain his or her imperturbability. And he or she, of course, would be eager to prepare a paper for publication in *The Lancet* or the *BMJ* on this exceptional case. I can practically write it myself:

> The micropenis has long been considered a clinical condition with its own fields of research, including endocrinology and psychiatry. The macropenis, by contrast, has hitherto not presented as a pathological condition and, indeed, the word does not exist in the medical lexicon. Although this condition has made a regular appearance down the ages in folklore and popular literature, in the medical literature it is mentioned only tangentially as a possible cause of dyspareunia or as a symptom in conditions such as precocious puberty, and then only in relative, not absolute, terms.[1] In the case of a forty-

[1] Fischer K., Mewlings P. F. and Mufftingler A., "Some psychiatric and behavioural sequelae in four cases of pubertas praecox," JAPEDA, vol. XLV, no. 14, pp.1121–7.

year-old patient, however, we enter uncharted waters with a symptomatology that includes abruptly raised Fibroblast Growth Factor and somatomedin/IGF-1 blood levels . . .

Even cloaked in anonymity I would find this sort of thing quite grim enough without the additional irony of serving to enhance somebody else's career by turning over all my privately collected data and standing around mutely wearing a paper gown. True, there are alternative possibilities, one of them being to capitalize on this personal disaster. *Think positively* (I ought to be telling myself while lighting a patchouli-scented joss stick): this is not an affliction but a benediction. We are *blessed* by our adversities . . . A likely tale. All I can hear is Émile Coué's famous maxim rephrased to mock me: "Day by day, in every way, I am becoming bigger and bigger." It is a pity that freak shows have fallen victim to amniocentesis and political correctness, otherwise I would be able to earn my living at fairgrounds alongside the Bearded Lady, the Fish-Scaled Boy and the Rubber Man. But one's afflictions can still command a market value. There may be a new career opening for me as the guest star in strip clubs or those DVDs with arch titles like "What—The Butler's Sore?" Would that really be worse than writing about Millie Cleat? The answer, incredibly, is yes. I can't even bring myself to explore possible avenues of succour on the Internet by summoning up some perverted penile helpline designed for ghouls and insomniacs. No. I have not yet reached so low a point. I just wish I could banish from my mind's eye an image in my school geography textbook of fat-tailed sheep in Australia obliged to tow their massive appendages in little carts. Well, the thing is not to become obsessive. I make a pact with myself that I will now take my tape measure into the bathroom only once a week, and carry on keeping a careful record. Whatever else, this is a scientific imperative. If I'm to make medical history, if not *The Guinness Book of Records*, I shall need impeccable data.

Right now I have more important things to think about, such as producing a culinary artwork from the calves' brains that are still sitting patiently in the fridge. Even at this altitude the weather is oppressive and I am disinclined even to think about heavy food. This is not the moment for seam-bursting winter fare. I bought the brains in Viareggio, you will remember, under the influence of my bedtime reading of Emmeline Tyrwhitt-Glamis's *Emergency Cuisine*. In this book she made several pithy asides about the iniquity in wartime of eating such things as lamb or veal. Sheep and cows, she explained, were factories on the hoof and their full output was essential to the war effort. She was wholly opposed to the slaughter of any creature that had not attained decent old age unless it happened to be wearing a Nazi uniform, in which case it was never too young to be culled. Naturally, by today's standards Dame Emmeline's hard line strikes us as disgraceful. For one thing, it helped perpetuate the Protestant streak in British cookery that has done so much to earn us the pity and contempt of more discriminating nations. By "Protestant streak" I mean the idea that it is sinful to allow notions of pleasure to contaminate the act of eating, which according to nonconformist zealots should serve only to refuel the machine. These people also consider it proper to maximize God's bounty by, for example, picking broad beans only when they are leathery monsters the size of big toes, or runner beans when they are a foot long and covered in fibrous green parchment, or pears when they are weeping bombs of wasp fodder. Dame Emmeline did not personally subscribe to this Calvinistic ideology. Indeed, her house in Berkeley Square became famous as a wartime haven for young naval ratings lost in the blackout, and there are ample accounts and memoirs to testify that she had no taste whatever for overripe fruit, being strongly inclined towards the invigorating hardness of comparative immaturity. Nevertheless, strictly from the point of view of wartime cooking, she did condemn as decadent the habit of slaughtering lambs and calves. In times of national emergency quantity must trump quality if it's available at all. Citizens should eschew rack of lamb even as they lamented the lack of ram. Anywhere other than on her own settee Dame Emmeline called patriotically for less veal and more beef.

> Not one whit less than our fighting housewives [she wrote], our British cows are part of the nation's great Victory effort. We already know our gallant head-scarved women working their dangerous shifts in a munitions factory are in the forefront of crucial war work. But you make a mistake if, the next time you see a herd of slow-moving Jerseys or Guernseys obliviously munching the lush grass of a shady pasture, you imagine they are mere shirkers and idlers living off the fat of the land. On the contrary, even as you watch them they are *making* the fat of the land in the form of best British butter: the essence of England to put heart and strength into our fighting men. What is more, these workers are mothers too, and in due course their offspring will be sacrificed at the Front in the war against hunger. What noble beasts are these! To watch them is to wonder what is going through their brains . . .

Ah yes, their brains. In our enthusiasm to get their brains into our stomachs it is important not to be carried away by primitive ideas of sympathetic magic, such as that somehow the dead brains of cows are full of the residues of green thought in a green shade. You smile indulgently, of course, knowing all about lark's tongue pâté and why oysters are supposed to be aphrodisiac; and you have sometimes wondered whether young David, having laid aside his trusty sling, was expected by his tribe to sit straight down to a barbecue of Goliath's balls to be sure of incorporating all his fallen foe's strapping manliness (and here I find myself wondering yet again about "orchic substance" and decide that I won't go there). Mediaeval nonsense, of course, although it's amazing how much magical thinking has made it in various guises into this supposedly scientific age. If you stand on the terrace here at Le Rocce and look down at the coast you can see, beyond the patchwork sprawl of greenhouses and Viareggio's outskirts, the very beach where in July, 1822, Lord Byron and Edward Trelawny burned the bodies of Shelley and Edward Williams. It had taken ten days for Shelley to be washed ashore, his friend a little longer. Classic floaters in a warm climate, they were in a pretty disgusting state and burning must have seemed a cleansing and dignified measure. Shelley's heart was raked out of the pyre unconsumed and in due course was buried in Rome. Can you believe that for two pins they'd still be at it today? In 2005 there was an official request for the heart to be cut out of Pope Wojtyla's corpse for burial in his native Poland. (DHL Rush Manifest: One (1) old pump. Donor value: Nil. Relic value: See attached estimate.) And here we are again, back in the primitive world of martyrs' thighbones and pieces of the Ark and bottles of water imported from the river Jordan. The whole thing is most peculiar, not least this enduring idea that the heart is the seat of the emotions and the soul, despite centuries of anatomists saying, "It's the brain, stupid."

The culinary truth is that the years of fizzing thought and passions that have passed through a brain before it dies leave no characteristic flavour. There is just the pulpy machine; the ghost has been laid for good. Which is why I now propose a dish that perversely attempts to resurrect it in a green and pastoral form:

Ghost soufflé

Ingredients
30 gm butter or olive oil
30 gm plain flour
500 gm fresh-picked clover
4 egg yolks and 5 whites
1 handful fresh basil leaves and stalks
250 gm calves' brains
1 sprig of mint
1 teaspoon coconut milk

You will be making a roux with a difference, for which you will need 160 ml of clover juice in place of dull, conventional, play-safe milk. The first task is therefore to pick the clover. Use the entire plant except the roots. Wash well and spin in a salad carousel to remove excess water. Depending on availability the clover can be eked out with tender, freshly cut grass, but do not exceed a proportion of fifty-fifty. This is also the moment to mix in the basil and the mint. Now you will need to have recourse to the sugarcane juicer you brought back from Southeast Asia because only it can apply real pressure. Forget the quaint aluminium apparatus slowly oxidizing at the back of the cupboard that you bought in a fit of meanness some years ago in the belief that it is possible to extract first-rate orange juice from fourth-rate oranges. Nor should you be tempted to use a blender to reduce the vegetation to mush: it will contain far too much cellulose and any grass mixed in will render it gritty. You are not expecting to lift out of the oven a mousse of compost. You are aiming to recapture the Spirit of Cow, to reimplant in the deceased animal's little brain a placid, ruminant ghost suggestive of lush, sun-dappled pasture and slow, cuddish thought. To that end it is best to ensure your butcher sells you the grey matter of forage-fed and not grain-fed animals. No matter what you do to it the meat of grain-fed cattle is never completely free of a hint of corned beef, a wartime standby that I believe is still in use for extreme eating purposes. Having gone this far I will confess that Derek once sent me a booklet that falls at the child-pornography end of cookery books: something to be hidden away and brought forth only at moments of shared hysteria in carefully chosen company. This is an illustrated collection of recipes entitled "The Great Taste of Spam™" that includes such creations as *Spam™ Stuffed Potatoes Florentine and Spam™ Fettucini Primavera*, the colour photograph of which looks exactly like what you find on the mat after worming the dog. You might infer that this is classic blue-collar cookery from something called *Hearty Spam™ Breakfast Skillet*. "Hearty" is a tinned-food adjective par excellence.

You should by now have a slightly foamy glass of green nectar whose smell suggests the drowsy whir of lawn mowers on early summer evenings when the shadow of the horse chestnut begins to topple across the base line at the far end of your grass tennis court. Before you begin the roux, however, you need to liquidize the brains together with the splash of coconut milk. This is perhaps the only curiosity in this recipe. At first sight coconut milk, even in such exiguous quantity, will seem the odd ingredient out. Yet I have found by experience that although it cannot be tasted as such in the final dish it has the ability to deepen the grassy note by roughly an octave. Season the creamy pinkish matter and set it aside in a chilled bowl. Now is the time for the roux. Do not be hidebound by the idea that a roux must always be made with butter: it works equally well with olive oil although care will be needed to choose one that is not so pungent that it swamps the green flavour you are aiming for. I would recommend using nothing from further south than 43° latitude, which excludes the whole of the Iberian peninsula. Once again, a slightly grassy-tasting olive oil can deepen the overall flavour by as much as a minor sixth.

When the sauce is ready, add the egg yolks beaten up with a little cold water, then the liquidized brains. Now carefully fold in the egg whites which you have previously whisked stiff and pour into a nonstick soufflé dish. If you bake it in a moderate oven (200°C) you should have between twenty and thirty minutes to lay your terrace table, have ready your cold bottle of prosecco and prepare yourself for a treat that would have gladdened the heart of Emmeline Tyrwhitt-Glamis. The poor lady would bitterly have envied you the fresh eggs. Trying for haute cuisine using wartime powdered egg was as doomed as the ill-fated attempt by Simpson's in Piccadilly to serve pemmican pie for lunch in 1944, the precise number of its victims being concealed for thirty years by the Official Secrets Act.

14

T. S. Eliot was wrong. *August* is the cruellest month, breeding Dionysiacs out of dead lands. Chianti addicts from shuttered northern Europe ebb southwards in awesome shorts. With seigneurial gestures bank managers and justices from Göttingen and Godalming, Hazebrouck and Haslemere, throw open the shutters of their Tuscan villas and farmhouses for the first time since Easter, disclosing heaps of bat guano staining the beds' white radiance. In local towns their translucent pink children squint beneath baseball caps in the drench of sun as they trail behind their parents beneath the scattered awnings of the weekly market. It is the kids' summer *hajj*: the obligatory pilgrimage through a blazing desert necessary for them to earn their reward of heavenly ice cream. Their eyes are downcast and in default of prayer beads their fingers, agile from years of devotion, skip nimbly over the buttons of their Game Boys. There is nothing for them in these markets except possibly Chinese rip-offs of Manchester United strips. They certainly don't care about the sun hats, scarves and handbags that so intrigue their mothers and which to them look the same as the ones on sale back home. No doubt ancient Athenians two millennia ago who dragged their children off to Egypt for a highly educational tour of the Pyramids were just as irritated to find their boys crouched in a patch of shade playing with a pocket set of knucklebones.

August is also the cruellest month because it breeds bric-a-brac out of Med lands. Models of the Leaning Tower of Pisa, packets of naughty pasta shaped like male genitalia, grappa in glass bottles of fanciful design and extreme fragility: all are crammed somehow into the back of the Volvo or the BMW, pride of place going by default to Daddy's prized bottles of wine that he has pronounced "a Billy bargain." Samper the sardonic, Samper the permanent resident, threads his way among these seasonal migrants, noting everything and saying nothing. He has given up trying not to feel superior. The truth is that since he has never had a proper five-days-a-week job he has never in his life had a holiday, either, and can't quite imagine what it would mean. Also, he thinks, for people whose normal way of life is one of constant gratification there can no longer be much distinction between levels of pleasure. So it is hard to imagine how much of a treat it really is to be shopping in Italy instead of at home: a thought that has probably crossed the minds—if not the larynxes—of the listless Game Boy players.

Maybe I'm being a touch disingenuous over this matter of holidays, since no sooner has Millie Cleat told Frankie that she thinks the new chapter will "do quite well for the time being' (grudging cow!) than I feel as though I'm at last on holiday. Thank God *that* job's over, I think, and break out carolling in my mountain retreat, causing buzzards to swerve in flight. It's true that *Millie!* is only the second of a three-book deal I have with Champions Press and I've not the faintest idea what the third book will be, but I refuse to let it bother me in August. My hopes of writing Max Christ's biography have faded ruefully. Such a project is obviously for the long term if it ever comes off at all. Equally obviously it would not be a Champions book. (For a moment I indulge the fantasy of submitting my biography of this celebrated conductor to Michelle Tost, my editor there. Poor old Weetabix, she'd be completely thrown. I could claim the text was larded with world records: the slowest-ever performance of the Adagio of Beethoven's Ninth; the record-breaking transfer fee for a piccolo player;

the infamous Last Night of the Proms that resulted in three fatalities from coins, fireworks and lavatory rolls hurled from the Dress Circle by middle-class music lovers exemplifying a social process known as dumbing up.) For the moment, though, I'm content to banish all thoughts of work and instead concentrate on having friends to stay, doing a bit of cooking and singing, and fulfilling one or two local obligations. These include translating a Camaiore restaurant's menu into English as a favour to the proprietor. It is a pleasure to be able to produce a neat, clean rendering completely devoid of editorial adjectives like "mouthwatering" and "succulent." It is an even greater pleasure to eat the dinner he gives me by way of payment.

In the middle of the month Adrian comes out for a particularly delicious week. I do like scientists. To me, Adrian's approach to everything seems thoroughly grounded in a sensible and weighty body of knowledge, whereas I just float over life's terrain like a gasbag or a hot-air balloon, periodically emitting loud blasts of music and invective and taking on haute-cuisine ballast to keep me from drifting away completely. Maybe this is also partly the effect of living in a house perched high on a mountainside. One can overdo this business of looking down on the world. Adrian arrives already quite bronzed, having just been on a ship in mid-Atlantic for fifteen days. He is a very glamorous figure indeed, almost exotic. One evening on the terrace, in a fit of candour brought on by a good deal of prosecco, he says the same about me and I'm glad it's dark and there's no one else around to see the hard-boiled Samper blushing. Our conversation then takes an awkwardly romantic turn, of which nothing more need be said. Unlike mishaps, shameless dalliance makes lousy and embarrassing reading. More important to the present tale is that Adrian has come bearing recent news about la Cleat, bane of my life, which plainly reveals that over these last six months while actu-

ally writing (as opposed to researching) her book, I have spent
too little time keeping up with her various non-nautical doings.

In common with most over-rewarded public figures Millie
earnestly fancies that her opinions on absolutely anything are
of value to the human race, and these she delivers loudly and
unstintingly. So much so that, out of sheer self-defence, I have
learned to let my attention drift when she informs me where
America went wrong in the aftermath of the Twin Towers
attack, why the current British Minister for Sport should have
his or her gonads removed with a rusty bread knife, and exactly what ought to be done to violent sex offenders. She also has
much wisdom to impart about the pharmaceutical industry,
Australia's cane toad problem and the right way to change a
light bulb if you have only one arm. From time to time I have
filtered out a good deal of her rhetoric on the subject of
Greenpeace and that mega-bore Cinderella of contemporary
discourse, the environment. Adrian now reminds me that by so
doing I have been missing a significant trend in Millie's life.
This is her increasing political interest in Bluedeep, a faction of
sea fanciers who broke with Greenpeace a few years ago on the
grounds that the latter were a bunch of landlubbers who
weren't interested in anywhere you couldn't plant trees.

I can easily see why the old sea bitch would be a Blue rather
than a Green, but Adrian tells me her current position is much
weirder. Apparently, despite their fervour, the Blues have also
had their factional tendencies (a problem common to all parties, even those as small as when two or three are gathered
together in Thy name). Accordingly, those whose approach to
the oceans is more mystical than scientific have become the
Deep Blues. Adrian says these are mostly cracked Atlantis
seekers, animal-rightists opposed to eating anything higher in
the marine chain than bladder wrack, and followers of the
Norwegian philosopher of eco-apocalypse Arne Naess. Now
these Deep Blues have formed a splinter organization of their

own called Neptune. This was surely an incautious choice of name since it gave the satirically minded the opportunity to dub them the "Loony Neptunies," a handle that took less than twenty-four hours to catch on.

But the amazing news is that Neptune has announced none other than Millie Cleat as its public figurehead. I am willing to bet her organization's name owes everything to that conversation she and I had in her Hilton suite a couple of months ago. According to Adrian, Millie has publicly declared her intention of establishing Neptune as a serious "envirospiritual" movement (for such is the dreadful epithet now bestowed on this brave new tendency). What is more, her Australian ally, sponsor and fetishistic lover, Lew Buschfeuer, is apparently putting a great wodge of his money behind it; so much, in fact, that the *Guardian* has acknowledged his bottomless pockets with the page-two headline: "Deep Lew to Fund Deep Blue." In other words, even as I was inventing her as a mildly spiritual yachtsperson for that final additional chapter of her book Millie was already solving the problem of her retirement by beadily taking on a role that will presumably keep her in the public eye until she ascends into heaven. Needless to say she has never given me, her biographer, the least hint of any of this. She has played it very close to her gristly chest. Nobody's fool, our Millie; although I'm willing to bet she also came under a lot of pressure from those pashmina'd girls down on the Solent. They must now be breaking out the Cristal to toast her elevation as the new patron saint of the sea, to say nothing of their own privileged position as her disciples.

Apart from this news, Adrian has brought with him a CD recording which he mischievously slips into the player in my kitchen the second evening after his arrival. It's a warm night and moonless. The French windows are flung wide onto the terrace, showing the table cleared of our main course and wait-

ing for my patented anchovy ice cream. Suddenly the room
fills with strange, ghostly noises that send a chill streaming out
into the velvety Tuscan night, seeming to cool it by twenty
degrees. Haunted chirpings and babblings are interspersed
with occasional moans, all of it echoing as though lost in an
immense void. It has the melancholy of those old war-film
soundtracks when tense-faced submariners, trapped on the
bottom by depth-charging destroyers, stare upwards at the
curved steel hull of what may become their coffin while the
enemy's sonar pings hollowly in the ocean around them. The
sound brings me out in gooseflesh. The more I listen to it the
more I hear, gradually becoming aware of a menacing twitter
running softly in the background. It is like one of those conversations or monologues one occasionally thinks one over-
hears within a steady noise such as a boat's engine: voices
always below the threshold of intelligibility, but insistently
talking. I can readily imagine that creatures from another
galaxy are quietly massing to invade my kitchen, and I remember Nanty Riah's conviction two summers ago that aliens had
landed over at Marta's house.

Adrian turns down the volume and shoots me an amused,
inquiring glance.

"I assume we're underwater," I hazard. "And very chill it is."
I have a sudden brain wave. "Oh, it's not those transponder
things that got washed off that ship?"

"Brilliant, Gerry. That's exactly what it is. This is what my
colleagues on the *Tony Rice* have to hear every day."

Even with the sound muted the noise seems to linger, so
powerful is its effect. I can almost imagine the benign summer
night outside replaced by black fathoms of water, pressing
inward to engulf Le Rocce while the kitchen's very rafters
transmit the mournful cacophony from no known place.
Adrian turns up the volume again and gives a running com-
mentary. For the first time I become aware of the expert skill

required to disentangle one stream of these noises from another. With surprise I realize how similar it is to his celebrated brother-in-law's ability to pick out a single clarinet or bassoon from an entire symphony orchestra, detecting a wrong note or an unwritten silence. Until this moment I have rather flattered myself on my own musical ear, but Adrian's ability to separate out distinct voices in this grotesque deep-sea chorus is uncanny and humbling.

"That sinister twittering? Those are the three-and-a-half kilohertz transponders talking to each other." Or: "Those ghostly squeaks are the ten kilohertz."

"And that *ghraw-ghraw* sound and those awful occasional moans? It sounds like the labour ward of Atlantis General Hospital."

"I've no idea," Adrian admits. "We've none of us been able to identify those. It'll be some animal in the water column, but it's nothing we recognize. Not surprising, really. The oceans are full of noises we can't identify. Lots of them we can, of course. Various cetaceans, the frying sound of snapping shrimps, the drummings and grunts and clicks of a lot of fish species. But every so often we encounter noises that are just plain baffling. Remember that when we do bathymetric or geological profiling like the EAGIS survey, we're pumping out some incredibly powerful sounds into the water column, especially air-gun bangs strong enough to bounce off rock three kilometres below the seabed. We're probably pissing off an awful lot of creatures down there. Quite often we get responses that aren't echoes at all. It's extraordinary: they sound as though something's deliberately mimicking or even mocking our signals. We've heard our ten-kilohertz "fish" sending out its single bleep being answered by a double or even quadruple bleep. We're stumped. We analyse the signals and it's absolutely clear: they weren't electronically generated. So what are we to think? That there are creatures down there sending us up?"

I am getting gooseflesh again. "I'd no idea there's so much noise in the sea. It's quite widely known about, is it?"

"Oh yes. But really only within the trade. Any oceanographer who's done a few years of survey work will tell you there are things down there we haven't a clue about. After all, nobody knows for sure why or how a mynah bird or a parrot can imitate the sounds it hears, even human speech, with such precision. And birds are right here to hand on dry land. You can study them as long as you like. You can experiment with them, you can dissect their brains. Imagine how infinitely less we know about the abilities and motives of audible marine species, most of which have probably never been identified. The oceans remain a planetwide mystery. They're why I became a scientist."

And still the soundtrack from however many leagues under the sea is filling the kitchen with its alien babble. As I lift my masterly anchovy ice cream out of the fridge I think how very appropriate to the occasion it has turned out to be: both fishy and chill. We take it out on to the terrace and indulge ourselves, from time to time pausing to gaze out speculatively towards Viareggio. On a night as dark as this the distant carpet of that town's lights appears laid with an edge straight and abrupt enough to make one believe in the abyss beyond it, like a sparkling nonslip mat glued to the lip of a high diving board.

"So, of course, a copy of that CD has to fall into Millie's hands."

"Well, that was your own malicious little idea originally, but we're certainly in agreement at BOIS." Adrian's look is still mischievous. "We reckon it's high time the Neptunies got to grips with the terrors of the deep."

"Obviously you're used to those noises, but to someone who isn't they're actually quite scary. Or not scary, exactly, but uncanny. Melancholy? Forlorn? Inscrutable? I don't know how to describe it, but they certainly make a powerful impression. Don't forget that when I first thought of trying them out on Millie I hadn't yet heard them myself. By the way, who are the 'we' at BOIS?"

"Oh, just hard-core, unregenerate types who'd enjoy seeing that woman keelhauled for screwing up our EAGIS data. The general public still have no idea what she did, have they? Vile seamanship, all that money wasted, several hundred scientists with ruined data and a further delay to our understanding a geological event that, if it happens, has the potential to cause havoc on both sides of the Atlantic. Trust me, Gerry, there are some very angry people at oceanographical institutions all over the world. But as time goes by and the woman is turned into a national symbol who can do no wrong, the EAGIS cock-up fades into the general hopelessness of trying to get the media to take *anything* scientific seriously. Some of us are thinking it's time to fight back. Didn't you mention 'The Face' made quite an impression on her?"

"I'll say. I'd just been lecturing her on Poseidon and Greek mythology and then I showed her the picture. It knocked her sideways. The real irony is that it was I myself who suggested her next book would be about her as the leader of a Neptune cult. Can you believe my idiocy?"

"Easily. Gerald Samper, the true inspiration behind the Neptunies. If you're very good I may keep that titbit from my colleagues, at least for the time being."

"It was only the *name*, for heaven's sake. I take no responsibility for her loony followers. And now with Lew's millions behind them they may not be so easy to debunk. Oh well, there's always the comic side. After all, it doesn't really matter if Millie and her disciples think there are fairies at the bottom of the sea, nor even if Cumbre Vieja does break off and drown millions. What were those extinctions you told me about? Permian? Late Cretaceous? Not to mention little human extinctions like Auschwitz. The planet will go trundling on, with or without us. And no matter what we do to it the sea will presumably go on producing life even if there are no humans around to know how to cook it properly."

"True. So we needn't be downhearted, need we? Meanwhile I'll send your Cleat woman a copy of this CD. No—on second thoughts you will send it. Better if it isn't traced back to me personally. As a thuggish reductive scientist I'm in the enemy camp. You can say it's been sent you by a closet sympathizer under deep cover in oceanography, something like that. Invent your own story."

"Right. And when she says, 'You see, Gerry? I always *sensed* it. There are *ur*-creatures down there completely unknown to us but who embody the wisdom of Gaia,' you or one of your colleagues steps in and says, 'Well, actually, Millie, that noise is not one of your familiar spirits of the deep but a two-hundred-hertz whatsit, and those chirps are a ten-kilohertz tiddlypush.' And so with the help of some carefully arranged media coverage and the EAGIS pictures of her trimaran cutting you up off the Canaries one night we bring her grey hairs down with sorrow to the grave. Is that the plan?"

"Something along those lines. We can fine-tune it as we go along. Didn't she once make an opprobrious remark about your bottom?"

"She may have," I say austerely.

"And your hair?"

"Possibly."

"You bloody well know she did. Go on, Gerry, you owe it to yourself. Think of all that aggro and rudeness you've taken from her over this last year. Flat-chested, monobrachial old besom. And think of her nice gay husband you were telling me about, and their two children—abandoned in Pinner, sacrificed on the altar of her overweening ambition. No, Gerry. It's time for the Empire to strike back."

I had almost forgotten how very nice it is to have some support. Being a perpetual loner can wear you down sometimes.

"Incidentally," says Adrian, "to change the subject: I forgot to tell you how much Jennifer and Max enjoyed your visit to them in Suffolk."

A muted pang of guilt stabs me lightly in the region of the anchovy ice cream. I become guarded.

"Well, obviously I very much enjoyed it too. Er . . . you've spoken to them recently, then?"

"Just the other day. They wanted to be sure I'd pass on their belated thanks for the delicious present you so thoughtfully left behind that evening. I think that's the message verbatim."

"You didn't detect a note of *irony* in the way they said it?"

Adrian looks a little puzzled. "No. Should I have?"

"I mean"—I need to be quite sure about this—"they weren't joking? No little edge of sarcasm?"

"Of course not, Gerry. As a matter of fact they found you charming: my sister's very word. Mind you, she's an impressionable girl and easily charmed. She once called Tony Blair 'attractive,' although admittedly that was back in 1997."

"Thank you so much." By now I am less than reassured. I'm reminded of my hosts' playfulness about Swythings and Crendles that left me at a loss that evening. This is a family with a peculiar sense of humour. It is clear to me that by now they must indeed have found the hideous time bomb I left behind in their spare room, put two and two together and have decided to play with me for humorous reasons of their own. Equally clearly, Jennifer would have told her brother, which means that Adrian's playing with me, too. This narks me considerably.

"It was one of those awful accidents," I say stiffly, staring out into the darkness. "What else can I say?"

"Heavens, Gerry, it doesn't sound too bad to me. It could have happened to anyone visiting that house. The state of the place is enough to distract any sane person. I can't think how they've put up with it for so long. I suppose Max is away a lot and Jen's always been something of a boho."

"Exactly," I say. "But imagine how I've felt about it ever since. Having blotted my copybook in such gross fashion I don't know how to make it up to them, especially now that so much time has gone by. That I should have done it to your own sister, of all people, and your illustrious brother-in-law . . ." I hear my own voice tail off more abjectly than I wish.

Adrian is now looking positively baffled. "Crikey, Gerry, it was just a bottle of prosecco. Aren't you making rather a meal of it? Jen told me about it. When the front door knocker came off in your hand, as it does in everybody's, you must have put the bottle down on the step in order to try and fix it and Jen opened the door and you forgot the bottle. She found it when she got back from Woodbridge next morning after dropping you at the station. No big deal. So judging by your overreaction," says Adrian acutely, "there must have been something else that evening. Come on, out with it."

Damn. Beneath that amused, handsome gaze I have no alternative but to confess the sorry saga of my *faux poo*. And to those who still take a Debrett's Guide approach to social etiquette I regret to say that within a minute both of us are helpless with laughter. In my case it is very much the laughter of relief, which as we all know can quickly border on total hysteria. In fact, I would like to think the confessionals in Catholic churches just as often echo with the hilarity of disburdenings as they do with the snivellings of regret. I bet they don't, though. Those awful stern religions of the Book mess fatally with the laughter glands—on its own a good enough reason to have nothing to do with them. Adrian and I wind up leaning weakly against the balustrade at the edge of the terrace, our arms around each other for support, still shaken with giggles. So he really *hadn't* known and it looks as though Max and Jennifer hadn't, either. Apparently the spare room next to

Crendlesham Hall's bathroom is now furnished and habitable and any old lavatories have long since disappeared with the rest of the builders' clutter. My reputation is unsmirched after all, except perhaps in the excremental and dinosaur-cluttered mind of Adrian's five-year-old nephew Josh. I can live with that.

The lights of Viareggio are dancing and wavering in the lenses of my involuntary tears. Down there, August goes on being the cruellest month with children of the tourist hajj playing with their Game Boys under cover of the tablecloth as their parents interminably eat weird fish dishes and talk mind-rottingly boring grownup stuff about the Priory of Sion and the Tuscan property market. Up here at Le Rocce a fresh bottle of prosecco pops like a merry firework and under its sparkling influence we shed more tears of laughter, the odd inhibition, and finally clothing. Very soon Samper is feeling considerably purged, and high time too.

15

Before he leaves I make Adrian promise not to tell Max and Jennifer the truth about my gaffe while I was their guest at Crendlesham Hall. This ought to bring the incident to a reasonable, if not actually happy, conclusion. Being British, it naturally never occurs to me to use the expression "closure": a piece of jargon appropriate to cod psychology and bereavement counselling. To me "closure" suggests unbolted stable doors and bolted horses, with maybe a stable boy breaking down in tearful remorse. In short, the Hollywood approach to regrettable incidents. The whole point is that these things never do end completely but go on echoing, often down an entire lifetime. I am proud to know I can live with this one.

The weeks go by peacefully. I remember to post off a copy of Adrian's CD to Millie with a covering note saying it had been sent me by some anonymous oceanographer working in the Canaries who couldn't explain these sounds but who thought I, as her biographer, might pass it on to her out of interest.

Derek phones me to say the owners of Josiah Corcoran, a.k.a. Blowjob, have promoted him to manage their new manicure and pedicure departments, already nicknamed Handjob and Ped-o-File, respectively, by their loyal staff. I force him to admit that "departments" really refers to a small back room that until recently was used to store industrial flagons of shampoo and conditioner, but he seems ecstatic about this upturn in his fortunes. I suppose it must be some compensation for the sad mishandling of his emotional life. It would be kind to think of Derek as merely fickle, but like a good deal of kindness it would be misplaced. Some years ago he deserted a penniless but devoted lover in favour of one of his clients at Corcoran's. The customer was a wealthy Harley Street specialist—well, not to put too fine a point on it, a proctologist—with a Lenny Bernstein mane of grey hair and a scarlet Ferrari. We all told Derek he was being a vulgar little gold digger and no good would come of this liaison, but he replied that he *liked* gold and that being driven around the Côte d'Azur in a Ferrari qualified as good in his book. The doctor was clearly besotted and lavished all sorts of fripperies on him and I'm sure Derek recompensed the man in his fashion by keeping his end up. Still, we all knew this was not the love of Derek's life. The truly devoted friend whom he'd thrown over went miserably to seed, pining in a bedsit in Palmers Green. He was a rather nice young scriptwriter whose modest fame derived from his having researched and written *The Rough Guide to the Cities of the Plain*, thereby scooping Lonely Planet who were still fact-gathering in Gomorrah. Meanwhile the Ferrari went, owing to a pleasantry by Derek in one of his moods to the effect that the only people who drove Ferraris were footballers and Russian mafiosi. It was replaced by a vintage Bentley Continental in which Derek sat bolt upright like a duchess with piles. The doctor, meanwhile, had successfully treated the piles of enough genuine duchesses to win a prestigious international proctology prize which the *Marylebone Tattler* headlined felicitously as "Bottom Doctor Wins Top Award." This gave particular pleasure to those who realized the headline could be reversed without losing any meaning. Derek basked in his glow.

But came the morning when he awoke to find the doctor stiff and stark next to him in their four-poster bed, carried off unnoticed by a heart attack in the small hours. Shortly afterwards he was dismayed to discover the true thickness of blood: the doctor had left his entire fortune to his own sister rather than to Derek, who practically overnight went from being a duchess to having to ask Corcoran's for his old job back. He got it, but only at the cost of some painful ribaldry. He also belatedly tried going to Palmers Green to rekindle the embers of his languishing friend's love, but in vain. Derek had revealed himself as a little too unscrupulous for comfort, and far too much so for love. Too late he learned the wisdom of Tennyson's observation that kind hearts are more than coronaries. There were those of us who felt there was something poetic about the way he was now reduced to paying rent to an immigrant colonic irrigator in the flat above him. At the time he salved his dignity by acting bereaved, exhausting the patience of most of his remaining friends. But sooner or later the moment comes when even a grieving duchess can't help noticing that one of the under-footmen bulges in all the right places and in due course Derek returned to his old ways, neither noticeably sadder nor wiser.

I now rejoice to hear he has been elevated to management status at work, and that he is happy and has rung me up to tell me so. I like to keep our relationship amiable. I no longer know so many people in London and it's useful to have Derek's flat as a bolt-hole when I'm being pestered and grilled by clients like Millie Cleat. There could hardly be a greater contrast between their two worlds. Not that he generically dislikes sailors. Far—very far—from it. But the demon blow-drier and back-comber of Jermyn Street is not what you would call an outdoors man. Having to tend a window box of geraniums would strike Derek as dauntingly agricultural. He prefers leafing through *Hello!*, going to musicals and, like *l'uomo magro*, eating Turkish delight in bed, although unlike poor Lieutenant Gasparo Derek never puts on an ounce of weight. As a counterbalance to the world of Millie Cleat his cosy little pied-à-terre feels to me like an island of sanity even if it does smell of Joop!

This last month I have been having a blissfully relaxed time "resting," as actors euphemistically put it. It is now early October and summer's hajjis have long returned to Dortmund and Dulwich, Cambrai Cambridge with their rapid tans and other souvenirs to die for. As a season autumn has lately been banished by global warming, but there is nevertheless a pleasant anticipatory sense of impending winter up here among the crags with the sun-battered leaves beginning to loosen their hold on the trees. I have constructed a rather nifty woodshed well stocked with logs for those roaring winter evenings when the icy tramontana blows down from places like Siberia and Voynovia. I have also replaced the lock on my own front door entirely without mishap.

From time to time I check Marta's house. These days, despite having reattached the knob to the inside of the lock months ago, I still can't go in through her back door without first propping a brick on the threshold so it can't slam shut. Neuroses have their value. The place is still fairly dry from the summer but I notice the first chill beginning to seep into the heavy stone walls. You can't abandon these old houses for too long before they begin to feel unloved and derelict, and Marta's has had a head start. I don't quite know what I'm doing as I stand there in the musty silence. My role as good neighbour seems imperceptibly to have elided into that of museum caretaker in one of those awful places where things are kept exactly as their famous owners left them when they died, like Puccini's claustrophobic house near here by Lake Massaciuccoli, or Cardinal Newman's oppressive bedroom in the Birmingham Oratory. However, I can't make my neighbourliness stretch to paying off Marta's various bills and getting her phone and electricity connected. What's the point without even knowing whether she's still alive? And nor does my curatorship extend to tackling the time bomb of her festering fridge, which must by now contain strains of bacteria toxic enough for biological weaponry.

I have also had some builders up here for the last couple of months, fettling up the sizable stone barn near the house that until now I've been using for nothing better than garaging the car. The barn turned out to be ten centimetres too low to qualify as a house, in the sense of being eligible for an official civic number. But my crafty plan has turned the upstairs into a marvellous studio or workroom. Since the building stands on the edge of the same gulf as my house the view from upstairs is nearly vertiginous, like something you might see from the window of an aircraft only without the sebum smears left by previous passengers' noses. Downstairs I've added a small bathroom and kitchen unit so the whole place could serve as a self-contained annexe if need be. The conversion has practically beggared me and I doubt I shall ever use the building myself but at least now it's finished, except for the decoration which I shall do myself with the customary Samper flair. Suddenly it's easy to see how property empires start. I realize that if poor Marta does turn out to be dead and her house comes on the market and I can afford it, I will buy it like a shot. Yet more space I would have no personal use for, but at least I would control it. It would be forever beyond the reach of Signor Benedetti and his baggy and dumpy clients. If ever I did allow someone to come and live there they would not have a piano named Petrof, nor relatives and friends who dropped by in helicopters at all times of day and night. A Trappist monk would suit admirably.

But you probably don't wish to know this. You would far prefer to hear the still more intimate details of my progress on the ProWang front. Well, it's very human of you. As a reliable form of pleasure, Schadenfreude is second only to that which shall be nameless. Specifically, you want to know if growth has continued and whether young Adrian noticed and passed comment. The short answers are "yes" and "yes," although it pains me to recall his words. Naturally, I told him everything. It's much easier to confide one's health matters to an oceanographer than to a doctor: they're far better scientists, for one thing. He did his best to listen gravely as I told him I'd embarked on the course of Pow-r-Tabs™ entirely in a spirit of scientific enquiry. When he could speak he remarked that he didn't believe a word of it. A little hurt, I then produced my meticulous records and demanded who, other than someone imbued with the heuristic ideal, would bother to keep such careful data? "Several hundred million fifteen-year-olds," was his reply. And when, finally, he was in a position to make a hands-on judgement for himself he merely observed that it fell "comfortably within the parameters of the unexceptional." Although I believe his dispassionate appraisal was intended as reassuring, I admit my crest fell. Sighs matter, they say, even if mine went unheard. We Sampers know how to dissemble beautifully, even as we chalk up the slight as something for future score-settling. I did wonder whether oceanographers have different standards from ordinary people and within a matter of minutes was happy to discover it wouldn't be surprising if they had.

But the long and the short of it is that the sudden growth belatedly triggered by that Chinese couple's remarkable pills *has* continued; and now, seven weeks later, even Adrian would surely have to concede that parameters were being stretched and that someone on the brink of his fortieth birthday might have reason for discreet alarm. As I keep saying, it's not just that. It's the worry about what else might have been set secretly in motion in the Samper physique that will burst out in the form of sudden breasts or buboes or something equally extravagant. Still, as you already know, I despise this age's narcissistic obsession with bodies and health and rattly bottles of pills. Plato was spot on when he remarked that "attention to health is the greatest hindrance to living." I must simply put these worries out of my head. Maybe if I give up taking my measurements growth will suddenly cease. These days even the dumbest scribbler has heard of the quantum effect whereby the very act of measuring something can influence the outcome. Maybe simply by taking my daily measurements I am actually stimulating growth even though the Pow-r-Tabs™ have long ceased working? I am rather struck by this thought and wonder whether as a layman I might not have stumbled on something that has been eluding the medical profession for centuries. I even think seriously about composing a letter to *The Lancet* or the *BMJ* and speculate about the Samper Effect in due course taking its modest place between "Sambucus" and "Sample" in the medical dictionary. True, there are one or two glitches in the theory to be ironed out first, such as that children whose parents don't periodically measure their height on the back of the larder door seldom turn out to be dwarves. I must remember to consult Adrian about this.

Then one day the phone rings and it is Frankie reminding me in unwelcome fashion that over in the real world there are still toads and commitments. Specifically, my contract with Champions Press, of which one title remains unwritten.

"Congratulations, Gerry. I think we've hit the jackpot," says Frankie breezily. "Arvo Bungis is in town and his father wants you to write his story. I suggest you drop everything and come over fast."

Even I can't plausibly pretend not to know who Arvo Bungis is. Back in June he won the Wimbledon title on his seventeenth birthday: the youngest-ever Men's Singles champion. Nobody can quite remember which of the Baltic states he's from, but I think he may be Estonian. Behind the ecstatic headlines it is widely admitted that his Wimbledon win was something of a fluke, greatly helped by biased umpiring and a lucky series of injuries that afflicted his opponents. The psychological advantage of being so young was strengthened by the common consent that he was by far the prettiest competitor of any gender ever to have stepped on to Centre Court. A dreamy blond who bounced silently around the court like rubber, earning him the predictable nickname "Bunjy," he easily outclassed in terms of his physical presence the cloned ranks of girls with sun-damaged cleavages and rawhide forearms who grunted and screamed and wailed each time they hit the ball. Young Arvo was a model of bashful modesty who, off-court, never once told a fawning interviewer that he'd "done real good." Even the most hardened commentators were captivated, and the boy instantly reached that pinnacle of public adulation where any worldly reward (starlets, riches, guest appearances in Rolex advertisements) seemed trashy and inadequate.

"Absolutely not, Frankie," I say firmly. "I can't possibly write an entire book about a teenaged tennis god unless it's a semiological deconstruction à la Barthes. Nobody can. Seventeen, for pity's sake: there's *been* no life to write about. What is there interesting to say about him?"

"Well, he's the great-great-whatever grandson of their national poet, Arhusis Bungis, if that's any good?"

"No."

"I looked him up on the Internet . . . Here we are: 'Arhusis Bungis (1803–57), 'The Sweet Singer of the Baltic,' whose autobiographical poems 'Erratic Boulder' and 'The Downcast Moose' are known to every schoolchild.'"

"Still no. Nobody would give a damn if he were a descendant of Shakespeare. What people want, although they're too wary to say so, is to see Arvo playing tennis with his kit off. They don't want a load of words getting in the way."

"Nonsense, Gerry. You'll find a way, you always do. Everyone's counting on you. I might mention that the alternative at the moment is a biography of Justin McPeach."

"*Who?*"

"He's the captain of our Ryder Cup team."

"I don't know anything about rugger, Frankie."

"It's golf, Gerry."

"You must be joking."

"He's keen for you to do it. Also he's thirty-four, so at least he's done some living. Quite a lot of it in bars, I fancy. And take it from me, nobody would want to see McPeach playing golf in the nude."

"Are those the sole choices?" Something is nagging me. I know Frankie of old, and there's more to this conversation than meets the ear. "Come on, Frankie. You're stalling, aren't you?"

There comes a Benson & Hedges moment at the other end of the line: great ochre gusts of coughing. Then, "It's the sainted Cleat, Gerry."

"Oh God, not again? *Now* what's up?"

"I don't know how well you're keeping up with the headlines in your Tuscan hideaway, but she's scarcely out of the news these days. So much so that Breakfast of Champions rang this morning to say they're going to rush *Millie!* out at the end of this week."

"Well and good. We get our publication advance that much sooner."

"True. But the real news is that Cleat herself definitely wants you to do the sequel."

"Of course she doesn't, Frankie. She knows I know she's bogus from stem to stern."

"Possibly. But she needs to cash in on her new public role as Queen Neptune, quick-quick. It means she can't afford to waste time looking for another writer of your reputation who also happens to be free and who already knows her story inside out."

"It doesn't sound like a book for old Breakfast."

"It isn't. This one will go to a general trade imprint in the same publishing group. It's too big and too nonspecialist for Champions Press. There'll be a lot of money in it, Gerry. You know the global interest there is in this sort of thing."

"Oh my God . . . Were you serious about the Bunjy-boy?"

"Oh yes, perfectly. His father has read your book on Luc Bailly and thinks you're just the sympathetic sort of biographer his boy needs. But naturally I never imagined you'd agree. I was trying to ease you into Millie Cleat, as it were."

Frankie mentions the sum of money he's proposing to ask for me to write yet another—and far more odious—book for this frightful Queen-o'-the-Seas. I am rather astonished. He assures me it's entirely feasible—ultra-short notice, and so on—and we've got her over a barrel, a time-honoured nautical posture. He adds that if the publisher balks, Lew Buschfeuer's billions could no doubt be deployed to good effect. In short, it's all over bar the shouting, of which I do quite a bit in an enraged sort of way once I've rung off. Can I really have got myself trapped into doing the one thing I vowed never to do? Yes, because this time it's serious dosh: serious enough to enable me to buy up the rest of my contract with Champions and thus free myself at last from the world of sport. Just think, Samper: no more people with syntax-free thought patterns and a vocabulary of five hundred words, every one of which is spoken in an uninflected monotone. No more having to hear how good they done. No more interviews snatched in private jets and hotel rooms, constantly interrupted by beady-eyed handlers wearing blazers and bearing news of the next photo-op or phials of the latest undetectable performance-enhancing drug.

In short, isn't this really a blessing, even if it does come heavily disguised as a one-armed harridan with mystical pretensions? Isn't this the break I've so long been looking for? Once I've written this book I shall be able to take at least the next couple of years off. I could literally afford to wait to write Max Christ's biography, which will only pay a pittance anyway. Of course, I can always hope that between now and then he will do something sensationally distasteful that will make my job easier and swell the potential readership. But for now it's a matter of ringing Derek at Blowjob, packing a bag, finding my passport and heading off to Pisa airport with gritted teeth.

16

If you join the motorway at Viareggio wishing to head southwards to Pisa, you collect your ticket and start by driving north, a counterintuitive challenge designed to weed out the faint of heart. Pisa, as the nearest major city down the coast, is naturally signposted "Livorno," and to get there you double back over what must be one of Europe's more lunatic flyovers when without warning the one-way system casually becomes two-way and for a heart-stopping moment you think you're in the wrong lane and about to have a head-on collision. All thought is blotted out by panic and the survival instinct. Despite my familiarity with this imbecilic piece of road planning it's the same again today. But once the Samper heart rate is back below fibrillation point and the car headed south I become freer to muse about the direction my life may be taking. With any luck, and with quite outstanding irony, the dreaded Cleat will turn out to be both nemesis and saviour. Just one more book and then I can be free? It seems too good to be true. To dismiss the ordeal of writing it as "just one more book" would be unguardedly blithe. The great question—and I suppose it has asked itself insistently throughout my lengthening and blameless life—is, how unserious can I afford to be in protection of my own sanity and still get away with it?

In a professional sense this question memorably posed itself nearly seventeen years ago when I was working as a scriptwriter for a commercial production company. The client was a cross-Channel ferry operator hoping to restore his passengers' confidence in the aftermath of the sinking of the *Herald of Free Enterprise*. In order to draw the attention of the travelling public—simple, suggestible folk—away from the irreducible fact that they would be going to sea, my company had decided that his ferry had best be presented reassuringly as a shopping mall that happened to be mobile. The client agreed and we went to work to produce a seductive video of the shopping facilities. As may be imagined, it was a film of devastating banality, tedium and outright untruth ("Our selection of familiar high-street outlets ensures that opportunities for bargain hunters are unrivalled." Thus the voice-over against shots of the usual dreary shelves of mass-market perfume, drink, teddy bears with nautical caps and nets of chocolate doubloons.) The trashy hucksterism of it all wore us down, as did the client, who couldn't even come up with a name for his shipborne arcade of boutiques and duty-frees that was supposedly his Unique Selling Point. In a meeting I suggested calling it "Mall-de-Mer" as a gesture towards the French who, after all, would also be travelling on the ship. Months later we discovered that the client had taken this seriously, emblazoning the cheery phrase all over the ship. The ferry company was duly hurt and baffled that, whereas the Mall did brisk trade with the Brits, the French passengers stayed away in droves. Moral: never overestimate other people's sense of humour, and never underestimate your employees' disloyalty. I shall need to be on my guard with Neptunia Cleat. The fervent don't *do* jokes.

Having my wits about me I ignore the exit to Pisa Nord, which is exactly where you don't wish to go if you want Pisa airport. Unwitting motorists are expected to divine this by telepathy; the first signs to the airport appear only several nail-bitten miles further on. Eventually I leave the car in the long-term park and discover my flight to Gatwick has been delayed by two hours. The reason being offered is "delay." I have time to stand around and reflect that the ineffable Leaning Tower is now one with the Great Wall of China, the Taj Mahal and the Pyramids. Pisa is on the global map as an experience to be experienced rather than as a place to be seen. Even in October the airport seethes with middle-aged tourists, most of them rushing, including those who happen to be standing still. What is it about modern air travel that drives anxiety levels steadily upwards when getting on a plane is as commonplace as hopping on a bus and even safer? The general frenzy is in marked contrast to the slow-motion process of flying itself, which is carefully designed to take up a day at the very least, regardless of the distance flown.

I can't imagine that anyone would ever call Samper a snob, but let me now formulate the theory that at least part of Britons' frenetic irritability as air travellers stems from our being obliged to forfeit our social bearings. We are forced into close association with the sort of people we have spent a lifetime trying to avoid. These days cheap travel shakes everyone together into a social emulsion; but as soon as the journey is over the immiscible fluids start to separate out again into their customary layers from the bottom up, the sedimentary denizens of ultimae Thules like Braintree settling out first. Even as I formulate the thought the Arrivals portal starts to gush a new batch of passengers from Stansted, dressed for the unseasonal heat wave apparently afflicting Britain. Merely to mention grizzled men in baseball caps and shorts with fading tattoos on their arms will alert you to the literary shorthand involved here, a brief *verb. sap.* acknowledging that no matter how alluring the Leaning Tower Experience, these are frankly the sort of people who have no business straying outside the Costa del Sol, Ibiza, or (if young) Ayia Napa. Their cheerful, floozy-like companions—wives, possibly—have upper storeys barely contained by straining pink hawsers, while below are pillars of cellulite. And drifting rapidly away from them are the honking middle classes, the men often wearing pale, broad-brimmed hats from Austin Reed, impatient with the queue to claim their hired cars. They are eager to be off to their houses—divinely restored—tucked into the hills behind Lucca, around Siena, or as far afield as Chiantishire. The degree of antagonism we Brits feel towards our fellow-countrymen abroad merits the attention of anthropologists.

One of the tattoos bins his *Daily Mail* and I glimpse a minor headline that makes me retrieve the paper once its previous owner has turned his back. Under the phrase "Death of a Sailsman" is the story of the sudden untimely demise of Millie Cleat's old yachting rival, Rufus Rasmussen. "The Dane with the mane," as this shaggy old Viking used to be known, was yesterday found dead and drifting in his favourite craft, an antique cutter of sorts (to judge from the picture), all dazzling sails, polished brass and gleaming teak and mahogany. He was eight years younger than Millie, who will be ecstatic although she will take care to weep crocodile tears in public. I never met Rasmussen, but from what I had gathered he was the better natural seaman as well as having no interest in the limelight. He was a loner in the Joshua Slocum tradition and an intense irritant to Millie, so I salute him on both counts. I down an espresso and mooch wearily "airside," as we seasoned travellers say in our quaint insiders' jargon that implies we have a background in military security. Just another of the little pretensions that enable us to believe we have some sort of control over our destiny, which ineluctably remains Putney Vale Crematorium or similar.

When Derek lets me into his flat the first thing I notice is the smell, which I immediately identify as Allure. I have evidently caught him *fragrante delicto*, splashing himself liberally from the bottle he's holding. Joop! has evidently been superseded, leaving me with an unwanted bottle of the stuff in my hand luggage: one of those dutiful airport gifts that mean so much these days now that the thought no longer counts. I give the air an ostentatious sniff fuelled by exasperation at having just wasted thirty euros.

"Since when the Chanel?"

"Oh, ages now. If you want to know, it's Pavel's favourite."

"Oho, so it's 'Pavel' these days, is it? I seem to remember when you last spoke about him you referred to him as 'Pauline.'"

"He's a very great pianist," Derek says sternly, "and a very close friend. His Bach concerts were a wild success, you know. Such problems we had with his hair, I can't tell you. Well, I can, actually," Derek adds with disarming professionalism. "He's losing it at a rate of knots. There was a time when I thought Wigmore Hall was all too appropriately named, but it's wonderful what can be done with blowing and combing and thickeners. That's Leoncine's problem now. I'm concentrating on his hands. Frightful responsibility, you know, a pianist's hands. These days he won't let anybody else touch them."

And to think that until recently I was hoping to write Taneyev's life. Somehow these invasive revelations kill the idea stone dead. Temperamental, we artists. "Obviously you're all performing a heroic task, keeping these great public idols groomed and manicured and back-combed," I say. "Josiah Corcoran needs a classy motto on its letterhead. How about 'Work on my looks, ye mighty, and despair'? The right Ozymandian touch, don't you think?"

But from his expression it is evident that Derek and Shelley are perfect strangers. Ah well. In any case I must hurry: I have been summoned to attend Millie in time for drinks. No mention has been made of dinner afterwards so I assume she is planning to allow me thirty seconds in which to make my case for not writing her a sequel, to be followed by an imperious five minutes in which she tells me why I shall write it and like it. In the last few months she has evidently shifted her base a little northwards up Park Lane from the Hilton to the Dorchester. The taxi drops me at the entrance and an illegal immigrant wearing a commissionaire's costume opens my door with a bow and extends a hand as though I were the slightly paralysed Ruthenian ambassador. Really, the whole charade of antique graciousness in front of a building put up in 1931 is so provoking I press a one-euro coin into the man's gloved hand. I then sail on through into what, after all, is no royal residence but merely an upmarket doss-house. Within minutes I find myself being ushered into The Presence by someone who looks suspiciously like a minder.

The décor tells me at once that something is up. Her Hilton suite's executive chic has been replaced by queenly tat: acres of powder-blue carpet pinned down by the rosewood legs of faux-Regency chairs. Heavy blue-and-maroon striped curtains are tightly drawn against the October evening and the clotted rush-hour crawl of traffic beyond the double glazing. If ever a room cried out for the Samper touch, this is it: a touch whose first stage would require a gallon of petrol and a match. Then I notice the Samper touch is already present in the form of a large reproduction of that nonexistent being, The Face. This is hung prominently in a gilt frame garlanded with flowers, looking ever more haunted and extraterrestrial. Her Majesty Queen Neptunia also looks like nothing on earth, standing in the midst of various courtiers who are sitting looking up at her like the disciples in one of those pre-Raphaelite paintings gathered eagerly around the storytelling old shepherd who turns out to be You Know Who. The marine monarch is wearing what appears to be an evening gown in black rubber; more eye-catchingly still, she now has two arms. When I was a small boy my mother, like any good parent, would scold me for staring at the afflicted in the street, especially amputees. But this amputee is doing her best to be stared at and my reaction is entirely that of my former and smaller self. Just as a child sees people wearing panes of glass on their noses and with little bonfires of dead leaves smouldering between their lips, so I see a woman in a rubber dress with fish swimming in her arm. For, since I last saw her, my famous biographee has replaced her missing right arm with a glass or polycarbonate replica, bent at the elbow across her body with the hand curved so it can conveniently hold what looks like a large gin and tonic. That the arm is hollow and filled with water is obvious because tiny coloured fish swim and dart in it like flakes of blue and ruby and gold. The harness she must be wearing to support the weight of this bodily aquarium is hidden beneath a black garment draped about her shoulders. This resembles a mozzetta, the skimpy cape worn by popes and cardinals, only even shorter, and I assume it's an integral part of her weird pseudo-ecclesiastical costume. Still, few clerics outside the sort of parties Derek attends would wear vestments made of rubber or neoprene, which it has to be because it doesn't move or hang like woven fabric. What is going on here?

"Good heavens, Millie!" I hear myself exclaim involuntarily. "Er, how do you keep the water oxygenated?"

"Dear Gerry. Straight to the point as usual. Tablets, actually, but the poor creatures grow sluggish after a few hours so I empty them back into their tank." I now notice on the far side of the room a large aquarium, a mahogany monster apparently from the workshop of Thomas Chippendale. In this the usual unfortunate creatures are soundlessly repeating the same syllable through the thick glass of their cage: *ob, ob, ob*. "Whenever I wear them they unselfishly give me some of their wisdom."

"That's good. Hey, I've only just heard about Rasmussen."

As predicted, Millie's face takes on a grave expression and her voice drops professionally like that of a newscaster turning to the three children who died in a fire in Bradford last night. "It was a terrible shock. Poor, dear Rufus. He was a fabulous sailor—a true seaman born and bred. It was an honour to have raced agai—"

"I gather he died peacefully in his sloop."

Millie turns an injured gaze on me. "It would pain me to think you were making a joke of it, Gerry."

"Certainly not. I only mean it wasn't such a bad way to go, on his own boat and well away from his family."

"Naturally I sent poor Helga a message of condolence this morning. But what am I thinking of?" Millie's internal newscaster becomes sprightly again as she rejoices in a surprise win for the English cricket team against the strongest eleven that Upper Volta has fielded for years. She turns back to her disciples or courtiers. "May I introduce Gerald Samper, who was an active consultant while I was writing my first book and has most kindly volunteered to be the same for my next? It was Gerry who passed on to me that CD of the mystical revelations off the Canaries which Tricia has done such valuable work in translating and which are giving our movement such incredible impetus worldwide."

While she was writing her first book? The woman is truly shameless. In fact, she's so outrageous I can't even feel outrage. At least it means that if she's claiming everything I write as her own work then I can afford to make her next book really prizewinningly mediocre. If it's to be my swan song then I intend to go out on a low note. Meanwhile, Queen Neptunia's courtiers are goggling up at me in a suitably fishlike manner and I simper back at them, weakly.

"How do you mean, 'translating'?" I ask Millie. "Surely those weird noises can't have been a language?" But silent glee begins seeping into my bloodstream. Can she really have swallowed it?

"Tricia Brilov is an actual professor of languages, Gerry. You've probably heard of her. She's a distinguished academic as well as a founder member of Neptune. She was the first person

I thought of when you sent me that wonderful CD, her being so brilliant." (Really, these autodidacts' reverence for anyone with some two-bit Ph.D. to their name! It's high time I began flaunting my A levels, gained at a time when they awarded them to people who could actually read and write and didn't think "good' was an adverb.) "She spotted at once that those apparently random noises really are a language. What do you think of that?"

"I'm amazed," I say truthfully. "But if it's a language, who is it talking down there at the bottom of the sea? Many experts believe this is impossible."

"Exactly!" Millie cries triumphantly. "The answer to that question could be the most important piece of knowledge the human race has ever been given. It could be absolutely crucial to our future and to the planet's survival. Tricia's partner, Isolde Tammeri, is her ex-student and a visionary of genius besides being a brilliant scholar herself. She at once confirmed it. Some kind of speech is going on down there and at the moment we can only guess at who or what might be responsible."

I am fascinated by this drivel as I am by a tiny scarlet fish that blunders into Millie's hollow thumb, turns around and bumps into a knuckle from inside. From where I'm standing the confusion of polycarbonate and Waterford crystal is such that I almost expect the animal to start swimming up the stem of the glass she's holding and choke to death in her gin and tonic.

One of Queen Neptunia's courtiers is nodding, a blond girl with a pronounced overbite and exopthalmic blue eyes. Just as I might notice a well-stuffed pair of jeans, I notice she is sporting a well-stuffed white T-shirt inside her black leather jacket. "It's incredibly exciting what Tricia and Isolde have translated so far," she assures me in the tones of Roedean or Cheltenham, managing to sound cool yet flirty at the same time. "True, we can't yet understand everything the voices are saying, but we're certainly getting a sense of it. I don't know how familiar you are with the field of logogrammatic assay, but standard linguistic techniques of bitword-frequency analysis and Junghans semantic algorithms have yielded some really suggestive stuff—more than enough to prove there's nothing imaginary or fake about this."

Millie is gazing at her fondly. "That's Debra," she explains to me. "She's absolutely brilliant, too. Give Gerry a drink, Debra, and then you can read him some of the translation and let him decide for himself." She waves a gracious hand towards a mini-bar that might have been thrown together by the same Regency craftsman who was responsible for the TV console in the corner. From this cabinet a reassuringly generous g-&-t is conjured for me and I am offered one of the scrolled and fluted chairs. A respectful silence falls as Debra plants her feet and begins to read to us from a folder in her beautifully modulated voice.

"'Many, many fear and is torrential, torrents in tribe our ciderpress family beseech. Turnip flagons walls with holes oncoming, coming on flying, flying tribe under many fear. Fear, fear, many ciderpress holes.'" ("We're not yet absolutely sure 'ciderpress' is right. Or 'turnip,'" she confides in a scholarly aside.) "Er, 'ciderpress holes push on red clouds. Veins, veins press together cider, dark mottles shot in the bottom. The mother many fearful lost under bottoms. Torrential fear in devoted shell-drift. Torrential bottoms over and torments dead tribe. Oh tubby unpushed turnips! Oh flagons family!'"

There is a pause. As is usual at moments of other people's high seriousness I am concentrating on not laughing. What this gibberish instantly reminds me of is one of those alleged translations of the Voynich manuscript, a mysterious document that was probably written as a scam by an Elizabethan con man. The Voynich's Renaissance hand is deceptively clear and the words appear in the normal patterns of a language, yet the language itself remains unidentified despite the best efforts of scholars and linguists with all the help that computers can bring. It is almost certainly meaningless: a brilliant simulacrum of a text designed to trick Rudolf II into buying this apparently ancient and impenetrably mysterious book for his royal library. This has not discouraged several amateur sleuths from presenting their own "translations," all of which are precisely the kind of nonsense that Debra has just been spouting to her respectful audience. It was the word "veins" that reminded me of a fragment of one Voynich translation that goes: "It is clothed with veinlets; tiny teats they provide (or live upon) in the outpimpling of the veinlets." It seems to me that Tricia and Isolde's rendering into near-English of the electronic blithering of a load of transponders shares that exact outpimpling quality. What is it about veins, anyway? Debra is watching me with an indulgent smile.

"I agree, Gerry," she concedes. "At first hearing it does seem obscure. But these are spirit voices. When you've worked on the text and studied it and lived with it as we have, something of its true meaning starts to come through. As I said, we have our doubts about whether we've read all the words correctly, especially "turnip" and "ciderpress," and we're not quite sure about "flagons," either. At first sight they don't seem to have many connections with the undersea world. Still, it's obvious that the first sentence has to mean there is a family, a tribe, living in extreme fear. Fear of what? What else can "walls with holes oncoming" describe but fishing nets, probably drift nets? To underwater creatures the nets would seem to be flying through the air even as they themselves are flying—or fleeing—the oncoming nets. Now look at "The mother many fear lost under bottoms." If you visualize the sea creatures' world and look upwards towards the surface, what do you see but bottoms? The bottoms of ships, obviously, the trawlers and factory ships deploying the nets that threaten the mother. Just look at her anguished face—" and Debra nods reverently towards the picture on the wall behind Millie. "We think the 'red clouds' might also refer to ships' hulls, which are commonly coated with red antifouling paint. Actually, that was Millie's own idea. It's a brilliant insight because it makes complete sense without straining the translation. And don't forget that a 'bottom' is recognized maritime terminology for a ship, notably in the insurance business, so it's technically right as well. And now we can understand the intense fear in the 'devoted shell-drift,' which is obviously the Great Mother's marine family, who lament the 'dead tribe,' meaning those billions of sisters and brothers they have lost to the brutal international whaling and fishing fleets. What we have here is an impassioned cry of anguish by the creatures of the sea who are hurting from the savage despoliation of their habitat. The kingdom of Neptune, if you like."

Debra pauses for breath, clearly moved by her own fervour. All eyes are on me except Millie's. Her attention is fixed on the little glittering creatures performing aquabatics in her arm: the Great Mother smiling at her flying tribe. My attention is taken by something else. In an awkward compartment of my consciousness an awareness has been growing that for no discernible reason Samper has acquired a stubborn erection. I take a grateful swig of gin.

"You don't think there may be some wiggle room in this interpretation?" I venture. "As it stands, it seems to leave out all the difficult bits. For instance, what was that stuff about mottled veins being shot in the bottom? It sounds more like a bad case of piles than a complaint about fisheries."

"Both Tricia and Isolde agree that sentence isn't fully clear at the moment," Debra says severely. "Still, it's obvious that whatever it means, it can't detract from the overall sense."

"That it can't." Lordy! Hook, line *and* sinker. Adrian will be ecstatic. Privately, I never really imagined that, uncanny as they are, those noises from the deep would fool anyone into believing they were made by living entities holding some sort of underwater discourse. I now appreciate that as a despairing marine scientist Adrian must be pretty familiar with Deep Blue thinking. And because he was around when the fundamentalist wing formed itself into the Loony Neptunies he would have understood much better than I that beyond a certain mysterious point any remaining ideological content in these movements becomes swamped by its nuttier members' sheer torrential outpimpling. Throw in a picture like The Face and suddenly Poseidon is back on his throne on the seabed somewhere off the Canaries, calling for an end to drift-netting with the voice of a transponder.

"Anyway," Millie says, still watching the tiny fish chasing one another in her forearm, "now they've broken the code so brilliantly the translation is coming along much faster. They hope to have the whole CD done by Christmas. But it's already clear what it will be. Yes—it will be repetitious. Of course it will, because it's a message to us, one that needs to be repeated over and over again until we arrogant humans understand it. It's both a cry of anguish, as Debra says, and a terrible warning we ignore at our peril. If it hadn't been for that moment of enlightenment, that sudden *satori* I was given when I was approaching the Canaries in *Beldame*, I, too, might still be oblivious to the awful damage we are doing our chances of survival on this planet. The sea is truly our Mother. It is She who ultimately gives us life. If we wreck Her, we will perish. Luckily, She spoke to me that night and told me not to fear, She would send me good winds and I was going to break the record. But in return She made it clear that I must make Her message known. She told me about the abominable slaughter of Her dearest children by longline-fishing fleets. It's truly appalling, Gerry. They catch all sorts of poor creatures other than fish, you know. Things like turtles and sea birds. Not even that magnificent wanderer, the albatross, is spared. Hooked, pulled under and drowned."

"So you might say these long-liners were committing alba-trossities?"

"*Really*, Gerry! I'm surprised at you. There's nothing remotely funny about it."

Her disciples mirror Millie's reprimand by jerking their heads slightly while making small sounds of disgust. No, Samper, this is not the way to win friends. You were right to wonder how unserious you can afford to be.

"I wasn't laughing," I protest.

"You made a bad joke of it, which is much the same."

"There are more ways of being serious than by being serious."

Millie looks at me pityingly. "Well, I agree it's hard for you to break with your old ways all of a sudden, Gerry. I myself have changed so much since writing my book with you and it's wrong of me to expect you to have done the same. But I promise the more we work together the more you will understand." Her attention is again caught by a tiny fish like polished shrapnel moving in her arm. I have to admire the old girl: her brachial aquarium is a real showstopper. "Look at that," she says in a hushed whisper. "It's like a flake of pure light. Sheer miracle."

Time for Samper to strike back. "Hardly that, surely," I say in a crotchety, rational tone. "Just evolution."

"You sound just like a scientist, Gerry," says Millie. It is not a compliment.

"Who, me? No, more of a cook, really. But thanks to you, dear Millie, in the course of *helping* you write your book I did meet quite a few scientists, so I suppose I must have picked up bits of this and that. Still, I can't help agreeing with the character in Norman Douglas who found everything wonderful and nothing miraculous."

"I have never heard of your Mr. Douglas," says Millie with a touch of her former Lady Bracknell. "But we mustn't be too hard. As I say, it's early days yet and I'm absolutely certain that when you know more about the true nature of the ocean you, too, will find your scepticism dissolving and will come to understand how miraculous it is. And that is the only word for it." She turns to her disciples. "Gerry and I get on famously, of course. But just now and then he loves to be provocative. I expect it's good for me, really, to be teased a bit. And we must none of us forget it was Gerry who introduced me to the Mother and Her message."

Everyone instinctively looks towards the flower-decked icon on the wall. It glowers back in an abstracted fashion, or as well as something entirely imaginary can. For the first time I notice a faint resemblance to whoever it was in Edvard Munch's painting before he or she quite pardonably began screaming.

17

Civilized readers will naturally be familiar with the scene towards the end of *The Magic Flute* where Tamino is about to undergo the last part of his initiation ritual and is confronted by two men in black armour, the eighteenth-century version of Men in Black. Against the steady tread of an orchestral fugato these two guardians intone in octaves the chorale melody *Ach Gott, vom Himmel sieh' darein*. In this way the music calls on God to look down from heaven and be merciful while the MIBs sing, "He who wanders these streets deeply troubled will become pure through fire, water, air and earth."

This captures pretty well my mood as I escape the Dorchester and walk in the direction of Marylebone High Street and Derek's flat. "Deeply troubled" is about right. When Adrian and I had planned our prank with the CD up at Le Rocce it never occurred to me that my future and fortune could ever depend on writing a final book for Millie Cleat. It's clear the prank has worked all too well. Not only has Millie been taken in, she seems entirely to have lost her marbles over it. I've never seen anything as preposterous as this superannuated old sailswoman standing there wearing a rubber dress and a false arm with fish in it, playing Queen o' the Fathoms while acolytes read out nonsense masquerading as revelation. Bad as it was working with Millie in her role as everybody's beloved sporting granny, it would be inconceivable to work with her in her newly transfigured state. A literary whore I may be, but even whores need to draw the line somewhere. So what began as a prosecco-fuelled joke has turned into an instance of Samper shooting himself in the foot or even, taking a cue from the Great Mother herself, in the bottom.

The awkwardness of my recent departure from Millie's suite is another reason to feel troubled, although in this case only mildly. In other circumstances it might have been comic. Yet it isn't easy for your middle-aged man of parts to get to his feet to take leave of all-female company while sporting a woody fit to poke a hole in his Stiff Lips jeans. And this, it goes without saying, without the faintest promptings of libido. It is hard to imagine a less erotic milieu than the one I have just left. No, it was a purely physiological event, like a touch of cramp, and equally hard to conceal. Not since the days of being suddenly invited by a teacher to stand up in class was it so necessary to perform odd contortions. Luckily, tonight I'm wearing a rather exquisite cashmere jacket (by Heavens To Betsy) which is long enough to have allowed crafty twitchings and drapings as I stood up. I don't believe anybody noticed anything except the blond girl Debra—she of the receding lower jaw and alleged linguistic brilliance. I can feel myself blushing even now at the memory of those pop eyes fixed on my discomfiture. Only once I had walked downstairs, run the gauntlet of the Dorchester's liveried doormen and passed into the night did I discover that the crisis below my supple Ferragamo belt was over and things were back to normal.

It is actually a fine October early evening and rush hour has elided seamlessly into night life. There is a sense of people hurrying towards undisclosed pleasures. I am not one of them. I solemnly tread the streets of Mayfair, determined there shall be no ordeal by water in store for me. I really had had no idea that Millie would have changed so much in a few months. I find myself looking back almost nostalgically to her former self: the sporting superstar with the hard-boiled egoism and inspired lack of irony who made my life hellish for well over a year.

Retrospectively, even that persona was preferable to her present incarnation as Our Lady of the Aquarium, able via interpreters to speak for the downtrodden creatures of the sea. "Ciderpress holes push on red clouds," forsooth. I'm surprised she hasn't got her busty acolyte Debra busy on translating the monosyllabic fish in that Regency tank of hers. No doubt she would claim they weren't saying *ob*, but *Om*.

No—it's too much to swallow, and too sudden. I'm remembering her husband Clifford in that peculiar pub out Hendon way, surrounded by displays of cricketing weasels and saying, "She won't retire from the limelight if she can help it," adding that he dreaded to think what she might do to stay in it. I bet goddesshood would qualify as living up to his liveliest dread. But the fraudulent old amputee can't fool me. You can't get to know somebody well enough to write their biography without acquiring a fair sense of what they themselves think is fit for public consumption. There's a thinnish line between a careful crafting of the facts and the invention of a largely spurious image. Millie crossed this line blithely and often enough to suggest that her current Queen Neptunia act is an act. I wouldn't mind if in private she had the grace to confess as much, and she still may. After all, who's she fooling? It's all showbiz: sport, politics, war, art, religion, you name it. The times demand we all be thesps in our way. But I suspect she won't come clean. Millie is always entirely the person she's playing: it's part of her single-mindedness. Whatever international worship accrues from her new role as the sainted figurehead of Deep Blue environmentalism, it will only intensify her conviction. Nor do I think she will easily be deposed from her new throne or dismissed with indulgent smiles as the Brigitte Bardot of dolphin sanctuaries. We might have to stake all on unmasking her as a delinquent sailor. But even this, newsworthy as it would be, is beginning to seem a long shot.

The question is, where does all this leave Samper, other than crossing Wigmore Street and feeling hungry? By the time I finished writing *Millie!* I felt compromised enough. But in order to write the sequel for much fine gold it will be necessary to resist the urge to lop off, excise and suppress, otherwise by the end there will be nothing left and I shall be like a cosmetic surgeon leaving the operating theatre after a long day's work, lugging a pail of polyps and wrinkles. Only in this case they will be exactly the bits the patient wanted left. I suddenly discover that I really do need the advice of an affectionate ally, which means speaking to Adrian as soon as possible and preferably seeing him. That it hasn't occurred to me until now shows how preoccupied I am. There's no time to lose. One way or another I must reach a decision before calling Queen Neptunia by the end of the week, as arranged.

Being so close, I make a small detour to pass Wigmore Hall, recent scene of Pavel Taneyev's recurring trichological crises disguised as Bach recitals. Judging by the notices outside, tonight's lucky audience should be in the middle of rediscovering its rural roots in a concert called "The Abandoned Ploughboy." This is described on the playbills as "an evening of songs by Finzi, Butterworth, Warlock and Quilter" (poems by the usual bucolic tragedians, Hardy, Housman *et al.*), sung by the celebrated Welsh baritone Brian Tydfil. Pride of place in this sumptuous spread of cherry trees and proud songsters (for which Emmeline Tyrwhitt-Glamis would have given you a good recipe) is a setting by Butterworth of Hardy's poem "The Knacker's Yard," the uplifting opening of which is printed on the playbill as an enticement:

"She's ploughed the headlands morn to dark
These twenty years, has this old girl,"
The knifeman says, hiding the blade
Along his leg. "We boys for a lark
Called 'un the Mare o' Casterbridge . . ."

All about the First World War, really, if we did but know it.

But there is something about the plangent recital even now going on inside that I know connects up with Millie and her ecobabble, if only I could work out how. I think it has to do with the Humanities bleating on about the essential humanity of nature so that art claims to speak for all the world that matters: the hapless priapism of a race constantly aroused by itself. The point about Millie is that her apparently loony position is obviously commonplace, even mainstream in less intellectual quarters. It's all based on agonizing about what we're doing to the world as if we weren't part of it, as if we didn't have exactly equal status with bacteria, barracudas and birch trees. Adrian tells me ninety-nine per cent of all the species that have ever lived on earth are now extinct. We're worried we'll soon become another of them and have become gracelessly obsessed with ourselves as the chosen race with the power to make or break the planet. And none more graceless than Millie's Loony Neptunies. Of course! Who cares that I stand deserted by the Men in Black with their promise of mystical enlightenment? I'm mesmerized by this playbill outside Wigmore Hall in which I can suddenly see a miniature version of our species' central problem. No wonder ploughboys become abandoned, poor dears. Lesser writers than I have sometimes taken as much as ten and a half chapters to write a history of the world. Samper can do you a history of *Homo sapiens* in a mere two sentences. They go as follows: The human race made itself King of the Beasts until there were no beasts left in the kingdom. Then one day in a fit of boredom it fought itself to the death, and won.

There, you see: a little *bonne bouche* of a fable, complete with moral sauce. That's lit. for you. And Greens and Blues and Neptunies. Meanwhile, inside the hall I would guess the Sweet Singer of Wysiwyg (for such, one gathers, is Mr. Tydfil's birthplace) will be well into some exquisite Georgian anguish along much the same lines, but tailored to the plight of the individual. For this is a world of solipsistic lament and the tragic inconvenience of having the wrong-coloured hair. ("*You should be so lucky,*" I can hear Derek's Pavel exclaiming.) Not tragedy, just genes and programmed cell death, just normal apoptosis. But Finzi and Housman don't do apoptosis, they order up tears:

> The lads have gone from Bredon,
> And nevermore shall heed
> How they themselves are peed on
> Who once on Bredon peed.

Ah me. *Eheu fugaces.* Alas, the fleeting years slip away . . . Which reminds me that I'm suddenly abominably hungry. I have not much confidence in there being anything of an edible nature in Derek's sordid little flat so I head for a toothsome bistro I remember up towards Marylebone Lane, only to discover a demolition site in its place: a tall yellow crane with a wrecker's ball hanging from it like an undescended testicle. Alas, the fleeting bistros slip away. Yet I'm not quite desolate because somewhere in these last ten minutes I may unexpectedly have taken a modest step towards an argument with which to face Millie, and therefore my immediate future. Within a minute I come upon a small restaurant pretending to seafood where I am urged by the waiter to try the squid. In due course I find myself tackling a tepid mound of fan-belt offcuts. Never mind, they also serve prosecco, and in between dealing with the fan belt and thinking about making my living I find that by the end I have consumed two entire bottles and feel a good deal better. My jaws aching, I pay for it all with my UK bank's much-touted Connect Card, based on an idea by E. M. Forster. Literature has its uses.

*

Two days later I am in Southampton, heading on foot through Dock Gate 4 towards the *QE2* terminal but soon peeling off in the direction of the block that houses Adrian's office in the British Oceanography Institute. I'm in high spirits at the prospect of seeing him, which as ever puts me in good voice. It is one of those days when lieder have it over opera hands down. Less grandiose? More private? Having just watched some very English fields speed past the window of my train from Waterloo, and doubtless still under Wigmore Hall's influence, I find myself choosing my namesake Gerald Finlock's music to express my cheerful mood. Unless it's by Peter Quiltworth? I do sometimes confuse them. Whoever it's by, "The Knot" is exquisite, starting like a gazetteer and ending with a tear.

> From Ludlow to Church Stretton,
> From Plaish to Acton Scott,
> The pretty lads would bet on
> The first to tie the knot.

> Once spoke a lad from Haydon:
> "I'd sooner lie in hell
> Than meddle with a maiden
> From Ashford Carbonel."

> We laughed and joked; but blighted,
> My hidden heart did sigh
> As one by one they plighted
> And home alone went I.

I notice some people giving me odd looks, but I'm used to the envy my voice arouses. It's thought perfectly all right in

Britain to set up a stall anywhere in public with some god-awful pop music blaring from loudspeakers, but singing as you walk, as people must have done for thousands of years, is looked on as mad, bad and probably dangerous. In Italy, of course, to sing in public is thought entirely natural; but then, they have a culture designed for human beings.

> I thought to hear their laughter
> As my own knot I tied
> And the noose beneath the rafter
> Swung dancing side to side.

> The lads who once were pretty
> Laughed from their marriage bed:
> "How can you write a ditty
> If you're already dead?"

Good question. But music banishes such nitpicking. Even as I hit that final, artfully skewed F sharp. I'm conscious of ambient interference. I round a corner and the building I'm heading for is besieged. A surge of people shouting and waving placards is narrowly divided like the Red Sea by bovine policemen and steel barriers. Bona-fide visitors, having established their credentials via a policeman's radio, are evidently required to walk between these foaming protesters. Fortunately, Samper is blessed with aplomb, and to be denounced at close range as a murderer and a torturer is water off a duck's nose or no skin off its back or something. How very much more offensive it would be if one were publicly accused of having bad breath or not knowing how to make a roux. I saunter provocatively towards the doors at the end of this corridor of bellowing yahoos. The jiggling placards turn my way like pallid sunflowers as I pass: Save Our Soles!, Eels *Feel*!, Hands Off Urchins!, West Sussex Thalassarians Unite!, Open The Cages!

"What on earth?" I ask Adrian, who has bravely come to meet me at the door. I notice he isn't wearing his white lab smock. Bravery has sensible limits.

"Just our daily maniacs," he says. "Are you O.K.? Sorry, Gerry—I should have warned you. We've almost got used to it here, even though they're no longer a joke. They're getting dangerous. They tailed a junior colleague home last week and threw bags of blood over his children. It was stinking stuff they must have got from an abattoir and left to rot."

"Who are they? And why here? You're oceanographers, not vivisectionists."

"I know. But we've got some animals in tanks in the labs here. One of my colleagues is working on oxygen transport in nautiloid blood so she's got a few cephalopods in a pressure chamber. Stuff like that. And over in the other block they're doing a lot of work on fish hatchlings so they've got vats of those. Essential research if we're ever to stop catching wild fish and rely on proper sustainable farming, but you can't tell these animal-rightists that. We're Nazi experimenters in here. Hey, it's great to see you. You're looking well, I must say." We pass two people chatting by a water cooler and Adrian's tone changes to breezy extrovert. "Still Mr. and Mrs. ProWang's model patient, are we?"

"Foucault's bloody pendulum, mate." Heartiness seems to be natural science's protective colouration. Adrian's ability to make me blush is among the reasons I feel affectionate towards him. To know someone well enough to embarrass him bespeaks a certain intimacy. I don't completely relax until we're safely through the door marked "Dr. A. Jestico." I note his yellow oil-skins still hanging inside. It's nice to discover a mild fetish on the brink of forty. Over a mug of something made from a jar of brown dust we catch up on the Millie saga. I explain my predicament. "So you see, I just need to write this one book and then I shall be able to afford to give up ghosting. But she's so far over the top these days I don't see how I can write it. At the very least I should have to pretend to take this Neptune lark seriously. How can I possibly manage that? I shall be exposed as an impostor, corrosively cynical, or else as an enemy mole in their midst . . . Really, Adrian, this coffee is unspeakable."

"But it's got the British Institution's Coffee kitemark. It's all very well being a Tuscan coffee snob, Gerry, but—"

"But nothing. There's no excuse these days. Proper ground coffee is everywhere available for ready cash. All you need is an electric ring and a little Bialetti percolator. If you can measure gas pressures in squid blood you can jolly well make decent coffee. This is not rocket science."

"I like it when you're cantankerous."

"Surely *nobody* these days slurps mugfuls of Nescafé as though they were trapped in a social-science department in the late seventies?"

"This is a government research department in the mid-noughts. Why should anything have changed? We British are conservative in our tastes and proud of it. When in Rome, drink espresso. When in Southampton—"

"Yes, yes, I get the message," I say testily.

"Revenons à nos moutons, or rather à nos Neptunies, did you notice they're well represented outside this building?"

"I was too busy being insouciant but I can believe it. As a movement, they're chock full o' nuts. Also, had you realized they're divinely inspired? That CD plan of yours worked too well."

"Your plan, I thought?"

"*Our* plan, then," I graciously allow, and give Adrian a vivid account of the scene in Millie's Dorchester suite the other evening. He is incredulous, which speaks well of his rationality but less so of his knowledge of the wilder fringes of human nature. Scientists can be charmingly naïve. After all, plenty of them believed Uri Geller could bend spoons by psychokinesis.

"It surely never occurred to us that they would mistake those noises for actual voices," he says. "We thought it would give a vivid impression of the uncanny and the unknown in the ocean. I mean, how can you translate electronic bleeps into *speech*?"

"Who knows? People spend their lives trying to break the codes of lost languages like Etruscan and Linear B and those Easter Island inscriptions, Rongorongo or whatever it's called. If you're determined from the start that transponder noises are really voices bequeathing wisdom instead of electronically generated data streams, then no doubt if you apply enough algebraic and statistical processes some sort of patterns will emerge that you can decipher."

"And if the messages are pure gibberish?"

"So much the better, because they need interpreting. Think of the Sibyl. Opacity is a prime requirement of the divine."

Adrian muses behind his desk. "When do you want us to go public with our film of Millie ruining EAGIS, then?"

"Oh, not yet," I say in alarm. "The book's coming out this week and we need to rack up some sales. Besides, if *Millie!* does well it can only increase interest in her, even give it some depth. The higher she goes, the further to fall and all that. Much better if we wait for the most damaging moment. Don't worry, we'll recognize it when it comes. By the way, what news of your illustrious brother-in-law?" (for one likes to keep more than one eye cocked to the future).

"Max? He's fine, I think. He's in America at the moment. Concertizing, as they say over there. Boston? Chicago? Jen tells me he'll be back shortly."

At this moment Adrian's phone rings and I turn to the notice board on the wall and the increasingly flyblown image of The Face saying "I can see your bow thruster!!" in the drawn-in speech bubble. As one who was recently privileged to learn professors Brilov and Tammeri's version of what the voice of the deep is really saying, I feel the bubble ought to be amended to read "Watch out! Torrential bottoms over!"

"*That's* good news, anyway," says Adrian, hanging up. "We've got a salvage ship on charter in Gibraltar, sailing tomorrow to see if it can raise that container-load of transponders."

"I thought you said it wasn't worth the expense?"

"It wasn't then. But we've since been in touch with the U.S. manufacturers. Apparently those batteries have at least a year's life in them and the din they're making is going to disrupt too many equally expensive research projects. Scientifically, it's quite a live area down there in the Canaries. So we've joined forces with some other oceanography centres in Germany, France and Spain and have agreed to split the salvage bill. Let's hope it works."

"If it does, someone's going to have to explain Neptune's sudden silence to Millie and her groupies."

"A job perfectly suited to your diplomatic talents, Gerry," Adrian says with the weightless sympathy of someone wishing an old friend well at the dentist's.

"You're a fat lot of help. What on earth am I to do? Not about the transponders, I mean *do*. About this book Millie wants written. About spending months having solemn conversations like the one I had at the Dorchester with people like the demonstrators outside this very building."

"That's simple. Grit your teeth and think of the money. Then when you're rich we can rush off to Las Vegas or Stockholm and get married and I need never work again."

"Be serious." But he *is* serious, it seems. Not about getting married, obviously—a nasty bourgeois business—but about gritting my teeth. I remonstrate feebly until at twelve-thirty a tall, bespectacled man in his late forties or early fifties wearing a stained tie breezes into the office. Adrian glances at his watch, springs to his feet and introduces him as Nick Vatican. He's new to me: not one of Adrian's colleagues I interviewed last year. True, it's not a very memorable face but I would never forget that name.

"Nick's head of our Cold Ocean Sciences department," Adrian explains. "One of our senior boffins who add lustre to this establishment. Never let it be said you came down to Southampton without meeting the quality. I should have warned you we're going out to lunch with him. He has disgusting table manners and a way with women."

"You're just jealous, Adrian," says this newcomer. "You too could have table manners like mine if only you'd loosen up." He turns to me. "So you're the writer who knows all about Millie Cleat, eh? That's exactly what we need here, some inside information. You saw those Neptunies out front? Bastards. Hey listen, you guys, the barf-barge awaits."

He leads the way through a warren of corridors and out the back of the building to the BOIS wharf. The breeze off the Solent buffets open our unbuttoned jackets and my nipples erect to meet the challenge.

"This is what we're driven to these days," Nick explains as we descend a ridged gangplank to a waiting motor launch. "There are perfectly good pubs up the road. But since the loonies took up residence outside the front it's as much as our lives are worth to go out that way. So we use our launch to escape. There's a very decent little pub across the water near Netley."

I'm sorry to hear it. After the civil sobriety of the Italian bars I'm used to I'm no great admirer of British pubs. Even when they're not actually carcinogenic with tobacco fumes they tend to have been gutted by the brewers, provided with new antique interiors in vinyl and given arbitrary and whimsical names like "The Leaking Marmoset."

"I hope you're a good sailor," murmurs Adrian as we go aboard the rocking craft. "This onshore breeze has put up a bit of a chop. Get inside the cabin, otherwise we'll be soaked. It's only a few minutes."

We wait for several more rumbustious scientists to pack aboard, then cast off. Glimpsed through thick panes the bristly water thuds and scuds as it flashes astern. The small cabin flickers with crumbling shadows. For the first time in my ill-starred relationship with Millie Cleat I can understand without effort the allure of moving swiftly over the sea even if the water we're crossing is largely fresh, brought down by the river Itchen. But the smell off Southampton Water is good and briny: the restless, aerated smell of travel. For a disloyal instant I wonder how much longer I shall be content to go on living at Le Rocce, reminding me that the urge to leave home is always there and will one day climb into my coffin beside me. The dis-content with contentedness sets the nibs of gurus and analysts scratching busily. Just when I was hoping it would last for ever the trip is over, we are climbing out and I must pretend to be hearty again. It's a good job Samper is a man of parts and can dissemble. I notice that not far out in the roads an immense white motor yacht is lying—a small ship, really, lustrous from radomes to waterline.

"A minor Saudi prince?" hazards Nick as he ushers us into Pegleg Dandy's, a pub whose interior is as relentlessly nautical as set-dressing can make it. The place is a riot of ship's wheels, binnacles, bells and Navy rum barrels, no doubt job-lotted in China in the same complex of factories that runs up horse brasses and corn dollies for English country pubs and, for all I know, cases of stuffed weasels for pubs in erstwhile Middlesex. If ever they find the Holy Grail it will have "Made in China" stamped on its base. When at length we're sitting with our obligatory pints and those strange English pies like roast Jiffy bags full of gravy, Nick asks what sort of pull I have with Millie. Adrian was quite right: Dr. Vatican's eating habits would make a hyaena appear dainty. Gravy is already spattering a ring around his plate like dollops of mud around a water hole.

"Pull? Nil, I'd think. Except that she does want me to write another book." I briefly outline the deal and my misgivings while Nick steadily widens the diameter of his water hole. "Why?"

"Professional interest. Self-interest, too. I'd like to know if there's anything we can do to get her to remove the pickets from BOIS."

"But I gather they're not all hers?"

"No. But that woman has recently acquired extraordinary clout. Practically overnight she's become the popular face of marine environmentalism. I should think she'd accept it's not going to do her image any good to be associated with righteous thugs showering small children with rotten blood. I must admit that until that EAGIS business I was a considerable admirer of old Millie. You know, one-armed granny sailing alone around the world and beating all comers. You've got to hand it to her: she was certainly different. What on earth's got into her?"

"I suppose what got into her were fame, fortune and Lew Buschfeuer, in reverse order. The better I get to know her, the more convinced I am he's the key to Millie."

"Cherchez le Lew, you mean?" says Adrian, rising. "Just as I'm about to do. Can I refill anyone on my way back?" He collects empty glasses and disappears. Nick has been polishing his plate with the side of his forefinger and licking it reflectively. It is now empty, surrounded by a ring of bright gravy. Methodically, he begins cleaning the table top around it in the same way. I charitably assume he has spent time either in prison or a decent public school.

"Do you know this Buschfeuer fellow, Gerry?" he asks, scrubbing vainly at his tie with a paper napkin.

"No. Oddly enough, I've never once met him. I've even wondered if this has been a deliberate policy of Millie's. Still, he's a busy tycoon."

"Another in the Rupert Murdoch mould, the papers say. An Aussie empire-builder. But what about her? What's she like?"

English draught beer may taste like thin glue but there is evidently enough alcohol in my pint to encourage indiscretion. "Ghastly. No, perhaps not ghastly, but I can't pretend I like the woman."

"Not like our Millie?" says Adrian, returning with fresh pints of glue and overhearing. "And you a product of this sceptred isle. This is treason. All the same, it can't be easy writing the biography of someone you don't like."

"On the contrary. The more you despise them the easier it becomes, especially when you realize they're even more venal than you are. Then you start to feel a slight affection, in a superior sort of way." I give Nick a thumbnail sketch of Millie's overweening vanity, ambitiousness and ruthlessness.

"The thing is," he says thoughtfully at the end, "I know all about her ruining that EAGIS survey, and I know exactly what most of my colleagues think about the Deep Blues and these Neptune idiots, and as a scientist I'm a hundred per cent with them. But had we thought she might actually turn out to be the ill wind that blows some good?"

"Radical, you see?" says Adrian to me. "Our pontiff here is radical. In a moment he'll bore you with the story about how his name comes from the Latin for the hill in Rome where the popes live. *Mons vaticinia*: the hill of prophecies. I do have that right, pontiff?"

"Correct, my son. It is for my God-given abilities as a seer that Adrian here invited me to have lunch with you today. When he told me you were Millie's biographer it made me give her some thought. After all, what she's doing and saying impinges directly on our lives and work as marine scientists, and I guess we oughtn't to become too knee-jerk about her. Granted, so far she's been a bloody nuisance. But I'm just about old enough to remember the beginnings of those social movements back in the late sixties, early seventies: black power, gay lib, women's lib—stuff like that. The thing they all relied on initially was consciousness-raising. Getting the inert mass of people to recognize the problem. It was in-your-face, it was embarrassing, it was humiliating. But in its messy, provocative way it worked, even though it was often on the very edge of causing a backlash. My point here is simply to wonder whether Millie mightn't have her uses as a consciousness-raiser about the sea. We don't necessarily have to approve her methods, but they may turn out to be effective."

"But isn't the parlous state of the oceans already a daily bleat in the world's media?"

"Yes," Nick agrees, "and daily bleats are no more effective than a nagging spouse. You switch off, don't you? Besides, what we're actually doing to the oceans is disastrous and brutal beyond anything the media say. Unfortunately, though, it's really only scientists like us who can give chapter and verse, and people tend not to listen to scientists unless we come with our hands full of miracle obesity cures or pills that will increase the human life span by sixty years. *Then* they'll listen. But not to yet more bad news from inaccessible parts of the planet they think have nothing to do with them. Really, we're in an impossible position: we get savaged for thinking we know too much, or we get dismissed for believing we know too little. The fact is, we know a lot more accurately about a lot more things than most people wish to hear. Believe me, it's hardly a pleasure for us each day to view from close up the steady decline of the oceans' larger biota."

Nick takes a deep gulp of beer and wipes his mouth on his tie. "Don't worry, this isn't a rant. I suppose I just wanted you to know that I'm not some wacky lone voice in this business. Adrian will bear me out when I say that virtually all marine scientists who study living things are environmentalists. And improbable as it may seem to animal-rightists, most of us come to love the creatures we study. I thought it might be worth suggesting that, even though they're nutty, Millie and these

Neptunies could still help spread the idea among ordinary landlubbers that we shouldn't go on savaging the oceans. God knows we scientists haven't yet got the message across. Now I'll stop. But I will have another pint if Adrian's paying."

18

B y the end of the week Samper is feeling emotionally unkempt, if not frankly despondent. He is sitting in one of those pointlessly expensive patisserie-cum-coffee shops that abound in Marylebone High Street, wondering how it is that espresso coffee made in England with an Italian coffee machine and using Italian coffee manages doesn't taste Italian. The machine's settings? The water? One of those trivial mysteries that so often displace weightier problems.

How I yearn to be home in Le Rocce. I think. Or maybe I just long to be free of my toad, of earning a living by such stupid means. How much more sense must life make in Africa or some place where the work you do is directly related to your survival. But nobody's working in this laid-back metropolis, not really working. Everyone's having coffee or shopping or just walking around in the glittery late-October air. Of course there are the huddled masses in their offices, but they're not working either. They're not planting potatoes or setting rabbit traps. They're gossiping as they process local authority forms, or dreaming up slogans to sell a new range of the same old chewing gum or hair lacquer, or writing drivelling speeches for the CEOs of drivelling companies. Supposedly it runs an economy but it makes no visceral sense. Deep down, we know our work is vacuous and unrelated to our survival. If we carry on we might get a small pension. If we stop we won't come close to starving. We've done nothing to deserve it but here we all are, drowning in food and goodies as though to the manna born. And one morning we're having overpriced coffee in Marylebone High Street, gazing unseeingly out at the frozen commotion of it all, and are suddenly overwhelmed by a disgusted urge to emigrate from the planet. At the same time we note the urge is not quite powerful enough to make us emigrate to Africa.

Even if I can argue myself into conceding that maybe the fatuous Millie might have her uses as a consciousness-raiser for the state of the oceans, do I really care? Of course I don't. It merely makes her all the sillier, vapouring on about spirits on the seabed as a sort of balls-aching metaphor for our commonplace awareness of consumer-led environmental ruin. We are the tribe with machetes. We will only stop when we run out of things to hack. The changes we've made are already irreversible. Fine. So let us concern ourselves with serious matters, like the horn parts in the 1841 version of Schumann's Fourth Symphony or the authenticity of the harmonium included in the posthumous edition of *L'uomo magro*.

What I'm really doing this morning is recovering from last night: another bizarre episode in what has come to feel like a lifetime of bizarre episodes. No sooner had I returned to London after visiting Adrian and his colleague in their scientific lair than I was summoned straight back to Southampton the next evening to see Millie and meet her Aussie mentor, the elusive Lew Buschfeuer. So wearily off I went again from Waterloo on yet another late-afternoon rail journey that gave me the opportunity to view firsthand Britons coming to terms with their chronic starvation, a sight by no means devoid of pathos. Once more I held myself aloof from the travelling rabble. It was only the second outing for my Blaise Prévert suit of chocolate corduroy and I preferred to stand and survey from a safe distance. As we set off I noticed my fellow travellers had to raise their voices to hear each other above the sudden storm of packaging being ripped frenziedly open and the tinny gunfire of ring-pulls.

Attentive readers who also take life's little ironies in their stride may remember that Millie had bought a house near Chichester, so they won't be amazed to learn that I was received on the very yacht we had seen at anchor from Pegleg Dandy's the previous day, the one we had assumed belonged to a Saudi princeling. I was met at the jetty by a cutter and whisked to the sugar daddy's personal ship, which grew in size as we approached until it towered overhead like the *Titanic*, although its lines were modern and so hideously unnautical it resembled nothing so much as a gigantic training shoe sitting on the water. As I trotted up the companionway of the *Vvizz* I was reminded of Jack Lemmon disguised as Daphne coming aboard Joe E. Brown's yacht in *Some Like It Hot*. The thought made me smile in anticipation. A steward in a white mess jacket escorted me to a lounge the size of a tennis court, wood-panelled and carpeted in green. What is it about chandeliers? *Titanic* again. But my attention was drawn to the twenty or so people standing around at the far end of the room in clumps. They were holding drinks and desultory conversation. I noticed some familiar faces, including that of the pop-eyed girl who had read out Brilov and Tammeri's inspired "translation" the other night and had beadily noticed my involuntary tumescence. Sandra? Debra? Barbra? Then I caught sight of Millie, who this evening was clearly regnant aboard her own royal yacht in her now established persona as Queen Neptunia.

Gone was the black rubber dress. Tonight she was sheathed in an evening gown of bridal white Lurex—or anyway some material woven with a sparkly thread. This time her mozzetta cape was gold satin. From under it her transparent right arm emerged, its water now tinted blue and full of some small white nektonic larvae that twisted like corkscrews as they swam, giving an impression of twizzling activity. She was surrounded by acolytes, including several thickset trousered ladies with gin-and-fo'c'sle complexions. I noticed one of them was going bald. Millie harpooned me with a look as I approached.

"Gerry!" she cried in the unnecessarily declamatory voice that people at cocktail parties affect. "Too good of you to come all this way."

Instead of only halfway, for instance? I shook her left hand rather than kiss the air beside her weather-beaten old cheeks with their riot of burst capillaries like a toper's nose. She indicated the balding lady.

"May I introduce Lew Buschfeuer? Lew, this is the famous Gerry Samper at last. I can hardly believe you two haven't already met."

"Gerry." His smile was friendly enough, at any rate. My having mistaken him for a moulting lesbian was explained by his being one of those men with fluffy cheeks who seem never to have shaved. Also, his way of going bald was not the traditional male pattern but an all-over thinning of wispy hair through which his sun-browned scalp gleamed in the light of his own chandeliers. He was a stocky figure wearing plaid slacks and a blazer. For a magnate of his calibre Lew was tastefully free of gold rings and hand-crafted chronometers waterproofed to nine thousand fathoms. In fact, he looked plausibly like the captain of a victorious women's golf team in the 1950s: confident and no-nonsense. "Welcome aboard." He gripped my hand as though trying to wring oil out of shale. "Congratulations, mate. Jist finished yer book. I don't pretend to have much literary taste but I reckon you've done the old girl proud."

The old girl, far from acidly putting her oar in to claim joint authorship as before, just stood there beaming while the spirochaetes milled in her arm. I made an effort to blush prettily and lie gamely.

"Thank you, Mr. Buschfeuer. It was an honour to have the opportunity."

The lady golfer frowned. "That's Lew, mate. There's no Mr. Buschfeuer on *this* ship. And there's just one Lew."

Resisting an opening like that is a mature skill and I returned his compliment by praising his yacht. If ever I become super-rich I can't imagine what I would spend my fortune on, other than ensuring that I never again write a book about anyone remotely connected with sport or popular culture. I really think it would never occur to me to own a private ship. Even a private aircraft would be less unlikely because at least that would mean my never again having to mix with the travelling public. Social emulsions are not for Gerald Samper, who is a niche creature par excellence. All the same, wealth of that sort presumably does lay one open to the envy and attention of criminals. I am still haunted by the image of poor Nanty Riah lying on the floor of his Lear jet, riddled about the rump by small-calibre bullets, watching thieves unscrew his Van Goghs. To own a private ship, though, would surely make one feel even more idiotically self-conscious. Imagine the sheer number of people needed to run it: the crew and staff whose sole duty would be to drive one person at whim about the world's oceans. I assume that is why wealthy yacht owners always seem to travel with a retinue of admiring guests, many of whom constitute a harem. At least these sycophants must dilute the embarrassment of being all alone on the ocean in a large ship, moodily looking for pleasure. Still, fundamentally silly as these playthings are, I couldn't help finding the *Vvizz* remarkable. Its flamboyant immensity and sports-shoe design somehow seemed at odds with its owner's unimpressive physical presence.

"I don't know how much Millie has told you about me," Lew was saying, "but the sea's in my blood. I was born to have my hand on my own tiller."

"She never mentioned that," I murmured.

"It's true, though. Like a lot of Aussies I was in and out of boats as soon as I could swim and I always wanted my own command. But I went into business and had some luck and you know how it is. The wealthier you become the less your time's your own, and it was getting so that months were going by without me even being able to take a day off to go for a sail round Sydney harbour. People think being rich opens all the world's doors, Gerry, but let me tell you it closes off just as many, especially the simple pleasures."

Ah, the poor wee plutocrat. My odious stepmother Laura, who worships God with a fervour worthy of a better cause, once informed me that it is easier for a camel to enter a rich man than it is for a needle to go through an eye, although it puzzled me at the time. I think she was quoting the Bible, a considerably opaque document whose text has always struck me as containing a high percentage of outpimpling and torrential ciderpresses. But she had definitely left me with the impression that life wasn't entirely a bed of roses for the rich, and here was Lew confirming it in a way that gladdened the heart.

"I guess it was Millie changed all that for me," he said. "We were two of a kind anyway, but just seeing what that lady could do with one hand made me ashamed at how much I couldn't pull off with two."

"She's certainly remarkably monodextrous," I agreed dutifully. "Although no matter how plucky and capable, she never could have done what she did without you, Lew. There was no way she could have afforded to build her own oceangoing yacht."

"The least I could do for her. As far as I was concerned we were shipmates from the start. Right from the moment I clapped eyes on her I wanted her hand on my tiller for the rest of my natural."

I couldn't have borne much more of this but there was suddenly a welcome distraction. A mess-jacketed steward had ushered in a late arrival: a small, egg-bald young man who was advancing across the acres of green carpet with a slight limp.

"*Nanty!*" I cried involuntarily. Talk of the devil. "What on *earth* are you doing here?"

"I invited him, what else?" came Millie's frosty voice from behind me. "But I didn't realize you two knew each other."

"Hi, Mills! Hi, Gerry, long time no see! Hi, Lew mate!" Nanty's greetings had the extravagant familiarity of someone far too famous to be socially rebuffed, or to care if he were. I noticed that although everyone in the room had glanced around, few appeared to recognize him since tonight he had come wearing nature's own disguise of total alopecia. Had he been wearing the blond wig he wore onstage most of those present would have known him at once as Brill, the lead singer of the boy band Alien Pie. To my certain knowledge Nanty was over thirty; but when nature takes away with one hand she sometimes gives back with the other, to the irritation of the majority from whom she only ever takes away with both. From enough feet away his face could pass for that of a teenager. Without his wig he looked for all the world like any other college kid who had shaved all his hair to piss off his parents. His exuberance and bonhomie were, I assumed, chemically induced. "So remind me: what's this you've got going here?" he asked, having been issued with a glass of something from a tray and raising it to Queen Neptunia. "A launch party?"

"That's just what it is," said Millie. "My book's out tomorrow and I shall be sitting all day in a London bookshop signing copies. The publisher says it will be a runaway best-seller. They're not usually wrong."

"Let's hope John Q. Public agrees. And it'll help keep old Gerry here in that stuff he was drinking up in that house of his in Italy. Fernet Branca, wasn't it? Let me tell you," Nanty said unnecessarily, given that nobody was trying to stop him, "that was just about the weirdest experience of my life. I mean, wacky or what? Blimey. UFOs disguised as helicopters, right out in the sticks up a mountain in Italy with a neighbour who was being porked by spacemen. I've never been so shit-scared in my life."

"Come on, Nanty, it was just a simple misunderstanding. There was a perfectly rational explanation for it all," I said, addressing Millie and Lew as much as my former house guest. I had never mentioned the episode to Millie and until a few minutes earlier I hadn't the slightest idea she and Nanty even knew each other. It was not obvious to me what a one-armed yachtsperson had in common with a hairless boy-band leader other than celebrity. Maybe these days that is common denominator enough.

"Nanty has turned out to be one of our most devoted supporters," Millie explained.

"You're a member of *Neptune*?" I asked him, not bothering to keep the incredulity out of my voice.

"Yah, you bet. Deep blue to the centre, that's me. Cool. Me and the boys are giving our services free in a couple of gigs to raise awareness. Gotta do something about these oceans, man."

I suppose I shouldn't have been surprised. Since I'd last seen him I'd managed to forget the strange mix-'n'-match ideological world he inhabited where Druidism segued into ufology which bled into New Ageism that incorporated deep ecology, any one of which might take precedence for a while depending on the guru he'd most recently met and the last psychoactive drug he'd taken. They have the attention spans of mosquitoes, these public figures, blown hither and yon by the winds of fashion, attracted as though by vagrant pheromones to alight briefly and suck up a draught of nourishing nonsense before pinging off for a different flavour elsewhere.

"So welcome to the club," Nanty was saying to me. "I didn't know you'd written this book about Millie until yesterday. Obviously you're one of us, Gerry. That's cool."

"Oh yes," chimed in Millie artlessly. "Gerry's one of our greatest and most loyal admirers. Right from the beginning he was an enthusiastic convert. In fact, he insisted on adding a chapter to our book which is going to be of the greatest importance to Neptune because it explains my spiritual side. That's the amazing thing about Gerry: his scope is so wide. He's also a person who instinctively understands the sports personality. It's extraordinary, seeing that he's not at all sporty himself. I mean, you only have to look at him" (and here she gave one of her famous laughs like smashed bottles pouring down a chute). "Yet his insight is uncanny. I don't know how he does it."

And that's how *she* does it. Any reader still wondering whether I haven't gratuitously blackened Millie's character out of sheer malevolence ought to note this unscrupulous farrago of lies, rudeness and moral suasion. Not to mention the liberal use of the royal "we."

"I'm with you, Mills," Nanty joined in. "He's just as good on musicians. Did you know we're going to do a book together? We got interrupted, though, when I got plugged in the arse. I've been meaning to get the project going again."

"Not before he's written *my* next book, though," said Millie firmly.

Lew caught my eye. "That's your future fixed, mate," he said with an amusement I didn't share. "Nobody says no to Millie."

High time somebody did, I thought in a considerable snit. The worst about being praised fulsomely is that it leaves no room for setting the record straight. To have attempted to deny any of her astonishing lies would only have made me sound insincerely modest. And to add injury to insult I had been aware for the last five minutes of a recurrence of my recent medical condition that was now obliging me to stand with one hand in my pocket with a great display of relaxed casualness. Glancing about me, to my horror I caught the pop eyes of Barbra or Debra or Sandra fixed on me. This was dire.

"I was really shocked to hear about your accident, Nanty," I turned hurriedly back to him.

"That was no accident, that was a carefully planned heist. Did you know the cops have got 'em?"

"The robbers?"

"Nah, not them. My Van Goghs, I mean. The Italians have these crack squads of fine-art detectives, right? They're hot shit, man. I don't know how good they are on your traditional bloodstains but give 'em a whiff of a pinched Picasso or a missing Monet and they're onto it like a shot."

"Talking of shots and bloodstains, what about you? Are you okay again?"

"Almost," said Nanty. "I've still got to watch how I sit down. I've got five holes in my bum, you know," he proudly informed the pre-dinner crowd around him, one of those pieces of information that really helps whet the appetite. "Two entry, two exit, and one dual-purpose. That one I've always had," he added gratuitously.

"The bastards *shot* you?" said Lew. "I hadn't realized that. That's a bummer."

"Sure was," said Nanty with a survivor's casualness. "Cheek to cheek. Twice. I swelled up like a splitting pumpkin."

"Dinner is served," announced an Aboriginal majordomo, turning as he spoke and raising a hand to draw attention to a piece of theatre. The wall behind us had divided and the two halves were silently withdrawing into the bulkheads to reveal a room hung with large works of Aboriginal art. Complicated snakes and salamanders full of spots predominated. I would have bet that the artists had been smoking something pretty potent as they drew, their brushes following tradition-hallowed patterns less songlines than bonglines. In the middle of this room was a gigantic round table, fully four metres across, much of it consisting of a Chinese-style lazy Susan. This black lacquered turntable was laden with quantities of odd-coloured food, not very much of which was instantly recognizable as edible. Beside each bone-white place setting on the periphery was a name, and with dismay I saw that an effort had been made to split up the sexes: a contrived and self-conscious practice if ever there was one, as though a dinner could double as a dating service. In this prandial lottery I had drawn on my left one of Millie's grizzled admirers who smelt strongly of dogs and gaspers. Her name was Joan Nugent. She had an anchor tattooed on her right forearm and I assumed she had once seen service as a Wren or something similar. And on my right, with remorseless inevitability, was busty old Popeye herself, revealed by her place card as Debra Leather. As the twenty-odd diners found their allotted seats, no doubt with impeccably stifled inner groans of social dismay, Debra made my own predicament clear.

"Gorgeous suit," she said in the tone of an innocently icebreaking compliment, running her great eyes lingeringly over Blaise Prévert's artistry.

"Thanks," I said gruffly as I endeavoured to slide contortedly into the chair beside hers. Suddenly I had good reason to regret my choice of clothes. Monsieur Prévert's corduroy is of exquisite softness and generously cut. Beneath it, Mr. and Mrs. ProWang's joint handiwork was of exquisite hardness and by no means as tidily confined as it would have been by my trusty Stiff Lips jeans. Veal revealed, in fact. I pulled my chair forward concealingly until my midriff touched the table edge. White-clad arms insinuated themselves between the diners and left behind tall glasses of Foster's lager. The dishes before us began to revolve slowly.

"Yer jist gotta grab it as it comes," came Lew's hearty admonition to his guests. "We don't stand on ceremony here. If you miss what you want it's tough titty and yer'll jist have to wait until it comes around again and hope it's still there. It's a bit messy but we're all shipmates here. We don't hold with formality aboard *Vvizz*, do we, old girl?"

I noticed he had his left hand thrust informally up under her mozzetta, presumably drawing strength from the thrilling and mysterious join where living flesh met polycarbonate.

"You'll have to be really careful not to splash that lovely corduroy, Gerry," Debra said. "I bet it shows every mark. Tuck your napkin into your shirt, I would, and sit well back. These buffet-style suppers are killers. What we all really need is a Big Dicky."

I nearly fainted. It took me a moment to realize she was merely referring quite harmlessly to a dickey, one of those false shirtfront things. But what malevolent fate could have put that dated phrase into her Neptune-cluttered head? As so often at critical social moments I sought refuge in food. When I had imagined myself coming aboard as Jack Lemmon's Daphne I had not unreasonably been thinking in terms of a private dinner for three, given that I'd been summoned from London for the occasion. I had been looking forward to a down-and-dirty but amicable discussion leading to some sort of agreement between Millie, Lew and myself as to exactly what they were expecting me to write, and the point beyond which I would not go. But in the present company of pop-eyed groupies, smoke-cured Wrens, boy-band leaders and white-jacketed Aboriginals I felt inhibited to the point of speechlessness. Add to that a thumping woody which for all its erotic potential might itself have been made of polycarbonate, and I was physically handicapped into the bargain. In the past Samper had occasionally found himself socially disadvantaged but seldom, I thought with a hot flush of rage, had he been so helpless a prisoner of circumstances. And all for what? Just so that he could write another damn-fool book? I stabbed moodily at a plate-load of rolled undergrowth in batter that was slowly drifting by.

"Don't forget the sauce," the ever-solicitous Debra was urging in her Roedean tones, drawing my attention to various silver pots of hectically coloured jam. "Spring rolls are made to be dipped."

"I'm in the market for something a good deal sturdier than bean sprouts," I said, casting hungrily about for suitable fare.

"The tofu will soon be coming around. Tofu's really good for you."

I can be unequivocal about tofu. As far as I'm concerned, eating things you dislike because you've been told they're good for you is about as silly as collecting things you're not interested in because you've heard they're a good investment. This is one of the many Laws of Samper.

"I never joke about food," I tell her. "What do you suppose that khaki sludge is?"

"Oh, that's delicious, Gerry. It's curried breadfruit from Bali. Lew always has it, it's a favourite. Go on—take some of that saffron rice and a good dollop of breadfruit. Quick, before it goes. Hurry! Oh. Tee-hee. Bad luck."

It is not a dignified way to dine, frankly, this snatching passing dishes at random from a carousel like some fairground challenge. The scene of my present disaster, whose puddled lumps on the table resembled something found under a lamppost in Piccadilly Circus after a rugby international, was pounced on and mopped up by Aboriginals before the dish was replenished with more of the same.

"Go for it, mate!" urged Lew from far away across the table. "Get stuck in, she'll be apples."

But I was waiting for great trenchers of grilled snapper or heaps of glazed spare ribs, and it was increasingly evident that I was waiting in vain. It reminded me belatedly that I was dining in the high temple of Neptunism and it was unlikely that any living creatures would have been permitted to make the supreme sacrifice for our pleasure. Trembling alps of semolina drifted past, pursued by heaps of knobbly pulses and a clutch of what looked like exploded leeks. All fine in their subsistence-level way, but needing something pretty dramatic to lift them onto even a modest plane of gourmet pleasure. In default of fatted calves I was still hoping for squid or tuna steaks. Instead, a gigantic tuft of deep-fried pubic hair swam into my ken.

"Oh, this you've really got to try, Gerry. It's a marvellous seaweed. I think it's a Fijian fucus. They say, *they say*, it's quite an effective aphrodisiac. Not that you'd need one, of course." And she actually giggled. Had she nudged me in the ribs I think I would have upended a passing tureen of strange puce broth over her blond head and stalked out, woody or no woody, career or no career. There are limits. Not, apparently, for her though, for at that moment I felt the hand with which she wasn't eating a Burmese bean pod begin to sidle across Blaise Prévert's foothills, heading peakwards. *Inconceivable.* Nobody behaves like that outside the movies or the pulpiest fiction. I brought my thigh up smartly against the underside of the table and sensed the satisfying crunch of knuckles. She gave a little gasp and dropped her pod.

"Oh, I'm frightfully sorry," I said. "I'd no idea that was you. I was just trying to get comfortable."

"Sorry, sorry, yes, and I was just trying to find my napkin. How embarrassing." She brought her crippled member into the light and inspected it tenderly.

"Maybe if you were to wrap something soothing around it? What are those things over there like bits of steamed tarpaulin? They've got a faintly therapeutic air about them, don't you think? I'm sure they can't be edible."

But the lady was licked. Apparently she was not about to drape her hand in Laotian water-hyacinth leaves or whatever they were. I began to feel very much better although still alarmed by my unyieldingly wooden state. Was it perhaps becoming ever so slightly painful? This was worrying because I had heard dreadful stories about priapism, such as that it could require urgent surgical intervention involving the insertion of large hollow needles for drainage. This is not something men like to think about. But at this point my tattooed neighbour Joan struck up in a confiding rasp.

"Something tells me you're not one of nature's vegetarians, Gerry."

"I'm not," I said briefly. "Neither am I ashamed of it. Most people are omnivores. You'd have thought that at least the odd shrimp might have found its way onto the table, wouldn't you? Perhaps even a hen lobster staring out wistfully from between her pink paws?"

"Keep your voice down." Her own was not unsympathetic. Her breath smelt of beer and nicotine, like the ancient mariner's on shore leave. "Even at boardroom level Neptune has its ideological differences, you know."

"It does?" I asked with faint interest. Maybe there was an article in this after all, even if not an actual book.

"Oh yes. One of them is raging at the moment, this business of what constitutes an ethical diet. Your dedicated Deep Blue wouldn't dream of eating seafood. The question is, what constitutes seafood?"

"Surely not seaweed." I nodded towards the bowl of green pubic hair, now much diminished.

"No. No one but the very deepest and dimmest ecologist thinks of weed as sentient. But I'm sure as a writer you're aware of the philosopher Peter Singer, who wrote *Animal Liberation*? He used to draw the line between animals that can and can't feel pain by saying that shrimps could and oysters couldn't. But I believe now he won't even eat bivalves. Personally, the idea of mussels in agony strikes me as a load of balls, but there we are."

"But I remember Millie telling me that on long voyages she used to spin for fish with a line over the transom. Anything for fresh food, she said."

"Of course. Any long-distance sailor does. Did you put that in your book?"

I tried to remember. "I think so, yes. But now you mention it, I believe it was one of those bits she cut out. I'd have to check."

"I shouldn't bother. She'll have removed it, bet you anything. This is all new, you realize." She indicated with her Bluto-like chin the food on the table and the assembled company, somehow even managing to imply the entire Neptune movement. Aha, I thought. Getting interesting. Of course: Millie's original groupies were fellow-sailors, not environmentalists, and some of them must be feeling badly upstaged by all these sudden new alliances. "Only a year ago we were having these bloody great fish banquets down in the harbour or on our boats. Whatever was fresh. Mackerel, sole, gurnard, tope, lobster, crab, you name it. Smashing nosh. We had great parties with the world's greatest sailor. But now . . . I wouldn't dream of giving my dogs most of this stuff. Not that they'd touch it. Got more sense."

Our voices had sunk to a conspiratorial murmur, lost in the general hubbub and Australian bonhomie as our eyes vainly raked the table for serious nourishment. A dismal floe of black jelly went mournfully by, highlights glinting from its quivering flanks.

"Christ," said my new friend with the ancient mariner's breath, "I miss those days, honest I do. And what's more, I bet old Millie does. I can't see this deadly purity lasting. Where's the moral issue, anyway? Fish eat other fish; big enough fish often eat us. Can't see why we shouldn't return the compliment. We're all animals and we all prey on each other. Right now I could prey on a decent steak-and-kidney pudding like the ones we used to get in the Navy after dives. Thick, rich gravy, suet and animal parts. That's the stuff to chase the cold away and put hair on your chest."

19

Having got so far with the admirably subversive Joan, I couldn't resist asking whether she knew about Brilov and Tammeri's translations of King Neptune's oracular sayings from the seabed. She shot me a warning look with a sideways glance at my neighbour on the other side, but Debra was now chatting earnestly to the moth-eaten man on her right.

"It's blithering bollocks, this food faddery," said Joan briefly, her square-tipped, nicotine-stained fingers closing conspiratorially about my wrist. "Not to mention the mystic stuff. It could be very damaging to Millie, you know, but I don't think she sees it. She played us a CD of these underwater noises and naturally I recognized them at once."

"Transponders?"

"Exactly. You've heard it too." She glanced at me sharply, obviously wondering how much I knew.

"Did you tell Millie that's what they were?"

"I haven't yet. It would have to be done at the right moment, and probably alone. You don't know where the recording came from, I suppose?"

"Not really," I said guardedly, and immediately regretted not having denied it outright. This lady who smelled of Sealyhams or spaniels was no fool. Nice as it was to believe one might have found an ally in this lair of lunatics, a breezy, over-the-dinner-table conspiracy might backfire fatally. I could easily be exposed as a traitor to my subject, who at the moment was being very queenly with Nanty over on the other side of the table. Her "aquariarm," as I'd heard her call it, was resting in full view by her plate and seethed with animal activity as though she embodied the very life-force of the ocean. Bogus old bat. The guileless Nanty seemed fascinated, possibly by his hostess's appalling oaths that occasionally ricocheted around the table. Meanwhile my pungent neighbour, like one of her own terriers, was not letting go.

"You know something, don't you?" she said nearly inaudibly. "Is someone setting her up?"

This was far too astute. I took a temporizing gulp of Foster's before replying.

"Oh no, I'm sure not. Why would they want to do that?"

"Ha! Don't be naïve. Politics, what else? This whole movement's a fucking minefield, pardon my French. Christ, you're her biographer. You must have discovered that by now."

"Well, of course," I said, a bit thrown by how far ahead this redoubtable old dyke seemed to be. "But basically my role is that of a hack. I write what I'm paid to write. The lady's an international sports personality, massively famous, much loved, blah-blah, and my job was to get her down on paper in a way that's going to warm the hearts of people who get given the book at Christmas by nephews who gave them golf balls last year. They're not an audience that appreciates complexity and they sure as hell don't want politics. They want a simple, straightforward heroine."

"Which she ain't. She's very much more."

"Agreed. And now I'm supposed to write another book about her and this whole Neptune business, and it's become dead obvious that it's politics up to the eyeballs."

"Too true. Me and the girls are none too happy about it."

"Let me guess," I said. "You think she'd do better to rest on her laurels as an outstanding sporting celebrity rather than risk derision if this Neptune caper blows up in her face."

"Something along those lines," my neighbour conceded. "As you must have noticed, dear Millie has an innocent streak in her. She can't believe that anyone as popular as she is might have enemies. But people are mean. You know—the tall poppy syndrome. There are plenty out there who want to see her cut down to size, believe me. Give you an example. The other week one of the girls here overheard some lunchtime table talk in a pub called Pegleg Dandy's. It's right across from where we're lying now. She thinks they were scientists from BOIS— you know, the oceanography institute here. It's a favourite place of theirs. One of them was speculating it would be possible to organize quite a neat smuggling racket using long-distance sailors like Millie. Diamonds, drugs, anything small and high value. All she'd need do is pick up a buoy dropped on her course and putting out a discreetly weak transponder signal. She could home in and pluck it out of the ocean while hardly reefing in. To be on the safe side she could hang it below the hull on a length of piano wire or nylon, just like the old Vietnamese boat people did back in the seventies when they were trying to get their valuables past the Thai pirates. Then she sails right over the finishing line and ties up. You've got TV coverage, cheering crowds, helicopters, a triumphal escort of a zillion yachts, interviews, the works. Who's going to bother with a customs inspection? Okay, some official might go aboard to satisfy the letter of the law, but he won't be thinking of contraband, will he? At most he'll be thinking of nicking a souvenir for his kids—Millie's sou'wester or something. Then later, when it's dark, a scuba diver comes and retrieves the bundle hanging underneath. Easy-peasy. She might not even have to pick the stuff up at sea: it could have been aboard from the start, even unbeknownst to her. All sorts of ways to work it, according to these scientists in the pub. Easy enough to put a rumour around, heh-heh. And it would be, too," said Joan. "No lack of folk wanting to believe it. I'm told Millie has acquired some dedicated enemies at BOIS, though I don't know why. Frankly, if she's put some of their delicate scientific noses out of joint, good on her, I say."

"She'll be all the easier to attack if she's seen to make an ass of herself over Neptune."

"Exactly."

All this was highly interesting, but I could no longer deny that my body was now demanding immediate attention. Oh dear, oh dear. For over the past hour my passionless protuberance had lurked at maximum elevation like a field gun beneath camouflaged netting and was now undeniably aching. As I had reflected at Crendlesham Hall, Italian habits and elapsing years between them have done much to ease my embarrassment at minor social crises (and which historical character was it I'd recently read about who, rather than excuse himself from the king's table, had sat there and allowed his bladder to burst, dying shortly afterwards?). I had no attention of suffering silently for etiquette's sake. Still, priapism does rather flaunt its own banner, the *Excelsior!* touch that gets its bearer noticed, whether by pious monks or Deep Blue environmentalists. But there was nothing for it. With a muttered excuse I stood up and turned quickly from the table, thereafter sauntering for the exit, one hand casually in my pocket. I don't believe I gave Debra a chance to focus those pop eyes of hers before I was out of range. Dusky gentlemen in white jackets pointed me through various doors before I arrived at one I could bolt on the inside. From within I conducted an alarmed inspection. This, then, was my punishment for having meddled with nature in the interests of science. The orchic substances were taking their revenge. It is unnecessary to go into detail but I admit I was shocked by my howitzer's appearance. The single adjective "empurpled" will convey everything of importance. Cold water appeared to help a little but I could hardly spend the rest of the evening leaning over a brimming hand basin aboard *Vvizz*. To think that my jocular experiment should have led to public humiliation and the dishevelling of my endocrine system! A ditty chants satirically in my mind:

> Amazing Disgrace, that I should fall
> A victim to my glands!
> That is now gross which once was small,
> What slept doth hotly stand!

I am referring here, of course, to my shame. I dried myself and left, and almost immediately met someone who might have been an off-duty officer. A dapper young man except for shoulder-length hair, he peered at me.

"Yer looking a bit crook, mate, if yer don't mind my saying. Can I help?"

"No, no," I said wanly. "I was having dinner and, well, I just thought I wouldn't mind stretching my legs."

"Up to you, but why not see the doc? Be on the safe side, you know?"

"There's a ship's doctor?"

"Sure is. You need one on a vessel this size. We've a crew of nearly thirty and there's Lew himself. Come on, I'll show you. Won't take a second."

He led off down a companionway, along a broad corridor, and knocked on a door. He must have heard an invitation to enter because he opened it, stood aside, said, "Guest feeling crook, Doc," and waved me in. I found myself in a brightly lit cabin. The door closed behind me.

"You're the, er, doctor?" I asked unnecessarily. She looked like a *Playboy* centrefold wearing a black leotard, sitting in front of a computer.

"G'day," she said and rose courteously to her feet. Or rather, to her foot, since her right foot was completely absent. I then noticed on the floor beside the desk an exotic pair of trainers, the right one being a racily designed orthopaedic job trailing Velcro straps. "I'm Steffi Toms. What's the problem?"

What indeed? "Well," I began cautiously, "I'm not really ill at all, you understand, doctor. I'm dining with Lew and Millie and . . . er, this *is* in confidence?"

"Absolutely. If it's about your health, that is."

"Um." All my worst premonitions about turning into a medical curiosity seemed to be coming true even though I was still clad in chocolate corduroy rather than a paper gown. "The fact of the matter is I seem to have acquired—only temporarily, I'm sure, and for no obvious external reason in the sense of the usual stimulation—a . . ."

"Yes?" she offered encouragingly. "Mr. . . .?"

"Oh, sorry: Gerry . . . An intractable erection." There, that wasn't so bad. Now, so long as she wasn't going to be breezy.

"How long?"

"About, er . . . oh, you mean *time*? The last hour and a half. Give or take."

"Any pain?"

"Far less than agony; rather more than discomfort."

"A very British answer." She smiled. "Sorry. It's just that I'm sure no one but an Englishman would have put it quite that way. We'd better have a look. These things need prompt treatment." Dr. Toms put on a pair of latex gloves, snapping them with relish. The distant sound of a zip. I stared numbly at the row of books beside her desk. *Famous Medical Errors* was one of the titles I registered. "Ah yes. Characteristic softness of the glans but rigidity of the corpus cavernosum. Classic stuff."

"Oh, that's all right then. You know how patients worry that theirs won't be a straightforward case. And I don't see why that shouldn't be 'cavernosus.' Corpus being masculine, I mean. And nominative."

"Don't gibber, please, Gerry. This is serious. It needs draining immediately. But before we declare a full-out emergency you might try a simple remedy that sometimes proves effective. Find some stairs and climb them for five minutes. It might do the trick. Failing that we'll call an ambulance and get the launch to take you over."

"Up and down stairs?" I said, gratefully zipping up Blaise Prévert.

"Yes. I suggest the ones you would have taken down to the dining room. They're nice and wide with good handrails. Get climbing, Gerry. By the way, 'corpus' is neuter, so 'cavernosum' is perfectly correct."

Which is how, when the first batch of dinner guests started to leave, they found me plodding wearily up the same flight of stairs, turning at the top and plodding down again, merely to repeat the process. To forestall questions I announced that this was an old naval punishment for leaving the table without the captain's permission. There was some dutiful laughter but I didn't care what they thought, and particularly not Debra Leather, who was giving the hang of my trousers the attention of her large blue eyes. I didn't care because for whatever hydraulic reason, Dr. Toms's emergency measure was proving effective and I was fast regaining the lineaments of normality. The pain had left, too, and it seemed the immediate crisis was over. I trotted back down to thank Steffi Toms who was down on one knee attaching her prosthetic shoe. Then she stood up, limber and tall in her black leotards but a foot short.

"Damned glad it worked, Gerry," she said after a quick peep inside the chocolate corduroy. "You must go and see your doctor tomorrow without fail. It needs investigating. And if it happens again tonight, get yourself immediately to the nearest A & E, okay? If it goes on for more than a couple of hours it'll cause permanent damage and you could well wind up impotent. How old are you? Forty. Really? Well, I expect you'd agree that's a bit young to lose such a useful member."

I couldn't help staring at her own orthopaedic trainer. "Coming from you, I shall take what you say seriously."

"Do. And in case you're wondering, I lost it to a shark in South Queensland."

"That's an odd coincidence. What with Millie Cleat losing her arm to a shark, I mean."

"No coincidence at all. The common denominator's Lew Buschfeuer. As a matter of fact the whole ship's crew has suffered a disfiguring attack by one predatory animal or another. Sharks, crocodiles, snakes, and in the case of one of the engineers a koala. It's a condition of employment on the *Vvizz*."

"Are you joking?"

"Not at all."

"Well, what about the young officer with the long hair who brought me to see you? He didn't seem to be missing anything."

"He lost one of his ears to a moray eel while scuba diving on the Great Barrier Reef. Sliced clean off. He's thinking of having the other one removed surgically. Fearful symmetry, and so on."

"And the Aboriginal gentlemen?"

"They're missing their entire continent, aren't they? We removed it from them without the benefit of anaesthetic many years ago."

I bade Dr. Toms good night, found my way to the upper deck and went outside. By now Millie and Lew were there seeing the last of their guests down into the ship's tender, all except for Nanty, who I gathered had already been picked up by helicopter from the helipad on the afterdeck. I was handed a note he'd left me which I pocketed while making my own farewells to my host and hostess at the top of the companionway. Far below on the dark waters of the Solent the launch waiting alongside burbled and rocked, probably not doing much good to the various digestive systems aboard it tackling their boluses of seaweed, toasted Burmese tree pith and deep-fried Sumatran pitcher plant. A steward was standing on the floodlit grating beside it holding the end of a painter half-hitched around a stanchion, obviously waiting for me.

"Touch of the squits, mate?" Lew asked me. "I saw yer make a dash for it. I guess some of our tucker is a little exotic for those unaccustomed to it. Never mind, eh? Yer can chuck a sickie tomorrow."

Until then I had been disposed to like Lew as a hormonally challenged tycoon with an informal, even engaging style. But this sally suggested he might be one of those men who take pleasure in setting up his guests for gastronomic dares, and those who know Samper will realize he is the very last person to take on. I bridled at this implication of weakness. After all, I had eaten nothing at his table more outlandish than had I been invited around for a quiet bridge evening with Tarzan and Jane.

"Not squits," I told him. "I'd forgotten I'd promised to call Max Christ during the interval—he's conducting *Don Giovanni* in Vienna tonight and I thought it less rude just to slip away up here and use my mobile. He and I are supposed to be doing a book together sometime and you know how it is—schedules to be fixed well in advance. I guess that's showbiz."

I stared out across the dark expanse of sea ringed with the blazing lights of the nearby town and felt satisfied I'd scored a point with this tactical fib. Lew's world was not confined merely to his ship of amputees and he would have to be Les Patterson himself not to know who Max Christ was. Queen Neptunia, on the other hand, was looking blank. She was shivering slightly in the chill breeze despite being draped in a politically dubious fur coat out of which her polycarbonate arm with its now sluggish organisms protruded stiffly, the transparent hand still curled to receive a glass. I noticed with pleasure that she was suddenly looking old. Her own ignorance and the cold evidently irritated her because she said brusquely, "I'll be at the Dorchester, Gerry. We'll talk tomorrow night after I've done this bloody signing."

"Okay. I hope the book goes well."

"We ought to be saying that to you too, mate," said Lew warmly. "It's in all our interests, isn't it? We realize you've got other writing commitments, Gerry, and we might have messed you about by not yet signing on the dotted line. But don't forget Millie got her foot in yer door long before the others. Yer can't rely on dainty manners when there's a queue for the dunny."

There is more than a hint of threat in this gem of Aussie wisdom and it almost goads me to reply quite sharply that we writers respond better to cheques through the letterbox than to feet in the dunny door. In other words, cobber, it's going to take hard cash up front to induce me to waste any more of my time on your girlfriend's three-limb circus. I tottered off down the companionway feeling not much like Daphne after all. She at least secured her future fortune, although at the cost of marriage under false pretences. Yet in other respects I felt our predicaments were not dissimilar. I reached the bottom and was handed down into the launch by the steward. As far as I could see he was physically intact, which only made me wonder which piece of his hidden anatomy might be missing. I rejoined my fellow guests inside, many of whom by now were queasy and impatient, except for Joan Nugent and her doggy cabal who had clearly never been seasick in their lives. During the short trip to shore she and I swapped phone numbers and once we'd landed she dropped me in her car at Southampton Central, from where I caught one of the last trains up to London. It had not been a successful evening, I reflected as I stared moodily at the black window beside me all the way to town while expelling noxious chickpea gas into the train's upholstery. Now and again a waft came to me redolent of Nilotic vegetation rotting beneath a tropical sun. The book business was still unresolved, the ProWangs' pills had revealed the sting in their tail and the ideological ins and outs of the Deep Blues were unfathomably footling.

And so . . .

And so to this mid-morning cup of overpriced coffee in Marylebone High Street and falling prey to familiar doomy thoughts about the inane things we do to earn our brief living in this madhouse. Nor are my thoughts any the less doomy for having booked myself a consultation with a doctor in Beaumont Street at two o'clock this afternoon: a man this time, but at least a specialist. Since my own doctor is hundreds of miles away in Italy I was reduced to asking Derek before he left for work this morning for the name of a reliable local practitioner. Over the years he has had ample opportunity to form close, often hurried, links with the medical profession and it was a source of much pleasure for him to winkle out of me sufficient humiliating detail in order to select the likeliest expert from his card index. So I shall be seeing a Mr. Benjy Birnbaum at two, a man Derek assures me has performed prodigies of surgery on the reproductive organs of many a world leader in the nearby Wimpole Clinic.

"One wouldn't have thought his case load could be all that heavy. It's a pretty specialized field."

"You'd be surprised," said Derek darkly. "Darling Antoine and he used to work in tandem"—this being a reference to his defunct proctologist. "Front bottoms and back bottoms. Below-the-belt surgery has profited vastly from the fashion for studs and infibulation, you know. They're always going septic. Things get wrenched off, too, or caught in Hoovers. Amazing the things people do to themselves. One of Benjy's patients took an angle grinder to a cock ring he couldn't get off. They had to transplant flesh fro—"

"This is breakfast," I interrupted sternly. "I don't wish to know."

"Oh, it's not always gruesome," the puckish manicurist persisted as he made toast for us in his bacterial kitchenette. "Benjy once had to embed a diamond in an Arab's knob. The

Arab later lost it to a hooker in Shepherd Market who faded into the dawn before he discovered it was missing. A whole carat, apparently."

"Lucky girl."

"Boy, I think. Contrary to popular wisdom, it sometimes pays to be a sucker. The Arab threatened to sue, claiming Benjy hadn't embedded the diamond securely enough, but he backed off when he thought about the publicity his case would generate. Not the sort of thing you'd want your folks in Riyadh reading about over their mint tea. Anyway, Benjy will sort you out in a jiff. Deftest blade in the business."

I winced. "And not cheap, no doubt?"

"Not actually *cheap*, no. But then, how much is it worth to you?" And with that Derek sailed off down to Jermyn Street leaving me prey to nameless panic, as no doubt he'd intended, the merry little ghoul. Ours is a curious relationship. You never fully plumb a friend's warped sense of humour until you find yourself having to ask him a delicate favour. Scrabbling in my pocket for enough cash to pay the patisserie's exorbitant bill my fingers now encounter last night's forgotten note from Nanty. I open it and find it's written in juvenile capitals and somewhat in the style of a text message. It is to this that the art of writing has sunk after a few thousand years of literacy: the pidgin remnants of a once mellifluous and precise method of human communication:

GD TO C U MATE. NOW IVE RECOVRD R PRJECT IS LIVE AGAIN
N WE SHD TALK SOONEST. CALL ME TOMORO. MOB # SAME
AS B4 NANTY

This style is as much affectation as practical, owing nearly everything to the fashionable whimsy that the world has moved on from the days of pen and ink, not to mention syntax and grammar. Nanty once gave me some perfectly literate notes he had himself handwritten towards his own autobiography and although they were hardly stylish they were expressive and showed a concern for accuracy. I find it ironic that the more people bang on about the vital importance of communication, the more slipshod its modes become. Utopia would be if everyone suddenly held their tongues and allowed a blessed silence to fall upon the earth. It would soon be appreciated that the world would be a better place entirely without communication, where nation didn't speak unto nation and the inanities of daily domestic discourse were stilled. And if that meant G. Samper would be out of a job, so much the better. Well, if I survive the ministrations of Mr. Benjy Birnbaum I will maybe call Nanty later.

Apprehensively, I present myself slightly early at the doctor's address. I should like to be able to report that the great man's waiting room is crowded with a mysteriously varied clientele including an archbishop, a veiled female newscaster and a small boy listlessly turning the pages of *Country Life*. In fact the room is empty of sufferers unless one counts a tank of tropical fish over by the window. On the walls are the usual framed diplomas and qualifications supposed to reassure nervous patients that their intimate parts will be in good hands. Mr. Birnbaum seems to have qualified at an inordinate number of medical schools in Switzerland, Israel, South Africa, the United States and here in London, where the Royal College of Reconstructive Surgery was pleased to elect him a Fellow in 1991. Moving to the end of a row of framed citations I note that the Ethical Latex Forum thanked Mr. Birnbaum most warmly for his keynote address to their Fourth International Congress in Denver, 2002.

I move over to the fish tank where the surgeon's set designer has recommended the Pirate Treasure scenario. From the copper helmet of an old-fashioned diver ascends the stream of bubbles that keep the water oxygenated. The diver is bent over a treasure chest he has found, its lid conveniently open and its freight of jewels and doubloons cascading across the aquarium's gravel bed. The plastic timbers of a pirate galleon protrude from behind some nearby rocks. Bent over as he is, the diver is unaware that he is about to receive a jolly rogering from a swordfish with an evil glint in its painted eye. Disposed about this mise-en-scène are the tank's living denizens, whose doleful lethargy suggests they have lately found the joke wearing thin. Ob, they comment disdainfully. *Ob, ob, ob.* At this moment a stout woman comes in to lead the way to her employer's next door consulting room so that I don't get lost.

As I enter I nervously note a trolley pushed against the wall and covered in crisp paper, screens on wheels and white net curtains to deter the prying eyes of Beaumont Street. Also many shelves of books. As with lawyers, I'm never quite sure what the thinking is behind these showy professional libraries. Are they meant to be the outward and visible sign of the erudition long embedded in the practitioner's capacious brain? If so, I'm unreassured. One has only to look back to student days to realize the hopelessness of trying to recall even a single verse of Thomas Hardy or A. E. Housman, which is why one needs to invent them. Or are the tomes meant to represent a ready reference library so that the expert is never stumped by a case? ("Why don't we see what those acknowledged authorities Pratchett and Finkel have to say, h'm?")

"Ethical *latex*?" I query, hearing the door close behind me.

"Ah, I've often wondered if anyone ever reads those things."

"Wonder no more."

We shake hands. Benjy Birnbaum is short and round and disconcertingly wearing a white nylon overall as though for protection against sudden squalls of urine. He is also wearing rimless spectacles with thick, perfectly round lenses. "Wonderful to see you, Mr. Samper. I gather this is at rather short notice. What seems to be the trouble?"

"There's no 'seems' about it." I start my doleful tale which I have been rehearsing ever since leaving the patisserie. I thought some harmless massaging of the facts might spare a few of my blushes.

"You say your motivation was medical science," Mr. Birnbaum observes at the end. "Are you by any chance a scientist? Or medical?"

"No, no. I'm a writer. Occasionally I'm asked to do some scientific journalism, and this present mishap is due to my foolishly overzealous attempt to find out what really lies behind those Internet advertisements about penile enlargement. Do they work? Are they dangerous? I was asked to look into it for one of the Sunday magazines."

"One of the Sunday magazines, I see. As for what really lies behind the advertisements, I should have thought the profit motive would be a satisfactory explanation."

"Of course," I agree, a bit rattled by the ease with which this little doughball has undercut the glaring plausibility of my story. "Profit—that's obvious. I really meant what lies behind *that*, in a larger sense. Are twenty-first-century men more worried about the size of their penises than their twentieth-century counterparts were, and if so, why? Is it due to the now ubiquitous pornographic imagery that might make some men feel inadequate? Or could it be that these days boys and young men seldom see each other naked, as they used to in the days of National Service and single-sex boarding schools, and consequently have less awareness of what constitutes a normally-sized cock?" This is more like it. Once I start ad-libbing like this I feel confident and inventive, knowing I can keep going indefinitely. Benjy Birnbaum listens impassively.

"You realized the risk you were taking?"

"I suppose I could paint myself in heroic colours, like a Morgan Spurlock living on McDonald's hamburgers for a month," I say. "But to be honest I didn't believe these pills contained anything harmful, if anything at all. I assumed the whole thing was a straightforward con: overpriced placebos with exotic-sounding ingredients that are completely inert, plus the patient's desire to believe, which would no doubt be reflected in his measurements, even if minutely."

Benjy Birnbaum sighs. "It's funny how often magazines commission these surveys nowadays. I've had several writers come in here and give much the same account. Odd how I never seem to see any of their articles in print. No doubt I read the wrong newspapers. I must say I'm impressed by the collective bravery of you journalists in offering yourselves as guinea pigs in a public cause. Well, do please come over here and lie down and we'll have a look-see. Pity you've finished the course. We might have had an analysis made of one of those pills. Orchic substances, you say."

I have the feeling I've already been stripped naked even before I climb onto the trolley and numbly unzip. I'm not wearing corduroy today, having discovered some small spatters of cooked vegetation adhering here and there. The awful Debra was right and the suit will have to be cleaned. Instead, I have chosen a lyrical pair of slacks by His Majesty in fawn mohair-and-denim mixture. We're talking a serious sum of money here, which may or may not be the right impression to convey in a private surgery in the Harley Street area. It could cut both ways. I watch as Benjy Birnbaum goes to a sinister-looking dispenser on the wall and sticks a hand into its brightly lit aperture. There is the gulping noise of a vacuum being released and then he repeats the operation with the other hand. Only when he returns to the trolley can I see that his hands are now covered by a nearly invisible film of latex, quite possibly of an ethical bent. Only a faint ring the colour of a rubber band around each wrist gives the game away.

"I suppose one could use that gadget to fit a condom," I say.

"Just relax."

It's strange how one can't watch a doctor examining one's

own body. Or I can't, at any rate. Just as I did last night while Steffi Toms was giving my veal the once-over, I stare off sideways at yet another row of books as though my body no longer has anything to do with me. *Handbook of Vascular Anastomosis; The Dysfunctional Penis* by Murray G. Intrilogator; *The Beyondness of Healing,* published by an outfit called *The Mystical Rose Center For Sexual Unfolding; Dicktionary.* Dicktionary?? A fat, coffee table-sized volume with a . . .

"Cough, please."

. . . peculiar colophon on its spine.

"Again. Good." He gives my veal a valedictory pat. "I think we can be pretty sure there's no permanent damage to the perioticular ostracon. And your melinges are sound, at any rate."

"In layman's terms, that will be five hundred guineas?"

"Ah, guineas. The dear, dead days. I'd like to do a blood test to be certain, however. I suspect these pills may temporarily have screwed up your hormonal system. Yes, yes, you can get up now. Mm, guineas." He returns to his desk. "How old are you?"

"Just about to turn forty."

"Are you sure?"

"I mean fifty. Did I say forty? Truth to tell, I've been a bit thrown by last night. I was quite worried for a while as you can imagine." It has taken a rotund Jewish surgeon in my pay to expose an entirely harmless deception that goes back at least, well, ten years. This is cruel and humiliating. It is something I was hoping to keep from my readers and myself alike, let alone from Adrian, who now seems to recede on the far side of a gulf of years. Suddenly everything looks bleaker, even slightly pathetic. Brace up, Samper. Get a grip. Beaumont Street's Hippocratic answer to the Pillsbury Doughboy is breaking out syringes and vials from sterile packaging. "I notice you have a book over there called *Dicktionary.* That big volume."

"Oh, that. I need hardly say it comes from California, like the spiritual twaddle next to it. Yes, the Mapplethorpe Press.

There's not a word of text in it. Just clench your fist? That's it. No, entirely pictures. Thousands of photographs. And do you know, no, hold still, it's a good vein and we'll take another twenty while we're at it, I've found it quite as valuable as most medical textbooks. Just press that hard for a minute or two and I'll stick a bit of plaster over it. We don't want to get our nice shirt all messed up. We'll have some results—what time is it now, two-thirty?—by this time tomorrow. And then we'll know how to proceed. But for now I think you haven't too much to worry about. I would recommend some form of erotic eventuality in the next twenty-four hours, preferably leading to climax. That way we'll know if you're draining normally. If not, call me immediately and find a flight of stairs to climb. Virginia in the office will give you my various numbers and deal with the paperwork. I'll see you again tomorrow."

On my way out I pass the open door of the waiting room where the fish are still frozen in their dimensionless limbo forty feet above a London street and the diver is for ever about to be shafted even as he revels in doubloons. Erotic eventuality? What kind of grotesque urban world have you strayed into, Samper, so far from the sanities of Le Rocce and its bucolic pleasures? You must hurry home and write whatever you want to write and stop waiting on other people's vagueness and indecisiveness, a bending lackey to their promises of loot to come. Either Millie and Lew make a straightforward proposal in the next two days or I'll sign up with Nanty. Not that he's so much better, pop stars being about as reliable as Hollywood filmmakers where airy promises are concerned. But cap-in-hand must now give way to cheque-in-hand. Samper has spoken.

20

This feeling of having taken a decision lifts my spirits, already somewhat buoyed by not having been despatched urgently by Benjy Birnbaum to the Wimpole Clinic for shaving and prepping prior to surgery. Still, he has left me some tricky homework to accomplish by tomorrow. Erotic eventuality? No matter how heartening an encounter with a cock doctor, the experience leaves behind it no quickening of the libidinal pulse. Rather the reverse, I'm afraid, and I don't quite see how I'm to fulfil this task in the allotted time. Sharing Derek's Allure-scented flat is often comic, sometimes sordid, but seldom stimulating since our amatory tastes in no way coincide. People cavil about having to follow their doctor's tiresome orders but right now I would be happy to forswear alcohol, sugar or salt if it also let me off having to experience orgasm before two o'clock tomorrow afternoon. I suppose that's what comes of being fifty rather than forty. Quite infuriating to have been found out, by the way. I'm still smarting as I walk down Beaumont Street towards Derek's rancid lair, but to take my mind off it I have already begun to sing Captain Thorogood's doleful aria from Gilbert and Sullivan's unfinished operetta, *Durance Vile*:

> The ides of March are iding,
> The cocks have all crowed thrice.
> The hours go quickly sliding
> With each fall of the dice—

With each fall of the dice!

If you have any familiarity with this scarcely performable but noble torso (which I rather doubt), you will remember that the Captain, unjustly imprisoned for cheating at cards, is now in the Tower of London awaiting execution for having throttled a succession of his gaolers, each of whom offered to cheer his spirits by playing games of chance with him and lost. Tonight it is the turn of kindly young Jack Lively, an apprentice gaoler barely out of his teens who has fallen in love with Pansy Thorogood, the Captain's comely daughter, who visits him daily. The Captain and Jack are about to play halma.

Ouija boards are weejing,
The palms have all been read.
And tea leaves in their legion
Have given up their dead,
Have given up their dead!

Young Jack survives, but barely. With extraordinary skill Sullivan manages to be simultaneously jaunty and sombre; and although we know there will be a happy ending (Jack will himself strangle Pansy in Act II when he visits her in Lowndes Square on his day off) a certain darkness tingles in the background. Impertinent burghers stare at me as I pass among them down Marylebone High Street, much as their counterparts did in Southampton the other day. There seems not much to be done about Britain's essential unmusicality—*Das Land ohne Musik*, as the Germans used to call us, and that was long before the Sex Pistols. Ours is today a riffraff culture of hooliscruffs and yobbigans with little original to say and scarcely any technique for saying it. It was not ever thus; and there are some who would blame our culture's demise on that of the Luton Girls' Choir in 1976. I myself would place the date a decade or two earlier, after which everything was swamped by the enduring deluge of social realism and conceptual art. But who cares? I shall be off just as soon as I've signed a contract and sorted out my woefully abused member.

Today I'm too lazy to clean up Derek's kitchen and prepare an inventive snack before his return from work. Instead I add to his phone bill by calling up last night's fellow diner, Joan Nugent. I've been thinking that on balance she could be more an ally than not. Anyway, I'm prepared to take a risk. I really do need to talk to someone about the Cleat problem, knowing the great yachtswoman is safely sitting in Hatchards or Borders or Waterstones laboriously signing copies of my book with her left hand. One of the minor inconveniences of losing your writing hand, Millie once told me, is that you also lose your scriptorial identity. All of a sudden bank managers, passport officers, the DVLC and supermarket checkouts refuse to believe you're you. But that, of course, was in the bad old days of being Mrs. Clifford Cleat. Once the nation recognizes you as just plain Millie it scarcely matters what hieroglyphs you scrawl.

"Hello?" rasps Joan's nicotine-pickled voice from the phone. "Get away, blast you, I'm feeding Sandy." A storm of yapping on the other end. "Go on, get away, Bo'sun. You've had yours. Greedy bugger. Who is this? Oh, Gerry. Sorry about that. Just feeding the dogs here. Bedlam as usual. Glad you've called, actually. We never did finish our conversation last night. I want to know what you know about those ruddy transponders, among other things."

"Even as we speak they're trying to retrieve them from the seabed."

"Ha! I was right. You do know more."

I tell her the story of the container that was swept overboard but lie when I say I have no idea how the recording of the transponders' electronic Babel came into Millie's hands.

"Huh, it'll be one of those marine boffins," says Joan astutely. "For some reason they've got it in for her. I don't yet know why but I'm going to find out."

Now tread carefully here, Gerry. There must be no mention of the EAGIS affair otherwise this old crony will warn Millie of the plot against her. "Don't quote me on this because I don't know anything for certain, but I suspect at least some of the scientists at BOIS will have taken against her over this Neptune business. It's all too flaky and New Age. I'd guess they feel it's squandering the opportunity of having a celebrity who might otherwise raise awareness in a serious and intelligent way. Possibly they think she's more interested in grabbing a new constituency of admirers for herself." "Suspect," "guess," "possibly." I hope I'm covering my tracks well enough, but this butch old girl at the other end is nobody's fool. "It might be a kindly act if you warn Millie about the transponders, at any rate. You obviously know far more about marine salvage than I do, but whether or not they retrieve this gear I'm afraid the story's going to break sooner or later. I'm sure Millie will want to distance herself from alleged recordings of the Spirit of the Ocean addressing the human race from the seabed. In short, if I were her I'd throw those nutty scholars—what's their names, Tammeri and Brilov—to the wolves."

There is a silence at the other end, unless one counts what sounds like a pack of the very wolves in question. Joan's terriers would surely make equally short work of the misguided linguists if thrown them at dinnertime.

"Right," she says at length. "Yes, I don't see she has any alternative. Not that she ever had. I'm afraid there's this streak in Millie that imagines she can get away with anything."

"You noticed."

"It's as if reality's never going to catch up with her."

"That shark did."

"Yes, but she's never spotted its more metaphorical aspects. She only thinks of it as having been an agent of change for the better in her life. I'll tell her, Gerry. That's loyal of you. While we're about it, do you know of anything else that might steal up and bite her when she's not looking?"

"Well . . . Not really, no." Why *is* it that conspiracies are so tempting to divulge? Why do we find it so flattering to hold some titbit of knowledge over somebody's head?

"May I ask how you come to have contacts in the marine sciences, Gerry?"

"Oh, sheer chance," I tell her. "Friends of friends. It came in handy while writing the book when I had to check some details about navigation. You can imagine—being a landlubber I needed to bone up on winds and tides and currents and compass bearings even if I didn't actually use the information." It's just like talking to Benjy Birnbaum. I'm so plausible when I ad-lib. We Sampers can think on our feet. I really believe there must be oratory in our genes. "You wouldn't credit the weird contacts and knowledge I've needed to acquire over the years while writing these stupid books. Skiing, competitive eating, motor racing, sailing—you name it."

"Competitive *eating*?"

"I'm afraid so. That was a few years ago. They were trying to have it accepted as an Olympic sport with strict rules, accredited trainers and regular testing for drugs such as regurgitation suppressants. As a matter of fact I believe they still are."

"You're having me on."

"By no means. Look it up on the Internet. It's still mainly U.S.-led, but the world champion hot-dog eater for the past five years has been a Japanese boy, and if you're thinking sumo wrestler you'd be wrong. He's quite small and hasn't an ounce of fat on him. Apparently it's all about training the stomach to expand. I had to learn a lot about the human digestive system, the vagus nerve, the physiology of the stomach lining, all that."

"What was your book called?"

"We never got that far, it all came to nothing. The cash wasn't there. Believe me, Joan, the money needs to be reasonable enough to supply incentive, at least. When I was still doing the preliminary interviews I once had to spend the night in the same small room as the reigning world-champion baked-beans eater." I thought back to those awful hours in a caravan behind a fairground outside Dewsbury. Never again; not least because the forty-stone Yorkshireman expired a month later, deafeningly, after losing his title in Oslo. He was only twenty-seven. It's a complete no-no, trying to write about people who are likely to up and die on you. I'd always thought motor racing risky enough when it came to writing a champion's biography, but since it's a wealthy sport the risk is probably worth taking. But competitive eating still inhabits the roustabout world of country fairs. Try as it might for Olympic status there's always the ghost of a barker with a megaphone in the background shouting, "Roll up! Roll up! Fifteen poundsa sausages in ten minutes, gennlemen 'n ladies! Fifteen *pounds*!" There's another aspect, too, from the would-be writer's point of view. Most sports are pretty sickening at close range, but competitive eating can be literally so. Try watching somebody stuff himself with a huge chunk of naked butter against the clock and without "regurgitating," as they euphemistically call throwing up. After witnessing a professional butter eater put away a kilo in five minutes, trying with his spare hand to stop it coming back down his nose, I ate nothing for a week and spent much of the time in a darkened room with cologne compresses reading Proust. We writers *suffer* for our art.

"So," I conclude, "my knowing the odd oceanographer falls well within the boundaries of normality for me. I can tell you honestly, Joan, that my boundaries are set pretty wide these days, but they definitely do not include the likes of Brilov, Tammeri and my other neighbour last night with the big, er, jacket."

"And eyes."

"And eyes, yes. Debra Leather, that's it. She's another of these mystical scholars. As I say, to the wolves with them."

"Definitely. I'll let Millie finish her book signing and then I shall get on to her and make that very point. Ciderpresses, my arse. Balls to Neptune! Me and the girls have been thinking it for a long time, mind you, but we couldn't find the right lever to move Millie. Really, she's been beyond reason in some ways, for Pete's sake don't quote me, but this time I shall talk her around. It will take two minutes, the way I'm going to do it. We'll simply put the blame on those blasted groupies for misleading her with all that mystic garbage. We Navy girls are about to reassert ourselves. You're a star, Gerry."

So there you are, Samper. Congratulations. For all the right reasons you have probably just talked yourself out of a plum contract, one that would have enabled you to step off the treadmill for a good long time. I have no doubt tough old Joan with her nautical tattoos will pound some sense into Millie and Lew. My bet is that Millie will pretty soon announce she's standing down from her short-lived leadership of the loony Neptunies for reasons of ill health. When her awful lapse in taste and intelligence has receded in the public's mind—in about a week, given that organ's attention span—she can maybe start lending her name to some serious marine enterprises and political initiatives. But the salient thing is she is no longer going to want me to write her a book about her awareness of divine presences twenty thousand leagues under the sea. I suppose I should keep ahead of the game by contriving a different book for her, an altogether more sensible book, a sort of David Attenborough-ish book about the ocean and its threatened future, as told by world-renowned yachtsmoll Millie Cleat. But I'm weary of the woman. And besides, the sea's future is in no way threatened. It will still be there long after Millie and the rest of our race

have vanished, washing its hands of us over and over on its
thousand shores.

*

Wise in the ways of the world, the next day I put off calling
Nanty until after midday. In my limited experience, boy-band
leaders are seldom up before noon and often not much before
4 P.M., depending on the toll taken by last night's gig. Slightly to
my surprise I catch him sounding frisky and compos mentis.

"Doin' me exercises, mate," he tells me. "Physio for the old
gluteus maximus. Bet you don't know what that is."

"I do, too. It's what you sit on." Minimus in poor Derek's
case, of course.

"I gotta hand it to you, Gerry, you know a lotta stuff. So
what did you think of that dinner the other night?"

"Inedible, mostly."

"Yeah. What about that neighbour of yours, though, eh?
Not the dyke—the one with the boobs? Tasty, or what? Giving
you the old eye, I thought. 'Wonder if old Gerry's up for it?' I
said to myself. 'She's making it a bit obvious.'"

"Well, Nanty, it can't be my body so it must be my mind. Or
maybe even my suit." Those pop eyes swim up into my mental
vision, reminding me of my passing ailment and by extension
of my repeat consultation with Benjy Birnbaum this afternoon.
I push them firmly under again. "Anyway, Nanty, I have your
note and here I am, calling you as requested."

"Cool. What I need to know, mate, is are you on ter write
this book about me? Thing is, me agent really went for that
plan of ours before I had me deliberate—that's what I call me
accident, because it wasn't; it was a carefully planned heist, like
the papers said. You remember: that idea of yours to build me
up for the future."

I certainly do remember. It was a plan of campaign for noth-

ing less than the later career of a rock star whose days as Brill,
the plausible leader of a boy band, are severely numbered.
There is a limit to how much longer a bald man of thirty-two
can continue to hold the attention of thirteen-year-old girls in
a way that won't lead to his arrest. With the famous Samper ad-
libbing skill and over a glass or two of Fernet Branca I had
sketched out a scenario for which any PR company would
probably have charged him at least fifty thousand pounds. It
was to begin with a best-selling autobiography and continue
with a plot to associate Nanty increasingly with the sort of serious mainstream artistic projects that get huge publicity. True,
they commonly give scant pleasure to anyone except the
celebrity in question, but at the barest minimum he usually
gets the OBE, much as the fat boy at the back of the class gets
a merit mark for trying. I rather think I suggested an AIDS
Requiem (African instruments, Liverpudlian guitars, Kiri Te
Kanawa and the singing strings of the LSO); but that could
now easily be transformed into a Mass for the Planet (words by
Nanty, translated into Latin and sung by the pious monks of
San Bernard augmented by Balinese instruments, Liverpudlian
guitars, selected Sperm, Blue and Minke whale soloists plus
the singing strings of the CSO under Max Christ). Whatever
project is chosen its theme should be agreeably tragic. It ought
to involve celebrity performers far enough past their sell-by
date to merit adjectives like "well-loved," and the whole thing
would have to contain that irreducible quotient of tackiness
that gives British public enterprises their unmistakable character. This, I reasoned, would propel Brill out of the kiddie-band
charts and Nanty into the wrinkled pantheon of those whose
eventual knighthoods in the Birthday Honours List elicit pep-
pery remarks such as "*Who?*" and "Good Christ!" in
Tunbridge Wells.

On the other hand, the project need not necessarily be musical. Obviously there is always room for another Holocaust

memorial somewhere—you can never have too many of them and they usually win prizes, too, like Paralympians. Possibly a little ambitious for the likes of Nanty, however. Maybe wacky as well as tacky was the way to go, with a postmodern "event" of sorts? From time to time I'd wondered if it was the right moment to resurrect the old idea of tear bottles: tiny flasks in which pining lovers once caught their tears as a way of quantifying their hurt. I fancied it might be possible to conduct a global weep-in on behalf of the environment. Well, if not actually global then confined to the EU or just to the UK, like Red Nose Day. Brill could lead a day of weeping in which people meditated on threatened species, dying pandas, starving koalas, bludgeoned seal pups and similar mammalian tearjerkers while catching their lacrimosities in little plastic vials which they would then drop off at collection points in shopping malls, post offices, etc. This would lead to a nationally televised ceremony when great vats of British blubberings would be poured into an empty swimming pool. Brill would compère the show while an immense ball-cock moved the hand of a Weepometer. Thus would the nation gauge the literal depth of its concern for environmental matters. A bit on the weird side but surely worth a CBE at the very least. By one means or another I was aiming for Nanty's regular inclusion as a well-loved figure in Christmas TV spectaculars by the time he was forty. Thereafter he was on his own and free to follow the normal trajectory of yesterday's celebrities: a divorce or two, a drug bust or two, a newspaper outcry following the assault of a paparazzo outside a nightclub, a crotchety letter to *The Times* about the scandalous unavailability of vegan food in motorway diners. Meanwhile . . .

"Does that mean you're keen to start?" I ask him.

"Oh yeah. Yeah, man. I wanna get going on this thing. Getting shot, you know? Makes yer think."

"Not about mortality, I hope."

"Give over, Gerry. Nah, just that there's so much yer can't

do while waiting to heal up yer may as well write a book, know what I mean?"

"Only too well, Nanty. We'd better get the formalities out of the way, then. Your agent contacts mine."

"Cool. But what about this other book you're supposed to be doing for Millie?"

"I promise that won't get in the way. In fact, between you and me, I don't think that will be going anywhere. I'm predicting her imminent change of heart about Neptune, though don't quote me. She's got herself in with a pretty flaky crowd."

"Sure," says Nanty equably, quite used to the idea of a sudden leap in midstream from the slippery back of one hobby horse on to that of another. I recall a similar equestrian feat he himself had been obliged to perform some years ago when his much-publicized, much-revered guru of the day, a sunny rogue from Benares with the usual robe, beard and mantras, failed in a foolishly undertaken test under laboratory conditions to make even a postage stamp levitate using the power of thought. This gentleman had previously convinced Nanty and another member of his band that within a month of embarking on his levitation course they would be able to rise two metres into the air while in the lotus position. The guru with the off-world powers was swiftly exposed as a businessman with offshore accounts. Nanty had leaped adroitly, although I can't now remember which fresh steed he'd alighted on: I shall need to find out when researching his book. "Yer know," he says, "I always did think there was something a bit daft about those voices on the seabed. Stands to reason."

Dear, brainless child. Why is their reason the last thing these credulous creatures ever actually consult? Let alone their agents? Talking of which, with any luck Frankie will be able to secure me a pretty good fee for writing *The Life of Brill*, though it may not be as munificent as the one Millie and Lew were offering. I am prey now to chiller thoughts than those I managed until yesterday to suppress. Fifty years old, and still hacking out biographies of people I essentially despise, although often amicably? So be it, Samper. The toad pays Le Rocce's bills and keeps you in suits of chocolate corduroy. Such parameters define life on earth, which makes the mind of a Divine Planner inscrutable indeed. However, the next item on today's agenda might be evidence that the Divine Planner has a quaintly human need for light relief. It is nearly time for Samper's appointment with Benjy Birnbaum, and no "erotic eventuality" has taken place in the last twenty-four hours. I turn up on his doorstep in Beaumont Street with an apprehensive schoolchild's feeling of being already scolded. I have to remind myself that not only am I about to turn fifty, but I'm also about to be billed by the good Benjy, meaning that he is in my employ.

The same empty waiting room, the same aquarium, the same fish glooming in a fossil dream. Even the plastic swordfish, poised in its proctological whimsy, seems to have lost hope of ever plunging headfirst into the rubber-suited diver, just as the diver's doubloon-inspired gloat has frozen into everlasting indifference to all loot. It is not clear how wise it was to have placed a tableau in a waiting room that so efficiently expresses the hopelessness of waiting. Perhaps it was an unconscious comment on the necessity to patients of patience, and the Latin denominator of suffering common to both. Suddenly the matronly Virginia opens the door, not a moment too soon, and together we once again succeed in finding the doctor's consulting room on the other side of the wall.

Benjy is gracious, even warm, maybe because we no longer share the stiffness of strangers. Inevitably I interpret it as an attempt to soften the blow he is about to deliver.

"Do please sit down," he says, waving me into one of those steel and black leather chairs that win design prizes and in which no one would ever instinctively sit. Today his nylon overall is pale blue and buttoned to the neck as though he anticipates another good drenching. His magnified glance passes damply over me. "Now, your results." The schoolchild feeling returns. Benjy Birnbaum flips through a sheaf of forms headed in red print. "Overall, I'm glad to say my original impression has been borne out and there's nothing much to worry about." *Great.* "However . . . " *As you were, Samper . . .* "However, there does seem to be a marked elevation in your moticular gammaparandrogens."

"Much as I suspected," I agree gamely. "Far too many of them."

The Doughboy lowers the reports and regards me through his thick lenses. His eyes swim like oysters on the half shell. "I'm happy our professional opinions coincide," he says amiably enough. "You know how awkward it can be when specialists disagree."

"No, come on, Doc. I've not the remotest idea what these vehicular pandagens are."

"Good. Then I can blind you with science. Basically, something in those pills you've been taking—rather nobly, as you describe it—has managed to raise a particular one of your hormones to a level more appropriate to adolescence. Sadly, as you have probably discovered, it won't have had an equivalent effect on your libido. I fear that trick works only once in a lifetime. In the intervening years we have acquired too much experience to be able to kid ourselves that we're still floating across life's surface on a raft so thin we're never more than a thought away from boundless and unplumbed deeps of erotic passion. In short, we've been there and done that many times too often. Hormones can do a lot of things but they can't reinvent novelty. In the present instance your flesh appears willing but it is the spirit that's weak. Would this summation describe the facts?"

"All too well."

"You're about to tell me of your failure to have brought about a climax as I requested yesterday?"

"I am."

"Nothing to be ashamed of. At fifty it should take more than a doctor's orders to set the pulses racing."

"I'm pretty sure the same would have been true at forty."

"And why not? Meanwhile, you've had no further recurrence of the priapism?"

"Not a smidgin."

"I think we'll just have one further look, if you wouldn't mind slipping onto the . . . excellent . . . and just lowering the . . . perfect." Again he retreats to the dispenser on the wall and comes back with freshly sheathed hands. His fingers begin squeaking busily.

Again the *Dicktionary* and other titles. This time I note Jackelby & Sprutt's monograph *The Ageing Male*, which takes my spirits several notches lower.

"Terrific," says Benjy Birnbaum. "Beautifully drained and flaccid. Tell me, as a curious medic, *have* you noticed any overall growth as a result of taking those pills? Honestly?"

"I did for a while. Might that have been down to early-onset priapism, or is that a new medical condition I've just invented?"

"The pills could well have begun to affect your capacity to drain fully, yes."

"Well, the tape measure cannot lie. But I haven't done any measuring recently. I've had rather a lot of other things on my mind."

"Like writing your article?"

"Er . . . exactly. Difficult to get the tone right, you know. Manly frankness? Veiled discretion? Brutal realism?" I climb off the trolley, zipping defensively.

"Well, I really would suggest no more unknown pills, Mr. Samper, not even in the interests of science or your readers. There's a real danger that some of those rogue pharmaceuticals could cause lasting damage. Much better content yourself with the entirely adequate and even quite elegant appendage which

nature has given you. Continue to keep a close eye on it and
don't hesitate to call me at the least sign of irregularity in its
behaviour. Since you tell me you're no longer a resident in the
UK you should take these lab reports with you as a record.
They are, after all, yours. I think you'll find Virginia has the
rest of your paperwork completely up to date."

"Not expressed in guineas, you mean?"

"No. But should you wish to pay in sovereigns I certainly
won't stand in your way. Failing that, I'm sure a conventional
cheque will serve most adequately."

We take leave of each other, not too sadly, and soon I am
standing once more on the doctor's doorstep, this time more
stunned than apprehensive. "Not cheap" was Derek's way of
putting it and he wasn't wrong. Still, Benjy Birnbaum's is not a
job I should care to have myself and he has definitely cheered
me up by ruling out surgery. Overall, though, I'm left with an
obscure sense of disquiet. Below-the-belt consultations undeniably represent a milestone. From now on such things will only
become more frequent, the dysfunctions more gross, the paper-
sheathed trolleys more familiar . . . *Samper! Get a grip! Think
"periodic checkup" and quit moaning.* And he did say the old
veal was not only entirely adequate but elegant as well: quite a
compliment from someone for whom genitalia are his daily
meat and two veg. He would hardly be in the habit of overus-
ing a word as precise as "elegant." One couldn't imagine him
saying the same thing to Derek, to take an example at random.
This is a thought worth singing about. Back to *Durance Vile*:

> The Fates are busy fating
> The moment of our dust.
> And e'en as doves are mating,
> Our cards fall as they must—
> They must, they must, they must!

My progress northward along the east side of Beaumont Street is marked by my mellifluous rendition of this little-heard number. As I come abreast of a stone portico a large lady in beige appears at the top of the shallow flight of steps and hurries down, her face bruised with rage.

"This is a *hospital*!" she hisses. "Disgraceful! Noise like that! *Private* hospital! Entitled to peace! And quiet! Certain patients! Gravely ill!"

With some difficulty I drag myself away from the Tower of London and return to the twenty-first century.

"Aha," I say, looking up at the building's dingy façade. "Isn't this where duchesses come on dark nights to give birth to babies fathered by gamekeepers? Or am I wrong?"

"Disgraceful! Din! Hospital! Some people . . .!"

Spirits appreciably lifted, I saunter onwards to Derek's perfumed pad to make myself a well-deserved cup of tea.

21

Ten days drag by, leaving me chafing. It is all well and good that I have apparently overcome the whole costly Pow-r-Tabs™ episode, but the ads—and worse—are still there each time I turn on my computer. How far have we sunk when we receive letters from total strangers beginning "Hey, cute dolls moan from harsh insertions. Click to hear"? Even more incredible that we now take it for granted, wearily? Apart from that, I suppose these are days of some minor importance to me since the events have direct consequences for the future of Samper Enterprises Inc. However, as I predicted these with flawless accuracy they lack the interest that might otherwise have compensated for my enforced stay.

First of all, stout Joan of the Sealyham terriers phones to tell me she has passed on my message to Millie about attempts being made to raise a container of mystic voices from the seabed off the Canaries. According to her, a long and thoughtful silence fell at the other end of the phone, as well it might. This is more than could be said for my conversation with Joan, which is sporadically interrupted by terrific outbursts of barking and rich naval expletives. For the life of me I can't understand why the unexceptional fact of being lesbian should so often entail living in conditions of canine mayhem. It makes ordinary human intercourse so difficult. However, I'm confident enough of how Millie will react to Joan's news to be satisfied we've reached a turning point. As soon as I've rung off I find myself extemporizing a triumphant little song:

Amazing Disgrace! How vile the cries
That plague poor Millie's ears!
Whom once they loved they'll now despise,
They praised whom now they'll jeer!

Next, Frankie rings in some alarm to say that Brill's agent
has been in touch to draw up a contract for the boy-band
leader's autobiography. I owe Frankie an apology for not having kept him abreast of developments. I pay this debt and
explain that I'm ninety-nine per cent certain Millie Cleat is
about to have a change of heart where her public role is concerned, and this in turn will almost certainly mean her pulling
out of our book project. I commiserate with him because, after
all, Frankie takes ten per cent plus VAT of whatever I earn and
a *Millie!* sequel would have kept the office in paper clips for
about seven thousand years, allowing for inflation.

"You're sure it's dead?" he asks plaintively, from the sound
of it coughing up live pulmonary tissue.

"It has to be." I recount what has happened. "Just wait,
Frankie. Have faith. The old fraud's got no alternative but to
recant."

"You realize *Millie!*'s selling a streak? Champions are
already reprinting. Another thirty thousand in hardback and
looks like building."

"If we're not careful we'll be earning out our advance."

"Didn't I tell you? The woman's a national institution. And
this isn't even the proper Christmas market yet. It's such a pity
about that sequel," he adds wistfully.

"Not to the man who was going to have to write it, surrounded by Neptune's courtiers, coral huggers and people
worried about whether clams might be more self-aware than
limpets. I've already gone the extra mile for Cleat, Frankie.
That chapter I added about her spiritual depth is not only a
masterpiece of tactful exaggeration, it says everything that can

be said about a small, ageing woman with one arm confronting the ocean's grand immensity and discovering that she is a small, ageing woman with one arm. Not to mention a dysfunctional family in Pinner. Anyway, Frankie, if you ask me Nanty Riah's a damned good prospect. I wouldn't care to say whether Brill is more or less of a celebrity than Millie, would you?"

"No. Different publics, but equally mega. Actually, Brill probably has the edge internationally. And he's got the kids. I doubt if too many teenagers see a one-armed sailing granny as a role model."

"There you are, then. It's up to you to cut a deal that will keep us all in paper clips to the grave and beyond."

I can't remember if it was that night or the following morning a shocked nation learned that on the advice of her doctors Millie Cleat was reluctantly resigning her position as the titular head of Neptune. She gave a careful interview to the *Guardian* in which she let slip having some mild misgivings about the direction being taken by certain younger activists working on behalf of the marine environment. She wondered (and here I could imagine a single brown forefinger laid pensively along her chin, another thespian gesture she'd picked up), she *did* wonder whether a small minority of the Deep Blue movement might not be risking their credibility by adopting certain controversial, even extreme, positions at a time when the urgent need was surely to unite blah-blah since only by harnessing concerned public opinion blah-blah hope to stave off disaster.

This was adroitly done as, with the spate waters of the river of lost credibility foaming dangerously around her suddenly limping thoroughbred, Millie leaped lightly onto the broad back of an exculpatory Suffolk Punch and lumbered safely to the shore. Just in time, too. For within a day Adrian called via Inmarsat link to announce that the container had just been retrieved, its babbling contents silenced, and that a great hush had at last fallen in the water column. Thanks to Millie's bareback—not to say barefaced—equestrianism, our plot to leak the Neptune-on-the-seabed story to the press is now in abeyance until I can see Adrian again and we can replan our campaign. However, the story's sheer absurdity ensures it will surface sooner or later. Old Millie has done a good job of getting clear in the nick of time, leaving the Brilovs and Tammeris and Debras to face the general derision when it comes. I fancy they will soon know what it feels like to cower beneath a torrential downpour of ciderpresses.

*

Once my contract with Nanty has been drawn up and signed there is at last nothing further to keep me in London. It is now November and I have been away the best part of a month: a fact brought home to me the moment I retrieve my slightly dusty car from the Pisa airport car park. Really, at that price the damned machine might as well have been lounging in the matrimonial suite of a provincial hotel on full board and room service. As usual, my mood improves as I gain altitude on the winding road up to Casoli and beyond. In my absence the forests have changed colour, leaves are thinning, the dark bones showing through. Another year passing, goddamn it. My house when I reach it glows in the afternoon sun but inside it has the dankness of a stone building that has not been aired. I bustle about, throwing open shutters and windows and laying in wood for the fire. By the time I have unpacked I need to close the windows again. At this altitude the waning afternoon sunlight is thin and there is a sharp dampness in the air outside.

The worst thing about arriving home after a trip is that it can lead to a banal and melancholy reflectiveness, as though occasionally one needed to be elsewhere the better to view one's normal life. Our brains are mawkishly wired up and I now try to short-circuit this process by taking an inventory of some-

thing much more significant, viz., the contents of my larder
and freezer. I had forgotten there is little enough. A tray of fish
lollies made from a base of the exquisite sorrel-flavoured juice
exuded by a baked halibut some months ago. An experimental
sausage, salami-style, made principally from doves I bought in
quantity from a man in Casoli who no longer wanted to keep
them. He also wanted to be rid of his late wife's four irksome
budgerigars, so I added them to the dove meat. But just at this
moment I'm not in the mood for cold dove-'n'-budgie sausage.
My mind keeps breaking off and coming to rest in recent
scenes, especially those connected with health matters. That
those humiliating encounters with doctors took place many
hundreds of miles away ought to make them less real, mere
episodes peculiar to *there*. But what with them and my imminent birthday—yes, all right, *fiftieth* birthday—the shades of
recent consulting rooms wield a psychic heft out of proportion
to their individual weight. And even as I think it, the thought
strands me in a cold house in autumn on the edge of a
precipice.

I light the fire and turn up the central heating and then
before it gets too dark find my torch and take a turn over to
Marta's place to give it the once over. When I unlock her back
door—not forgetting to trap a cobble in the jamb—the air is
actually colder inside than out. Both smell and silence are of
the tomb. In the last month it has slumped from being an abandoned house to a forgotten burial chamber. No smell of corruption as such, more the breath of blind, vegetal things that
feed on the thin amino-acids corruption once left behind.
Entering the kitchen I notice the family-vault smell is stronger
and I remember the fridge with the great grey nodding fungus
I briefly glimpsed inside during the summer. In the torchlight
it looks as though the fridge door is no longer sealed completely shut. Can there be a hairline gap between the grey plastic gasket and the surround, as if some slow but implacably

growing mycelial muscle is shouldering its way out? I resist the temptation to push the door experimentally with a fingertip, not wanting to send whirling puffs of spores up into my face. Marta's problem, I say to myself as before. But truthfully, I no longer believe she will come back. The utter deadness of her former home is freighted with the implication that she, too, has long been in her grave. Jackals have already crunched the last marrow from her bones somewhere in the Syrian desert. Or she has been bulldozed into an anonymous pit together with others, their wrists bound behind them in the contemporary manner of political killings. I very much fear I have seen the last of poor Marta.

I lock the back door behind me and as I turn towards my own house I spy a glimmering of white on the ground among the leggy brown remains of summer's hollyhocks nearby. Had this been the Shropshire of my childhood home I would have expected a windblown scrap of paper with a message in faded biro reading "Two pints please" in my mother's hand. This being Italy forty years later, however, it is a business card: a little flabby with damp and with a snail's silver tread crossing it. The print is perfectly legible. It reads: "Studio Benedetti. Soluzioni immobiliari," with various phone numbers and his office address in Camaiore. Oho, so our weaseloid house agent has been back, has he? And this despite my having told him in front of Baggy and Dumpy that Marta's house is emphatically not for sale?

But maybe it is, I think with alarm as I close the door in the fence behind me and thread my way back through the dark trees towards my own home's welcoming lit rectangles. Maybe this time he really does know something about Marta's fate. Perhaps a member of that sinister Eastern-bloc family of hers has already put it on the market? Which means I ought to move pretty smartly if I want to ensure my new neighbours won't be second-home owners from Leatherhead or Linz or

Liège with teenage boys eager to practise their drum kits amid the uncomplaining wilderness of these hills. By comparison, old Marta is belatedly beginning to feel like my ideal neighbour, her own occasional electronic sounds and Petrov piano noises merely the signs of a fellow professional at work. How well we got on together! She played and scribbled, and I scribbled and sang. And if my memories are not of complete neighbourly harmoniousness at all times, our late rapport was becoming practically conjugal. Better, actually, from my experience of most people's marriages. All of which makes it imperative that I pay Benedetti a visit after the weekend.

In the meantime the pleasure of being home again seeps into every pore, like one of those alleged muscle relaxants you add to bathwater to soothe away aches. Friends like Derek used to express incredulity that I could ever live outside London, let alone in a place where English is not the first language. I have long since grown tired of explaining that my reasons for living here are not so much because I find Italian culture, cuisine and general approach to the art of living superior to those of contemporary Britain—though I do—but because it is still a place where one can affordably combine those advantages with non-negotiable essentials such as silence and being able to see the stars. Almost the only lights visible in the night sky in southern England are those of police helicopters and passenger jets stacked for Stansted, Heathrow and Gatwick. I doubt if the Milky Way has been visible to Londoners since the blackout during the Second World War. What kind of a place is that to live? Of what use the intellectual delights of libraries, cinemas, galleries and concert halls if one's whole sensory apparatus is dulled and occluded, one's pores irretrievably blocked? Tonight, it is true, I can't actually sit out on my terrace because it is too chilly. But when I turn off the kitchen lights and sit by the window I can see a canopy of stars despite the ever-growing puddle of lights far below spreading to blur Camaiore into

Viareggio. And I need only step outside the door to hear the night breeze finding its way through the grasses and the leaves letting go autumn's branches. For reasons I can't explain, such things are important to see and hear; and not just once (seen that, heard that) but as a daily constant, as necessary as my pulse. Hence my horror two or three years ago at discovering I had a fat, frizzy-haired Voynovian neighbour and my fury over Benedetti having lied to me about her when I bought this house. Now as I wash up after a scratch meal I reflect on the irony that the mere passage of time has lent him a spurious veracity. Mouse-quiet Marta certainly is these days. And as for her frizzy hair, I can't help seeing it bowling like a pathetic fragment of tumbleweed across the dry bed of a wadi.

Over the weekend I find I am, after all, not remotely dismayed at losing the second Cleat contract and having signed up for Nanty's company instead. The truth is, I rather like the fellow—a first for me when ghosting someone's autobiography. He feels honest in a way none of the others have, Millie Cleat least of all. Nanty seems to maintain an endearing surprise at the way the cosmic lottery has plucked his number out of the hat; and although he is streetwise he is not at all worldly wise. By contrast there is something hard and opaque about Millie. I shall never know to what extent she believed in herself briefly as Queen Neptunia. The "aquariarm," the claque of courtiers reverently spouting drivel, the picture of The Face bathed in hallowed light: was that the sudden, naïve awakening of a long-comatose soul? The discovery of a spirituality remarkably in tune with the Age of Aquarius and beyond? Or was it merely a convenient platform designed to keep her in the limelight, an ambition her own husband, Clifford had dismally predicted?

Speaking as the woman's biographer, I honestly can't say which of these alternatives describes Millie's intentions. Maybe she inhabits that middle state peculiar to "personalities," which is neither quite artless nor quite steely. Armed with a certain charm or ability, such people treat everything as a try-on. They sniff the prevailing wind, pick a direction and sail. If they find the going favourable they scud along; if not, they put about and try a different tack. But no matter how often they change course before the fickle winds of public approbation, they never lose face. No setback is too damaging to be beyond repair. Like successful politicians, they have the hides of rhinoceroses. And like politicians, they have the further enabling disability of proceeding as though they will never be held accountable for anything they have said or done in the past, or for any ideological position they ever took. This is because they live in a sociopath's world where each day starts with a clean slate. Nothing they did yesterday has anything to do with them. This attitude amounts to a conspiracy that is successfully dependent on the public's gnatlike memory span and general credulousness. After all, these days you need not even be a "personality" in your own right: merely *resembling* one is good enough. People who know perfectly well that the Queen's double is not actually Mrs. Elizabeth Windsor will still turn out in droves to cheer her, just as people who know that Elvis Presley is dead as mutton will scream hysterically at a look-alike from Tulsa or Tulse Hill. It is this determined fantasy that makes possible the public fortunes of the averagely untalented. True, Millie is exceptional by virtue of her prowess as a sailorette; but she is also typical in her yearning for continued limelight and the gratifying shenanigans it entails.

By standards such as these Nanty Riah, the bald man in his thirties who dons a wig and turns into Brill to the adoring screams of the faithful half his age, is strangely genuine even though he, too, hankers for respectability and a knighthood. Underneath it all the boy from Harpenden is in some way indifferent to the fuss. He remains hotly devoted to his retarded sister and even to his wife, more or less. So it is not too hard to talk myself into almost looking forward to nailing him to the page. He will not find Samper unsympathetic even though I may be properly acid from time to time. He has, after all, chosen to live among the bubbles that continuously dance and burst above the slow, odorous churning of the public wash. It would be hypocritical of me to pretend I haven't, too.

On Monday morning I drive down to restock the larder and pay a call on Signor Benedetti. Camaiore exemplifies the general rule that first thing Monday mornings is not a good time for shopping in Italy. Most food shops blearily drag their shutters open at around eight, but plenty of other shops won't do so until about four-thirty in the afternoon. I suppose it's not unreasonable when you consider they were open to all hours on Saturday evening, but it's still an incitement to apoplexy when you need a reading lamp or a sofa in a hurry. Estate agents like Benedetti seem to open or not, according to whim, although with the vanishing of the summer hajjis there's little incentive to be punctual. Not a lot of people house-hunt in November. To my surprise, though, I find him in his office on the Corso reading *Il Tirreno*, that fascinating source of local stories concerning such things as the discovery on Saturday of an apartment in Viareggio full of Brazilian transvestites, many of them dwarves. From the neatly pomaded strands of the tangled web on his head to the single highly polished shoe cap visible to one side of his desk, Benedetti appears his usual spruce self. On my entry he folds his newspaper and civilly lays it aside with no outward sign of the displeasure he is undoubtedly feeling. We have long played a game of cloaking our mutual dislike in heavy folds of conversational brocade.

"Signor Samper!" He shakes his draperies out first and a few conventional moths flutter weakly in the bitter light cast by the computer monitor on his desk. "I was only just thinking this newspaper was not doing quite enough to raise my spirits this Monday morning and that exactly the right thing was lack-

ing and lo! in through the door you walk to personify my missing pleasure." His smile, which resembles that of a weasel siz-
ing up a baby rabbit, suggests the phrase "Get out of that one,
clever-clogs."

"*Ingegnere!*" I exclaim. "Preoccupied as my head was with
the banal reflections peculiar to Monday mornings, my feet evidently retained more sense because they have led me through
the one door in Camaiore where they knew such thoughts
would at once be salved and cheered." Not too bad an effort, I
think, closing the door behind me. This baby bunny punches
above its weight. I glance ostentatiously around the well-
appointed office, which is entirely empty of other people. It is
a pretty undercroft, barrel-vaulted with old but recently sand-
blasted mezzane, very pink, with fresh white walls in which a
few pieces of ancient stonework have been allowed to stand
forth. At a guess, the town house of which this is the ground
floor is seventeenth-century, maybe slightly older. I have to
admit that Benedetti has created an office that is surprisingly
tasteful. There are the inevitable desks with computer termi-
nals for his absent assistants: teenaged shysters who generally
wear slightly too large Armani suits and always have a mobile
phone plugged into one ear. There are the equally inevitable
grey filing cabinets that bespeak active commerce. There are
three of those steel and black-leather designer armchairs like
the one in Benjy Birnbaum's consulting suite. There are tasteful lights to illuminate the brick vaulting from below, and a
coconut sapling is sprouting in one corner from an unhusked
nut in a terra-cotta pot. It is a perfect set for dramatic acts of
conveyancing, but just at this moment the stage is empty.

"So how is business?" I innocently ask. "Frankly, *ingegnere*,
I'm surprised you ever manage to sell your houses because any
prospective client, once having glimpsed these superlative
premises, could scarcely covet any building other than this."
Benedetti, having risen punctiliously to his feet, makes an

elegantly dismissive gesture with one hand. The rosy light reflected by the naked brickwork overhead cruelly picks up the pink of scalp gleaming amid the skeins of his web. I give it another year and then he'll have to admit defeat and go for a toupee. The old warp and weft are fast disappearing and soon only an unabashed rug will suffice.

"You are your customary kind self to enquire," he says. "This is, of course, early Monday morning so naturally things appear slow. But in general, I'm happy to say, business becomes steadily more propitious. True, the economic climate is gloomy, and investors everywhere are maybe not as sanguine as they were a few years ago, but—yes—I dare say that sanguine is the overall mood of my modest enterprise. I can't, of course, speak for my competitors; but from the perspective of this office enough people, both from within Italy and from outside, seem to want to move to Versilia to keep my humble affairs here afloat. Discreetly so, but definitely afloat, the blessed Madonna be thanked."

"I hadn't realized she took such an interest in real estate."

"That British humour of yours, Signor Samper!" he wags an admonitory finger while smiling his rodent smile. In the usual manner of our conversations the initial brocade is beginning to wear thin.

"Since you so courteously indulge it, *ingegnere*, might you humour me further by explaining how I have just found this lying outside the back door of my neighbour's house?"

He studies the muddy, snail-trailed card I hand him as though it were a mystifying artefact lately unearthed in Pompei.

"It would appear to be one of our own cards," he concludes cautiously.

"My very own impression," I agree. "Unless of course an unscrupulous rival is counterfeiting them for his own arcane purposes. Call me credulous if you will, but I find myself assuming this to be the genuine article. In which case I further wonder how it came to be up at Le Rocce, given that on the last occasion we met I distinctly remember having told you my neighbour's house is not for sale. Of course, my memory is not infallible."

"No, signore, your memory is as excellent as ever. 'A gem' is how I describe it whenever you are mentioned. 'Signor Samper is blessed with a veritable gem of a memory.' I can only hazard that I must have dropped this card on that occasion and it has lain there unnoticed ever since."

"It hasn't."

"A hasty conclusion, surely, signore? A small puff of wind, the activities of a mouse—anything might just now have brought it out of hiding."

"Have you been up to that house since the summer?" I ask point-blank.

"No," he answers, equally so. For an instant we stare at each other through the holes in the brocade.

"Then it is indeed mysterious," I'm reduced to saying lamely. Damn.

"Without doubt. Except of course that anyone might carry one of our cards and drop it by chance. It is not in the interests of my business to ration them. However . . ." He goes into a thoughtful pose, tapping the card edgewise against the manicured nails of one hand.

"However?"

"However, it is conceivable that a *galoppino*, in the course of his researches, might have dropped such a card. These people often do carry an assortment of house agents' cards, depending on which of us might be interested in a particular property. Yes, the more I consider it, the more likely it seems. I am, of course, as distressed as you about such promiscuous littering of that veritable paradise of yours up there in the mountains."

"I am less concerned with litter, *ingegnere*, than with this impression everyone seems to share that my neighbour's house is for sale. Once again I must ask, do you know anything I don't about Marta? To be frank, I'm now seriously worried about her." A *galoppino*, I already knew, is a man who gallops about, nosing out likely and unlikely properties for sale and passing on the information for a cut of the sale price: in effect a sort of freelance estate agent working mostly for private buyers, although he will sometimes be employed by an official agency like Benedetti's. It is perfectly possible that a freebooting galoppino has been making his rounds even in a place as remote as ours, such is the demand for houses in this area. Isolated houses with a much-prized *vista mare* go at a premium, especially to those twice-a-year holidaymakers from Wiesbaden, Winchester and Willebroek.

"Am I to understand, Signor Samper, that you have still heard nothing of the lady's whereabouts?"

"You are."

"I'm naturally distressed that you are distressed. But as I told you before, I have no news of la Marta."

"Since you last saw her at Pisa airport."

"Ah no, signore. If you examine that gemlike memory of yours, you will immediately recall that I said I saw somebody who *resembled* her at a distance. The more I think about it, the more I doubt it was the lady in question."

"Well," I say resignedly, "I'm baffled."

"While not presuming on the depth of your relationship with her, might I suggest that she gave me the impression of very much having a life of her own?"

"You mean, like being a prostitute?" This is a goodly thrust, an exasperated reference to the canard Benedetti himself spread around some time ago, probably to curry favour with the local police and immigration officials but also from sheer malignant weaselry. But almost as soon as I've made this bitter remark I regret it. Benedetti quite properly lost a good deal of face over that incident, and that ought to have closed the matter with honour all square. Now, eager to make a debating point, I have unbalanced the ledger once more. I need to make immediate amends. Damn again.

"I apologize, *ingegnere*," I say pacifically, noting that the rodent glitter in his eyes has intensified. Ours is clearly not destined to be one of those deep and abiding friendships. "I spoke hastily and out of turn and I was wrong to do so. Please accept my sincere assurance that it is purely my worry for the lady that lends heat to my words." Enough, Samper. There's no need to lick the man's highly polished shoes.

"I accept your apology, signore," Benedetti says stiffly. "I trust that if and when you hear news of your neighbour I shall be among the first you tell."

Mercifully, at this uneasy juncture one of the Armani boys comes whistling in to work, hair painstakingly tinted and tousled and with a considerable love bite visible on the very back of his neck. Yes, I've often wondered about *him*. Ritual greetings defuse the moment. I take my leave and head for my favourite bar for a much-needed espresso. Sometimes I emerge triumphant from these bouts with Benedetti, but today I feel obscurely bested. I'm exhausted from cudgelling my brain into inventing florid insincerities in Italian, and I've learned absolutely nothing new. Maybe (I think as my caffeine receptors shift into overdrive), maybe that really *wasn't* Marta he saw at Pisa airport all those months ago. Isn't it more likely that in time, blood being thicker than water, she simply repented of her apparent desire to distance herself from that evilly handsome helicopter pilot brother of hers and went off to see him and her newly married sister? And maybe got picked up by Interpol along with the rest of her nefarious clan? Maybe (for under the influence of a second espresso, which has caused my caffeine receptors to go to afterburners, both heart rate and imagination are now racing), maybe after all she has swapped the shaky career of a composer for a better paid life of crime, or else is simply living on the ill-gotten gains her father had apparently been stashing away for her and her siblings in numbered accounts around the world? Perhaps even at this moment Marta is sunning herself in Barbados after extensive cosmetic surgery, a Voynovian beach bunny with a string of taut-stomached paramours in tow who don white dinner jackets to escort her to casinos after dark . . .

The sheer implausible vulgarity of this sub-James Bond fantasy makes me giggle. Nico the barman glances at me with raised eyebrows as though I might be calling for an impossible third espresso. He is clearly thinking that if this peculiar foreigner is going to have an *infarto* it would be far better if he had it off the premises. But my mirth is simply for the absurdity of my imaginative flight. Marta is not that kind of girl. Besides, the cosmetic surgeon doesn't exist skilled enough to transform that fat, frizzy bat of forty-plus into any sort of beach bunny that didn't look as though it had myxomatosis. No. But none of this explains what has become of her, any more than it explains why I should care as much as I so obviously do. Her house. That's it, of course. It matters very much to me what becomes of her house. Think Wiesbaden, Winchester and Willebroek. And here we are again, come full circle.

22

A nd now begins what Sherlock Holmes might have called a singular concatenation of events. The first is a furious outburst of barking and a fusillade of shots early one morning. It jerks me out of bed, the raw cucumber compresses falling from my eyes, as it were. As it isn't, actually; although ever since Benjy Birnbaum's brutal unmasking of my age I have taken to the gentle masking of my face with horrendously expensive creams applied nightly. Quite soon the panic and vanity will wear off and I shall present to my sixth decade a brave if rugose face. It is a visage both surly and lined that I now poke around the back door to find a platoon of middle-aged men apparently making a Vietnam movie by dawn's early light. They are all heavily armed and wearing dark olive or camouflaged fatigues girt about with bandoliers of glittering ammunition. They are high with triumph, unable to stand still and grinning madly. They pause occasionally to prod a large hunched mass on the ground with their toe caps like a prospective buyer kicking the tyres of a secondhand car. Their guns swing in all directions. They look crazy enough to turn my anger at being disturbed into an appeasing fear. Full mental jackets are what I should like to see them all safely strapped into, prior to being hauled off to the nearest Bedlam. However, this isn't going to happen and in the meantime I recognize several members of the local boar hunt. When they spot my whey-faced presence, clad as I am in a becoming pair of Count Mara pyjamas, their killers' grins turn to bluff bonhomie.

"Buongiorno, Gerri," says Mannue', a man of about my age but well beyond the aid of face packs and cucumbers, besides missing several teeth. As he speaks, he and his companions contrive to shuffle together so that their huddled victim is concealed behind camouflaged legs.

"Emmanuele," I acknowledge with a brief nod. Some hounds are roaming about, rangy and mangy, sniffing at whatever lies behind their masters' legs and baying excitedly. "What's that you've killed, a *cinghiale*? Well inside the hundred-metre radius around a house specified by the law, wouldn't you say?" I add with an attempt at a proprietorial sternness.

"Ah, no, Gerri. We shot it at least a hundred metres away but with its last energies it ran here and expired."

"You're sure you didn't all miss it and the beast simply died of a heart attack?"

The men laugh dutifully. "We never miss," says one of them. "Whatever we aim at *dies*."

"Well, it would, sooner or later." The strengthening light is beginning to reveal glimpses of stained fur on the ground between their legs. "Unusual looking boar, that."

"Ah, they come in many varieties up here. Once my father shot a—"

"With *fur*?"

"Sometimes," Mannue' agrees darkly. "Sometimes more furry, sometimes less so. I remember—"

"So what is it you've just shot in my own back yard?"

"It was a mistake, Gerri. The light was not good and the dogs—"

Emboldened now, I move toward them on slippered feet, the dewy grass cold against my ankles. Not knowing what to do, the men fall back slightly and reveal the bloodstained corpses of a large badger and one of their own dogs, its back legs still twitching. I'm thinking how lucky I am they haven't shot one of their own party. Not a season goes by without fatalities among Italian hunters, many of them genuine accidents. Whatever else goes wrong with my humble plans for quiet bucolic harmony up here at Le Rocce I am determined there shall be no human cadavers. It seems little enough to ask. "A fine *tasso*," I say. "Heavily protected, of course."

"And rightly," says Mannue' virtuously. "They're good animals. No one would ever shoot one deliberately, not these days. Unfortunately, up here in these wilds and woods regrettable accidents happen."

We've reached the subtle part of the proceedings. As locals, these good old boys will know about the helicopters and film moguls and carabinieri who haunted Le Rocce for some months only a couple of years ago. They know I have connections and that it is theoretically within my power to cause them trouble. But they also know I won't because the same goes for them and it would only start a feud that would cause me greater grief in the long run. Hunters here have age-old rights and, besides, I'm an interloper in their territory. In recognition of this standoff, in which I am technically the wronged party (if one discounts the badger and the dog), they will be in a mood to be pacific.

"Badger meat can be delicious," I observe. The men's expressions soften into enthusiasm.

"Ah, stewed, *in umido*, like boar."

"No, roast with rosemary," says another. "My wife—"

"Even minced and made into *polpette*," volunteers a third. "During the war, according to my grandfather—"

"Perhaps you would like some, Gerri?" asks Mannue', stepping forward and unsheathing a huge knife.

This is exactly what I want. Softly, softly, catchee badger. "True, a good haunch would do well in my freezer. And maybe even some of that dog, too. Meanwhile, I assume we could all do with a coffee?"

I go back into the house to put on some rugged attire suit-

able for breakfasting with hunters and to make the coffee.
Through the window I catch occasional glimpses as they
adroitly but messily skin the animals. One of the men goes off,
no doubt to his parked Russian UAZ jeep, to fetch a spade and
a tarpaulin. Two of them then disappear into the woods with
the skins to bury the evidence while the roughly jointed car-
casses, a beautiful bright red in the early sunlight, glisten in a
heap on the tarpaulin. They drink the hot coffee heavily *corretto*
with grappa and Vecchia Romagna brandy from their hip
flasks and a curious peace falls over us, of death and a new day
and an honourable pact. I take the cups from them and then
the dripping, still warm haunches which I dump in the kitchen
sink before following them to their jeeps parked haphazardly
just outside my drive. I was right: three of them are UAZ and
one a Land Rover. The tailgates of two are already down and
covered in drying blood from a brace of small boar. I'm betting
the owners will leave the blood on for a day or two as public
witness to their rough-and-tough machismo. We shake hands
all round and wish each other well and I return home satisfied
that my relations with the locals have been further cemented.
Up here in the wilds you need all the goodwill going. You
never know when your car might slide off the road on a patch
of ice in winter and need a tow.

It's a bit of a shock being jerked from one's bed in this brutal fashion, but the compensatory hunks of flesh in the sink
have made it worthwhile. I have only ever eaten badger once
and was impressed by its subtle, if gamey, richness. I can't say
I find dog meat overexciting, but it can be turned into wonderful pâté with the right herbs and diligence. I carefully wash,
pat dry and bag both haunches and put them into the freezer.
At the back of my mind is a plan to make badger Wellington as
a possibly outstanding winter recipe using a meat all too rarely
eaten these days. The old people around here are a fertile
source of ideas for cooking badger, porcupine, squirrel,

marten, hedgehog and similar woodland delicacies, although they won't eat mole. So much of an animal's flavour depends on its own diet. (As anyone will know who has eaten puffin. I remember from my childhood that earthworms taste bitter as well as gritty, so I imagine they might well pass on this quality to the moles that prey on them.) No doubt it was only the absence of badgers in wartime central London that prevented Dame Emmeline Tyrwhitt-Glamis from bequeathing us a toothsome way of preparing them. Her fox rissoles are a treat. In any case I believe Juri Picacs (however you pronounce him) has several fox and wolf recipes as well as sixteen ways of cooking the bears his late employer, President Tito of Yugoslavia, shot by the hundred. Picacs was Tito's game master at Slub, and in retirement supplemented his state pension by writing an unexcelled game cookbook, although Western palates may find some of his flavours a little on the robust side, especially those involving quantities of paprika, juniper berries and slivovitz. I have long wished to get my hands on a haunch of bear in order to have a go at bear Wellington (which I suppose in Britain would inevitably become known as bear Paddington). I am encouraged by excitable accounts in *Il Tirreno* of European bears as well as wolves making a slow but steady comeback in mountainous regions, suggesting it is only a matter of time before they stray across to Le Rocce from Garfagnana. At which point they will inevitably wander into the grappa-blurred sights of Emmanuele and his mates and sooner or later wolf Stroganoff will once again feature on local menus. Until then, badger Wellington remains a plausible alternative.

The second of the events I mentioned earlier is a call from Adrian inviting himself to Le Rocce for my birthday which is now in a mere three weeks' time, on December the second. I notice that this year it happens to fall on a Saturday, which gives us the weekend in which to celebrate this deeply unwelcome anniversary.

"You surely couldn't have been proposing to pass such a notorious milestone on your own?"

"Forty-shmorty," I say bravely. "It's just numbers."

"Fifty-shmifty," he corrects firmly. "I can add up better than you can, you old fraud."

"A harmless deception" is my attempt to laugh it off.

"Oh, harmless, yes. Sure, *harmless*. I'm merely saying it wasn't much of a deception, given that you leave your driving licence lying around. Your picture's peachy enough, the date of birth less so. I always thought you came on a bit world-weary for a stripling of forty."

"Ah, well." I'm suddenly diffident. "I'll just have to put on a stronger shade of lipstick and wear butcher jeans."

"Mutton dressed as ram? This I must see. Anyway, you can expect me at Pisa some time on the Friday."

"Good," I say, secretly overjoyed, although I can't quite bring myself to say so, not without warning, not to this brisk scientist speaking from his room in BOIS with the oilskins on the back of the door, The Face pinned to the cork notice board and bone-white specimens of the cold-water coral *Lophelia pertusa* lying around. It's hard to sound convincingly affectionate to the person who has just wrong-footed and unmasked you.

The third event is almost more marvellous. Adrian's sister Jennifer calls on behalf of her husband: the great Max Christ is wondering whether there's any chance of his being able to see me over the weekend of the second of December.

"You mean in England?" I ask, thinking, Just my luck: it *would* be that weekend.

"No, there in Italy. What he'd really like to know is, is there any chance of his being able to stay the night on that Saturday? I know it's an awful impertinence, inviting himself like that, and you must say at once if it will be too difficult, what with it being your birthday and your living out in the wilds. But he has just been asked to do a concert in Florence at short notice that week and he's been wanting an excuse for yonks to go back there and look at a manuscript in someone's library. Max hates hotels, so he thought he might combine it with a visit to your famous eyrie."

"I don't know what to say. Oh, yes I do: how did you know about my birthday? I suppose Adrian ratted on me, curse him."

"Certainly he did. And why ever not? Is it a state secret, or are you just being bashful?"

"I was, but it's no longer worth the effort. Will you be coming as well?"

"I can't, Gerry, unfortunately. I've still got the last of the builders to supervise here, plus there's Josh, who just at the moment doesn't like leaving his dinosaurs. These days it's as much as I can do to get him into Woodbridge, and when I do he's anxious they'll start fighting among themselves in his absence. You should see his bedroom. It's a Jurassic theme park. On the rare occasions I go in there with the Hoover I feel like Wilma Flintstone."

"Did you ever get the one out of the downstairs lavatory?"

"I don't remember. Which was that?"

"I've no idea. But there was a crisis when I came that night. I think he'd decided his stegosaur needed a poop and it had jammed in the S-bend."

"Good lord, we have crises like that every day at Crendlesham Hall. At the moment I believe we've got plastic dinosaur eggs in the car's heating system. When I wasn't watching he somehow managed to feed them into one of those swivelling-eyeball duct things, don't ask me how. So when we put the blower on it sounds like hailstones inside. It's completely deafening. Josh said he thought they would hatch faster where it was warm. Perfectly logical for a five-year-old. Anyway, what should I tell Max?"

"That I shall be delighted."

"He'll be so pleased, Gerry."

"What's he conducting in Florence, anyway?"

"Golly, he did say but I wasn't really listening. Some dutiful Respighi, I think. Anyway, a largely Italian first half. Then some Chausson and Bartók Three. Taneyev's playing that. Apparently the Italians love Taneyev—all that romantic hair and those Byron collars. Oh, thank you, Gerry. Max will be thrilled."

She rings off, leaving me stranded somewhere between ecstasy and total panic. Christ himself up here at Le Rocce! The logistics are going to be horrendous. Food. Beds. Fetching from airports. Then it strikes me that maybe I should invite a guest of my own. Whether or not Derek will anyway be coming to Florence to hear Taneyev play (and I doubt he's at much liberty to travel around behind his paramour, what with having to earn his crust at Corcoran's), Samper can score maximum points by having Derek to stay that weekend. Russian pianists with rapidly thinning romantic hair, no matter how adored by the Italian concertgoing public, are effortlessly outranked by a conductor of Max Christ's stature. The casual fact of Christ overnighting in my house will not be lost on Derek, I'm happy to say, but I should like it to come as a surprise. So I phone him and suggest he might like to join a little house party I've decided to give on my birthday.

"Ooh, your fiftieth, of course! Yes, that would be lovely, Gerry. I think Pavel's playing in Florence that week and it'll be perfect. One stone, two birds, you know."

Oh, how I know. "I look forward to your gracing my humble nest with your presence," I say with a slight edge. Lost on him, no doubt, but I can't go too far or else he will remind me of all the hospitality I've taken off him recently in London.

"Fifty!" he witters on blithely. "Fancy that. It's been at the back of my mind for ages. For the last ten years, actually." Okay, so maybe my harmless deception hasn't deceived anyone but me. "I shall have to find something appropriate for you."

"Too kind, Derek. But do bear in mind you're not so far behind yourself. I shall be waiting."

"No you won't. You'll be too busy heading for sixty. Sixty. Imagine! It will be like living in one of those black-and-white Movietone news films where everyone wears hats."

All of which is our way of being quite pleased that he will be coming for the weekend in early December.

Those of you who have kept up with the Samper chronicles so far will know that mine is a rough-and-ready approach to social events. We tend not to stand on ceremony up in these regions off the beaten track. Potluck is the normal order of the day for visitors here, although even I can see that in the past certain guests faced with some of my more experimental dishes may have considered themselves pot unlucky. I would be the first to admit—although as it happened I was the third to admit—that the cuckoo sorbet I once dug out of the freezer for stepmother Laura and my father was a culinary failure on the nitpicking grounds that it was inedible. It's possible that the cuckoo had been off or else that I had burst its gall bladder while preparing it. Even so, the fuss they made seemed out of all proportion to the dish's sheer inventiveness. These things happen. No doubt even in the sunny, food-is-fun world of the TV cheffies the aproned idiots must occasionally find themselves stuffing burnt quiche down their waste-disposal unit and hoping the extractor fan will clear the fumes before their guests arrive. None of it need have happened had not Laura, in a burst of geriatric energy, insisted on coming to Italy to see the Leaning Tower of Pisa before either it or she collapsed irreparably. At the age of seventy-seven my father, faced with the alternative of a severe pussy-whipping (to borrow an appalling but apt American expression) wisely acquiesced. They used Le Rocce as their base shortly after I'd bought it a few years ago. I suppose over the decades I have grown almost fond of my father in a distant sort of way, as fond as I'm able while despising him for having imagined he could replace my mother with a creature like Laura. People generally do what they're going to do but in the case of family there's the additional burden of having to pretend one approves of their action. The scriptures, as so frequently quoted by Laura, claim that many waters cannot quench love. Obviously tsunamis don't read the Bible, nor did the wave that swept my mother and elder brother Nicky off the Cobb at Lyme Regis some forty years ago. It certainly quenched any possibility that I would love my mother's stand-in. Meanwhile the Good Book remains Laura's daily helpmeet for making sense of her world. This antique compendium of jokes will form a fitting accompaniment to her final years in a hospice for the terminally bewildered.

In any case, soi-disant experts on the human unconscious will naturally claim I quite deliberately fed my father and stepmother with a less than top-hole cuckoo sorbet as a way of showing the aggression I felt, Laura quite clearly being the cuckoo in our family nest. As usual with such smart-arse diagnoses this is hopelessly overdetermined. Actually, there had been two polythene tubs in the freezer marked "CS," the other one full of the sumptuous cashew sorbet (with hints of caraway and cardamom) I was intending to serve and which was of a more or less identical mottled beige colour. By the time it was thawed enough to be scooped I realized I had picked the wrong tub but deemed it too late to bother about. Within minutes we all wished I hadn't. Certainly I was not doing my unconscious any favours by sampling it myself and even gaily persevering for several spoonfuls while eulogizing its fascinating flavour and digestive properties. The upshot of this unhappy episode is that I am determined nothing of that nature will happen at my forthcoming birthday dinner. When grandees like Max Christ are guests it behoves the host to produce something rare and memorable without being remotely hazardous. A sorbet that induces projectile vomiting is no gracious way to end a meal, as

Gayelord Hauser cogently observed. This means I am already giving careful thought to the menu.

I am also giving careful thought to accommodation. Adrian will share my room, naturally, and Max Christ will have the main guest room. There is a third bedroom in the house which under normal circumstances would be quite good enough for Derek. I am now very glad I had the barn converted this summer. Knowing him of old I'm familiar with his habit of turning up with some unexpected creature of the night in tow, so it will be far safer to segregate him in the barn. He'll have a brand-new bedroom with all mod cons so he can hardly complain. Mind you, if he does bring some uninvited partner I shall probably never speak to him again, but we'll face that if and when. He's better than he used to be, I will say that for him. Old age, I suppose. He went a little wild after seeing his proctologist through the gates of Putney Vale but has since calmed down considerably. Maybe it's the sudden influence of classical music on his life or else a general withering of the glands.

The more I consider the menu the more convinced I am that badger Wellington will fill the bill most admirably. Here we have a meat that I already know to be excellent, recently killed and ready to hand. Why go to the expense of buying pounds of dreary old fillet steak in a Camaiore butcher's? There's no doubt we shall be needing a sturdy main course. We will be a minimum of four or five sitting down and who knows what the weather will be like in early December? In the past we have had early snow up here in November, and even without snow it can get pretty cold. I also have to take logistics into account because it's not clear how the various guests' arrivals can be synchronized. All in all it will require a substantial dish that will stand keeping warm while meeting the minimum Samper criterion of novelty. Since we're on the subject I may as well impart the secret even as I remind you that it remains my intellectual property.

Badger Wellington

Ingredients

1.53 kg badger fillet
249 gm sliced mushrooms, button if nothing better available
40.5 ml decent olive oil
51 gm unsalted butter
321 gm gun-dog pâté
38 gm foie gras
Several juniper berries
Small clove fresh garlic
403 gm frozen puff pastry, thawed
6 fresh bay leaves
Pepper
1¼ beaten eggs to glaze
1 boiled empty shotgun cartridge (optional)

This is a very straightforward dish indeed and I hardly know why I bother explaining it to any cook worth his or her salt. (Which incidentally should be the ordinary granular kitchen variety. Don't let the organic brigade dupe you with faddist nonsense about sea salt, as though in some mysterious way it's more healthy or flavourful. It's merely evaporated seawater, which is exactly what all salt deposits are, duh. In fact, regular salt mines tap into prehistoric salt deposits laid down by long-ago seas unpolluted by human fallout, and therefore have claims to be considerably healthier than modern salt. Kitchen salt is the same stuff as sea salt even when it comes in flaky crystals in packets including the words "Nature" or "Neptune" and costing eight times as much as ordinary salt. It *is* ordinary salt: no more, no less.)

Anyway, what you do is thaw out and bone both your badger and gun-dog haunches, remembering to remove any whitish pieces of tendon. Marinade the badger overnight in salted water (not too strong) together with the half-dozen bay leaves. This will remove any faint vestiges of its late owner's musky scent while not interfering with the characteristic flavour. Pat it dry, trim it up and tie it into an oblong with string. Heat the oil. Season the fillet with pepper and fry it briskly to seal the meat. Then roast it for 25 minutes at 220°C. Let it cool and remove string.

The dog, too, should be briefly fried and roast for 29 minutes. When it is cool you should mince it as finely as possible, continuing to pass it through the grinder until eventually it attains a pâté-like consistency. Then blend it with the pounded juniper berries, the pounded garlic and the foie gras. Only you can say how you like your canine pâté. Personally, I favour it velvety smooth and not too highly seasoned so that an educated palate might even make a good guess at the breed. As to the breed of this particular hound, I should think a single sperm from a springer spaniel blundered into its ancestry round about 1876. The rest of its inheritance was the genetic emulsion that leads to leggy, vaguely liver-and-white Italian hunting dogs with the eager intelligence of toadstools, an attribute they generally share with their owners.

Now slice the mushrooms and fry in butter until soft. I only specified button mushrooms out of pity for urban cooks without access to anything better than those overpriced scabby brown Japanese fungi with the risky name. The truth is, and despite a global conspiracy to pretend otherwise, button mushrooms *have no taste*. None. Zero. Nada. They are empty texture. What you *really* need for badger Wellington are fresh chanterelles or blewits. This is an autumn or winter dish and ought to taste as though it has spiritual roots in the rich loam of damp woods rather than in the bins of an all-night deli. Anyway, once your interesting fungi are soft, cool them and blend with the doggy pâté.

The rest is easy. On a floured surface roll out the pastry (if you're cooking this in Italy, puff pastry is known as *pasta sfoglia* and is easily obtained). Aim for a rectangle 35 x 30 cm and 0.5 cm thick. Transfer it to a baking sheet. Spread the dog down the centre of this pastry strip. Align Mr. Brock on top of it and brush the edges of the pastry with the beaten egg. Fold the pastry over lengthways and turn the entire parcel over so that the join is now underneath. Tuck the ends under the meat on the baking sheet and if you can be bothered decorate the thing with leaf shapes cut from the pastry trimmings. Bake at 220°C for 50 minutes, covering with foil after half an hour. The thoroughly cleaned and boiled cartridge case—it should be 12-bore but 20-bore will do at a pinch—can be cut down and inserted cap uppermost in the top of the pastry just before serving if desired. It strikes a suitably venatorial note. On no account allow the cartridge to go in the oven. Modern ones are made of plastic which will melt disgustingly and ruin everything. What one is aiming for is the brightly polished brass cap embedded in dog pâté and sticking jauntily up through the lusciously browned puff pastry.

On this occasion I am preparing the main dish several days in advance, half-cooking it and putting it into the deep freeze to await the day. It's always a great relief to be that much ahead of the game. It gives one time to assemble the dinner's lesser elements. These, I decide, will be strictly conventional, consisting of the sort of things visitors to Tuscany expect to find. We will start with assorted *crostini*—and I may even cheat and buy the various spreads made by my favourite grocer, although I shall certainly mix some hound pâté *crostini* in with the normal *fegato* ones. After that I feel we might skip the obligatory pasta course owing to the substantial nature of the main course. An intricate salad will do quite well instead. With the Wellington I shall serve rosemary-roasted potatoes and broccoli spears. Frozen peas, I'm sorry to say, are common. Even cheffies will only reach for the mushy variety. To add a thawed block of peas to a carefully crafted dinner is an admission of failure. You might just as well add monosodium glutamate.

*

As the day approaches I seem to be spending inordinate amounts of both time and money on what are essentially my own birthday celebrations. This feels wrong. On the other hand, having Max Christ to dinner feels right for both social and professional reasons. Once again it looks plausible to think of myself as his future biographer. Still, a mood of brainless bonhomie does not come naturally to me. I'm not fond of playing host at the best of times but the background rumbling of the wingèd chariot's wheels makes it that much worse. No doubt I ought to be pleasantly surprised that anyone wishes to visit me and celebrate my birthday; but it all feels too ironically like being thrown a life belt from the deck of the *Titanic*. Consequently, I'm finding it hard to enter into the spirit of the thing. What exactly *is* the spirit of turning fifty that any mortal could possibly enter into with rejoicing? These days the years succeed one another like quick, identical drips from a diminishing icicle.

But this is familiar territory to the last and most philosophical of the Sampers. I suppose watching one's mother and brother being swept to oblivion by a freak wave adds a sobering note to any nine-year-old's life. But I am certain that even before that memorable incident I could never really suppress bleak thoughts, especially the most inopportune ones, a habit that has persisted. For instance: called upon to view a friend's newborn baby, the precious bundle from which protrude adorable bits of infant anatomy, I always find myself wondering (even as my voice supplies the requisite pleasantries) whether it will grow up to be force-fed human excrement and drowned in a barracks latrine, as uncounted Russian Jews were in the Second World War. Or else is it destined to die of a drug overdose at seventeen, choke to death in a restaurant in its thirties or fall victim to a hit-and-run driver while walking the dog? In short, there is nothing like the sight of new life to make me wonder how it will end. This must be one of those yardsticks of a person's basic character, like the one that supposedly distinguishes optimists from pessimists (is the glass half full or half empty?). Is this baby alive or merely laggard in its dying? It does add a dimension of pity to what is otherwise a flat and goofy spectacle of unapprehensive love. And I am powerless to stop it.

I am also powerless to stop the sudden phone call that adds a new dimension to my dinner-party plans. It is Nanty Riah, and there are five days to go.

"See, Gerry, thing is we had this gig on Saturday, right? In Oslo, right? Turns out the Danes, or are they Swedes, are like *really* fussy about communicable diseases and they've postponed it. Prolly after Christmas, now. So what I was wondering, suppose we have a go at starting this book? Few sessions with a tape recorder, know what I mean?"

"You have a communicable disease, Nanty?"

"Nah, not me, just the boys. Nothing to ping off the walls about. Just a bit itchy."

"How revolting. What have they got?"

"Scabies. I mean, whoever made a fuss about scabies? It's like having nits, right? Which half the schoolkids in Britain have got. Not me, of course. One of the few perks of alopecia. No lice, no crabs. So these Swedes or Oslogians are saying it's an E.U. health directive or some bollocks 'cos scabies can lead to something else."

"Like scratching?"

"Dunno. Anyway, are you up for this or what?"

And before long Nanty, too, is on my guest list together with whatever of Alien Pie's parasites are able to hitch a lift on his body. When I tell him Max Christ will be there he knows exactly who he is, which is a good sign. A few years ago he either wouldn't have known or would have affected not to know. I think he must be taking this image face-lift seriously. He can have the third room in the house. He seems unbothered about returning to the very place where a couple of years ago he was so terrified by imaginary UFOs that he fled to London the very next day. He says it will be all right if there are other people there besides me. This is possibly not much of a compliment but he can stay on after the others have left and see how his nerves stand up to it.

Apparently Max's concert is on Thursday and he will be staying that and Friday night with friends close by in Empoli, enabling him to spend a whole day free in Florence, plus most of Saturday. Then he will come on to me by car. I shall myself collect Adrian and Nanty from Pisa airport. Derek havers mysteriously over the phone and can damn well make his own arrangements. This is typical of him and I shan't waste time worrying. No doubt I shall get an excited call from him just as we're moving from the festive prosecco into the crostini course, saying he's in Barcelona with this *fabulous* boy and not to worry. Worry? Me? With a birthday meal to prepare and the nightmare of arranging the roughly simultaneous arrival of at least four guests at an obscure house somewhere up a pitch-dark mountainside in Tuscany? Absurd.

But heavy sarcasm doesn't become me. Even as I buckle to, making beds and rounding up those curious balls of dust that grow in the darkness beneath them, I have to admit I'm now beginning to feel more chipper. I'm still registering what a huge relief it is at last to be free of Millie and her preposterous entourage. The thought that I shall never again have to write another book with her is a tonic to the soul. In addition—and to satisfy the inquisitive—I can reveal that I have had no further manifestations of a priapic nature and I really think my body has finally shed the last residues of Mr. and Mrs.

ProWang's magic toxins. I instinctively sense that the internal storms have subsided along my hormonal coastline. An uncanny peace has fallen over my ravaged endocrine system and my islets of Langerhans are once again sunlit offshore jewels set in an ocean of dimpling blue. Feeling that these days a tourist brochure might represent my interior more accurately than an MRI scan, I bustle about the house making it minimally salubrious.

23

Adam and Eve, the world's first householders, had their lease on Eden rudely foreclosed and were obliged to relocate to one of Mesopotamia's less fashionable parts, of which—then as now—there was no shortage. Eve later remarked that aside from the occasional snake Eden hadn't been a bad place to live. "The fruit was fabulous. Basically, though, just too many trees. We weren't that sorry to leave, actually. If you wanted any sort of social life, well, forget it, the place was dead. But *dead*. We couldn't throw even the smallest dinner party for a few friends because we simply didn't have any. There was literally no one else to invite apart from some old gardener with no conversation who turned nasty at the end."

There must be something of the old Eve in me because although Le Rocce is in many ways a paradise there is not much in the way of society up here for those rare evenings when one feels the itch of sociability. Very occasionally the mood does come upon me and I have the urge to shine a bit. Frankly, certain people are better at playing host than others and I rather fancy I have underused talents in that direction. If I can temporarily overcome my utter disdain for most of the human race I can generally enter into the spirit of the thing and lay on a memorable occasion.

On the day of my grand dinner—yes, my birthday party if you insist—I find I am definitely in the mood, having arranged everything to perfection. My cantina is stuffed with prosecco

and other drinkables. My larder shelves groan with edibles.
The house is clean without being prim. The beds are made.
And as the day progresses my guests start arriving. By means
of cash, cajolery and threats the local taxis have managed to
bring some; others I have fetched myself with split-second tim-
ing. So by the time we sit down to dinner I at last feel I can
relax and indulge the spirit of revelry that liberal quantities of
prosecco have already done much to encourage. Everyone I
invited is present and correct, even Derek, who has earned
additional Brownie points by arriving with the celebrated
Pavel Taneyev and not with some ragamuffin stranger he has
scooped up en route. The *crostini* topped with the gun-dog
pâté that I cannily intermingled with the ordinary liver ones
have vanished with cries of rapture. I have now served the first
two bottles of Chianti Classico, San Fabiano Calcinaia's Cellole
Riserva 2000, which is a superb blend of Sangiovese, Cabernet
Sauvignon and Merlot grapes. With a muscular alcohol content of 13.5% it falls companionably into step with a robust
meat dish. And so it is that I finally help myself to a sturdy portion of badger Wellington and sit down at the head of my can-
dle-lit dinner table. I still can hardly believe it has all come to
pass.

It is a charming, even glittering, scene. I have to admit it is
the first time this house has really come into its own as a setting for the sort of company I have always known to be my
proper milieu (except for Derek). So if you detect a note of
preening in my description you will have to excuse it. Picture
a large farmhouse kitchen with chestnut beams and an open
log fire on a raised stone hearth along one wall. Seated on my
left, the world-renowned conductor Max Christ, whose startling presence made Derek's jaw drop satisfyingly when he
arrived. It was just as I'd foreseen. Taneyev is no doubt a royal
card, but my ace in the hole was Max, who trumped him perfectly. Neither Max nor Taneyev had known the other was

going to be here so it came as a surprise to them, too, a mere couple of days after they had played the Bartók concerto together in Florence. Last night, of course, Christ stopped at Empoli, which now I think wouldn't be a bad title for a movie. On my right is Adrian, who arrived first and has provided sterling help with the food. Derek, to his intense pleasure, is sitting on the left hand of Christ while opposite him in a miasma of Allure is his Byronic Russian hero, whose performance two nights ago was so wildly acclaimed by the Florentines. A daemonic poet at the keyboard he may well be, this prodigy son of a Soviet aeronautical engineer, but at the festive board he is revealed as a solid trencherman of peasant-like proportions. I keep trying to forget that the staff at Corcoran's know him as "Pauline." As for Derek's verdict on his hair, I can only concur. Pavel's genes have unfortunately fated that his hair go the same way as Sig. Benedetti's. Still, he has one great advantage over that smooth little estate agent. If someone can play Balakirev's *Islamey* electrifyingly you don't bother about his expertly tousled hair being less substantial than its dimensions pretend. On the other hand it is precisely the finicky grooming and utter ordinariness of someone like Benedetti that makes the eye zoom in cruelly on his woven web.

Opposite me at the far end of the table is Nanty, perched on cushions to ease his gluteal zone. He is in high old form, I'd say, now and then giggling to himself or inviting Max to join him in renditions of some classic rock number from the sixties. To everybody's pleasure Max minds not at all, and having actually been alive in the sixties (unlike Nanty, who was born in 1973) and blessed with a musical memory of stunning accuracy, he performs better than the boy-band leader. I imagine that after Nanty's previous experiences in my house two years ago, when he foolishly arrived without a single pharmacological crutch, he has made sure on this occasion to pack plenty of mood-elevating substances. My own experience of recreational drugs is that, like drunkenness and senility, they do not encourage some startling new character to emerge. On the contrary, they simply display the same old character but in a form no longer inhibited by shame, social mores or self-censorship. If people appear to become suddenly mean in their cups or nursing home the chances are the meanness was always there, which may well make their friends and family look back with new insight. In Nanty's case he simply disseminates an amiable, comfortable presence much like that of a prolapsed old family Labrador, now following the conversation (and people's forkfuls) with a sort of blank alertness, and now staring at the fire with something approaching alert blankness. I am more than ever convinced my judgement of his character is sound and that he will prove a comparative delight to work with. Compared with Millie Cleat, I mean. I shall always need to remember that Nanty is also a public figure, with the drawbacks that entails. But at the very least he has a lovable streak. Just before dinner he came downstairs with a present for me: a flat presentation box of polished walnut in which, on velvet lining, lay a bright metal disc. This turned out to be a platinum pressing of his band's theme song, "Alien Pie," which was in the charts for a near-record number of months some time ago.

"'Ere y'ar, mate," he said as he thrust the box into my hands. "Didn't want you to think we'd nicked your idea without any acknowledgement."

"Huh?"

"It was your idea, remember? It was you came up with Alien Pie as the new name for Freewayz. In the business they say it's the most successful-ever exercise in rebranding. Ever, Gerry. That's not nothing, mate. So 'ere y'ar."

This gift is not only touchingly useless but has the additional virtue of being unplayable on any audio equipment I own. But I suppose you don't *play* platinum discs. Quite what you do with them I'm not sure. Presumably you stick them on the wall of your downstairs lavatory to intrigue and impress your guests, much as Benjy Birnbaum advertises his repute in the field of ethical latex to give nervous patients a talking point before he starts to loosen their clothing.

As to the food on this auspicious evening, the badger Wellington is an unqualified success. The fillet is tender and delicious, the hound-and-foie-gras pâté in which it is lapped intriguingly unidentifiable and divinely rich. The only tiny deviation I have made from the stated list of ingredients concerns the mushrooms, which I picked in the woods myself since absolute freshness is essential. Chanterelles are unfortunately nonexistent around here because it's simply too dry for most of the year. Blewits, both wood and field varieties, are also quite uncommon. What we usually have is an abundance of parasols, although on my early morning ramble I failed to find a single one. But I did gather a mixed bag of woodland goodies, including a couple of small porcini or ceps and six or seven chestnut boletus—which each year grow sparsely beneath a particular group of oak trees near here. These have a delicious hazelnut flavour and I was pleased to have found them. On the way back I also spied three fresh, leggy specimens of *Panaeolus semiovatus* growing on a mildewed lump of what may have been fox dung, and just as I skirted the grassy area Marta had once cleared for her brother's helicopter I found two sound survivors from a deliquescing group of Liberty Caps (*Psilocybe semilanceata*, in case you need to know). Both these last varieties are of small dimensions and somewhat hallucinogenic. I have found that when cooked together they induce a most agreeable euphoria combined with mild but interesting sensory disturbances which last a couple of hours or so: long enough to ensure an evening's success. It is, of course, utterly irresponsible to incorporate such things into innocent guests' badger Wellington, but I trust no one has ever accused Samper of responsible behaviour except in identifying the fungi I pick in these woods. I never take chances. There is nothing in this dish that could cause even passing queasiness, let alone projectile diarrhoea, and still less kidney failure. Don't worry—we country boys may be out of our depths in big cities but up here in the wilds we are in our element.

As any good hostess knows, the presence of an illustrious guest at the dinner table can sometimes actually dampen the occasion because the other guests hardly dare strike up a conversation with him or her for fear of appearing either sycophantic or stupid. Tonight, of course, we have no fewer than three bona fide celebrities, at least two of whom easily qualify as household names, depending on your household. This is really an advantage because none of them needs to impress anyone else so they can turn with relief to the sort of ordinary topics that make for light conversation. If Derek hoped he was going to hear gems of stage-door gossip from the two classical musicians present tonight he must be disappointed. Over the main course Max and Pavel suddenly discover each other to be Tom and Jerry aficionados. Pavel is not seriously let down by his English, the holes in which he patches with an occasional French or German word.

"Non, Max, the first is 'Puss Gets the Boot' and is from 1940. The cat, he is not yet Tom."

"Quite right, he's called Jasper, and Jerry is Jinx. The producer was Rudolf Ising. But from the second cartoon onwards, in 1941, they were all produced by Fred Quimby until the mid-fifties. The great years."

"*Genau.* The best of *animation*, the best of *dessin*."

"But what interests me," says Max, who is now beginning to conduct his own words with a fork and a pronged roast potato, "is the use of classical music in cartoons of that period. Right from 'Fantasia' onwards, which was 1940, you get that Hollywood urge to set cartoon antics to well-known classics."

"'*Fantasia*' is a *travestissement, ganz geschmacklos*, terrible."

"Agreed. But did you ever see Bugs Bunny in 'Bunny Baton'? He has to conduct Suppé's 'Morning, Noon and Night in Vienna' and the matching of the music with his actions is simply wonderful, especially when a fly starts to pester him. In the space of about five minutes he parodies every conceivable 'great conductor' mannerism. I tell you, Pavel, if ever I feel I'm becoming pompous in front of an orchestra I remind myself of Bugs Bunny."

I endeavour to punctuate this scholarly exchange with offers of stronger wine and madder badger. Substantial though my dish may be, nobody's appetite seems to have slackened yet and everyone comes back for seconds. I pluck the gleaming brass cartridge base out of the puff pastry and begin carving the badger's second half with the inner glow of the host who suddenly sees his much-dreaded dinner party becoming a great success. There are other reasons, too, for pride. Like both Derek and Pavel, Max Christ has obviously been bowled over by the house and on arrival paid me some very pretty compliments. Coming from the owner of a grand pile like Crendlesham Hall such enthusiasm was doubly gratifying and made me suddenly feel that all that hard labour I put into the place when I bought it has at last been fully rewarded. And throughout the evening, I've been noticing, Max seems completely at home and at ease. I can't not believe that this makes our future working partnership substantially more likely. I already imagine long sessions taking place in this very room, Max leaning back in his chair while I take careful notes as a tape recorder slowly twirls its spools between us. Once I've got Nanty's book out of the way I can at last embark on a project I needn't feel ashamed of.

But enough of the satisfactions of the future; the good host must attend to satisfying the present. There is a good deal of merriment around the table, I notice, with bits of salacious repartee threading their way amongst the Christ–Taneyev thesis of Hollywood cartoons. There is also a moment of potential awkwardness when Derek—it would be Derek—finds a piece of lead shot in his meat and asks if it is usual for Italians to hunt cows. Not at this time of year, I tell him, so the pellet must have fallen out of one of the mushrooms, which Tuscans hunt assiduously in November. The moment is mercifully lost in giggles and conversation continues.

" . . . *parodie* of Italian opera. Example: 'The Cat Above and the Mouse Below.' Tom, he is Figaro singing 'Largo al factotum' and Jerry, he is under the stage and trying to sleep. But by the end they have changed places. Once more, the action is so beautifully *synchronisiert* with the music."

"They also used 'The Barber of Seville' earlier in the series. If I remember correctly it was in 'Kitty Foiled' . . ."

Once normally unpompous people start saying things like "if I remember correctly" at a dinner party it's time for the host to start worrying that the conversation is in danger of becoming a monologue. But right on cue Nanty, who has been singing "The Blue Danube" to himself in a falsetto at the end of the table, now remembers a Tom and Jerry cartoon in which Tom retires to an attic to teach himself to play the piano. This is so he can lure Jerry out of his hole because the mouse can't resist waltzing by himself when he hears music.

"Ah, yes," Max says at once, "'Johann Mouse.' It won an Academy Award. In that one the musical satire's aimed at extreme pianism. You have Tom playing these incredible roulades à la Josef Hofmann or Horowitz but with his *feet*, even as he tries to hit Jerry over the head with a poker. It was actually Jakob Gimpel playing his own paraphrase of 'The Blue Danube.' He was a sadly underrated pianist."

"But much earlier than that is 'Cat Concerto,'" Pavel puts in, his hair an enthusiastic aureole that seems to give off a glow. "Tom, he is in tails, par excellence the romantic maestro. I think that is from 1947 . . ."

Adrian and I discreetly lurch to our feet to open more wine and fetch a second tray of rosemary potatoes from the oven. I notice the floor suddenly seems unstable and bright shimmers frame everything I look at. It's a very pleasant sensation, this dreamy swaying and the opulence of my vision. We both simultaneously clutch at the marble work surface.

"I'm afraid I must be getting a bit pissed," Adrian confesses. "Also, do you know, I feel mildly stoned."

"Me too. Don't tell anyone," I say conspiratorially, "but not everything lurking beneath that puff pastry would have been approved by Mrs. Beeton."

He catches on fast. "You rotten sod," he says with a giggle. "You've doctored it."

"Nothing much. Just a little something to help th–"

But at this moment there is an imperious knocking on the front door. By now Max is holding forth about how American culture in the forties and fifties had felt itself still overshadowed by the grand European artistic canon and sometimes felt obliged to poke gentle fun at it with an artistry all its own. But at this knocking he, too, breaks off and a sudden hush falls. "Who on earth can that be at this time of night?" he asks for all of us. "This is hardly the sort of place where neighbours just drop in."

"It's probably the Grim Reaper," says Derek. "He's come to tell Gerry that he's actually sixty after all and that his time is up."

More people laugh at this tasteless remark than I should have wished, but I suppose alcohol dulls the wits. I'm out in the passageway and opening the door to a squat lump with a halo. Can this be the Marian apparition I have long dreaded? I then notice that everything I look at has a halo, which probably has more to do with magic mushrooms and Chianti than with innate divinity, but who can tell the difference? The figure's features come suddenly into focus and—

"*Marta!!*"

"Gerree! I'm sorry to—"

"You're *back*! At last!" and incredulously I fall on her and give her a great big hug. She smells faintly of Etro's Gomma, a remarkably sophisticated scent for her to be wearing and by several light years an improvement on her usual Musky Temptress or whatever it was called. "Oh, Marta, I'm so pleased to see you! I—I thought you were dead."

"*Dead?*"

"Well, I mean, you just walked out leaving your house unlocked and the gas on and your car in the garage and blood-stains in the kitchen; what else were we to think? I was sure you'd been kidnapped and taken off to one of those horrible CIA 'black zones' to be tortured to death."

"But I was in California. Writing film music."

"California? How was I supposed to know that? You might have left me a note, Marta. I do think it was mean of you not to tell me. I've been off my head with worry."

"Oh, Gerree, I'm so sorry. I remember now, the taxi arrived early and muddled me and I cut myself taking the trash out." And she squeezes my hand. Hers, I notice, is stone cold.

"Never mind that." What *is* there to say to anybody as absentminded and ditzy as Marta? "You poor thing, you're frozen. Come in, come in. When did you arrive? We're having a bit of a party here. Some quite distinguished people, actually," by way of preparing her for the social disparity she's bound to feel. I am, of course, ecstatic to see her again, but I do rather wish she had chosen any evening other than this for her resurrection. Though doubtless distinguished in her way, I'm not sure that Marta exactly fits into Samper's natural milieu of world-class artists, not to mention a world-class scientist and, less probably, a world-class hairdresser. Frankly, old Marta diffuses about as much glitz and glamour as a debtors' prison. Still, all this while I'm leading her into the kitchen and in the doorway I pause and raise my voice like a butler announcing a late arrival.

"Er, guess what, everyone? This is my neighbour Marta, returned from the dead. I still can't believe it." But my disbelief has only just begun because Max rises courteously from his chair with the easy warmth of an old acquaintance.

"Hullo, Marta," he greets her. "This is a surprise! I didn't realize you were Gerry's neighbour. Long time no see."

"You *know* each other?"

"But of course, Gerree," she says. "Max and I met in Boston in April. We were sort of sharing an orchestra briefly, weren't we, Max?"

"Good God . . .!" I begin but the rest is drowned by squeals of delight from Pavel, who springs from the table and flings himself into Marta's arms. There follow some interminable Slavic endearments from which the pianist eventually emerges.

"We were bestest friends in Moscow," he explains.

"Oh, that's right, so you were." It all comes back, now, her telling me about camp, gossipy times in student digs a long time ago. Gradually things calm down.

"You I know too," Marta tells Nanty, who all this time has been beaming vacantly from the end of the table like a Labrador with its nose out of a car window, ears blown back in the slipstream. I fear he's rather far gone. "I saw you on Gerree's terrace here."

"Yah," he agrees. "You're the one kissed that bloke from the UFO."

"That was my brother Ljuka. And it was a helicopter."

"Whatever," says Nanty equably. "You stick to your story. Don't go away. I'll soon need a bit of beaming up myself."

Meanwhile I have been trying to take stock of old Marta. In some ways she's exactly as she was when I last saw her a year or so ago: the same frizzy mane of derelict hair that looks as though insects are probably hibernating in its depths, the same bollard-like physique like that of a bargee on the River Volga more familiar with liverwurst than liposuction. But her clothes have climbed several rungs up the fashion ladder in the interim, even if they plainly spend the night on her bedroom floor. And now there is about her a general air of easy internationalism, partly reflected by her now almost fluent English with a faint American accent. She feels less—what can I say?—Voynovian, somehow, no longer the bumpkin fresh from the steppe.

"So what is this party I've crashed?" she asks brightly. "I must apologize for coming over but I've only just arrived and I can't get into my house. None of my keys will open the door."

Of course! I'd overlooked that. "Oh God, I'm sorry, Marta. I'm afraid I took it upon myself to change your back-door lock, and bolt the front door from the inside. Can't be bothered to go into it now, but you remember that estate agent of ours, Benedetti? I found him sneaking around inside your house with prospective buyers. Turns out he'd kept your keys, mine too, probably, so I changed our locks. But how did you get up here?"

"By taxi. I just had the man drop me, assuming I could get in. But I can't."

"Actually it's Gerry's *birthday* party," Derek puts in, obviously dying to answer her question. "That's why we're all here. It's up to you to guess his age and you're not allowed to cheat by using radiocarbon dating."

"Gerree!" she squeals at me, instantly reverting to olden times. "I'd no idea! Many happy returns," and she presses me to her dugs before I can evade her grasp. Out of the corner of my eye, amid psilocybin shimmers, I catch Adrian's look of amusement.

"My dear, you can't possibly stay in your house tonight," I tell her when I can disentangle myself. "Out of the question. I was over there a week or two ago just to check on it and the place is an icebox. Apart from that your electricity has been cut off so there's no light and no water. The phone's off, too, and there's a creature from another planet living in your fridge. We'll tackle it in the morning. You must stay here tonight. We've heaps of room." (Those careless gestures of hospitality that come well before an actual counting of beds!) "Pull up a chair, now, and have something to eat. Vino. Where's the vino? I'll open some more."

"I've left my bags outside my house."

"It's not raining, is it? Don't worry, Adrian and I—this is Adrian, by the way, he's a world-famous oceanographer—will fetch them over once you've had something to eat. Golly, Marta, I still can't get over it."

"Oo, Gerree, you're not thirty-nine again, are you?" she asks roguishly, and Derek gives an unpleasant guffaw at which she rounds on him and says she thinks I'm "very youthful-looking" and that I still have "a great ass." What on *earth* sort of company has she been keeping this last year? But thank you, Marta; and put that in your pipe and smoke it, Derek, the man whose own ass got up and walked out on him a good ten years ago. That'll teach you to make a mock of the birthday boy.

And now the evening really begins to mellow. Despite my earlier misgivings I now realize Marta has actually been the party's missing element, the absentee member of this group. All the feelings of vexation amassed over the past year's care-taking of her house evaporate as I watch her demolish several thick slices of badger thigh and wash them down with copious draughts of Chianti. That's certainly the Marta I remember, she of the terrifying native delicacies: the dreadful *shonka* sausage, dense *kasha* balls and a sort of satanic haggis whose name I never did learn. Also a Voynovian cheese like spreadable lep-rosy. Obviously a bargee's appetite is something she shares with the poet of the keyboard sitting next to her. Maybe it's in their east-European genes, an urge to gorge themselves and store fat against the long winter months of hibernation while Siberian winds howl outside their caves and woolly mammoths trumpet mournfully in the taiga. This picture may be a little fanciful because, as I keep pointing out, I have yet to discover where Voynovia actually is. But watching them put the badger away I'm sure I can't be far wrong. Marta's mammary shelf is soon supporting a dandruff of puff-pastry flakes, and so authentic a reminder is this of my old neighbour that I suddenly feel immense affection for her, as for all my friends at the table who tonight have come from far and wide across the universe wearing haloes to celebrate my humble birthday. It's so very warm and comfortable, sitting back with all my friends in this gently undulating, glowing room. A couple of logs collapse noisily in the hearth and from somewhere comes a dull rumbling, but this is exactly what one expects after eating a really good badger Wellington. Adrian is telling me the latest on the Cleat front, which is that Lew Buschfeuer has also had a rethink and has withdrawn his financial support from the Deep Blues, and the loony Neptunies have moved to California and formed a new sect, their object of worship being The Face as the oceanic Great Mother, a.k.a. the mother of all mothers. Max and Marta are reminiscing about an oboist in Boston who shot a concertgoer for blowing his nose. Derek is bent over Pavel in a shared cloud of Allure and tutting over the state of his fingernails while Nanty is apparently mesmerized by the gleaming brass cartridge cap that lately decorated the pie. With a fatuous smile he watches it slide gently across the polished table until it is arrested by a puddle of wine.

"Very clever, Nanty," I shout down the table. "I saw that. You moved it just by using the power of your mind. It's called something kinesis and it could win you a million dollars from that American magician with the beard, James Randi."

"I've already got a million dollars, thanks," says the bald pop star mildly. "I've transcended money, y'know. I shall never, never need money again. From now on I'm *renouncing* money."

"This is not what your biographer wishes to hear," I begin, but this time the rumbling noise is much louder and the glasses on the table chatter. This provokes some expressions of mild interest but by now even the appearance of the Angel Gabriel would be accepted with good-natured equanimity.

"I shouldn't worry," I tell them in the relaxed tones of an old hand. "Probably just a minor earth tremor. We get them now and again. The whole of Italy's seismic."

"One of the joys of living in an orogenic area like the Apennines," Adrian comments languidly. "It's the bit the estate agents tend not to mention." I notice he has his eyes closed as though in rapt contemplation. "Basically, you know, the trouble is your African plate's sliding beneath your Eurasian plate. The whole mess dates back to Mesozoic rifting in the Tethyan areas, which foreshadowed the Mediterranean's Tertiary and Quaternary subduction zones . . . I learned that from a Christmas cracker."

"Well, thank you, Professor," says Derek, who has dropped Pavel's hands and has been squeaking on and off like a true urbanite who just *knows* he should never have left the safety of London.

"Pour yourself some more vino," I tell him firmly, "and Adrian and I will go and fetch Marta's luggage. At the same time we'll do a recce to convince you that this is nothing out of the ordinary. Come on, Adrian."

I grab a torch and turn on the porch light. Outside it is chilly, slightly misty, damp. Everything looks entirely normal if one doesn't count the faint psychedelic rainbows. Adrian and I let ourselves through the gate in the fence and retrieve three substantial bags from outside Marta's back door. Only as we stagger back through the gate do I become aware that something is different.

"The world is truly a very different place tonight," agrees Adrian, dropping Marta's luggage to urinate copiously against a lime tree. "Oh, very, very different. And yet, somehow, strangely the *same*."

"No, be serious. I mean, doesn't the house look more, I don't know, *isolated* or something? A trick of the mist maybe."

"Thanks to Max and Pavel I keep thinking we're in a Tom and Jerry cartoon. Tom is suddenly going to come flying out through the back door leaving a cat-shaped hole in the woodwork. Then he's going to whack into this fence and become corrugated all over before he pings back to normal and whizzes back inside to carry on the chase. Or else Butch or Spike or whatever the bulldog was called will come roaring out of his kennel by the garage over there and . . . You're absolutely right, Gerry. Something does look different. Where actually *is* your garage?"

And it isn't long before we're standing not too close to the raw edge of a precipice into whose benighted depths my ex-garage has entirely vanished. There is a strong smell of fresh earth and smashed rocks and popped tree roots. I say ex-garage because of course since its summer conversion my old stone barn has—had—become the charming self-contained annexe in which Derek and Pavel Taneyev will shortly—would shortly have been sleeping. Suddenly the psychedelic effects dwindle and fade and an awful sobriety invades us.

"That's not terribly reassuring, is it?" says Adrian as my house is revealed as now standing on a small, crude promontory on the edge of space. It is obvious that the moonless dark is doing us quite a favour by not revealing the full extent of the chasm on whose lip we are poised.

"How safe do you think it is?" I ask faintly.

"I should say it could go at any moment," he replies. "Mind you, I'm speaking as a marine scientist and not as a professional geologist. Speaking as a human being, I'd say we'd better get everybody out, pronto."

Slowly, we try to run.

24

The room is silent. Outside the window a freezing January afternoon has darkened to invisibility a Suffolk landscape of sodden fields and bleak twigs. The bed on which I am lying is exactly beneath the pitched ceiling where two sets of oak rafters meet to form a sort of Tudor tent. A cup of tea that Jennifer brought me with kind intentions half an hour ago is cooling untouched on the bedside table. *Tea.* I am waiting for my six o'clock dose of opium tincture. And after that, if I can summon the energy, I am supposed to read to Josh before he goes to bed. He likes little rhymes; but although Crendlesham Hall is now gleaming and builder-free, most of his mother's books are still in boxes. I have managed to find only a battered copy of Wordsworth's nursery poems, *Now We Are Seven,* well loved by all except me and Josh, who has made it quite clear that he wants bedtime verses about dinosaurs. He is as little diverted by the doings of Pecksy Redbreast as I am:

> By a freshet of the Dove
> Young Redbreast piped his lay;
> And unseen on a branch above
> Joined in his brother gay.
> A shepherd heard their birdie song
> And tried his best to sing along . . .

I mean to say. It is not much of a challenge to reconfigure this sort of thing so as to accord better with Josh's interests and primitive sense of humour. Ad-libbing such verses on demand is now my chief form of intellectual exercise.

> Into a tree beside a stream
> Young Terry Dactyl flew.
> It was so cold his breath was steam,
> His feet and claws were blue.
> But cold or not, he had a hot
> And urgent need to poo . . .

How have I come to this pathetic invalid state? I almost can't remember. These days I can scarcely tell what is feverish memory and what pure nightmare induced by *Papaver somniferum.* Today, not quite four weeks later, I am still incapable of giving any further account of that appalling night up at Le Rocce. To do justice to the full horror that within minutes turned a cheerful birthday celebration into ruin and despair would require the brush of a Géricault, even though *The Raft of the Medusa's* victims were clearly from an underclass accustomed to brutal reverses of fortune.

The stampede to evacuate my sweet house, the subsequent nail-biting tiptoeings back inside it to retrieve the essentials of survival and the interminable hours spent cowering under mouldy blankets in Marta's dank and freezing slum, ready at any moment to dash outdoors—over it all my lacerated spirit draws a merciful veil. Sometimes, while lying here in the bedroom in Crendlesham Hall that was intended for Adrian's occasional use, I am prey to nightmare images that punctuate my laudanum-aided stupor. We were cut off in quaking mountains without even a mobile-phone signal for company and because of the mist unable even to tell if the lights of Camaiore were still lit down below. Most hideous of all is the memory of standing with my huddled guests at first light, almost insensate with cold and shaking with hangover, driven in panic from

Marta's house by yet another tremor in time to see my own home disappear with an uncanny lack of noise and with—my eyes brim as I write this—a kind of jaunty dignity, the entire pergola cocking up at the last moment in ironic salute.

Well, whereof one cannot speak, thereof one must be silent. I can't improve on the late Mr. Wittgenstein's unheeded advice to journalists.

I thought I should never smile again. And yet a single event over Christmas has proved me wrong. With something of the inevitability of a Greek tragedy it concerns Millie Cleat: the one person who, no matter how devastated my own life, reliably bobs up to hog the headlines. In this instance I can't really complain because she has provided a spectacular distraction from my own woes—so spectacular, indeed, that had she been a fictional character one would have accused the novelist of going too far. But that's Millie all over: too far is never quite far enough. At the same time I can't help wondering whether she hasn't become something of a fixation with me. From time to time I've thought about her obsessive quality. Has she really been very much ruder, more arrogant, more egotistical than any other of my sporting subjects? Now and then over this last month, when admittedly reduced by grief and opium to a state of profound mental weakness, I have briefly entertained the possibility that I might actually be jealous of her. *Jealous?* Of that one-armed old harridan? Unthinkable under normal circumstances, naturally. But when viewed from the pit of utter dejection Millie's popularity has occasionally seemed enviable. How could it not? Wherever she has gone in the last few years people have surged to touch the hem of her rubber garments, have cheered themselves hoarse when she passed by, have flocked to become her disciples while according her practically canonized status. This has been bitter for her biographer to contemplate, lying as he is in abject obscurity in a shuttered room in the wilds of East Anglia. Had *Beldame* sunk beneath

Millie she would at once have been presented with a bigger and better yacht, expense no object. Whereas Samper's poor house can capsize into a ravine, taking with it all his clothes and possessions, and who cares? "Minor Tremors Shake Versilia," reported *Il Tirreno* heartlessly. "Limited Damage and No Casualties."

Still, survivors do sometimes have the last laugh, as the episode involving Millie on Christmas Day demonstrated. It was a piece of theatre that must surely be as seared into the memories of a million television viewers as it is safely stored digitally in image banks around the world. As everyone now knows, Australia decided to mark this Christmas with a huge regatta in Sydney Harbour to celebrate that country's maritime history. The ships taking part ranged from a faithful recon-struction of a prison hulk to the latest "stealth" warship built for the Department of Immigration. As a special gesture they gave Millie Cleat pride of place, deciding that *Beldame* with her patriotic green-and-gold sails should lead the grand flotil-la and be first to pass beneath the famous bridge. By now most people Down Under had either forgiven Millie for being British or assumed she was Australian, just as they took it for granted she was the wife as well as the consort of the country's best-known tycoon. As we know, she was neither Australian nor Lew's wife, but nobody bothers with the truth on national occasions.

In due course viewers worldwide saw *Beldame* approaching the magnificent span of Sydney Harbour Bridge. Should a few patriotic eyes have been failing to fill of their own accord, com-mentators and journalists drew attention with their customary inspiration to just how small a craft she was, how toylike by contrast with the great fleet following in her wake, how frail and flimsy in comparison to the world's oceans she had so gal-lantly traversed. It was a beautiful blue breezy day and little *Beldame* was nowhere near under full canvas otherwise she would easily have outstripped half the vessels behind her, especially the prison hulk which, we later learned, was leaking authentically. It was a spectacle fit to gladden the heart of the Minister for Tourism who was watching, glass in hand and tear in eye, from the Prime Minister's residence, Kirribilli House. There were the nested white sails of the Opera House, there the fire tugs moored on either side with their cannons spraying creamy rooster tails of water into the cloudless summer sky. There were the crowds cheering and the lusty booming and wailing of a thousand ships' sirens and hooters. The cameras zoomed in on *Beldame* to catch Millie alone at the helm in her best Horatia Nelson pose, her slight figure ramrod straight and her left arm held in rigid salute. I noticed her right arm, too, was equally rigid so today she was evidently wearing one of her polycarbonate versions bent at the elbow across her chest, which must have made it a nightmare trying to get into the jacket of the naval uniform she was certainly not entitled to wear.

Given her trademark amputee image, I wondered why she had decided to strap on a false arm at all for this occasion. I was idly speculating about such things as her indomitable vanity and Lew's enthusiasm for prosthetic limbs when the extraordinary event took place. She was still a hundred yards short of the bridge when *Beldame* heeled slightly beneath a clout of breeze. Millie evidently decided she would shorten sail or something and we glimpsed her reaching for the various electronic controls with which the yacht was festooned. Another lurch of the boat threw her against the base of the mast. In an instant she was seen to be bodily hoisted off her feet and carried briskly at an awkward angle to the top of the mast where there was some sinister floundering and thrashing. Even as we watched it happen I surmised the automatic hoist she had had installed for carrying out masthead repairs in mid-ocean must somehow have malfunctioned, snagged her false arm and run away with her. Maybe it will turn out that the gearing had recently been repaired and wrongly reassembled— only the inevitable inquiry will reveal such details. In any case it was the shocking speed of the transition that stayed in the mind. Within a matter of seconds Horatia Cleat at full salute was whipped a hundred feet skyward as a flailing marionette, her cap falling off and twirling down into *Beldame*'s wake.

Taken by surprise, the cameras did their best to follow her in close-up but by now the yacht was in the bridge's shadow and viewers were left with a confused impression of Millie's left hand waving—or was it trying to reach a halyard? It had all happened so fast that most people assumed this unconventional manoeuvre was planned, an extra piece of drama designed to heighten the triumphal pageantry. They were mildly intrigued to see what would happen next when the trimaran emerged on the far side of the bridge. Perhaps Millie was going to lead the regatta from her masthead? It was a gesture that would surely transcend mere pluckiness and reach the level of the heroically dotty.

From his vantage point in Kirribilli House the Minister for Tourism, despite his reactions being lightly retarded by Bundaberg rum, must surely by now have had a blurred premonition of disaster. For when the cameras picked Millie up again, once more bathed in brilliant sunshine, it became apparent to everybody that something had gone badly wrong and that the uniformed figure who appeared to be kissing the mast at a cramped and unnatural angle might be beyond making gestures of any kind. Before the cameramen had the presence of mind to jump back into long focus viewers had the impression that Millie was actually pinned by the neck to the hollow titanium mast by a wire rope; but amid the blurred confusion of rigging it was impossible to be sure. We now know, of course, that she was already dead. While the commentators slowly caught on to the fact that this good old Millie they were still chuckling over and praising for her cheeky sense of drama was in fact a corpse, the cameras continued to follow her. The last thing viewers saw in close-up was the slogan on *Beldame*'s foredeck: No Worries. Thereafter it took several minutes for a police launch to summon the nerve to officially spoil the regatta's dignity. It ran alongside the yacht while men in orange life jackets swarmed aboard her. One took over the empty helm while others wrestled with the fused machinery in a vain attempt to bring down the grotesque figurehead. In the event there was nothing for it but to tow the yacht to shore. This was done and a crane jib was extended over her from which dangled a man with cutting equipment. Even now something else went wrong. Before he could get a sling around the defunct mariner the harness of her prosthesis finally snapped and her released body tumbled all the way down to the deck leaving her bent right arm dangling aloft, trailing straps. All in all, the passing of Millie Cleat lacked solemnity.

In fact, the gross and global outburst of mawkishness that ensued has made it impossible to view Millie's demise other than as high comedy. Adrian tells me many of his BOIS colleagues phoned to interrupt each other's family Christmas, eager to ensure that all had heard the news and seen the footage and to urge the opening of yet more champagne. "That'll teach her to ignore COLREGS" was the general tone, and plans were made for the prompt release to the media of the film of Millie's near collision in the Canaries to counterbalance the lying and fawning obituaries. Heartless it might sound; but as her biographer I am in a much better position than you, dear reader, to know how frightful she really was. And if the flippant among us choose to see the hand of the Spirit of the Deep in her downfall, I would be the last to dissuade them. If you will elect to pollute the stately ocean with torrential ciderpresses and mottled mothers shot in the bottom, it's your own lookout. Neptune is not mocked.

As for Millie's own malicious maxim that it is an ill wind that blows somebody else more luck than her, I can only agree it has held true. For the same ill wind that sent *Beldame* heeling in Sydney Harbour and hanged its skipper from her own masthead has puffed billowing life into my own sales. I have always said that in my line of business a really dramatic and punctual death can do wonders for a book and *Millie!*, having sold very briskly in the two months before Christmas, has now taken off like mad. I gather Champions Press have cudgelled their holidaying printers back to work and are rushing out another hundred thousand copies. The most unlikely countries are at this very moment struggling to translate my prose into their motley languages to catch the tide.

Just as well, too; for my own future is a black book into whose pages not even regular tinctures of grappa and opium can yet nerve me to peer. I simply glean a debilitating impression of rootlessness and insurance claims. Plus, of course, the same old toad demanding that I keep on scribbling foolishly. Still, Samper may pull through and his fifty-first year could yet turn out to have been cathartic. Worse for some, I reflect, as a verselet rises unbidden to my lips:

> Amazing Disgrace, so bitter-fanged,
> Has brought low poor old *Millie!*
> Admirers saw her hubris hanged
> While cheering themselves silly!

ACKNOWLEDGEMENTS

Not for the first time I have to thank Mrs. Maribel Ongpin for her generosity in providing me with that near impossibility: a quiet retreat in which to work in Manila. The closing chapters of this book were mostly written in her hospitable home, whose calm and serious tenor is so innocently at odds with the antics of the egregious Gerry Samper.

I equally wish to thank Mrs. Monica Arellano Ongpin. Over the years her house in Italy has been a locus of friendship, improper conversation and gin: an exhilarating and frequently inspiring combination.

Once again Quentin Huggett has earned my gratitude, as have other of my friends at Geotek Ltd., in particular John Roberts and Sally Marine. Between them they have answered my questions while supplying ideas of their own. Those, as usual, ranged from the invaluable to the frankly barking. It is for the lack of anything in between that I most thank them. Nor can I forget that when we were aboard R/V Farnella fifteen years ago, Quentin and I were present at the moment The Face first manifested itself: an ineffable apparition that immediately sparked an irreverent train of thought.

Finally, Ken Thomson was an obliging and witty consultant on Australiana and Ozisms in general.

About Europa Editions

"To insist that if work is good, no matter what, people will read it? Crazy! But perhaps that's why I like Europa . . . They believe in what they are doing above everything. Viva Europa Editions!"
—ALICE SEBOLD, author of *The Lovely Bones*

"A new and, on first evidence, excellent source for European fiction for English-speaking readers."—JANET MASLIN, *The New York Times*

"Europa Editions has its first indie bestseller, Elena Ferrante's *The Days of Abandonment*."—*Publishers Weekly*

"We certainly like what we've seen so far."—*The Complete Review*

"A distinctly different brand of literary pleasure, thoughtfulness and, yes, even entertainment."—*The Ruminator*

"You could consider Europa Editions, the sprightly new publishing venture [...] based in New York, as a kind of book club for Americans who thirst after exciting foreign fiction."—*LA Weekly*

"Europa Editions invites English-speaking readers to 'experience all the color, the exuberance, the violence, the sounds and smells of the Mediterranean,' with an intriguing selection of the crème de la crème of continental noir."—*Murder by the Bye*

"Readers with a taste—even a need—for an occasional inky cup of bitter honesty should lap up *The Goodbye Kiss* . . . the first book of Carlotto's to be published in the United States by the increasingly impressive new Europa Editions."—*Chicago Tribune*

www.europaeditions.com

AVAILABLE NOW FROM EUROPA EDITIONS

The Jasmine Isle
Ioanna Karystiani
Fiction - 176 pp - $14.95 - isbn 1-933372-10-9

A modern love story with the force of an ancient Greek tragedy. Set on the spectacular Cycladic island of Andros, *The Jasmine Isle*, one of the finest literary achievements in contemporary Greek literature, recounts the story of the old sea wolf, Spyros Maltambès, and the beautiful Orsa Saltaferos, sentenced to marry a man she doesn't love and to watch while the man she does love is wed to another.

I Loved You for Your Voice
Sélim Nassib
Fiction - 256 pp - $14.95 - isbn 1-933372-07-9

"Om Kalthoum is great. She really is."—BOB DYLAN

Love, desire, and song set against the colorful backdrop of modern Egypt. The story of Egypt's greatest and most popular singer, Om Kalthoum, told through the eyes of the poet Ahmad Rami, who wrote her lyrics and loved her in vain all his life. This passionate tale of love and longing provides a key to understanding the soul, the aspirations and the disappointments of the Arab world.

The Days of Abandonment
Elena Ferrante
Fiction - 192 pp - $14.95 - isbn 1-933372-00-1

"Stunning . . . The raging, torrential voice of the author is something rare."
—JANET MASLIN, *The New York Times*

"I could not put this novel down. Elena Ferrante will blow you away."
—ALICE SEBOLD, author of *The Lovely Bones*

The gripping story of a woman's descent into devastating emptiness after being abandoned by her husband with two young children to care for.

Troubling Love
Elena Ferrante
Fiction - 144 pp - $14.95 - isbn 1-933372-16-8

"In tactile, beautifully restrained prose, Ferrante makes the domestic violence that tore [the protagonist's] household apart evident."—*Publishers Weekly*

"Ferrante has written the 'Great Neapolitan Novel.'"
—*Il Corriere della Sera*

Delia's voyage of discovery through the chaotic streets and claustrophobic sitting rooms of contemporary Naples in search of the truth about her mother's untimely death.

Cooking with Fernet Branca
James Hamilton-Paterson
Fiction - 288 pp - $14.95 - isbn 1-933372-01-X

"A work of comic genius."—*The Independent*

Gerald Samper, an effete English snob, has his own private hilltop
in Tuscany where he wiles away his time working as a ghostwriter
for celebrities and inventing wholly original culinary concoctions.
Gerald's idyll is shattered by the arrival of Marta, on the run from
a crime-riddled former Soviet republic. A series of hilarious
misunderstandings brings this odd couple into ever closer and
more disastrous proximity.

Old Filth
Jane Gardam
Fiction - 256 pp - $14.95 - isbn 1-933372-13-3

"Jane Gardam's beautiful, vivid and defiantly funny novel is a
must."—*The Times*

Sir Edward Feathers has progressed from struggling young barrister
to wealthy expatriate lawyer to distinguished retired judge, living
out his last days in comfortable seclusion in Dorset. The engrossing
and moving account of his life, from birth in colonial Malaya, to
Wales, where he is sent as a "Raj orphan," to Oxford, his career
and marriage, parallels much of the 20th century's dramatic history.

Total Chaos
Jean-Claude Izzo
Fiction/Noir - 256 pp - $14.95 - isbn 1-933372-04-4

"Caught between pride and crime, racism and fraternity, tragedy and light, messy urbanization and generous beauty, the city for Montale is a Utopia, an ultimate port of call for exiles. There, he is torn between fatalism and revolt, despair and sensualism."
—*The Economist*

This first installment in the legendary *Marseilles Trilogy* sees Fabio Montale turning his back on a police force marred by corruption and racism and taking the fight against the mafia into his own hands.

Chourmo
Jean-Claude Izzo
Fiction/Noir - 256 pp - $14.95 - isbn 1-933372-17-6

"Like the best noir writers—and he is among the best—Izzo not only has a keen eye for detail but also digs deep into what makes men weep."—*Time Out, New York*

Montale is dragged back into the mean streets of a violent, crime-infested Marseilles after the disappearance of his long lost cousin's young son.

The Goodbye Kiss
Massimo Carlotto
Fiction/Noir - 192 pp - $14.95 - isbn 1-933372-05-2

"The best living Italian crime writer."—*Il Manifesto*

An unscrupulous womanizer, as devoid of morals now as he once
was full of idealistic fervor, returns to Italy where he is wanted for a
series of crimes. To avoid prison he sells out his old friends, turns
his back on his former ideals, and cuts deals with crooked cops. To
earn himself the guise of respectability he is willing to go even
further, maybe even as far as murder.

Death's Dark Abyss
Massimo Carlotto
Fiction/Noir - 192 pp - $14.95 - isbn 1-933372-18-4

"A narrative voice that in Lawrence Venuti's translation is cold and
heartless—but, in a creepy way, fascinating."—*The New York Times*

A riveting drama of guilt, revenge, and justice, Massimo Carlotto's
Death's Dark Abyss tells the story of two men and the savage crime
that binds them. During a robbery, Raffaello Beggiato takes a young
woman and her child hostage and later murders them. Beggiato is
arrested, tried, and sentenced to life. The victims' father and
husband, Silvano, plunges into a deepening abyss until the day the
murderer seeks his pardon and he begins to plot his revenge.

Hangover Square
Patrick Hamilton
Fiction/Noir - 280 pp - $14.95 - isbn 1-933372-06-0

"Hamilton is a sort of urban Thomas Hardy: always a pleasure to read, and as social historian he is unparalleled."—NICK HORNBY

Adrift in the grimy pubs of London at the outbreak of World War II, George Harvey Bone is hopelessly infatuated with Netta, a cold, contemptuous small-time actress. George also suffers from occasional blackouts. During these moments one thing is horribly clear: he must murder Netta.

Boot Tracks
Matthew F. Jones
Fiction/Noir - 208 pp - $14.95 - isbn 1-933372-11-7

"Mr. Jones has created a powerful blend of love and violence, of the grotesque and the tender."
—*The New York Times*

A commanding, stylishly written novel that tells the harrowing story of an assassination gone terribly wrong and the man and woman who are taking their last chance to find a safe place in a hostile world.

Love Burns
Edna Mazya
Fiction/Noir - 192 pp - $14.95 - isbn 1-933372-08-7

"Starts out as a psychological drama and becomes a strange, funny, unexpected hybrid: a farce thriller. A great book."—*Ma'ariv*

Ilan, a middle-aged professor of astrophysics, discovers that his young wife is having an affair. Terrified of losing her, he decides to confront her lover instead. Their meeting ends in the latter's murder—the unlikely murder weapon being Ilan's pipe—and in desperation, Ilan disposes of the body in the fresh grave of his kindergarten teacher. But when the body is discovered, the mayhem begins.

Departure Lounge
Chad Taylor
Fiction/Noir - 176 pp - $14.95 - isbn 1-933372-09-5

"Entropy noir . . . The hypnotic pull lies in the zigzag dance of its forlorn characters, casting a murky, uneasy sense of doom."
—*The Guardian*

A young woman mysteriously disappears. The lives of those she has left behind—family, acquaintances, and strangers intrigued by her disappearance—intersect to form a captivating latticework of coincidences and surprising twists of fate. Urban noir at its stylish and intelligent best.

Minotaur
Benjamin Tammuz
Fiction/Noir - 192 pp - $14.95 - isbn 1-933372-02-8

"A novel about the expectations and compromises that humans create for themselves . . . Very much in the manner of William Faulkner and Lawrence Durrell."—*The New York Times*

An Israeli secret agent falls hopelessly in love with a young English girl. Using his network of contacts and his professional expertise, he takes control of her life without ever revealing his identity. *Minotaur* is a complex and utterly original story about a solitary man driven from one side of Europe to the other by his obsession.

Dog Day
Alicia Giménez-Bartlett
Fiction/Noir - 208 pp - $14.95 - isbn 1-933372-14-1

"Giménez-Bartlett has discovered a world full of dark corners and hidden elements."—*ABC*

In this hardboiled fiction for dog lovers and lovers of dog mysteries, detective Petra Delicado and her maladroit sidekick, Garzon, investigate the murder of a tramp whose only friend is a mongrel dog named "Freaky." One murder leads to another and Delicado finds herself involved in the sordid, dangerous world of fight dogs. *Dog Day* is first-rate entertainment.

The Big Question
Wolf Erlbruch
Children's Illustrated Fiction - 52 pp - $14.95 - isbn 1-933372-03-6

Named Best Book at the 2004 Children's Book Fair in Bologna.

A stunningly beautiful and poetic illustrated book for children that poses the biggest of all big questions: why am I here? A chorus of voices—including the cat's, the baker's, the pilot's and the soldier's—offers us some answers. But nothing is certain, except that as we grow each one of us will pose the question differently and be privy to different answers.

The Butterfly Workshop
Wolf Erlbruch
Children's Illustrated Fiction - 40 pp - $14.95 - isbn 1-933372-12-5

For children and adults alike: Odair, one of the "Designers of All Things" and grandson of the esteemed inventor of the rainbow, has been banished to the insect laboratory as punishment for his overactive imagination. But he still dreams of one day creating a cross between a bird and a flower. Then, after a helpful chat with a dog . . .

Carte Blanche
Carlo Lucarelli
Fiction/Noir - 120 pp - $14.95 - isbn 1-933372-15-X

"Carlo Lucarelli is the great promise of Italian crime writing."
—*La Stampa*

April 1945, Italy. Commissario De Luca is heading up a dangerous investigation into the private lives of the rich and powerful during the frantic final days of the fascist republic. The hierarchy has guaranteed De Luca their full cooperation, so long as he arrests the "right" suspect. The house of cards built by Mussolini in the last months of WW II is collapsing and De Luca faces a world mired in sadistic sex, dirty money, drugs and murder.